TED ALLBEURY
THE SEEDS OF TREASON

THE MYSTERIOUS PRESS • New York

Copyright © 1986 by Ted Allbeury
All rights reserved.
The Mysterious Press, 129 West 56th Street, New York, N.Y. 10019

This Mysterious Press Edition is published by arrangement with the author. First published in Great Britain by New English Library.

Printed in the United States of America
First Printing: July 1987
10 9 8 7 6 5 4 3 2 1

Library of Congress Cataloging-in-Publication Data

Allbeury, Ted.
  The seeds of treason.

  I. Title.
PR6051.L52S4 1987   823'.914   86-62784
ISBN 0-89296-181-3

To Julian and Carole—with love

Go search for people who are hurt by fate or nature—the ugly, those suffering from an inferiority complex, craving power and influence but defeated by unfavorable circumstances . . . The sense of belonging to an influential, powerful organization will give them a feeling of superiority over the handsome and prosperous people around them. For the first time in their lives they will experience a sense of importance . . . It is sad indeed, and humanly shallow—but we are obliged to profit from it.

From a lecture to KGB officers by
KGB General Pavl Anatolevich Sudoplatov

One

He had always known at the back of his mind that they would come sooner or later, but he hadn't expected that it would be quite so soon. There had only been a couple of paragraphs in one of those pieces on the security services in the *Daily Telegraph*, and there had been no name given. Just a brief reference to a former officer of MI6. There had been no follow-up story but it would have gone over the wires from the press services, and that would have set people ferreting through the records. The story had appeared in the paper a week ago.

They had bought the farmhouse when they moved to Spain and they had chosen it because of its remoteness and inaccessibility. The plaque over the door said *Hacienda di Santa Anna—1872* and it was much the same now as when it had first been built. It was on the *sierra*, the mountain ridge behind Malaga, about two miles up the pot-holed mountain road from El Palo to Olias.

There were two cars and a small white van and he could see them pulled up on the lower ridge by the village of Jarazmin. By the time they had made their enquiries about his house it would be another fifteen minutes before they arrived. There was still light, but there was the tell-tale pink of sunset across the Bay of Malaga toward Torremolinos, and

1

the glowing red heads of the geraniums were already taking on the shades of mauve and purple that came with the evening.

It looked as if it was a TV team. He'd always imagined that if it ever happened it would be with a journalist, quietly and in his control. But TV interviews were never like that. They were brash and short, with every second significant. He could refuse to see them. Send them packing. But if he turned them away there would be others. And if he didn't say anything to any of them they would just put the Establishment point of view plus the usual speculation and distortion. Chambers would have a field-day with noncommittal statements that hinted without saying anything out loud. And Paula would loom out of the past to cash in on it without needing too much encouragement from "investigative" reporters. All the venom of the years unleashed as at long last she could try to even the score. He shivered despite the warm air, and turned, walking back through the big, double front doors to warn Anna. It was cool in the house as he stood at the foot of the stairs and called up to her.

She wasn't upstairs and as she came through from the kitchen she stood in the archway that led to the dining-room and he realized that that was almost exactly how he had seen her that first time. All those years ago. Before it all began. Standing under the wide archway of one of the reception rooms at the hotel in Berlin. She looked no older now. Calmer perhaps, less tension in that slender neck and the large brown eyes. But her mouth was the same, wide, and the dimples ready to deepen when she smiled. That first time she had been wearing a black silk dress and her dark hair had been swept up into a chignon held by a tortoiseshell comb. Neither of them knew the other but for a moment their eyes had met and held before he was past her. It could only be hindsight but he was sure that at that moment he had known that their lives would be entangled somehow. She was much younger than he was and she was very beautiful, but it wasn't just that. In those days he went in more for long-legged blondes with well-filled sweaters.

"They're almost here, my love. It looks like a TV crew."

"This is very soon, Jan, isn't it?"

"Yes, but I suppose it doesn't matter. Shall I send them away? Refuse to be interviewed?"

She walked across to him and put her hands on his shoulders as she looked up at his face. "What do you want to do?"

"I want to be left alone. With you."

"But what . . . ?"

"I don't understand."

She smiled. "If that was exactly what you wanted you wouldn't have asked me what you should do."

"I'd just like people to understand how these things happen."

"It might be good for you to talk it out. Good for you, I mean." She paused. "But don't expect people to understand. They won't."

2

"Are you sure?"

"Quite, quite sure."

He heard the car engines and then Jackie, their German Shepherd bitch, barking at the strangers at the gate. He turned to go outside but she held him, kissing him gently on the mouth. "Don't get upset, Jan, if they don't understand. You don't have to explain."

He sighed. "There may be somebody else someday. It could help them."

She smiled and shook her head. "They wouldn't be like you, Jan. You're just a shade too much Polish for the British to understand."

As he walked across the patio he could smell the jasmine and the mimosa. The cars were drawn up in a line on the rough track outside. A man stood in shirt-sleeves and denims on the other side of the big wrought-iron gates. He had seen him somewhere before. On "Panorama" or some such program.

He didn't open the gates and as they faced each other he noticed the TV man put his hands on his hips. The small action of readiness for an aggressive move was revealing. He smiled. "Mr. Massey? Jan Massey?"

"What do you want?"

"My name's Bartram. Tom Bartram. We met briefly when British Forces Network Berlin opened their new studios. It must have been five or six years ago. BBC television has sent me over to interview you." He paused. "I expect you've seen the papers."

"I don't wish to be interviewed. I have nothing to say."

The man shrugged. "I could save you a lot of hassle. We've got here several days before anybody else is likely to find you. Give me an exclusive and we'll sell it to all the others. It would save you having to deal with anybody else. You could tell them that this is the only interview you will give. I'm authorized to offer you a fee of £5000. We could double that for an exclusive."

"What sort of questions have you got in mind?"

For a moment the man hesitated and then, looking at Massey's face, he said quietly, "Only one."

"What's that?"

"Just tell me how it all happened."

"That would take days, not ten minutes."

"So I'll stay for days, if you'll allow me to."

There was something about the choice of the word *allow*. He could have said "if you'll *let* me." But *allow* was different somehow. It acknowledged that Massey had a choice, and control over the situation.

"I don't want my wife disturbed by all your crew and lights and the rest of their paraphernalia."

Bartram smiled. An amiable smile. "It's odd. I only learned the real meaning of that word paraphernalia about ten days ago. Maybe you already know the real meaning. The legal meaning?"

3

"No."

Paraphernalia is the old legal description for the things that a husband gives to his wife before and during the marriage that can never be taken from her by him or the courts."

Massey looked at the TV man's face and then said quietly, "OK. I'll talk to you, Mr. Bartram. I'll see how it goes. Just you and me. Not an interview at this stage. Just a chat. Off the record." He paused. "Provided you send your crew away and they don't talk. To anyone."

Bartram nodded. "That's OK. I'll take them off now. What time could I come up myself in the morning?"

"Let's make it ten. But if I'm not happy about how it goes there'll be no cameras."

"It'll be up to you, Mr. Massey. I assure you it will be played straight down the middle."

"And no long lenses or hidden cameras?"

"None. I promise."

As if it were quite normal they shook hands through the iron-work scrolls of the gates and the BBC man turned and walked over to the cars. Massey watched him bend over, talking at one of the lowered car windows, and then the cars backed to the edge of the track, turned and drove away down toward Malaga.

Massey turned and looked across the valley. There were lights on in the cluster of houses in Jarazmin below, and the sunset was, as always, theatrical almost to the point of vulgarity. A range of reds, mauves and purples that shaded through that end of the spectrum and touched the creases and folds of the mountains. Around the bay the lights of Torremolinos and Marbella danced and twinkled on the dark waters of the Mediterranean. And everywhere was so still and quiet that he could hear the cassette that Anna must have put on. It was Victoria de los Angeles singing the "Baïlèro" from *Les Chants d'Auvergne*.

They sat on the patio. A bottle of local white wine and glasses on the marble table between them. He had put out the upright cane chairs for them so that he could be continuously reminded that it wasn't a friend he was talking to. It was almost half an hour later when Bartram got round to the first question.

"You were in Berlin for nearly six years according to what I could find out. Isn't that longer than SIS usually leaves their agents . . . their officers, in one place?"

Massey looked at him and smiled. "I signed the Official Secrets Act a long time ago, Mr. Bartram. They never release you from that. There's very little I can actually tell you. Nothing that would interest the public."

"Could we talk about the more personal aspects of what happened? Your feelings and your wife's feelings. Your present wife, that is."

4

Massey smiled. "You'd end up with a sort of 'This is Your Life' piece. You wouldn't want that, would you?"

Bartram shrugged. "I just want to understand. To show people how these things happen. That it isn't all as black and white and cut and dried as it seems."

"You really mean that?"

"Of course. Why shouldn't I?"

"The Establishment wouldn't like that very much. They might stop you showing it anyway if it doesn't go along with the official point of view."

"To hell with them. They wouldn't stop me. I'm a freelance. And as a matter of fact I don't think they'd try."

"What makes you think that?"

"I talked briefly to several people before I left. They didn't put up any barriers. On the contrary."

"Who told you where to find me?"

The TV man didn't avoid his eyes. "Does it really matter? We knew you had been in France and that you had recently moved to somewhere in Spain. It wouldn't have taken long."

"Was it someone in MI6 who told you where to find me?"

"Yes."

"Chambers?"

"Yes. But I don't think he told me out of spite."

Massey laughed. "Chambers never does things out of spite. None of them do. It's not their way. It's either in the line of duty or in the public interest."

"It didn't sound like that."

"Of course not. That's why he's in SIS. They're not the fools that you journalists try to make them out to be. They know how to put the words together. And they're used to dealing with much more cynical people than even journalists are supposed to be."

"You don't like the people in MI6?"

It was almost impossible to explain to an outsider. Massey shrugged. "Like any other organization there are people you admire and like, and people whom you don't like. People who care more about the rules than human beings. People who are more active against their colleagues than against our enemies."

"You think Chambers is one of those?"

"I didn't say that."

Tom Bartram smiled. "How do you want to do this?"

"I'm not a TV man. You tell me how you want to do it and I'll see if I can cooperate."

"OK. Let's play it very loosely. How about you give me two or three days of your time? No recordings, no filming. Just you and me on our own. You tell me what you choose to tell me. Just as background material for me. Then, if I feel I can make a worthwhile program from it, we'll go over it again. On camera. The parts that really tell the story."

"Will it be a sympathetic treatment?"

"It'll be honest and balanced, but that won't necessarily make it sympathetic. How it comes out depends on the facts."

"And when I've talked and you've filmed it I can have the final say about what goes in?"

"No. But after we've talked privately you can say an absolute no. And when we film, if you don't want to answer a question you don't have to. But the viewers would see that you hadn't answered."

"Let's just talk and see how it goes. Where do you want me to start?"

"Back on square one. Tell me about when you were a child. Your parents. Your life. Anything that you can remember."

Two

Jan Massey's father, Adrian James Massey, had qualified as a doctor in 1940. He was then twenty-four. He was called up by the army immediately after qualifying and was commissioned in the Royal Army Medical Corps.

Other people had told Jan Massey that his father was a very lively man in those days. A good sportsman and, despite that, something of a scholar. Because of his fluent French he was transferred into Special Operations Executive where he eventually became part of a network on the outskirts of Paris. When the Paris networks began to fall apart he was brought back to England with several other officers and given a refresher course before being sent back to lead an SOE network in the Angoulême area.

It was during his refresher course at Beaulieu that he met Jan's mother. She was being trained by SOE as a radio operator and was eventually parachuted into France as his father's operator three months after he took over the network. She was then twenty-one years old.

Her name was Grazyna Maria Felinska and she had been born in Warsaw. Her parents had sent her to Paris just before the Germans invaded Poland in 1939. She had been recruited in Paris for SOE and was sent to England for training.

Long after the war was over Jan Massey had spent a sad afternoon shortly after he had joined SIS, looking through their old SOE files. Most SOE files had been destroyed within weeks of the war ending but about a hundred or so had been preserved. Nobody could tell him why those particular files had been kept. It could well have been no more than chance. His father's file read like his school reports. Everything he did he did with enthusiasm. He was commended for his bravery and his inspired leadership of his group in the Dordogne.

His mother's file was very different. The training staff at Beaulieu found her defiant, reckless and disobedient. They conceded that she was courageous and an efficient operator, but they saw her as a liability to any unit in the field. In addition they noted that she was far too attractive not to cause trouble in a network and almost certainly too noticeable to Germans as well as Frenchmen.

No reason was given in her file as to why, after all these negatives, she was posted to his father's network, but his reports on her work made clear that she was a valuable member of the network who cooperated well.

They were married by a local priest in Brantôme in the summer of 1943, and Jan's mother was obligingly brought back by an SOE Lysander in February 1944 so that her child could be born in England. He was, in fact, born in Edinburgh, where his grandparents lived.

Two weeks after D-Day his father was shot in the chest by a German patrol. His men carried him to a farmhouse where he was treated by a local doctor. It was at a time when the Gestapo and the *Sicherheitsdienst*, the SS, were reacting ruthlessly against the Resistance, and his father, despite his condition, had to be constantly on the move. Reports came back to Baker Street that Adrian Massey's health was deteriorating and that he was in a state of deep depression. He was considered too vital to the network's morale to be brought back to England.

In defiance of contrary advice from all quarters his mother insisted on being dropped back into France so that she could care for her husband, and in the end a reluctant SOE agreed.

In July 1944 his mother was parachuted back into France with new drugs that could help heal his father's lung. Nobody ever established whether it was through inefficiency or because of a leak, but the Gestapo from Angoulême were waiting for her. The pilot reported later that the guiding lights had been correctly placed and the signal had been in code with the correct password. The only evidence as to what happened to her after her capture was the camp records at Mauthausen concentration camp. His mother and two other SOE girls had been burnt in the ovens at the camp sometime in February 1945.

A month before the German surrender Adrian Massey was brought back to England. Even with proper medical treatment it took a year before he was fit to be discharged.

With his savings and his service gratuity he bought a half share in a general practice in the small town of Tenterden in Kent. His son stayed with his grandparents until he was five, and then went to live with his father.

Dr. Massey was a lonely man. A sad man, despite his obvious efforts to cope with a child and only a modest income. As the years went by their relationship became close. The boy seemed to recognize that he was much loved, and accepted the lack of any social life for what it was. The residue of sadness, not indifference.

There was a photograph of Jan's mother, in a silver frame on the mahogany table beside the fireplace in their home and a similar one on the tiled window-ledge in his father's bedroom. Even as a small boy he could recognize that she was very beautiful.

He frequently asked his father to tell him about his mother. The things she had said and what they had done. He was about ten years old before he realized that although his father obviously liked talking about her it always made him quiet and withdrawn for several days afterwards. It was then that he stopped asking about her. Looking back he thought that it would have been better if there had been some churchyard, some grave that his father could visit and tend. To be with her or feel that he was with her. His father often walked to the parish church in the High Street on summer evenings, to sit on one of the benches in the churchyard and read. It was generally the blue-bound Oxford version of Palgrave that he took with him. But they had no church and no grave for a pilgrimage. Not even a date that they could hold for remembrance. He couldn't recall his father actually saying it in so many words but he got the impression that his father felt that the British hadn't appreciated her enough because she was a foreigner. And these days his father defiantly wore a cheap metal badge, white with *Solidarnosc* in red script across its face. He was still strongly pro-Poland and the Poles.

Jan Massey identified early with his mother. He supposed that originally it was just a child's wish to be different from other children. He boasted about her and her courage, and got beaten for it by other boys. When he was old enough to fight back and do real damage he imagined himself as a knight in armor defending his lady's honor.

There were several Polish families in the town and on Saturdays and Sundays he was taken to one of the houses and was taught Polish. He learned quickly, and was treated by the Polish families as if he too were Polish. To them his mother was a heroine. A Polish heroine. For years he assumed that all heroines were Polish, and that all beautiful Poles were heroines.

They had a housekeeper who came in every day to cook and clean. She was from one of the Polish families at the far end of the High Street and his father was always mildly amused that she fussed far more over the boy than over him. He said it was because the boy was half Polish while he was just a "foreigner."

When Jan was twelve years old his father's partner died and Adrian Massey was able to take over the whole practice. His income was much improved and they were able to spend most of their evenings together. Walking over the marshes on spring and summer evenings, playing chess or reading in the winter months. Jan tried to teach his father Polish but although he spoke fluent French and German he absorbed very little Polish.

At eighteen Jan had the chance of going to university but decided that he would rather join the army. He was accepted for a short-service commission in the Intelligence Corps, and for the few days before he was due to report to the depot in Sussex his father talked to him as if they were contemporaries. It was in those talks that Jan realized the dichotomy in his father's ideas about Poles and Poland. And the Polish temperament. He was worried that his son was so like his mother. Impetuous, over-romantic, defiant of authority when it was unimaginatively applied and, as he put it, "always ready to cut off her nose to spite her face." His father warned that what was just tolerable in a pretty girl who was a foreigner would not be tolerated in a young man who was British and in Britain. He seemed to take comfort from the possibility that the army would knock off some of the young man's rough edges.

The army, and particularly the Intelligence Corps, is less clumsy and heavy-footed than civilians and the media imagine. It looks its new boys over with a quite benign eye. Both at their faults and their virtues. The Intelligence Corps is flexible enough, and shrewd enough, to use its members' vices as well as their virtues, and Jan Massey enjoyed his time in the army. He served in counter-intelligence in Germany, France and Hong Kong. A few months into his fourth year he was offered a permanent career in the Foreign Office—the euphemism that the Establishment sometimes uses for describing MI6 or SIS, the Secret Intelligence Service. His command of Polish, Russian and German was the attraction.

He served the statutory two years in Moscow as assistant military attaché before being posted back to London. His paper on the structure and organization of the KGB impressed his superiors with its insight into Soviet thinking and attitudes, and under an assumed name he spent a year at Oxford at St. Anthony's College studying the history of the Soviet Union. Back to normal duties, he was posted to the special unit that dealt with Soviet and Warsaw Pact defectors. There were one or two senior people who felt that his understanding of the Slav mind was based not only on understanding the Soviet system but on at least a mild sympathy with the system itself. But his success in the initial contacts with potential defectors was too good to be ignored. His amiable and seemingly relaxed debriefing of turned agents seemed to produce more information than the usual more formal methods.

In the aftermath of the arrest and exposure of George Blake, the whole of SIS's organization in Berlin had to be torn apart and put together again. Jan Massey was responsible for the evaluation of and proposals for the new set-up. Most of his recommendations on both organization and personnel were accepted. A year later he was promoted and sent to Berlin to take charge of the organization he had himself devised.

For two years Jan Massey controlled the SIS operations in Berlin with skill and success. The Berlin appointment was one of SIS's key posts. With the KGB and the Soviet military intelligence organization, the GRU, just across the Wall, and the East Germans' security service, the HVA, encircling the city, it was a hotbed of espionage and counter-espionage not only for the British but for other European countries and the U.S.A. It was also a diplomatic minefield where a wrong move could give the Soviets an excuse for another move to oust the Allied occupying forces. But Massey's reading of the Russians' minds proved successful in sending back a flow of vital information and controlling the KGB's crude efforts in West Berlin. Century House congratulated themselves on their shrewd appointment.

The only black mark on his record was in his private life, and his record was enough for it to be overlooked at the time. It wasn't forgotten, because it showed that there were areas where his judgment was all too obviously unsound. But there were no security aspects to the personal disaster and it didn't affect his standing. At least not his official standing. There were even critics who saw it as a sign that Massey's Slav mind was human after all.

In 1976 he was on leave in England. He'd gone to a nightclub. It was either the Embassy Club or Churchill's. He couldn't remember which. He met a girl there who was with an old friend of his, an officer in naval intelligence. The old friend was already well away when he waved Jan over to their table. Just before midnight they had to half-carry, half-drag, his naval friend out to a taxi and take him back to the man's flat in Holland Park. She was very efficient and very pretty and as they tucked him into bed she offered to do the Florence Nightingale bit and keep an eye on him until the morning.

He had tried a hundred times since then to try and work out why he did it and he still hadn't found a satisfactory answer. The bald fact was that the girl and he married a month later. People tended to smile and say that it was just because she was very pretty and good in bed. Whatever it was, it was a total disaster. Not a gradual deterioration but right from the very first day.

One of the first precepts of intelligence training is that everybody tells lies about something and it pays to find out as quickly as possible what area of life your particular adversary tells lies about. It's not difficult. You dig a few verbal pits and wait to see which particular one they fall into. If it's done skillfully they don't even notice they've fallen. If you're wise you

11

try to avoid doing this in your private life. If you're unwise, as he was, you ignore the signals even when you see through the lies without digging a pit. It had started on the day they married and went on right into the divorce court. Pointless lies. Lies just for the hell of it. And lies to cover up the liaisons with other men. It wasn't a marriage, it was a mental hurricane that bent the mind and depressed the spirit if you were on the receiving end.

The Polish bit was dragged out by both sides in the divorce court. Her counsel did a smarmy piece about the problems of mixed marriages and what he called the explosive Slav temperament. Suggesting that the "brutal assaults" on his client's adulterous lovers were all part of that unfortunate temperament. Jan's own chap did an impassioned five minutes agreeing that even a thrice-cuckolded husband should not take the law into his own hands, but suggesting that where honor and the sanctity of the marriage bed were concerned the Poles were second to none in their respect for the law of the land. It was a cross-petition case and he won that round. But the financial settlement was bitter and long-fought. To Jan Massey it seemed typically crazy and typically British that a woman who admitted three separate adulteries and was perfectly capable of earning her own living, should be able to consider the wronged man as a lifetime meal-ticket. Fortunately she married another sucker before it was settled, but he got landed with her lawyer's fees as well as his own. He sometimes wondered if the British divorce laws weren't intended to cloak the fact that Brits don't really like women but try to make up for it when they get rid of them. Professor Higgins's little ditty about women in *My Fair Lady* wasn't all that far from the Brits' ideas about women.

He knew it was a waste of time thinking about all that. It wasn't significant. It had nothing to do with Anna and him. But the newspapers would dredge it all up and he was sure that Chambers wouldn't have forgotten it either.

Three

It was still only the last week in February but there was an indefinable feeling of spring in the Berlin air. There were no buds as yet on the trees in the Kurfürstendamm but the sky was cloudless and blue. And the sunshine was bright enough to cast gaunt shadows from the ruins of the Gadächtniskirche and light up the windows of its modern replacement.

But it was the people who made it seem suddenly spring. As if, after a dreary winter, the Berliners' natural optimism was beginning to come back. There were small gray heaps of snow still edging the bases of the trees, and a drift of thin snow on the spoil from the excavations in the road. But there were girls without coats, stopping to look at the new season's fashions in the shop windows. It looked as if people might buy fine china and jewelry again. Or Hermès scarves and Gucci shoes.

It was the day that would change Massey's life, although he didn't know it at the time. Even looking back on it, it seemed an ordinary enough day.

He stopped the taxi outside the travel agency and when he'd lifted out his case he paid the driver and walked across to the door next to the travel agency's entrance.

His flat was on the top floor, the fourth, and when he had let himself in he dumped his case on the bed and looked at his watch. The flight from

London had been half an hour late arriving at Tegel but there was time for a wash and a shave before he needed to start for the meeting.

He washed, plugged in the shaver, staring at his reflection in the mirror. He seldom noticed his reflection in the mirror but that day he was aware that he looked older than he actually was. He had had a birthday while he was away, his thirty-eighth, but the face in the mirror looked much older. His mouth looked set and grim, the muscles each side contracted, giving an impression of aggression. He remembered that his lawyer had nudged him as they sat in the judge's chambers. He'd whispered to him to relax and not look so aggressive. The hearing was going his way, don't spoil it. It was her obvious vindictiveness that was creating a bad impression. Keep calm. And look calm. He switched off the shaver and tried to bring his mind back to Berlin.

There would be time to phone through to the house in Grunewald before he went to the meeting at Spandau. It was a meeting he didn't want to miss. A chance to look over the new Russian.

They met only when one of the occupying powers had a complaint to lodge, so most meetings, including this one, were called by the Russians. Although the meetings were solely concerned with the Spandau prison, the representatives of the four powers were, in fact, career intelligence officers. Except Maguire, the American. He was a U.S. Army major, a couple of years from his army pension, who'd been given the post as a well-earned sinecure. Bourget, the Frenchman, was SDECE, the Russian was always KGB, and himself SIS.

According to the files the Russian new boy was Alexei Andreyevich Kholkov. Aged twenty-eight. Newly promoted to captain in the KGB. No previous record of contact with any Western intelligence agency. Believed to have been mainly occupied on training case officers on the handling of agents, couriers and cut-outs. Married. No children. His name corresponded with one on central archives giving details of a man previously employed by the Bolshoi reserve theater group, and suspected of being a KGB informer. No photographs available. No further information.

Sitting on the edge of the leather couch he reached for the telephone and dialed a local number. It was Howard who answered.

"Signals Security."

"It's Jan. I'm back. I'll be over to see you early this evening. Tell Cohen and the others, will you?"

"How did it go in London?"

"Fair to bloody."

"But you won?"

"Kind of. I'll tell you when I see you."

"OK. And welcome back."

"OK. See you."

"Cheers."

* * *

14

As he drove to the prison in Spandau he wondered what the Russians would be complaining about this time. The elderly Nazi in Spandau, its solitary prisoner, had long been a bone of contention with the Russians, who insisted that despite his senility and sickness he should stay there until he died. It wasn't just a question of revenge. It gave them one more access to West Berlin and one more chance to create dissension among the allies. That was why, except for the American, the representatives were intelligence officers not administrators. It gave them opportunities for meeting their opposite numbers, and sometimes a chance to test the water for minor deals and cooperation.

He parked his car in the courtyard and the security sergeant checked his card carefully before opening the side gate to the governor's office.

Maguire and Bourget were already there, drinking coffee from a Thermos on a silver salver. They chatted as he poured himself a coffee, and then the Russian arrived. The escorting officer introduced him.

"Gentlemen. The Soviet representative. Mr. Kholkov."

There had been a brief bow or two but no handshaking as the Russian was waved to a seat at the table. Maguire did the basic courtesy of offering the Russian a coffee, which he declined.

They briefly discussed the first of the two items on the agenda. As Maguire read out the MO's report on Hess's deteriorating health, Massey looked at the Russian.

He was tall and good-looking. Almost elegant in his Italian silk suit and his Hardy Amies tie. The fingers on the notepad were long, tapering and well manicured. Massey guessed that he must be one of the KGB's new-look officers. The old-time thugs had had their uses but they didn't blend well into Western civilian communities. But Alexei Kholkov could get by successfully in Paris, London or Washington. Even Berlin.

Indifferent to the prisoner's state of health, the Russian sat ostentatiously not listening to Maguire reading out the medical report, his eyes on some distant horizon. When he caught Massey's eye, he hesitated and then nodded an acknowledgment.

Maguire passed on to item two. A complaint from the Soviet representative. The American nodded toward the Russian.

"What's on your mind, Mr. Kholkov?"

The Russian turned toward Massey. "My superiors wish to lodge a formal complaint against the British authorities concerning a grossly defamatory article in the *Sunday Times* regarding the Soviet attitude to the Nazi prisoner, Rudolf Hess. We wish to remind the parties concerned that the Soviet Union suffered twenty million dead in the Great Patriotic War and—"

Maguire interrupted. "Mr. Kholkov, don't let's go through all that jazz once again. We don't indulge in that sort of propaganda at these meetings. I'm sure Mr. Massey will deal with your problem if you say what it is."

Massey saw the flush of anger on Kholkov's cheeks as he leaned forward aggressively.

"Is it the official view of the United States that twenty million Russians killed fighting the Nazis are of no significance?"

Massey intervened and said quickly, "Mr. Kholkov, we are solely concerned here with Rudolf Hess and the conditions of his imprisonment. And maybe it would put your mind at rest if I remind you that when Rudolf Hess flew to Scotland in 1941 the Soviet Union and Nazi Germany were allies." He leaned back in his chair. "Perhaps you could bear that in mind when you frame your complaint."

He saw the mixture of embarrassment and frustration on Kholkov's face. His mouth half-open to speak but no words emerging. Then the Russian took a deep breath and launched into his well-rehearsed party piece.

"The newspaper article was aimed solely at discrediting the Soviet people by suggesting that our insistence on complying with the sentence passed on this leading Nazi is inhuman, unjust and vindictive."

As Kholkov paused Maguire said, "It bloody well *is* inhuman, unjust and vindictive."

Kholkov's anger broke, his frustration desperate and obvious. He wagged an inappropriately elegant finger at Maguire and said, "You remember that statement, Mr. Maguire, when your Secretary of State next complains about articles in *Pravda* or *Izvestia* criticizing the United States' warmongers."

Maguire smiled, but not benevolently. "Just go back, Mr. Kholkov, and tell your masters that you delivered their complaint and it was duly noted."

"And what action will be taken?"

Maguire was lighting a cigar and waved the lighted match toward Massey, who said, "We have a free press, Mr. Kholkov. If you want to put your own views forward I suggest that somebody in Moscow send a letter to the *Sunday Times* making out the Soviet case."

Kholkov's anger betrayed him. His fist beat on the table as he looked at each one of them in turn. "Our people are right, you bastards don't give a shit for our people."

There was a moment's silence and then Maguire said amiably, "I must congratulate you, Mr. Kholkov, on your command of the English language." He looked around the table. "Gentlemen. Is there any other business?"

There was none, and the meeting broke up.

As he walked back toward the guardhouse Massey found himself alongside the Russian. "Have you got time for a cup of coffee, Mr. Kholkov?"

Kholkov turned to look at him, the surprise obvious on his face. He shrugged. "Time, yes. But I'm not allowed to move around in West

Berlin. I have to go directly to our liaison unit or your people will arrest me for breaking the rules."

The SIS man smiled. "Phone your people or give your driver a message. Tell them you're with me. I'll take full responsibility for returning you in an hour or so."

"Why do you suggest this?"

Massey shrugged. "We're going to cross paths quite a few times, Mr. Kholkov. It could be sensible for our masters if we had reasonable communications."

"You call it reasonable communications what you did in there?"

"It should be a lesson to you."

"How?"

"That you need to do your homework before you put your case."

"Homework? I don't understand."

"You need to prepare your case, not just bounce it on the table. That might work in Moscow, but not here."

Kholkov looked at his watch. "OK. I'll tell my driver."

Ten minutes later they were in Kempinski's and as Massey stirred his coffee he said, "I let you off lightly today, my friend."

"In what way?"

"I could have pointed out that Stalin murdered as many Russians as the Nazis did. Not only before the war, but while it was still going on." He paused. "That's why you had no experienced commanders when the Nazis invaded you. He'd had them executed because he was scared. Scared of the Soviet people turning on him. And it was that that made it possible for the Finns to give you a bloody nose when you invaded them."

"Why should you care what Stalin did?"

"Because the present men in the Kremlin would do it again if they needed to."

"Why are you saying all this?"

"Someday you might come to one of the meetings with a genuine complaint. Something that could be worked out. But if you don't recognize that cheap propaganda and table-thumping doesn't work with experienced people, then you'll never stand a chance of putting things right."

"But you and the Americans never would put anything right. If you knew something angered us you'd be delighted."

"What did you do before you were KGB?"

The Russian's dark eyes looked at his face and he said softly, "Who said I was KGB?"

"The Soviet liaison officer is always KGB. You were promoted to captain before they posted you to this job."

Kholkov shrugged. "So why ask about me if you know already, Major Massey, SIS?"

Massey was amused at the knowing schoolboy retort.

"It's Alexei, isn't it?"

"Yes."

"Where did you learn such good English?"

"At Moscow University."

"Did you know Yuri Rostov, your predecessor?"

"I met him briefly."

"He took the hard Moscow line in our meetings but it got him nowhere in three years. But he was a peasant, you're not."

"So?"

"I imagine that if Moscow had wanted another hardliner in Berlin they wouldn't have chosen you. So maybe it would pay you to prepare your case better when you have a complaint. Especially if it's genuine and not just propaganda."

"I still don't understand, Mr. Massey. Why are you telling me all this? Why should you care whether I succeed or fail?"

"It's part of my job."

Kholkov laughed. "What? To train the new KGB man in how to succeed?"

"In a way. It helps keep things from boiling over. The more we understand one another the less tension there will be. Unless one side or another actually wants the tension."

"And the American? Maguire?"

"He was fighting the Nazis before you were born, my friend."

"And hates the Russians."

"Only the nasty ones."

"Like KGB captains."

Massey smiled. "Try some charm next time. It may not work but it won't make things worse like you did today."

"You think Hess should be released?"

"I'm not sure. I could be persuaded either way. But not by propaganda." He paused. "Is this your first posting that gives you direct contact with the West?"

Kholkov hesitated, then nodded. "Maybe you really know already. But yes, I've been outside the Soviet Union but only inside Warsaw Pact countries." He shrugged. "And to answer your other question, I was an actor before I was recruited. With the Bolshoi company."

Massey smiled. "Don't you wish you were still an actor?"

"No. I was only in the reserve company. My wife wishes I was still an actor, of course. But she's an intellectual. Are you married?"

"I was. We got a divorce."

"It's not easy to keep a wife happy in this sort of job."

Massey smiled and shrugged. "I guess it depends on the wife. Anyway, I'd better take you back or your people will be getting worried."

Kholkov smiled. "I don't think so. Actually talking with the opposition will improve my status."

Massey said in Russian, "They're not fools, your bosses."

Kholkov looked amazed. "You speak Russian?"

"Why not?"

"So few foreigners speak Russian. It's very rare. And you speak without an accent. Or very little. You could be Ukrainian."

"More a Georgian by temperament, Alexei."

Kholkov laughed as he stood up. Georgians were the hot-blooded men of the Soviet Union. "We must cooperate where we can."

Massey phoned Max Cohen and told him that he'd leave their meeting until the morning. He read his mail and went early to bed.

Four

The sign said simply, and deceptively, BRITISH FORCES COMMUNICATIONS UNIT BERLIN. The Counter Intelligence sergeant checked his pass and identity card and the big gates were swung open. He had done it hundreds of times before but it made no difference.

There was coiled Dannert wire and a net of electric fencing on each side of the drive until he came to the second guardbox. His documents were checked again and a message phoned through to the house.

The house had once been the home of a furniture manufacturer. Built of stone, it sprawled over a vast area where wings had been added over the years, and now there were raw, new, windowless concrete blocks that had been added for its present occupants. There were ten acres of parkland to guard, with their complex of aerials. Long criss-crossed wires of antennas, an enormous radome, parabolic microwave dishes and a group of high, slender pylons that were strung with wires like giant birdcages.

Below ground was a vast complex of rooms spreading beyond the foundations of the buildings above ground. Living quarters, working areas, offices, generating plant, air-conditioning and a computer room. And several million dollars' worth of state-of-the-art electronic surveillance and decrypting devices. Most of the gathered information went straight to GCHQ at Cheltenham, and a lesser amount to London Communications Security Agency. A separate section covered the local surveillance and communications needed for local intelligence operations.

Jan Massey, as Head of Station, was responsible for all its activities, not just the GCHQ outstation. He was not involved in the day-to-day operations of the electronic surveillance unit; that was the responsibility of Max Cohen. Massey was much more involved with the convoluted and complex espionage and counter-espionage operations that were run by Gordon Harper. His deputy and personal assistant, Howard Fielding, was responsible for keeping him informed and updated on problem areas and planning.

He had his own quarters on the top floor of the house, the small flat on the Kurfürstendamm and another larger official apartment near Checkpoint Charlie in a block off Wilhelmstrasse. None of his people knew of the place on the Ku'damm. He paid the rental himself and the name on the door was J. Felinski. There were times when he needed to be alone. To spend a night or a couple of days away from the pressures of the house in Grunewald.

Massey walked up the wide staircase to the first floor and along the corridor to Max Cohen's office.

Max Cohen had no known living relatives. At the nearest Cohen could assess, twenty-seven of his family, including both his parents, had been gassed or burnt in one concentration camp or another. That was also the reason why he had never married.

He had been a brilliant science student at Cambridge and a total failure as a don at his own college. He walked out one morning and a few days later took a job at a small firm making advanced aircraft communication systems. He was spotted a year later and recruited by GCHQ. He had specified and partly designed the total radio surveillance system that was installed in Berlin, supervised its installation and was then put in charge of the operation. He and Massey got on well with each other without any undue effort on either side. They recognized and tolerated each other's idiosyncrasies and found common ground in their resistance to being molded into the typical Brit character. The Jew and the Pole, who might well have been antagonistic in any other European community, exchanged their sly but amiable jokes at their British colleagues' expense. It defused their antagonisms and afforded them a small enclave of relief when stiff upper lips or some routine Brit hypocrisy set their pulses pounding in frustrated anger.

Max Cohen's hatred for Germans was controlled but chronic, and active enough for him to feel guilty when he slept with German girls or listened furtively to almost any Wagner music from *Tristan* to *Parsifal*. He loved it all.

Cohen was talking on the phone and Massey stood looking at the bunch of sit-reps clipped to the white board on the wall. Status reports on equipment. Changes of personnel on listening shifts. A list of current names and words to be alerted to the evaluation section. A leave roster for Russian speakers and a similar one for German speakers. A list of four new Red Army units which had moved into Leipzig in the previous twenty-four hours, with their current frequencies in brackets, and a reference number of the files that would give all recorded information about their status and function.

When Cohen hung up, Massey sat down on the chair in front of the trestle table that Cohen used as a desk.

"Any new problems, Max?"

"No. Some old ones getting worse."

"Which ones?"

"The shortage of KG4 microchips for upgrading the special tape recorders. We're ten days behind schedule. And we had a break in recording GRU traffic yesterday. One of the Racal 6790s was on the blink. The RAM 'keep alive' memory on one band went down. We lost about an hour."

"Did you miss anything important?"

Cohen shrugged. "Who knows, Jan? Probably not."

"Any problems in Harper's area?"

Cohen smiled. "That's the only part you really care about, isn't it?"

"It's the only part where people who work for me can get killed because of mistakes." Massey smiled. "And it's the part I understand. Anyway, you keep your end up pretty well without me. Your friends at Cheltenham were full of praise at the Joint Intelligence meeting last week. There was talk about an MBE or some such thing in the next honors list—services to industry."

"I'd rather get a guaranteed supply of microchips."

"So what about Harper and his boys?"

"Which do you want first—the good or the bad?"

"The bad."

"I want to sack one of your radio operators for bad on-air discipline and I want you to discipline one of Harper's men for the same thing."

"What happened?"

"Malins had sent a surveillance team into East Berlin to take a look at the KGB HQ in Normanenallee. He'd heard that there was building work going on there and London wanted them to see what it was in aid of. We gave them a frequency and a code and they were warned to use it only in an emergency. One of them, a chap named Rawlins, came on air—in clear—and asked the operator to tell his girlfriend he'd be an hour late. The operator responded—also in clear—and contacted the girl by phone. It was irresponsible, Jan. Harper's people see themselves as being above rules and regulations and it's going to cost you dear one of these days if we don't stop it. I've sent you a memo about it."

"OK. I'll deal with it."

"Toughly? No excuses."

"Exactly how you want, Max. I agree that there are no excuses but there are reasons why they behave like idiots."

"Tell me. I'd like to hear them."

For a few seconds Massey was silent. "When they go through the Wall into East Berlin or over the frontier into the GDR it takes a lot of guts, Max. If they're caught they know what'll happen to them, so there's a lot of adrenaline flowing. What they're doing is illegal and dangerous, and they're on their own with every man's hand turned against them. This place seems a long way away. And the routine rules and regulations are far away too. They've got an in-built disrespect for the law. We train them that way. They're special—and they know it. And sometimes they act irresponsibly. Not excusable, I agree. But just about understandable."

"You don't need to do a hearts-and-flowers job on me, Jan. I can imagine what it's like, but if they want to end up in a KGB cell at Karlshorst, bad radio security is a quick way of getting there. My boys aren't the only ones with headphones on twiddling the knobs up and down the short wave frequencies."

"I'll deal with them, Max. Don't worry." Massey paused. "What's the good news?"

Cohen picked up a transparent plastic folder and tossed it across the table. There were half a dozen A4 pages inside it.

"We've broken the new Moscow code in record time. They changed it a day early and in the middle of a transmission. We only missed seven minutes. It's interesting stuff. I wasn't going to pass it to Evaluation until you'd seen it. It looks like a major reshuffle of KGB staff in East Berlin." He shrugged. "Anyway. See what you think of it."

"Thanks. Did Loftus cooperate on the courier problem you had?"

"Yes. He moaned a bit, but he's increased our nominal roll by two extra couriers for the next six months."

"No other problems?"

"Dozens, but none that you need to worry about."

"I'll see you at the meeting this afternoon."

"OK."

In his own suite of office and living quarters Massey went through the various piles of accumulated memos and reports. A mass of information on what was going on in the city of Berlin, both East and West. Reports on living conditions and morale in East Germany and the GDR. Transcripts of selected intercepts of Soviet military and civilian telephone and radio communications. The operations covered not only the Russians and East Germans but all diplomatic establishments in Berlin including its German government and all the representatives of other countries' intelligence and diplomatic services.

There was a single-page daily summary of items drawn to his attention and compiled by his assistant, Howard Fielding. Fielding was thirty, a history graduate from Aston University who had specialized in Soviet studies. A calm, unflappable academic who had learned how to act as a safety net and defender of his more volatile boss.

Harper had stayed behind after the general meeting and filled him in on the details of a few operations that were too confidential to be discussed in front of other section heads. Massey ordered him to downgrade the two offenders mentioned by Cohen and transfer them back to London without waiting for replacements. Harper saw the look on Massey's face and abandoned the defense he had prepared for the field agent. Massey in that mood wouldn't be impressed by the fact that the man's girlfriend was pregnant.

"I think Bourget is anxious to speak to you. He's mentioned it to me a couple of times. I told him you were in London."

"What does he want?"

"I've no idea."

"What are the French up to at the moment?"

"The Mission is buttering up the Germans on orders from Paris. The Mitterand–Kohl axis. And the SDECE—well, you know them as well as I do. Rushing off in all directions to no particular purpose—apart from impressing Paris."

"Are they operating in East Berlin at all?"

"Just casual line-crossers. In and out the same day."

"How do they go in?"

"They use the usual tourist coach trips." Harper smiled. "They check the prices of fruit and vegetables and a few household goods and call it economic intelligence. They chat up a waitress or a barman and that's evaluating public morale."

"How does Bourget stand with Paris these days?"

"OK, so far as I know."

"I'll let you know what he's got to say when I've spoken to him."

"Don't forget I'm in London for two days next week."

"What for?"

"Routine medical."

Five

Heidi Fischer walked back slowly from the Justiz Palast in Vienna toward the History of Art Museum, her backside rolling provocatively and her blue eyes alert and vigilant for any sign of interest from the few men who passed by in the narrow back streets. She was eighteen and well built, with long legs and firm breasts. She wasn't pretty but she was attractive with a neat turned-up nose and pouting, almost petulant lips. She was Viennese but looked more German. Solid, and without the chic that most Viennese girls managed to contrive with a scarf or a belt or even a smile. But the rather stolid farmgirl appearance seemed somehow to emphasize her obvious sexual attraction. There would be no swinging from chandeliers but she looked as if those long legs would open eagerly enough to satisfy a man's lust.

Despite its being the middle of summer a slight drizzle began to fall and that gave her an excuse to stand in the shelter of the shop doorway of Apotheke Ludke. Twenty minutes later a U.S. army jeep slowed down as the driver looked her over and then stopped. A few minutes bargaining and she climbed in over the tailboard and the canvas flapped to behind her. Arthur was never worried about the men but he objected to her taking them back to the room when he was there.

An hour later her high heels were clattering up the stone steps to the

25

fourth-floor room in the old house in a cobbled alley off BreiteGasse. He was sitting there smoking, his battledress blouse hung over the back of the chair. Signalman Arthur Johnson was twenty-three, with a raw, fleshy face and a body already showing a tendency to flabbiness. He glanced at her as she came into the room and then looked back at the black-and-white TV. The sound was turned down because he couldn't speak German and the football game had a German commentary. While he was watching she made coffee for them both and a plateful of corned-beef sandwiches from an army ration tin.

When the match was over he said, "How did you get on?"

She smiled. "OK. Thirty marks."

"How many fellows?"

"Two. One British and one Yank."

He watched as she counted out the money before putting it in a china vase on the small table under the window.

"I got news for you, Heidi. I've been posted."

She turned quickly. "Where to?"

"Berlin."

"When?"

"The day after tomorrow. Friday."

"Can I go with you?"

He shook his head slowly. "I shouldn't think so. You're not even proper German."

The girl's eyes blazed with anger and her voice was shrill. "Is that all you care? You said you'd marry me. You said we'd have a proper life. No more street work for me. I'd be your wife. We'd have a place of our own. And now you just sit there calmly and say you're off to Berlin without me."

"Calm down, for Christ's sake. I'll just have to work out how to get you there when I've settled in and know how to do it."

He pulled her into his lap and kissed her avidly as his hand went under her skirt. It was several minutes later when she struggled and took her mouth from his. "You bastard. You're just like the others. You just want to screw me and you—"

Her words were smothered by his mouth on hers and five minutes later they were both naked on the ramshackle bed.

Signalman Arthur Johnson sat in the underground room and checked the computer print-out of incoming stores against the print-out of the official order. He didn't know what most of the items were, and nobody explained them to him because he didn't need to know. And "need to know" was paramount in the house in Grunewald. He had never been beyond these rooms, apart from his shared room in the big house upstairs. It took several minutes of elaborate electronic games to get into or out of his small office. He had only the vaguest idea of what went on in the labyrinth of rooms and cubicles beyond the metal door. Nobody would ever tell him, and part of the reason why he'd been posted to the unit was that he was too oafish to care but bright enough to do several of the routine jobs that had to be done. The fact that he didn't know or care what the difference was between gallium arsenide and recrystallized polysilicon was, to the man who had recruited him, a virtue in itself.

Arthur Johnson was born in Handsworth, a suburb of Birmingham that had once been a cut above its neighboring district, Aston. Handsworth had then been a place for the upper working class—skilled craftsmen and foremen, many from Scotland and Wales, who worked in the nearby foundries and big industrial plants and saw it as proof of their status that they could move to Handsworth and bring up their families in such a pleasant environment. Flower shows and bands in the local park, a good tram service to other parts of the city, and a quiet respectability that suited their temperaments. But the trams went and soon the respectability went. And Handsworth became the fief of immigrants and the unemployed. Nobody knew why they had chosen Handsworth but in five years they had taken over.

He never knew who his father was apart from the fact that his name was Joe and that his mother hated him. She hated her son too. Inevitably he did badly at school but that wasn't unusual by local standards. By the time he was fifteen he seldom went to school and spent his time running errands for local bookmakers and prostitutes. He lacked the street-smartness of his contemporaries and that was an advantage. As it turned out, this lack of enterprise continued to stand him in good stead in the future. He seemed too dull and too stupid to be mistrusted.

When Arthur was sixteen he had gone home one night to find his few possessions in a cardboard box on the front steps. There was a note from his mother telling him that she had given up the house. It was being sold by the landlord and he'd have to find somewhere else to live. She wouldn't be back. She wished him luck and there were two pound-notes in the envelope.

He had picked up the cardboard box and walked round to Johnny's place. Johnny had been an all-in wrestler using the name Tarzan but now he was keeper for two girls who plied their trade up near the recreation ground. Arthur wasn't actually made welcome but he wasn't turned away. He cleaned the house, ran messages and chatted with the girls when they weren't occupied with their trade. And in their own odd way they became surrogate sisters and mothers to him, and shared their innermost thoughts with the young man: ambitions for hairdressing salons or smart boutiques, and their anecdotes of customers and their funny ways. The older of the two girls granted him her standard favors a few times but it was always her initiative, not his. He was energetic but undemanding.

It was Johnny who fixed him up with the job at the radio shop.

Customers bringing in their radios and TVs for repair mistook his silence for hostility and eventually the boss put him out of sight in the small back room to help the repairman. By the time Arthur Johnson was eighteen he could fix most of the routine breakdowns himself. He could even use the test instruments without understanding even the rudiments of electricity.

He saw the display in the window of the recruiting office in the city center but only stopped to read the noticeboard after he spotted the chassis of a radio set and a television. It happened to be a recruiting campaign for the Royal Corps of Signals and he went inside. After half an hour of questions and chat he signed the papers and was given a travel warrant to Catterick Camp. At the end of the course he wasn't surprised when he failed. The technical stuff was far beyond him and the practical side little better. He was used to domestic appliances, not the high-flown electronics that the army used.

But he was in the army and somehow a job had to be found for him. He had a few virtues that could be of use: he did what he was told, he was uncomplaining, and he could read and write. Signalman Johnson was trained as a clerk and was posted to a small specialist unit in Cumbria. After several other postings he was eventually sent to what was called the Composite Signals Unit in Vienna. One of the small but vital links in a chain that led back to GCHQ in Cheltenham.

The Kit-Kat Club in Berlin's Uhlandstrasse has no pretensions. Dimly lit, to hide its tattiness and the identity of its habitués, it offers expensive drinks and cheap food and a harbor for petty criminals and prostitutes. Arthur Johnson had tried most of the clubs in the area and found the Kit-Kat less of a rip-off than its neighbors. And the girls were pretty and uninhibited.

He had never had a relationship with a girl other than a prostitute. Not that he was either a pervert or particularly sex driven. But, perhaps due to his earlier experiences, he was drawn toward prostitutes because it avoided responsibility. They had their own places and they earned their own money. And in their turn the girls, recognizing his weak but amiable character, found him an undemanding companion. He didn't want to take any of their earnings, his sexual demands were normal and intermittent. And he was male, and someone to talk to.

Johnson's new girlfriend earned her living between performing an uninspired strip act and casual prostitution. Being both several years older and far more worldly than Johnson, she was aware that she was less a mistress than a mother substitute for him. She listened to his complaints about how the army treated him and he brought her cartons of cigarettes and tins of coffee from the NAAFI. And on Sundays, if he was off duty, he had her for ten minutes of crude urgent lust before they went to a cinema or for a meal in a restaurant. Otherwise, he spent his off-duty evenings with her as if they were brother and sister.

Signalman Johnson would watch her act as he waited for her on his free nights with the feeling that he was part of show business. An impresario, or perhaps a talent spotter for some Hollywood studio. That particular night she was doing the coy version of her act. Twirling the paper parasol as the tape played "Raindrops Keep Falling on My Head" and undoing the buttons on the yellow plastic raincoat with her free hand.

He was sitting sipping a beer when a shadow fell across the table and a girl's voice said, "Hello, Arthur." He didn't look up at the girl, assuming that she was one of the other regulars. But when she pulled out a chair and sat down he turned briefly to see who it was. For long moments he just stared, his mouth open, his eyes screwed up in disbelief.

"Heidi. What the hell are you doing here?"

"You said you'd send for me."

"I tried, Heidi. I couldn't get anywhere. It's bloody difficult."

"You glad to see me?"

"Of course I am. Where're you staying?"

"I've got a room near Checkpoint Charlie. I've been here two weeks. Looking for you."

"Let's go there. It'll be easier to talk."

She smiled. A knowing, experienced smile. "Saves paying thirty marks for screwing one of these chicks, you mean."

"Come on, Heidi, you know it's not just that."

She shrugged. "OK. Let's go."

Heidi Fischer had slept with five different officials to acquire the permits and documents she needed to get to West Berlin. Two in Vienna. One in Bonn. And one in West Berlin who was ready to keep her documents up to date in return for more sex. An impartial observer might wonder if Signalman Johnson was worth all the trouble. He was neither handsome nor wealthy, nor did he have the affection or charm that most girls would consider worth competing for. But he was British and a soldier and he had one unique virtue so far as Heidi Fischer was concerned: he was the only man who had ever, no matter how obliquely, hinted that he might marry her. With a large surplus of women in Austria and Germany, men who mentioned marriage were rare. And with such a marriage she would become a British citizen with a legal passport of her own. A British subject, not an ex-enemy alien.

As she undressed slowly and professionally she could tell that he wanted her and that was a relief. Although he was never demanding, when they had sex he was crude and clumsy. But her attractive face and the thing between her legs were the only assets she had.

29

When it was over and he lay smoking a cigarette beside her on the bed she said, "How've you been getting on?"

He leaned up, reaching over her to stub out the Lucky Strike in the metal ashtray. "Still in the same old grind. Three chaps been promoted over my head. I been thinking of getting out. Going back to civvy street."

"Why didn't they promote you?"

"Christ knows. They think I'm just a zombie."

"What's a zombie?"

"A mad person. Crazy."

"Poor old Arthur."

"I'll get my own back on the bastards one of these days. You mark my words."

"How would you do that?"

"I've got ideas, girl. I'm not just bluffing. Maybe you could help me."

"Oh, Arthur. I'll help you. You know I will. Any way you want."

Johnson looked at his watch. "I'll have to go, Heidi. There's a service bus back to the unit at midnight."

"Can you see me tomorrow?"

"I ain't sure. I'll try. It'd be about eight if I can make it."

It had been a bad day for Johnson. A document wrongly registered, a rollocking from the CSM, and a snotty interview with Meyer. Just one bloody document and all that fuss. And the same question again and again. Why had he registered it under Karlshorst intercepts instead of GRU? Why keep on asking him? If he could have told them why it had happened he wouldn't have done it in the first place. He'd just mistaken the network coding index, but they behaved like he'd started World War III. They always had to have somebody to blame for their cock-ups and it was always him.

He was still in a bad mood by the time he got to Heidi's rooms. But as she cooked him a meal and he sat drinking a coffee, the first glimmerings of how to strike back at the bastards filtered slowly into his mind.

As Heidi placed the plate of sausages and potato in front of him she noticed the change of mood.

"What have you been up to, Arthur?"

"I've had enough of the army, Heidi. I'll never make enough for us to get married. They don't give a damn about me."

"What you got in mind?"

"You and me are going to Moscow, kid."

She looked amazed. "Moscow? What the hell for?"

"I'll do broadcasts against the British and the Yanks. Tell the world how they really treat people. I can tell the Russians how to do it. Propaganda. I'll give press conferences, go on radio and TV. Write for the newspapers, the lot."

30

"D'you know any Russians?"

"No. That's where you can help me."

"How?"

"Go through the Checkpoint. Find a Russian officer and tell him I'm ready to come over."

She looked shocked. "I couldn't do that. I don't speak Russian. How would I find a Russian officer?"

"They're all over the place, girl. Just give one the eye and tell him the tale. We could make a fortune. I'd be like Philby and what's-his-name, the queer. Questions in Parliament. God, they'd see I wasn't just a dumb cluck after all. I'd show the bastards."

She shook her head in disbelief. "I couldn't do it, Arthur. I wouldn't know how to go about it. I wouldn't dare."

Johnson looked at her. "If you want to marry me, kid, you'll do it. It's the only way."

Heidi Fischer shook her head. "I'll think about it. But I don't fancy it. It's scary."

"Try. Just try. See what happens. There's no harm in trying."

"What if they don't believe me?"

"They'll give it a go, girl. They want people to go over to them. They make them into heroes. They do."

"And if it works we'd get married?"

"Why not, kid? Why not?"

Six

Massey had slept that night at the flat in the Ku'damm and drove back to the house in Grunewald the next morning.

There was a note on his desk that there had been another call for him from Bourget. The Frenchman had left a number for him to call. It wasn't the usual SDECE number.

Like most British and American intelligence officers he walked very cautiously when he was dealing with the SDECE. They were tough and energetic but in Berlin they were riddled with KGB plants. There had been scandal after scandal ever since SDECE had been founded in the early nineteen-sixties. Narcotics dealings, counterfeiting and particularly bloody assassinations. And on top of all that they were unreliable, disreputable and, from an intelligence point of view, insecure.

He dialed the number that Bourget had left and a girl answered. A sleepy bedroom voice in German not French. He had to wait a couple of minutes before Bourget came on the line.

"Jan?" His voice sounded like she'd had to wake him up.

"Yes, Pierre. What can I do for you?"

"What time is it?"

"Nine thirty."

"Do you know Au bon Bistroquet?"

"On the Ku'damm?"

"Yes. How about we meet there in an hour? Say a quarter after eleven?"

"OK. But I can't stay long."

"Just a coffee, my friend, or a bowl of soup."

"OK."

Bourget had booked a table but when Massey got there the Frenchman hadn't arrived. They showed him to the table and brought him a glass of red wine. He guessed that that bedroomy voice had held things up.

Bourget came in looking as villainous and attractive as ever. It was one of those very lived-in faces. Tanned, heavily pock-marked, but undoubtedly attractive to women. He was a Hemingway man, strong, energetic and hairy. Massey didn't like the type though he quite liked Bourget. But he suspected that sooner or later the Frenchman would end up on Devil's Island or wherever the French put their naughty boys these days.

"Well, my friend, I made it," Bourget said, as if being late was some special achievement.

"I've got twenty minutes, Pierre. No longer."

"Bouillabaisse?"

"Fine."

Until the girl brought the soup he was given the benefit of Bourget's views on Berlin and the Germans. Bourget wasn't a fan of either. Then, hunching his shoulders as if that gave them greater privacy, he got down to business.

"Got a problem, old friend. Think you could help."

"What is it?"

"What KGB have you got at the moment? Not defectors I mean."

Massey smiled. "You don't expect me to tell you, do you?"

"Why not?"

"It'd be in the local papers in two days. Your outfit leaks all over the place."

"No way. Just between you and me."

"Why do you want to know?"

"I think I got somebody from the other side."

"Who?"

Bourget shrugged. "I can't say you. Is not finished yet."

"So let's wait. We can talk when you've got him."

"He's more important to you than to me. Maybe we can cooperate. You went to the meeting in Paris, yes?"

"Yes."

"So we can cooperate."

"It doesn't need a meeting in Paris to make us cooperate, Pierre. But I can't do a deal about some unknown man who might defect but hasn't as yet done so."

Bourget looked troubled. "You want to know who he is?"

"It's up to you, Pierre."

"Is Kuznetsov."

Massey hesitated. "Tell me more." He paused. "Are you sure he's not a plant?"

"No. I'm not sure. That's why I like cooperate with you."

"Why does he say he wants to defect?"

"He don't say."

"What's he want?"

"Wants to go to your people or CIA. New identity, cash and pension."

"So why didn't he approach me or Autenowski at CIA?"

"He got no choice, my friend." Bourget smiled. "He talk with me or nothing."

"When are you meeting him again?"

"Any time you want."

"Where can we meet him?"

"My villa."

"He'd never go there. There's people watching your place all the time."

Bourget grinned. "I got him there now. We picked him up two days ago. We been working on him."

"Why don't you just pass him over to me?"

Bourget grinned. "No way, Jan, no way." He paused. "Maybe I sell him to you. A private deal."

He didn't like the sound of it but it was typical SDECE. "How much do you want?"

"Fifteen thousand U.S. dollars in cash."

"London would never agree to that."

Bourget smiled. "I can get more than that from others."

"Who?"

The Frenchman shook his head. "You think about it, my friend. Let me know when you want to do a deal."

"Let me talk to London and see what their reaction is."

"They don't let you decide these things here on the spot?"

Massey smiled because the jibe was so obvious and naïve. "I like to keep them in the picture, Pierre. By the way, who's the girl with the sexy voice?"

The Frenchman grinned, his strong uneven teeth gleaming. "You want to try her, my old friend. Leni. Blonde, not yet twenty. Long legs, beautiful big tits. I make you a present of her if we do a deal, yes? What do they call it? A goodwill gesture, yes?"

"You're a thoughtful, wonderful man, Pierre, but I'm too old for young blondes."

Bourget was looking down at the table crumbling the remains of a *brioche*, and without looking up he said, "What d'you think of Kholkov?"

"He's hard-working. He knows what he's doing."

"Would you trust him?"

"I'd never put myself in a position where I needed to trust him. One way or another."

"Would you trust him in an exchange deal?"

"Provided all the *t*'s were crossed and the *i*'s were dotted, yes."

"What does it mean, the *t*'s crossed and dotted?"

"It means that I'd want to go over every possible detail and angle first. The Russians usually deliver when they've made a deal but they drive a hard bargain first."

Bourget shrugged. "Is best you think seriously about what I say, my friend."

Massey stood up. "I'll think about it, Pierre, and I'll be in touch. *Soyez sage.*"

Bourget nodded and turned away to beckon to the waitress.

As Massey walked back to the flat he thought of what Bourget had said about Kholkov. He had met Kholkov three or four times since that first meeting six months earlier. They had been routine meetings at the Kommandatura but he had had a meal with Kholkov after one of the meetings. He had felt then that there was something odd about the Russian. He was cool and sophisticated and he talked fairly freely for a KGB man. But Kholkov's operation in West Berlin was hopelessly inefficient. His people were being pulled in by Harper's men at a rate of almost one a week. He might have been good as an instructor but it was different doing it in the real world. In the real world sex, money and fear were factors that lectures and training manuals only mentioned as hazards. In the real world they were a large part of life itself.

He wondered why Bourget had Kholkov in mind as a contact for some exchange deal. Maybe Bourget knew something about Kholkov that he didn't know. But Bourget's story of having picked up Kuznetsov must be a figment of the Frenchman's imagination. Kuznetsov never ventured into West Berlin. He didn't need to and his KGB bosses wouldn't have let him.

Massey breathed a sigh of relief as he let himself into his flat in the Ku'damm.

He switched on the hi-fi. There was a program of Viennese songs on RIAS Berlin FM and he hummed along with "Sag beim Abschied" as he stood looking out of the window.

The British and the Americans were putting on a cocktail and buffet party that night at the Hilton. He had often tried to remember afterwards what it was in aid of. He thought it was to commemorate the anniversary of the Potsdam Conference, but it could have been something quite different.

He disliked parties of any kind but there were some he couldn't avoid without causing real offense. Twenty minutes of doing his duty, then maybe a call to the art student he'd become friendly with. She was an American. Very young and very pretty, and she was having a year in Berlin before heading back to Chicago and the graphics department of her father's advertising agency. She was collecting scalps on the way in case she never got to Europe again. Berlin in the eighties had become like Paris in the twenties for Americans.

He switched off the radio, passed the Hilton telephone number to Cohen and Moore, then walked a few yards down the Ku'damm until he found a taxi.

When he got to the Hilton he was glad he hadn't backed out. His absence would have been noted. Consular staffs, military missions, NATO and visiting brass from Paris, London and Washington were there in force. There was too much of a crush for any serious talking but Massey dutifully did the rounds. When eventually he made for one of the exits he saw Kholkov talking to Bourget and the Frenchman's current girlfriend. He nodded to them as he passed, smiling to himself at the brashness of the Frenchman, who defied the ban on Germans at the party by bringing a German girl—and a callgirl at that.

It was then that he noticed the girl in the black dress. She was standing alone as if she was waiting for someone. He registered that she was beautiful before he passed her.

He was almost at the cloakroom when Kholkov caught up with him. "Massey. Jan. Come and meet my wife. She's with me tonight." He smiled. "Special dispensation from the Kommandatura."

Massey hesitated for a moment but was aware of the Russian's enthusiasm.

"Of course, Alexei. I'd very much like to meet her."

She was still standing there, just outside the crowded room, and she definitely was beautiful. Stunningly, breathtakingly beautiful. Almost as tall as her husband. Black hair in a chignon, heavy-lidded brown eyes, and a wide, sensuous mouth. She was wearing a black silk cocktail dress that emphasized her slender, elegant neck.

She put out her hand, smiling as Kholkov said, "Anna, this is Jan Massey."

"Kak pozywacie."

"Jak pozywacie."

They both laughed at the Englishness of the greeting and response and then Kholkov said, "You two talk while I go and say my bread-and-butter thank-yous."

They stood silent for a moment and then she said, "Alexei told me that you're English." She smiled. "I would have said that you were a Pole."

He smiled back. "Why would you say that?"

"You speak very good Russian but you said jak instead of kak so you must be more used to speaking Polish. And nobody actually bothers to learn Polish."

"Do you speak Polish?"

She laughed. "I *am* Polish." Then she shrugged. "Or I was Polish. My mother was Polish."

"My mother was Polish too."

She lifted her eyebrows. "Was?"

"She's dead."

"Oh. I'm sorry." She paused. "My momma's dead too. Four years ago. In a car accident in Leningrad when the roads were icy." Then she said softly, "When did your mother die?"

"A long time ago. In the last few months of the war."

"What happened? Was she ill?"

"The Nazis killed her in one of their camps."

"Was she Jewish?"

"No. She was in the Resistance."

"Is your father still alive?"

"Yes, he's a doctor in a small town in England. And yours?"

"He teaches music at the Conservatory in Moscow."

Then Kholkov was back, smiling amiably. "We'd better go, Anna."

Massey hesitated for a moment, then said, "Why don't you both have dinner with me sometime next week?"

Kholkov looked at his wife. "OK, Anna?" She nodded and Massey said, "How about next Friday? Seven o'clock at Café Wien?"

"Fine. We'll look forward to that."

They said their goodbyes and after they had left, Massey went to the bar for a drink before he walked to the foyer and stood waiting for a taxi. He didn't phone the art student but went straight back to his flat.

The dinner was not a success despite the good food. Even the traditional questions asked of new acquaintances were taboo. No questions on background, previous life, work, politics, relationships but could be seen as probing for information for a dossier.

They talked about music and art, but even in those areas Massey was conscious of the fact that in the Soviet Union the Politburo could decide that a painting or a symphony was anti-Soviet propaganda.

They ended up talking about ice-skating, athletics and gymnastics. Sports where the Russians were world leaders without controversy. Subjects that not one of them cared about but were acceptable for their neutrality.

Anna Kholkov did her best to make it seem normal and less tense. She had been a ballet dancer before they were married and she was able to amuse them with anecdotes about dragonlike wardrobe mistresses and autocratic directors.

Massey drove them back to Checkpoint Charlie just after eleven and watched them pass through the barriers on both sides. A car was waiting for them on the East German side and the girl turned and waved to him as the driver opened the door for her.

He stood for several minutes, looking but not seeing, before he got back into his car and headed for Grunewald.

Seven

Massey waved Harper to one of the leather armchairs in his office and pulled its twin to face his visitor.

"Have you had anything out of SDECE recently, Jimmy?"

Harper looked surprised. "Nothing but the usual gossip."

"Personal gossip or business gossip?"

"Personal. They've been playing footsie with one of my chaps recently but it's only a mild fishing expedition. Hoping to get something they can use to pad out their reports to Paris." He smiled. "We feed them a scrap or two to keep them happy and a bit of disinformation to keep the boys in Paris on the hop." He paused. "Have you heard something?"

"Nothing that I could believe . . . but I heard a rumor that a Russian had come over and was holed up with Bourget."

Harper shook his head. "I don't believe it. Any Russian would come to the CIA or us. Any Russian who knew the business, anyway."

"Could you get your people to do a little sniffing around?"

"Of course. Anything more to go on? Name, when, how, et cetera?"

"I'm afraid not."

"Any priority?"

"Days, not weeks. A nil report could be as useful as anything else for my purposes."

"Can you tell me your source?"

"I could but I'd rather leave it."

"A classification, maybe?"

Massey smiled at Harper's persistence. "Let's say . . . unreliable but close. OK?"

Harper laughed softly. "Sounds like Bourget to me. And he was trying to contact you for some weeks. I passed the messages to Howard Fielding as they came in."

"No comment." Massey smiled. "Any new problems?"

Harper looked quizzically at Massey. "Are you sure you want to hear?"

"Of course."

"I need another evaluator, preferably two. Mason's team can't cope with the traffic now we're getting all the transcript summaries."

"You asked for it that way . . . and you were right . . . it saves thirty-six hours on anything you need."

"I know but—"

"I'll get you one—let me know if you need another. Evaluators are in short supply and you'll need to spend at least a month before the new one's any use to you."

"Can I tell Mason?"

"Sure. I'll speak to London today."

When Harper had left, Massey still sat on in the armchair. He couldn't stop thinking about what Bourget had said about Kuznetsov. He didn't believe it, but it worried him that the Frenchman's lie had been based on Kuznetsov. There were dozens of other Russians he could have picked on. Was it some sort of hint? Or a threat? Not even Harper knew about Kuznetsov. Only Chambers and himself. He couldn't mention it to Chambers at this stage. He looked at his watch. It was time to go to the CIA meeting, the Joint Intelligence Liaison Committee where SIS and the CIA exchanged as little information of their operations as diplomacy would allow. If there was anything important that one side had to tell the other it would be done in Washington or London, not in West Berlin.

The Kholkovs had invited him to dinner that evening and they were waiting for him at the barrier on the East Berlin side of the checkpoint.

It was a warm, pleasant evening and they walked to the Café Warschau on Karl Marx Allee.

Anna ordered the meal for the three of them, choosing only Polish dishes—*barszcz, kotlet, nalesniki,* no wine but two bottles of *sliwowica.* She had teased her husband because she had to translate for him.

As they ate, Massey was constantly aware that Kholkov was watching him and he wondered if the Russian was more suspicious and less friendly now that he had had time to absorb what went on between the two sides in Berlin. When the girl photographer was doing the rounds of the guests at the tables, Anna Kholkov angrily waved her away when she attempted to take a photograph of them. He felt grateful to her for the partisanship but he knew that there would be plenty of photographs of him already on the KGB files.

A small orchestra was playing for dancing and he watched as Kholkov danced with his wife. They looked a handsome pair. It passed through his mind that it must be very nice to have a wife who was so beautiful and so intelligent. He asked her to dance with him when they came back to the table. When they were on the small dance floor she said, "I apologize about the photographer. I don't think Alexei had arranged it."

Massey smiled. "It doesn't matter, they'll have dozens on the files already. But thanks all the same."

She smiled up at him. "Do you recognize what they're playing?"

"I recognize the tune. It was on one of my mother's old gramophone records. What's it called?"

She sang very softly, "*Ptynie Wista, ptynie. Po Polskiej krajinie—Po Polskiej . . .*"

And then he remembered it. The gentle little ballad that said that while the Vistula river still flowed Poland would always be free.

He smiled. "Are they allowed to play such songs now?"

She shrugged. "This place is mainly for Poles. I doubt if the Russians know what the words mean. I'm sure they'd stop it if they knew."

"Any news from your father?"

"Are you trying to change the subject?"

Massey laughed. "Yes. But for your sake not mine."

"My father disapproved of my marriage. I never hear from him. He's cut me out of his life."

"What did he object to?"

"Oh, two things. The main one was Alexei himself. He didn't like him."

"And the second?"

"The fact that Alexei is KGB. My father despises them. All of them."

"But your father's Russian not Polish."

"All Russians don't go along with the system." She shrugged. "But I guess I don't need to tell *you* that."

"Does Alexei know his views?"

"I'm afraid he does."

"Maybe your father's attitude to you is to protect you from being associated with his views."

"That's what I tell myself when I'm lonely and unhappy."

"You don't look unhappy—ever."

She sighed. "That's part of the system, Jan. You know that. That's how one survives."

"What are you unhappy about?"

41

"Just being alive."

"Oh, Anna. Don't say that."

"Why not?"

"Because you're young and beautiful and far too intelligent to despair like that."

"I heard a song by Frank Sinatra once—called 'Come Fly With Me.' I wish I could just fly away like it says in the song."

"Where would you fly to?"

"Anywhere. Somewhere quiet and peaceful. A small village. In France maybe."

"We'll have to see what we can do."

"We?" And her brown eyes were on his face.

"I'll think of something to cheer you up."

She smiled but said nothing, and when the music stopped he walked her back to the table.

They both walked back with him to the checkpoint and when he turned on the Allied side to look back she waved to him and he waved back. He saw a big black Merc pull up behind them and he stood watching until its tail-lights faded as it drove away.

In the flat on the Ku'damm he poured himself a whiskey and switched on the radio for the news from the Voice of America. But he didn't listen. He was thinking of the car's red lights disappearing into the grim darkness of East Berlin. And of Anna Kholkov. She must trust him implicitly to have been so outspoken. And he wondered what was the root of her unhappiness. Living under the Soviet system was depressing enough. Especially for a Pole. But people did live under that system and survive. Without feeling such despair. It must be more than that.

The Joint Allied Intelligence meeting in Paris had been much as usual. The French pressing for a free exchange of intelligence from Berlin and he and the American choosing their words carefully so that their evasions gave the least possible offense. When the meeting closed in the early evening Massey had strolled back to the hotel with Maguire.

As they walked down the Faubourg Saint-Honoré he saw something in a jeweler's shop window that made him stop and look. It was a model made in plaster displaying a pearl necklace. The slender neck of the model reminded him of another neck. Maguire stood a few paces away. Hands in pockets, watching him, waiting for him. When Massey joined the American again, Maguire said, "Who's the lucky lady, Jan?"

Massey smiled. "Nobody. I was just interested by the display."

"It's about time you got yourself a girlfriend, anyway."

"I've got several girlfriends already."

"I mean a real one."

"You mean a good Irish-American?"

"You could do a lot worse at that."

"How long before you get back to Boston?"

"Ten months four days."

Massey laughed. "You must have found our games in Berlin a bit of a contrast to the U.S. Army."

"Not really. I did a stint in the Pentagon. That's a bit like Berlin when you get behind the scenes."

"How do you get on with Bourget?"

Maguire laughed softly. "I hit the town with him now and again just to look friendly. He's OK. A bit of a bull in a china shop, but he's got guts."

"Do you exchange much with him?"

"Just penny-ante stuff to keep him happy. He couldn't offer us anything we don't know already."

"And what's the official attitude to cooperating with the Brits these days?"

"The official attitude is that that's for Washington and London. But I've always had the green light to cooperate with you personally on Berlin matters."

"Any problems with my people at the moment?"

"None. My guy keeps in touch with Harper and Mason and I leave it to Fort Meade to liaise with Max Cohen. No, no problems—you want a drink?"

"Just a quick one. I've got somebody over here from London and I want to leave before midday tomorrow."

"To London or Berlin?"

"Berlin." Massey grinned. "I don't go to London unless I'm called for."

Eight

Eric Mayhew was forty-eight. A shortish, slightly built man of a usually mild disposition. Acquaintances and colleagues at work had sometimes been surprised by his reaction to a casual and not ill-meant joke about his size or his intelligence. The response was never open anger but he harbored grudges permanently. With a sharp, almost vindictive, tongue he harassed offenders long after they had forgotten the original cause.

He had been routinely bullied at school, but his teachers' praise for his skill in mathematics had compensated for most of it. His career had been a matter of steady and continuous progress. Appreciated by his superiors, almost unknown to his colleagues, he was considered as a solid, respectable, middle-class man of reasonable means and reasonable views. His salary was well above average but his bungalow home was of modest size, furnished in the tradition of three-piece suites and Athena prints. The few visitors were mainly fellow members of the local short wave radio club of which Mayhew had been honorary secretary for almost ten years.

With the pattern of his life so uniform, he had grown into his new role with some confidence. Readier to speak up for himself and less willing to be put upon. Normally mild, he could show sudden bursts of defiance or anger if someone attempted to take advantage of his placid nature.

Everybody who knew him was amazed when he first announced that he was about to marry. And even more amazed when he showed them photographs of his bride-to-be. Young and pretty with a figure to match. Male acquaintances began to see Eric Mayhew as something of a dark horse, and their wives exchanged significant looks and murmured about still waters running deep.

Eric Mayhew was proud of his pretty, young wife but permanently conscious that he was twenty-four years older than her. When she had her birthday in two weeks' time he would be only twenty-three years older. He was well aware that in fact she liked him being older. She had told him that she liked his maturity. He knew what to do about everything. Arguing about the price of things, sending food back in restaurants when it wasn't properly cooked. Jenny Mayhew had been brought up in a Bristol orphanage. She had been on the cosmetics counter at the local Boots' store when he first met her, and for her, Eric Mayhew was her rock and salvation. To outsiders it was obvious, but the man himself lived on a permanent rack of self-doubt. Were younger men staring at her well-filled sweater as they walked together down the street? Were people ignoring them because they were such a mismatched couple? Were other men trying to make him look small in front of her? It was a constant torment, no less tormenting because it was unfounded.

Jenny Mayhew had seen a pair of second-hand Parker Knoll chairs in the furniture shop. They had paid for them and today was the day they were to collect them. It would save £4 to pick them up in their own car.

The small bungalow, which the previous elderly owner had called The Cottage, was in a close near the grammar school in Cheltenham. Ten minutes' walk from Eric Mayhew's place of work.

PC Brian Bull was hooker for the police rugby football team and built accordingly. He was also a fine cricketer with an excellent eye and a pair of shoulders that could clout a short ball over the pavilion. And he had a temperament that matched his physique.

That Saturday morning two things had happened that set his mood for the day. At breakfast he had quarreled with his wife about the housekeeping allowance he gave her, and, although he had passed his exam for promotion to sergeant two years earlier, he had learned after inspection parade that a fellow constable had been promoted over his head and out of turn.

When he saw the small car parked outside a shop on double yellow lines he didn't hesitate. He leaned down at the open window, but noticing that the girl in the passenger seat was very pretty told her politely enough that she had to move the car. When she said she couldn't drive, he straightened up and as he turned to look in the shop for the driver a man hurried out.

"What is it, Officer?"

"Is this your car?"

"Yes."

"It's parked on double yellow lines."

"I'm loading some furniture."

"You should know better than that. It's illegal. An offense. You've gotta move it. Loading or no loading."

"It'll be a couple of minutes. No more. I promise."

"You'll move it now, mate, or I'll book you."

"How can I carry two big chairs down to the car park, tell me that?"

"Better do some press-ups, Dad. Anyway, move the banger off the yellow lines."

"I could have moved the chairs while we've been talking, for heaven's sake."

PC Bull reached in his pocket. "OK, mister, if that's the way you want it, I'll book you. Name and address."

Being called Dad in front of his young wife, and the two-year-old car being dismissed as a banger was too much for Eric Mayhew. Quivering with anger he said, "Go to hell," jumped in the car and drove off. PC Bull lifted his mobile radio and pressed Speak.

At three o'clock that afternoon a patrol car pulled up at The Cottage. A policeman delivered the summons which would be heard in the magistrates' court in ten days' time.

In that ten days, Eric Mayhew rehearsed the courtroom scene a dozen times. It was a subtle mixture of Henry Fonda in *Twelve Just Men* and Winston Churchill's "Some chicken, some neck" speech to Congress. And all the time he seethed with anger at the policeman's bullying arrogance. He longed for his chance in court to square the account, and was sufficiently convinced of the rightness of his case to ignore a friend's advice to hire a solicitor.

His hour of drama turned out to be ten minutes in front of three magistrates. The policeman didn't need to exaggerate his case. Mr. Mayhew had parked his car illegally on double yellow lines, and been warned twice. He then became abusive, had attempted to avoid the proper procedures and had been traced to his present address.

The senior magistrate looked at Eric Mayhew.

"Do you dispute any of those facts, Mr. Mayhew?"

"I was only going to load—"

"Do you dispute any of the facts, Mr. Mayhew? Please answer me, yes or no."

"I want to explain—"

"Mr. Mayhew, if you refuse to answer I shall take a very serious view of your behavior in court. Are the facts as stated correct? Yes or no?"

"I didn't say 'for Christ's sake,' I said 'for heaven's sake.' He said that just to—"

"Is that the only point you disagree with?"

"I want to make a statement to the court—"

"Twenty pounds fine for the traffic offense and ten pounds for attempting to avoid a summons." He paused. "I am sorely tempted to fine you for abuse of a police officer in the course of his duty but in view of your previous good record I shall treat it as no more than a display of that behavior toward law and order which is becoming so common today among certain hooligan elements in society. Step down, Mr. . . ." he looked at his pad ". . . Mayhew." He turned to the clerk. "Call the next case, please."

A more balanced man would have said his piece to his friends about the law having nothing to do with justice, paid his fine and perhaps hoped that the policeman would be thumped in some back-street riot sustaining severe fractures to the jaw. But for Eric Mayhew, the humiliating scene in court only added to the policeman's humiliation of him in front of his young wife. The phrases "previous good character" and "certain hooligan elements" echoed in his mind like a mad tape recorder. It was a month before he calmed down at the thought of how he could take his justifiable revenge on the Establishment of phoney law and order which had treated him so grossly unfairly. He wasn't sure how to go about it but he knew quite definitely what he was going to do. A short, sharp lesson was what they needed.

He found the address and telephone number that he wanted on a card on the information board in the public library.

The small room stank of cats and stale food and the elderly man in the wicker chair looked pale and emaciated but he listened intently as Mayhew said his piece. When Mayhew was finished the man turned his head stiffly and with a grimace of pain to look at Mayhew.

"I don't see the connection, my friend."

"You people want to change society. Make it fair and just for everybody. I'll help you do it."

"How?"

"I'll join the party and help you fight the Establishment."

The old man's watery blue eyes looked at him. "What do you do, Mr. Mayhew? What's your job?"

"I work at GCHQ."

"At Oakley?"

"No. At Benhall."

"Doing what?"

"Cryptology. I'm a mathematician."

"Can I give you some advice, Mr. Mayhew?"

"Of course."

"Go back to your home and your young wife. Get on with your job and forget all about politics, whether it's Tory, Labour or Marxist."

"Does that mean you don't want me in the party?"

"I'm afraid it does."

"But I want to help. I want to help you people change society."

The old man sighed. "And so you shall. We all play our small parts and in the end we shall succeed. Meanwhile, be patient. It takes time."

Mayhew thought that it was just one more symptom of the crazy world that they didn't want him. He'd expected to be welcomed with open arms. He had a brain. He was a thinker. And had put himself at their service. It was ridiculous. Like when they did those psychology studies where people in the street were offered genuine pound-notes for fifty pence and they wouldn't buy them.

It was almost six months later when Mayhew's wife told him one evening that a man had been asking about him at the paper shop. The shopkeeper had told her himself.

"What did he want to know?"

"Did you pay your paper bill promptly. Did you have any money problems." She smiled. "He asked if you were interested in girls or fellas."

Mayhew shrugged. "You know what he is?"

"No. What is he?"

"He's doing a positive vetting. They never warn you."

"Can I tell them that at the shop?"

"Yes, if you want to."

The man who spoke to him two weeks later had a foreign accent. Mayhew had just backed the car into the concrete driveway when the man came up to him.

"Mr. Mayhew?"

"That's me. And who are you?"

"Some friends suggested we spoke together."

"What about?"

"Is perhaps more private in your car. We go for a spin, yes?"

It was a long time since Eric Mayhew had heard anyone talk of "going for a spin" but he shrugged and said, "You can come in the house."

"I don't want to disturb your wife."

"She's at my mother's."

"OK. We speak in your house."

48

* * *

She was back just before eight and he took her to the cinema to see *The Sting*, but he said nothing to her about his caller. He would have to make some excuse to go to London when they told him the date. He could always say no, but there was no reason why he should. It was everyone for himself in this world. At least somebody appreciated that he really was prepared to help alter the way things were done. There would be some risk, of course, but it was easy enough if you knew how. People nicked old reels of tape to record pop music. They would only be scrapped anyway.

Nine

Lieutenant Barakov was not amused at having his free evening interrupted by such trivialities, and it showed in his brusque questions and his dismissive reactions to the replies. He stared implacably at the man sitting facing him on the other side of the desk.

"But I don't understand, Mr. Johnson, why you want to come over."

Johnson shifted uneasily in his chair. "But I told you. I hate the army. They don't give me a break. Nothing."

"Many soldiers don't like being in the army. They'd rather be sitting on their backsides playing cards and drinking vodka. How do you think you could help us, anyway?"

"I could go on TV and radio and denounce them. The British and Americans. Tell the world what they're really like."

"You think the world would be interested in the grievances of a private in the British Army?"

The telephone rang on Barakov's desk. He reached for it, said his name, listened for several minutes and then hung up without speaking. As he turned to look at Johnson, the signalman sensed a change in the lieutenant's attitude.

Barakov said, "Of course we appreciate your willingness to help us,

50

comrade." He shrugged. "But maybe there are other ways, better ways, that you could help us and we could help you."

"I don't understand."

"You're at the house in Grunewald, aren't you?"

"How did you know that? I didn't say where I worked."

Barakov smiled. "We have to know these things. We have to check. You could have been sent to trick us by the British. We have to be cautious."

"They didn't send me, mate, that's for sure."

"Tell me about your work. The kind of things you do."

"I register the transcripts and route them to the data base."

"Do you read them?"

"Jesus, no. There's thousands of them pouring in. Hundreds a day. And they're in code anyway."

"Do you know what they're about?"

"They're the transcripts taken down by the monitors in the listening-room."

"Do you know what they listen to?"

"It's radio and telephones."

"What radio and telephones?"

"I don't know . . . everything . . . you people."

"You've no idea?"

"No."

"How many people work at the house?"

"There's four shifts working round the clock. About a hundred. Maybe more."

"How long can you stay with us?"

"I've got to be on duty on Sunday night."

"I'd like to put you and your girlfriend up for a couple of nights at one of our best hotels. You and I can talk tomorrow. There are other officers who would like to talk to you. We'll see how we can help each other. Yes?"

"My girlfriend didn't come with me."

"We'll contact her and get her over here for you. Meantime, you must be hungry, why don't we have a meal together?"

Johnson tried not to be openly impressed by the magnificent suite on the top floor of the Berolina but Heidi had no such inhibitions. There was a magnificent sitting-room, a large bedroom and a palatial bathroom. The KGB girl who had contacted her had taken her to a shop on the Ku'damm and bought her a dress, shoes, and underwear.

She lay with her eyes closed in the marble bath and hoped that it would last.

Later that evening, Barakov took Johnson to a house in the suburbs by the river and they talked with two other Russians. They were friendly, treating him as an equal, discussing every detail of what he knew of the operation in Grunewald. And back at the hotel another KGB man talked with Heidi. She could be paid a hundred marks a week for acting as a courier for them and sometimes accommodating someone at her rooms for a night. He was young and good-looking and his eyes wandered from time to time to her legs with obvious interest. She was used to that but was flattered all the same, and readily agreed to his proposals. It seemed that at last there was going to be some security in her life. Not just Arthur but these new people as well.

Although his first contact was, in ignorance, with the GRU, Johnson had been passed over to the KGB. He got on well with Kholkov, who had taken him over since Johnson worked for Massey's organization. Johnson had only vaguely heard of Massey but Kholkov found it amusing to have contact with both ends of the spectrum at the house in Grunewald. Whenever possible he met Johnson in West Berlin in case the British security men at the checkpoint should notice Johnson's frequent crossings. Numbers of Allied troops crossed the border to buy fresh fruit and vegetables in East Berlin but Johnson had no such excuse as he was fed at his place of work.

They met that night in a club near the Brandenburg Gate. Johnson had passed the three rolls of exposed microfilm in a packet of Benson & Hedges cigarettes, but Kholkov seemed in no hurry to leave.

"Does the code RA 4901 mean anything to you, Arthur?"

"We get a few registrations under that code. Not much."

"Where do you route it?"

"It goes to Mr. Howard's people. And then it goes to London. Not from me but from them."

"I've got good news for you, Arthur. They're very pleased with what you're doing for us. Moscow have given orders that if the good work continues you'll be officially recognized in a couple of months' time."

"What's that mean?"

"It means you'll be an officer in the KGB. A lieutenant."

Kholkov saw the mixture of disbelief and pleasure on Johnson's face as he said, "You mean for real?"

"Of course. Next time you're over here I'll show you your uniform and insignia. You can wear it inside our HQ whenever you are on our side of the wall."

"That's great!"

"One other thing. You seem to be giving us material that's always from the same code sectors. Why is that?"

"It depends on what shift I'm on. But it's quieter at night and I can hear them unlocking the doors to come down the stairs if anyone's coming down. I take night shifts when I can and those are the sectors that come through at night most of the time."

"OK. Leave things as they are for the moment. How are things with you and Heidi?"

"What made you ask?"

"She's been complaining to her contact. He's a little worried about the situation."

"What's she complaining about?"

"Says you promised to marry her if she made contact with us for you."

"That was a long time ago."

"Can't be more than a year, comrade."

"I'm not interested in marrying her. Nor anyone else for that matter."

"She's a valuable operator, Arthur. We'd like to keep her happy."

"What about keeping me happy?"

"We want to do that too."

"How?"

"She wants a British passport and British citizenship. We could provide the necessary documents for her but they'd have to be in your name as if she was married to you. You won't actually be married to her, of course, but she doesn't need to know that."

"How would you do all that? It would need birth certificates, marriage certificates . . ."

Kholkov smiled. "Leave that to us, comrade. But it would help us if you cooperated."

"OK." Johnson shrugged. "If that's what you want."

She was in her late fifties and she had obviously once been handsome rather than pretty. Gray-haired and well dressed, with a beige jacket and skirt and a brown felt hat, she could well have been one of those ladies the TV cameras pan across at Tory Party conferences. She had an air, not perhaps of authority, but of expecting immediate cooperation from public employees. And she had found a young assistant at the Registrar General's office in St. Catherine's House to lift down the heavy leather-bound volumes for her and carry them to the nearby table.

Slowly and carefully she went through the register of deaths for the months of June and July in 1949. An hour later she paid £8.25 for copies of three certificates and the clerk slid them into a stiff brown envelope.

During the next two weeks the lady drove in her well-preserved Rover 105 to the small town of Dorchester, the village of Wadhurst in Sussex, and Richmond in Yorkshire. When she returned to London she revisited the Registrar General's office and paid for a photocopy of the birth certificate of Agnes Mary Andrews, infant, born May 19th, 1948, died June 6th, 1949.

Heidi Fischer, now Heidi Johnson, and her new husband had four days' honeymoon in the luxury suite at the Berolina Hotel in East Berlin and

Arthur Johnson wore his KGB lieutenant's uniform. Not out in the street but in their suite of rooms at the hotel. There had been no ceremony but she had the documents. The British passport. The birth certificate in what was supposed to be her maiden name and a marriage certificate as Mrs. Agnes Johnson, née Andrews.

Eric Mayhew had lied to his department head and lied to his young wife. He had claimed four days of accumulated leave from his boss and that had been willingly agreed to. And to Jenny Mayhew he had said that he was being sent away for four days on an assignment in Northumberland.

When the plane touched down at the airport in Vienna he had done exactly what they had told him to do. First buying the copy of *Stern* at the bookstall, then walking over to stand under the departures information board. It was almost ten minutes before he saw the man with the meerschaum pipe and the copy of *Railway Modeller*. Mayhew followed the man to the car park until he stopped at a gray Volkswagen. The car door opened and he got into the passenger seat alongside a tall man in a blue suit who took his bag and reached over to put it carefully on the back seat.

"A good journey, friend?"

"The plane was crowded but it was OK."

"I'll take you to the house and hand you over to my colleagues. They're looking forward to meeting you."

Half an hour later he was being introduced to an elderly man who spoke excellent English and reminded Mayhew of his old headmaster. He was shown to the small bedroom but the instruction started straightaway. The training program was modular and reminded Mayhew of the style of some of the Open University programs he had seen on TV. No previous knowledge was assumed, and the man he knew as Josef never moved on to the next step until the previous section had been mastered.

First came the use of the pads of stationery with specially treated carbons for invisible writing on top of a normally written letter; then the more complicated instruction on the preparation of microdots using the miniature Minox camera and the microscope with its reversed lenses. The technical process he grasped quickly, but he had to practice again and again, using the hypodermic needle to lift the dot out of the emulsion and place it as a full stop on a typed letter, until the KGB man was satisfied. Mayhew was not good with his hands.

The next morning Josef made him go over the whole process a dozen more times before he was satisfied. The afternoon was spent on the less complicated use of one-time pads.

Two whole days were spent on radio procedures, frequencies, transmission timetables and tape recording. The decrypting of the transmissions was no problem for Mayhew—he had listened to those monotonous voices reading out the five-digit groups for hours on end in his job at

Cheltenham. He was amused at the simplicity of two codes that GCHQ had not yet broken. A neat, elegant piece of mathematics that used a combination of a log-table and a fourteen-hour day as its variable.

He was shown the equipment that would be provided for him in England. The camera, the reverse microscope, the stationery, the modified Sony tape recorder and the black leather attaché case and its secret hiding-places. He was left to buy the ICOM IC-R70 himself in London as they were in short supply in Moscow.

The final day was spent with a different Russian who gave his name as Max. Mayhew never really understood what he was there for. Just chatting, amiable and joking. Admittedly there were questions about security routines at Cheltenham, and questions about heads of sections and divisions, but it was fairly obvious that he already knew the answers. For most of the time it was just gossip about the people who worked with him. The Russian asked about his childhood, his hobbies and his possibilities of promotion.

Max offered to take him to the Opera House or a cinema and when he declined, the Russian smiled and asked him if maybe he'd like a pretty girl. He was taken for a meal at a small restaurant that evening and Max offered him a sightseeing tour of Vienna to round off his visit. He said that he'd rather not see the city so that he could never be trapped into talking about it. The Russian complimented him on his foresight.

The whole time he was treated as an important and valuable member of a team. It was the first time in his life that he felt an accepted member of a group. Accepted and respected. Praised, and not derided, for his cautious virtues.

John Hooton was thirty-five and Tony Moore, his boss, was forty-nine; Massey looked at them both from his side of the table.

"Who's their cut-out this side of the Wall, Johnny?"

"The butcher by the station. Franz Lauterbacher, they used the code-name Emil for him."

"And on their side?"

"A girl who works as an assistant in the KO store."

"Are you sure of that?" Massey asked.

"Pretty sure."

"How many sources confirmed it?"

"Only one."

"You know it's a favorite ploy of agents who haven't got any real lead to pick on somebody at the KO. It's the main place in East Berlin where Allied servicemen go. It looks a suitable place to provide cover for a cut-out but we've never had a confirmed target yet." Massey paused and looked at the older man. "What do you think, Tony?"

"I've got a hunch she really is a cut-out, sir. She's always on the counter for fresh fruit and that's where most servicemen go. She seems to work at odd times. Sometimes not more than an hour a day and sometimes she's not there for several days. Works like she's there by arrangement."

"Any signs of anything being handed over?"

"It's impossible to tell. It could be put in a bag or coded on a receipt. There's hundreds of ways something could be passed over."

"Why don't you pull in the butcher and see if you can squeeze anything out of him?"

"It would mean pulling in the whole of his network."

"How many?"

"Five."

"Who are they working to?"

"We think it's Kholkov."

"What are they covering?"

"Only low-grade stuff so far. HQ telephone directories. The Oberbürgermeister's clerical staff. And U.S. Army Air Force people."

"Have you kept CIA informed?"

"No. That's up to Mr. Harper. But we think they know at least two of the agents."

"Any photographs?"

Hooton pushed two ten-by-eight glossy prints across the table and Massey glanced at them. It was a young face although the girl was very plain. A tense mouth and alert eyes. The second photograph was very grainy and it showed the girl handing change to a British captain. He pushed them back across the table to Hooton.

"What do you want to do, Tony?"

"I'm inclined to do as you said. Pull in Emil and the rest of them and see what we can get."

"And you, Johnny?"

"If we pull them in, then they'll just send new boys over and I've got to go through the jazz all over again to find them from scratch."

"So leave one of them free. Somebody fairly bright. And they'll form the new network around that one. It's the lazy way, but that's how Kholkov works."

"OK, sir. I'll do that."

"Tony, you'd better decide the timing. OK?"

"OK. I'll fix it with the team."

Massey sat there after the two had left. His office at the house in Grunewald was modern but windowless, and unlike his subordinates' offices there were no personal touches. No photographs of families or Sussex cottages, no holiday postcards tacked to the cork board spreading across one wall. No flowers in looted KPM vases. There was nothing that gave a hint of Massey's private life or interests. Not even a paperback on the double bookshelf. Just dictionaries and other reference books, a microfiche reader and a gray plastic box of fiches, while a crude, metal MOD-issue bookend underlined the reticence.

He realized as he sat there that with the expansion of Max Cohen's division he was being drawn away from the day-to-day SIS operations that were his normal work. He was becoming more and more an administrator, less and less involved in the long-running contest with the Russians and East Germans. In fact, he had more free time than ever before—but he was too used to having a heavy workload to use it creatively. He was on the edge of boredom.

Ten

The KO stores, Kaufhaus des Ostens, were the show-piece of East Berlin and most British and American wives, encouraged by both the Allied and West Berlin authorities, went there once a week for the top-class fruit and vegetables that were always available and cheaper than in West Berlin.

He had bought oranges, lemons, potatoes and lettuce, and had recognized the girl who served him as the suspect girl in the photographs. There was nothing suspicious about her apart from the fact that the other girls who laughed and joked among themselves seemed to ignore her. He walked to the cheese counter and as he looked at the array of cheeses and yoghurts a quiet voice said, "Hello, Jan."

He turned to look and it was Anna Kholkov.

"Hello, Anna. How nice to see you."

She smiled and said in Polish, "Buying the wicked Marxist fruit, I see."

He smiled. "Pleasing both sides at the same time. Saving the West Germans freight charges and providing hard currency for the proletariat." He paused. "Anyway. How are you? How's Alexei? Or shouldn't I ask?"

"He's busy and fine. I'm bored and fine."

"Have you got time for a coffee?"

She smiled. "I'm afraid that on this side of the Wall with you in uniform that could be a problem."

"Have you got your Kommandatura pass with you?"

She nodded. "Yes."

"How about I meet you in half an hour on the Allied side of the checkpoint at Brandenburger Tor."

For a moment she hesitated, her eyes on his face, and then she said quietly, "Why not? In half an hour."

"I'll be there."

He saw her come through the Allied control post and hesitate until she spotted him when he waved.

She hesitated again for a moment when he opened the door of the taxi for her, but then got in. She turned to look at him as he climbed in and sat beside her. "Where are we going?"

He put a finger to his lips and she obviously understood. They talked about the weather, and the taxi stopped for them at the junction of the Ku'damm with Lietzenburger Strasse. As he turned from paying the driver he said, "Follow behind me. Wait until I've unlocked the door."

She stayed a few yards behind him, watched him unlock a door and then followed him through the doorway. He closed it behind her and stood there looking at her.

"I hope you don't mind me bringing you here. I thought it might be . . ." he hesitated ". . . better if we weren't seen together by too many people."

She smiled and said softly, "No, I don't mind. You were going to say safer not better, weren't you?"

"Yes."

"And the only one of us in danger is me."

"I'm afraid so."

"Won't people be watching this place just because it's yours?"

"Nobody knows about it. Not even my own people."

"Is this what they call a safe-house?"

"No. A safe-house is official. This is mine. I pay the rental and my mother's name—Felinska—is on the contract and on the door. I've never mentioned this place to anyone nor brought anyone here."

"You must trust me a lot."

"I do."

"Why?"

"I don't know exactly. Experience? That you're a Pole? And the usual reason."

"What's that?"

"I want to trust you." He paused. "Let's go up and have that coffee."

She looked around the living-room as they walked into the flat, and while he made the coffee she looked at the cassettes and records. When he brought in the tray she turned, smiling.

"All jazz and German schmaltz. No Chopin. I'm surprised."

"Why surprised?"

She shrugged and smiled. "I always think of you as being so very Polish."

As his brain absorbed the words "I always think of you" he looked into her face.

"I always think of you just as you. Not Polish. Not Russian."

"Is that good or bad?"

He shrugged. "Neither. Just human and normal."

"Not me as the wife of a KGB man?"

"No. Never."

She was standing very close to him, the big brown eyes looking up into his own, and she said softly, "I'm glad. Very glad."

He looked back at her. "You said you always think of me as a Pole."

"I do."

"Not as a man?"

"Oh, yes. Very much as a man."

Then his arms went round her, his mouth on hers, her warm body clinging to his. When eventually she drew back her head to look at him, she said, "Do you think of me often, Jan?"

He sighed. "A dozen times a day, every day."

"Tell me what you think when you think of me."

"I think of you that night at the Hilton. Your lovely face and your beautiful neck. Your eyes and your mouth."

"Do you want to make love to me?"

"I do. But that wasn't why I brought you here."

"Why did you bring me here?"

"So that I had seen you here and I could think of you in these rooms with me when I'm alone."

"Were you going to tell me that?"

"No."

"Why not?"

He shrugged. "How could I?"

"Why not? Because I'm a KGB man's wife?"

"No. Just because you're another man's wife. It would have been the same if he was English."

"I've imagined this so many times, my Jan."

"Tell me."

"You with your arms round me. Then both of us naked. Making love."

"And where was all this happening?"

She smiled. "In Lazienki Park by the Chopin monument."

He laughed softly. "That's a bit public, isn't it? But very romantic."

"Have you ever been to Warsaw?"

"No."

"Will you go there with me one day?"

"I'm not allowed to, honey."

She smiled. "Call me honey again."

"I love you, honey."

"You don't have to say that."

"I mean it."

"How can you mean it? You don't know me."

"It's got nothing to do with knowing you. I love you, and that's a simple, truthful fact."

"But why?"

"I don't know. I just do."

"I know why I love you."

"Tell me."

"Take me to bed and I'll tell you."

As they lay naked an hour later on his bed, he leaned up on one elbow and said softly, "You said you'd tell me why you love me."

"So I did."

"Tell me."

"Say honey to me again."

He smiled. "I love you, honey. But you're a tease."

She shook her head. "That first time we met at the hotel I knew you were attracted by me. And I knew that it was because of me you asked us to dinner. I liked that but I'm used to that. But two people said nice things about you. So I looked at you that night at dinner, and listened. I thought they were right in what they said. Not everything, but in the things that mattered. And you're handsome. And you're Polish. I found I couldn't stop thinking about you. Hoping we should meet again. Hoping something might happen."

"Who were the two people?"

"One a man. One a girl."

"Who was the man?"

"Alexei."

"I don't believe it, you're joking."

"I'm not. He'd already told me what you said the first time he met you. The meeting about Hess. He said you were either very foolish or very kind. When I saw you I knew you weren't foolish. Weak men sometimes see gentleness as weakness. Alexei is a weak man."

"And who was the other one? The girl?"

"She's a friend of mine. An American. You know her. Judy Campbell. She studies at the Kunstschule here in West Berlin. She came to a seminar at Humboldt University. She painted me." She smiled. "And one day I looked through some of her canvasses in her flat and there was a face I knew—you, my love. So I interrogated her about you."

Massey smiled. "What did she say?"

"Nice things. All of them nice. They fitted the picture I had in my mind."

"Tell me."

She laughed. "You have a very strong Polish ego under that simple outward appearance of yours. I shall say no more. Ask *her* if you want."

"We can use her as an excuse for you coming into our zone."

She nodded. "Yes. But we must tell her. She knows Alexei too."

"Does she like him?"

"You must ask her yourself."

"How long can you stay?"

She looked at her wrist-watch and then at his face. "Another hour."

"Can I see you tomorrow?"

"You can see me any day for the next ten days. Alexei is in Moscow."

"Can I see you every day?"

She smiled. "Yes, please."

"Let's talk about Alexei."

She closed her eyes and said, "OK. You talk."

"I know what he does and he knows what I do. That gives us an extra problem. So I suggest that we do a deal. I will never ask you anything about him that has anything to do with his work. And we won't ever talk about my work. OK?"

"Of course. You're very honest."

"Only with you, Anna."

"Love me again."

"Can I say something else about us?"

"Yes, of course."

"I don't know what's going to happen to us. But for me this isn't an *affaire*. I won't say that I never had fantasies about you. Not in the park in Warsaw. Here, on this bed. But if it made any difference to you or to us I'd be happy to do nothing more than hold your hand."

The brown eyes looked up at his face and she said softly, "It's not an *affaire* for me, Jan. Not even my fantasies. We have to wait and see what happens with us both. But I'm happy to wait. Afraid, but happy."

"Why afraid?"

"Afraid because my husband is a KGB man."

"That's all?"

She shook her head. "It must be comforting to be so . . . so self-assured."

"I love you so, Anna. I won't let you come to any harm."

Judy Campbell was twenty-two. She was a painter, and she already knew that she wasn't an artist. She painted well and several people had bought canvasses from her, and she got more commissions for portraits than she could produce. She looked a typical dumb blonde but like most dumb-looking blondes she wasn't at all dumb. She was easygoing and good company, and seemed to have a knack for being at home with all the different kinds of people she spent her time with. She never disguised the fact that she liked men and liked sex. But she wasn't promiscuous. She did the choosing and there were no smooth words or pressures that could get her into bed if she didn't want to. The men she slept with mattered. They were usually good-looking but that wasn't the only criterion. They tended to be creative rather than football players, although they could all be classified as mildly macho. There had, in fact, only been six altogether in her life. Only the first was a real dud and that had taught her a lesson. It only worked out at point seven five of a man a year. It seemed more to onlookers merely because she had the rare talent of retaining the friendship of men who had once been lovers. They didn't come back for "afters" because they weren't available; it was genuine friendship because Judy was loyal and likable.

She wondered why Jan Massey had been so insistent that he should see her that evening. She'd had a cocktail-party date which she'd canceled and she'd promised to phone a major in the U.S. Marines later to let him know if he could take her out for the rest of the evening.

She poured them both a whiskey and grinned as she raised the glass. "What the hell is it you say, Jan? *Naz* . . . something or other?"

"*Na zdrowie.*"

"And the same to you, lover boy." She looked at him over her glass. "Why so serious, Jan?"

"Because I've got something serious to say . . . and I don't know how to say it."

She shrugged. "Better just say it right out."

"You know what I do in Berlin?"

"Your job, you mean?"

"Yes."

"People have told me that you're the top guy in the British spy set-up. Like the CIA."

He nodded. "That's more or less right. And you know who we're mainly concerned with?"

She rolled her eyes, smiling. "The wicked Reds. The boys from Moscow."

For a moment Massey wondered if he wasn't foolish to go on.

"You know some of them, don't you?"

"Not really. A few Russians, but I wouldn't think many of them are spies."

"You know one Russian who's a very senior KGB man."

"Have you been spying on me?"

"No way. But I'm sure the CIA keeps tabs on you."

"Who's this mystery guy?"

"Kholkov. Alexei Kholkov."

"You mean *he*'s a spy. I can't believe it."

"He is, Judy. He's quite senior."

"And you're going to ask me not to see him anymore."

"No. It's not that."

"What is it? You want me to lure him into bed and ask him for the secret code." She saw the look on his face and she said quietly, "I'm sorry, Jan. I don't mean to be flippant. Tell me what you want."

"I want to tell you something. Something confidential. Something personal. But if you passed it on to anyone else, accidentally or otherwise, it would be a disaster for someone we both know."

"You mean Alexei?"

"No."

"Who then?"

"Anna. His wife."

"You're in love with her and she's in love with you."

"What made you say that?"

"The penny just dropped. Two pennies. I can remember how she looked at the portrait I painted of you. And the questions she asked about you."

"What was the other penny?"

"I just realized. You're both Polish and you're very like one another."

"In what way?"

"Now I come to think of it . . . except that she's a girl and you're a man, you're the same in every way. She's beautiful, you're handsome. She's quiet and calm on the outside but inside there's a volcano. And the same with you." She shrugged. "So how do I come into it?"

"She needs to be able to say she's coming over to see you when we meet."

"Is this for real, my love?"

"Yes. For both of us."

She stared at him for several moments. And then said softly, "What the hell are you both gonna do about it?"

"We're going to work this out. That's partly why we need your help. To give us time."

"Is she KGB?"

Massey smiled. "Of course not. She's just Kholkov's wife. She was a ballet dancer before they were married."

"I know. She told me. OK. Let me be your auntie."

"Do you mind about deceiving Kholkov? I know you've met him."

"Good God, no."

"Why so sure?"

"Feminine intuition."

"What's that mean?"

"I already knew they didn't love one another."

"How did you know? They've always behaved amicably enough when I've seen them together."

"You can often tell what a man is like if you watch the expression on a wife's face when her husband's talking. Try it sometime. It works."

"Anything else?"

"Yes," she said slowly. "I'd say he was queer. He puts on a good act but most of that charm is because he isn't after the girls. It works because women know instinctively that he's not looking for a prize. Not the one that most men are looking for anyway."

"Thanks for saying you'll help."

"I'm not just saying it. I will help. Any way I can."

"If anyone over there found out, she'd be in a Gulag camp two days later."

"Do they really do that?"

"They really do. She'd be dead in months."

"I won't talk, Jan. You can rely on that. I like your Anna."

"Can I take you for a meal or a drink somewhere?"

She smiled and shook her head. "I've got a U.S. Marines major jumping up and down waiting for a call to say tonight's the big night." She stood up and walked across to a stack of canvasses. She bent over, looking through them. She came back with two. She handed them to him. "With love from me to you." One was the portrait of him, the other was an almost finished portrait of Anna.

Eleven

Nobody could actually recall when James Vick was first called Jimbo but it was agreed that that was what his family called him before he was five years old. There is a wide variety of diminutives that derive from the name James, and each has its own particular aura. Jimbo carries implications of bounce and youth that need living up to. Jimbo Vick had lived up to them to such an extent that at thirty-two years old he still had the looks of a quite handsome all-American boy complete with freckles, and chestnut hair that was the envy of every girl who noticed him.

Jimbo was born and brought up in the small town of Montpelier on the edge of the Napa Valley. The town was small but not because it lacked attraction; it was, in fact, a fine example of what purposeful planning could do when combined with utter selfishness. The seven men who were the original founders of the town would have been surprised but not disconcerted by an accusation of selfishness. They saw themselves as no more than a group of like-minded men who wanted to live in a certain way. A way that nobody could describe as ostentatious—two of them were Quakers. But they wanted to maintain what they always referred to as "certain standards." None of them would have been able to put in words what they meant by the phrase, but they all knew instinctively exactly what they meant. They had never discussed the exclusion of Jews. There was no need to. No more than the question of blacks or Hispanics at a later stage in the town's development. Even today money alone would not buy you a place in Montpelier. It would be difficult to advise a potential newcomer of the criteria that applied. But the say-so of the present head of any one of those founding families would mean that you were half-way there. One more nod of approval would be enough. But apart from descendants of the founding families the nods had not been given to more than three or four suppliants a year so the town was still small enough to be manageable to the unspoken ethos of its founders.

The Vick property was on Prospect Avenue which in most other towns would be reckoned to be the best road in town. In Montpelier it was merely typical of that far-sighted original planning and no finer than most of the other avenues in town. The house itself had originally been mostly Gothic, but over the years it had been transformed into honest and quite awe-inspiring Colonial, while the remains of the original Gothic building had been converted into servants' quarters and indoor pool with facilities for squash, tennis and gymnastics.

The Vicks had always been bankers and Joss Vick, Jimbo's father, was both respected and liked. Gregarious and given to acts of careful generosity, he was popular not only in Montpelier but in San Francisco, Los Angeles and New York. There was a touch of the twenties and Scott Fitzgerald in both his dress and his attitudes. Athletically built and handsome, it was accepted that he had both charm and style enough to make women adore him and men eager for his company. The charm was natural and genuine, the envy of his men friends and the delight of most of the women he met.

Joan Vick had been the belle of Montpelier, a Hudson from one of the founding families. Intelligent and beautiful though she was, their circle had not expected the marriage to last. They were both too attractive to be left in wedded bliss. But despite both gallant and cruder attempts at seduction they had remained an inviolate pair. Neither lechers nor charmers could make any headway with Joan Vick and, although obviously appreciative of pretty faces and nubile young bodies, Joss Vick admired without wanting to own or touch. Men gave up trying for Joan Vick and only the very young females still dreamed of luring Joss from the strait and narrow. They had looked a pair on the day that they married and they had stayed a pair. Seemingly without effort or temptation. Joan and Joss, referred to by their friends as the Jaybirds. They were envied by everyone who knew them.

By the time that Jimbo Vick was sixteen the envy had become substantially diluted. Jimbo was a classic example of the spoiled brat. Clever at school but a natural cheat. Leader of a group of middle-class kids from the next town who were mesmerized by his audacity and his money. Worldly wise far beyond his years and detested by the school staff.

Openly defiant of all authority from his parents to the police, who knew him as Smart-ass and avoided him whenever possible. Two psychiatrists had given up the unequal struggle, confirming as they did so that he was intelligent, clever and uncontrollable. Jimbo had offered to help the second psychiatrist with his own emotional problems.

He was eighteen when it all came to a head in a meeting with his father and the family lawyer, when Jimbo had finally tried the patience of the local police once too often and had been arrested for drug peddling. The ten-thousand-dollar bail had been no problem; his father had not only paid up willingly but had made a contribution to the hospital funds for an additional dialysis machine. The police captain's wife ran that particular appeal. But Joss Vick knew by instinct that this was a time when his local esteem and popularity would not be enough. He phoned Jackson in L.A. to arrange a meeting.

Jackson was a senior partner in a large and successful Los Angeles law firm. Despite Los Angeles's reputation his knowledge of drug offenses was limited to a mere knowledge of the law and procedures. His speciality was high-stake divorce and, for a few special clients, tax avoidance. Joss Vick fell into neither category. Jackson was the son of Joss's father's lawyer and was called on solely for matters concerning the various family trusts and Joss Vick's estate.

The meeting took place in Joss Vick's study. It was more a personal museum than a study. The walls were lined with photographs of various Vicks in the company of politicians, diplomats and captains of industry. Those of Joss Vick were all informal, featuring him with the Beautiful People on yachts, at polo matches, the races and social functions.

"Where did you get the stuff, Jimbo?"

"What is this, Dad, a courtroom?"

Jackson said crisply, "These are the sort of questions you'll be asked in court, Mr. Vick."

The youth turned a languid look on the lawyer. "You don't say? And what do you know about drugs, mister?"

"I know about courts and the law," Jackson said quietly.

"You'd better pay attention to all this, Jimbo. Or you'll end up in jail."

The boy shrugged. "So what?"

Joss Vick sighed heavily. "So I don't want my son in jail. If I can prevent it."

Jimbo grinned. "Would you and Ma visit me?"

Jackson intervened. "Even as a first offense you'd get a very long sentence if you were found guilty. I think you should bear that in mind."

"Oh, I have, old friend. I have. But you're being paid to keep me out. The family's expecting a lot from you, old sport."

"Jimbo. Mr. Jackson isn't to be talked to like that. I won't have it."

"You're paying this guy, Dad," Jimbo shouted angrily. "He wants me to plead guilty. No way do I do that."

Joss Vick shrugged helplessly. "It could help when you're sentenced."

"You take it I'm guilty, then?"

"I'm goddam sure you are. The police showed me the evidence that they've passed to the DA."

"Those creeps have been trying to frame me for years. I know enough about Captain O'Keefe to put *him* behind bars for years."

"Is there some other attorney you'd prefer?"

"No. I'll handle my own case. My own way."

Joss Vick stared at his son for long moments before he spoke.

"When this business is over, Jimbo, I'll make you a reasonable allowance and you can go your own way. I've had enough of getting you out of trouble. You're just a spoiled brat."

"How much allowance?"

"We'll talk about it some other time."

"Why not now? Are you embarrassed because of this guy hearing?"

"Just leave the room, boy, before I lose my temper."

Jimbo grinned. "Make it a thousand bucks a month and I'll leave this dump today."

"I'll make it two. Don't come back."

Jimbo stood up, grinning. "I'd like it in writing. Jackson could draw it up while I'm packing."

As the boy left the room with a swagger, Jackson was aware of the tears at the edges of Joss Vick's eyes.

Jimbo Vick drove off in the Mustang convertible that afternoon, its rear seat and trunk piled high with leather cases. His thinking was too superficial to have any regrets about leaving his home and he had no sense of obligation or affection toward his parents. When cornered in some minor delinquency he had always weaseled out by saying, "I didn't ask to be born, folks. You had me so you owe me. That's what parents are for."

From a ten-year-old the apparent logic had amused Joss Vick, but as the years went by it was too obviously specious to be amusing any longer. It wasn't the plaintive protest of a child but the cold, selfish shrugging-off of personal responsibility by a teenager and then a youth.

So many people had longed to see Jimbo Vick get his come-uppance that when he left home they saw it as the beginning of the end of his reign of defiance of both the law and decent behavior. Unfortunately it was no such thing. Jimbo Vick's defiance of the way things were was without any element of bluff. Getting what you wanted was just a question of working out how easiest to get it. Unlike most upper-class kids he was not only street-smart but extremely shrewd, resourceful and intelligent. The fact that these qualities were misapplied made no difference to their effectiveness.

The charges for drug peddling were never pressed and his card in the local police records were inexplicably mislaid. The new card gave no details of the previous reports of vandalism, drunken driving or participating in the gang-bang of an out-of-town black girl.

His father knew nothing of all this, neither did he ever discover how his son managed to become a student at UCLA. While he was still at university Jimbo had a small but elegant pad in a good block in Marina del Rey. One of the two girls who lived with him was also at UCLA but Jimbo was quite impartial in fixing them both up with local businessmen who wanted discreet services from pretty, young call girls. They paid him half their earnings toward the cost of running the apartment and they were available for sex whenever he wanted. It was one of Jimbo's repeated boasts that from the age of fifteen he'd never paid for sex. Most of those who heard the boast assumed that he had been sexually precocious to have such experience so early, but in fact it was merely accurate since he had paid for even earlier experience at the rate of a dollar a time with the daughter of the school janitor. Jimbo Vick always impressed some small group of his contemporaries. He knew what he wanted and took it one way or another.

At UCLA he majored in math and electronics, and, surprising even himself, turned out to have a genuine gift for those subjects. His professors, unaware of his vices and seeing him as an achiever, encouraged him. So, for the first time in his life, Jimbo Vick, always the show-off playing to his audience, actually found himself working far beyond what would just allow him to get by. After graduating, he was invited to join a team that was financed by one of the newly arrived computer companies in Silicon Valley. A year later he was recruited by the company for its own research department. Much of the equipment that they designed and manufactured was for government departments, and he spent a lot of his time briefing the ultimate users of the high-technology equipment. When he was sent to Washington he assumed it was one of those routine briefing sessions.

There was a message for him when he booked in at the hotel, welcoming him and telling him that a car would call for him the next morning.

The car pulled up at what looked like a private house in Georgetown, and in a sparsely furnished room two men interviewed him. The questions were mainly technical but the older man chatted with him while they were eating lunch alone, about his friends and how he lived, his interests and his ambitions. He slept in the house that night, on a small camp bed with a man sitting outside his room in the corridor.

The following day they gave him a variety of tests. Mainly mathematical problems with a smattering of questions on advanced electronics.

Late on the second evening they invited him to join the National Security Agency at Fort George Meade. He smiled at them both as he refused, a smile that was almost a sneer. When they asked him why he refused, he laughed derisively and shrugged, saying that he wasn't interested. He added gratuitously that if he *had* been interested he would have gone to someone at the top, not half-way down.

Back at his normal job he was outraged when he was made redundant at the end of the month. He had several interviews for other senior jobs in the area, interviews where the selection panels were obviously impressed. Three of the panels informally told him that he would be appointed. None of the seven companies eventually pursued his application. Two that he phoned were curt to the point of rudeness. When one of the two NSA men who had originally interviewed him called at his apartment one evening, saying that he was just passing through and had wondered how he was getting on, Jimbo finally got the message.

"You creeps have fingered me, haven't you? You told them to shove me out, and you've warned all the others not to give me a job."

The man smiled amiably. "Between you and me, why *did* you turn down our offer in Washington?"

"Because I don't like being questioned. Who the hell do you people think you are? I've got a private income, and there's no way I'm going to be cross-questioned by two jerks who think they're doing a favor to some small-town hick."

"Is that what it seemed like to you?"

"It sure did."

Hank Lowther was a trained and experienced psychologist and he had picked up the vibes from Jimbo Vick as soon as they had started talking. It hadn't been so obvious at the original interview. The juvenile aggression, the need to be offensive and derogatory to prove that he resented any kind of evaluation. He was still the boy gang-leader despite his age. But he was what they needed and there was no doubt that he could be tamed. Apologies and some show of deference were called for. As between equals.

"In that case, my apologies. That wasn't what we intended. We thought that you would have realized that just the fact that we spent so much time with you and tested you so thoroughly must mean that you were potentially very important to the Agency."

"You could have fooled me, buddy."

"Why don't we go back to square one? No more questions from us, we'll tell you what we had in mind for you. It's a very important and senior assignment." He paused. "Especially for a man of your age. We should normally have been looking at professors, maybe heads of faculties, for a post of this nature." He paused as he looked at Jimbo's face. "You'd be leading a team of specialist code-breakers on top-secret work."

He saw the instant response in the young man's eyes to the phrase "leading a team."

"How many bosses would I have?"

"Two. The director of Signals Intelligence Operations, a civilian, and beyond that the director of the National Security Agency himself."

"What would be my title?"

"Officer in charge of Special Cryptanalytic Mathematics."

"Sounds not bad. How much does it pay?"

Lowther talked for another hour and arranged for Jimbo Vick to spend a week in Washington at the Agency's expense after he had signed the appropriate documentation. It was almost midnight when Lowther sat on the edge of the hotel bed and dialed the Washington number. There was no rejoicing, it was just one more assignment dealt with. Another note to add to Vick, J.'s file. Lowther hesitated between the descriptions "immature" and "unstable" and felt that the latter word might be going too far. Among the thousands of men and women who were employed by the NSA there were representatives of most of humanity's frailties. What mattered was knowing that the weakness existed.

Twelve

He had arranged to meet her by the Kongresshalle in the Tiergarten. The sky was overcast as he waited for her. For a moment he wondered if there was some restriction on her Soviet pass that could prevent her from coming. But exactly at ten he saw her walking toward him. He checked automatically to see if anyone was following her but they seemed to be the only people in sight.

As she stopped in front of him, smiling, he sat quietly, still looking over her shoulder, "How long can you stay?"

"As long as you want."

"I'm going to give you an envelope. There's money for a taxi and two keys. Ask the driver to take you to Steiner Travel on the Ku'damm. On the left of their entrance is another door. You'll recognize it. It's my place. The big key is for that door. Go to the top floor and you'll see my name, Felinski, on the door. Let yourself in with the other key. Make yourself at home. I'll be there soon after. OK?"

"OK."

"Just look at your watch and then shake my hand and walk away."

She was standing by the window untying the red ribbon, peeling away the flower-patterned wrapping-paper, lifting out the long, narrow, blue-leather box. It was embossed with some coat of arms in gold and the words Étienne et Cie, Paris, Faubourg Saint-Honoré. He watched her open the box and look at the pearl necklace. The three strands of pearls. Then she looked up quickly as if she had only just realized that he was there.

He smiled. "Do you like them.?"

"Oh Jan, they're beautiful. But they're from Paris. How could you have known? When did you get them?"

"I had to go to Paris for a meeting a few months after I first met you. I saw them and they made me think of you. I bought them for you then."

"But that was a long time ago. How could you have known . . . about us?"

He smiled. "I didn't know about us. But I knew about me. I just hoped that one day I would have some excuse to give them to you."

She smiled. "You really are a Pole, Jan. Not at all English."

He reached in his pocket, pulled out a thick envelope and handed it to her.

"There's a British passport in there. In the name of Anna Taylor. The photograph is not you but it's good enough to pass. There's also a security card in the same name. If ever you need help this side of the Wall just show that and they'll contact me." He paused. "You'll need to keep them hidden very carefully."

"Is all this a problem for you, Jan?"

"No. No problem at all."

The clear brown eyes looked intently at him. "Are you sure it's worth it? There are bound to be problems. Maybe more than just problems."

"Sit down, honey. Let's talk about it."

She sat beside him on the leather couch and he took her hand. "It's easier for me," he said, "because I've imagined all this many times before. I'm more prepared for it than you are. And I've no ties. I'm not married to someone else, and my movements aren't restricted as yours are. There's no danger for me. But there is for you. I want to make sure that you have time to think about it. The sacrifices are all yours and I want to be sure that you understand what they are."

"What are the sacrifices, Jan?"

"Sooner or later it should mean that you leave him. It means the end of all your contacts in the Soviet Union. Your father. Other relatives and friends. You'd be in a strange country. A different way of life. Once you've come over, there could be no going back." He paused. "And . . . I'm not sure that I'm worth it."

"Would you do it for me?" she said softly.

He nodded. "Yes. But that's different. I know you're worth it."

"So what do we do?"

"How easy is it for you to come through the Wall?"

"It's not difficult if I have an excuse. I've got my Kommandatura pass."

"What sort of excuse?"

"Shopping, sightseeing, concerts." She smiled. "But I have to notify the Allied Control Authority through the guard at this side of the checkpoint."

"Do they ever stop you going where you want?"

"Not so far."

"I'll check on that and see that it doesn't happen. If you use the British passport they'll know you're OK."

"How?"

"There's something in the number."

"Sounds just like the KGB."

"Yes, it does." He paused. "That brings me to the last problem. How much do you care about Kholkov?"

She sighed. "If you mean do I love him, then no, I don't. I don't hate him. There are good things about him. But not good things for me."

"You won't regret leaving him someday?"

She smiled and shook her head. "No. Not at all."

"If we didn't have these problems I guess I'd ask a lot more about him. But because of what he is, and what I am, I won't." He looked at her face. "Is what I have said good sense?"

She nodded, smiling. "You're a good man, Jan Massey."

"Why do you say that?"

"Because for my sake you're prepared to be British and cautious and patient. And in your Polish heart you'd rather I just stayed here now and never went back. And to the devil with all the problems."

He laughed. "You seem to know me very well."

"I told you. I've thought about you a lot, my Jan. Every day."

"Since when?"

"Like I said. Since the three of us had dinner together the first time."

"Why then?"

She smiled. "Because I wished that it was you that I had come with, and you that I was going home with." She looked at his face. "How can I contact you?"

"You can phone me here. But not from your home. That will be monitored. Use a call box. I'll give you the number." For a moment he hesitated, then he said, "D'you know the bookshop on Unter den Linden?"

"The one that sells old books?"

"Yes. If you want to write to me you can take it there. Ask for the old man, then ask him for a first edition of *War and Peace* in Russian. He'll tell you they haven't got one and then you hand over the letter. I'll get it about four hours later up to midnight. Then the checkpoint is closed. After midnight I'll get it early the next morning."

She put her hands on his shoulders. "Do you like your work, Jan?"

"Most of the time. Not always." He looked at her lovely face. "I've told Judy Campbell. You can use her anytime as an excuse."

75

"Is she safe?"

"Yes. I'm sure she is. I told her how serious it would be if anyone at all ever had even a vague thought about us."

She shivered as she looked at him. "What shall we do today, Jan?"

"I'm going to take you to a lake in the forest. There's a nature reserve there and we can have a meal and I'll row you on the lake."

She smiled. "It will be like being a little girl again. I'll like that." She kissed him gently. "Can I see you tomorrow?"

"Of course. What time?"

"Shall I come here about two?"

"I'll be waiting for you."

Maybe they had got too used to meeting every day, for when they met on the last day before Kholkov was due back they stayed at the flat. Most days they had made love but on that day they just talked and listened to records until it was almost time for her to go. There were tears in her eyes as she stood at the door.

"When shall I see you again, Jan?"

"Whenever you can. You can pick up the keys at the cigarette shop. If ever I'm going to be away I'll leave a note for you here. You've got the phone number where you can always get me. Just say the name on your British passport and they'll get to me and I'll come here."

"I feel terribly sad today."

"So do I. But I'll be waiting and thinking about you all the time."

Thirteen

Harper had stayed behind after the weekly heads-of-sections meeting had finished.

"About Bourget, Jan. You asked me to check on their comings and goings."

"What did you get?"

"There's been no evidence of anybody there permanently apart from the French. But there have been a number of visitors. We've identified most of them. The majority are Germans. Maguire of CIA has been there a couple of times but it always looked like a social visit. A few girls have been there, all Germans. Two of them known prostitutes but the others were just party girls."

"You sound like that's not the end of the story."

"It's not. There have been two visitors who we haven't been able to identify. One is about forty and we covered him back through Checkpoint Charlie. He lives in a flat near Humboldt University. He seems to be a free-lance journalist named Hans Bayer. That's the name he uses anyway. We've found pieces in two East German newspapers with that by-line. He's a sports writer."

"And the other one?"

"There's a guy who's been there three times. Always at night. We can't identify him."

"Does he matter that much?"

"I think he does."

"Why?"

"Because all three times we've had him under observation, when he left Bourget's place we lost him. The first time could have been carelessness on the part of Ridge's men. The second time it was a two-man team and he lost them after fifteen minutes. The third time they deliberately set a trailing pattern that would indicate whether he was deliberately avoiding a trail or not. He was. They lost him." He paused. "A man who can lose professionals three times is a professional himself." He paused again. "Even their descriptions of his appearance are almost useless. They never got a good look at his face."

"What description have they got?"

"About five eleven tall. Dark complexion. Dark eyes. Hollow cheeks. Thin but with broad shoulders. Age about mid-fifties—but that's a very crude guess."

"Are Ridge's men still watching the place?"

"Yes."

"You'd better boost the team for at least the next two weeks. I want to know who that man is. It's important."

"Can I be frank, Jan?"

"Of course."

"You obviously had some tip-off that something was going on at Bourget's HQ. Why can't I be told what you know?"

Massey stared back at Harper, his face impassive, his eyes hard and his mouth set aggressively. "Just do what I want, David."

For a moment Harper hesitated and then he nodded, stood up and walked out of Massey's office without speaking again.

Five minutes later Massey locked his office and walked down the corridor and the stairs to the front entrance of the house. The CI sergeant handed him the book and he signed it before he stepped out into the garden.

He walked away from the main house past the new blocks to where a group of apple trees clustered together where the grass was not mown. The ground under the trees was covered with the pale pink petals of apple blossom. There were daisies and dandelions and a clump of thin-stemmed field poppies. Behind the trees was a wide tall sweep of rhododendrons in full bloom and at the edge of the orchard was a small pool with a paved surround. Its surface was green from a dense mass of oxygenating plants, and at its fringes were irises and a kind of water celandine. A black and gold fish nosed at the pads of the lilies and a dragon-fly danced and hovered low over the still, dark water. There was a white painted bench angled across the paving stones facing a small

78

marble statue of a young girl. Massey brushed a few stray blossoms from the bench and sat down.

The description was too general to be significant. Only one thing definitely fitted Kuznetsov—the hollow cheeks. The rest could describe thousands of men. But the hollow cheeks and the expertise made Kuznetsov a possible. Except that he could think of no possible scenario that could link Kuznetsov with Bourget. Unless something had gone wrong. Terribly wrong. He would have to be really desperate to have anything to do with Bourget. Massey closed his eyes for a moment to help him concentrate, but all he was aware of was the sound of the birds and the peacefulness of that almost wild section of the gardens. There were two things he could do. Contact Bourget and fish around, or contact Kuznetsov using the emergency plan. He stood up slowly and walked back to the house, still thinking about Kuznetsov.

Aleksandr Dmitrevich Kuznetsov was born in October 1930 and now, in his early fifties, he was a senior officer in the First Chief Directorate of the KGB. There are five sub-directorates and twenty departments in the First Chief Directorate and all of them specialize in the penetration of foreign intelligence services including those of fellow members of the Warsaw Pact. The Directorate's responsibilities also include the control of KGB agents in all parts of the world outside the Soviet Union.

The administration and control of such a tangled web requires liaison between departments that jealously protect their fiefdoms and bitterly resent any interference in or control of their operations. Kuznetsov had previously been responsible for liaison between Directorate S and three of the departments—the First, Third and Fourth Departments. Between them, these covered KGB operations against the USA and Canada; the United Kingdom, Australia, New Zealand and Scandinavia; and the Federal Republic of Germany and Austria.

It is inevitable that operations of departments can leak into areas where others are both responsible and jealous of their responsibility. Kuznetsov had been responsible for minimizing the conflicts of interest. He was part of Directorate S and not answerable to any of the chiefs of departments which he observed. He had powers of inspection that overrode all security and was responsible only to Moscow and the five controllers of the First Directorate.

Kuznetsov was born and brought up in the city of Yaroslavl on the banks of the Volga River. His mother was a professional violinist and his father a foreman at the local factory which produced heavy lorries. About a hundred and sixty miles from Moscow, the city had stubbornly stayed provincial despite the industry that developed in the mid-twenties. People still made the journey to see its beautiful old churches. Those that were damaged during the war were eventually restored.

It was said afterwards that the bombing raid which killed his parents had been a mistake. The Junkers had been intended to bomb Rostov but a new deception device had put them far north of their target. Four hundred and seventy-five people died that night. His parents and many others at the works' social club, more in a tenement block building near Professor Pavlov's old house.

Aleksandr was adopted by the family of one of the brass players in the local orchestra, a man who had once been in love with Aleksandr's mother. It was they who changed his name from Davidov to Kuznetsov and registered themselves formally as his parents. They had no children of their own.

In later life he realized how much he owed them. Not just the care and affection that they gave him but his new identity. His mother had been Jewish and there would have been no career with prospects open to the son of a Jew. Especially in the KGB. He was well on in his career before he first understood the significance of the change of name. His new parents had thought neither of deception nor protection any more than he did himself in always proffering the registration papers to any authority concerned. It was only when he heard a lecture about dissidents and Jews on his initial training course with the KGB that he remembered about his real mother. He decided that even his life might be in danger, not just his career, if he revealed his true origins. However, there was virtually no chance of his secret being discovered as the documentation in cities like Yaroslavl had all been destroyed in the fighting.

Kuznetsov studied foreign languages at Moscow University and like many linguist graduates he was offered a job as a reader of foreign publications for an organization that appeared to be part of a publishing house. It was in fact part of the KGB, and in due course he was recruited openly by a KGB colonel into a special unit that was responsible for providing cover stories for KGB illegals in Germany and Britain.

For the first year he was part of line N, briefing Illegal Support Officers who were responsible for recruiting low-grade agents in Germany and Britain. He was sent on a course and then posted to the Soviet Trade Mission in London to operate a group of agents previously handled by a KGB man who had been recalled to Moscow. His next move, after nearly two years in London, was to Directorate K, known to field agents as Line K. He was based in Paris at the Soviet Embassy but his responsibilities were still concerned with operations in London, those of the KGB's top field agents in Britain and the Republic of Ireland.

Kuznetsov showed a resourcefulness and leadership that almost led to his undoing. The internal rivalries of the First Chief Directorate led to a bitter battle for his services between Directorate S and Directorate K and the eventual compromise saw him promoted to lieutenant-colonel and made deputy head of a new directorate to be called Directorate R, with responsibility for analyzing all KGB field operations in Europe, Canada and the U.S.A. The huge and unwieldy overseas operations had become almost uncontrollable. Kuznetsov was to sort them out and control them, discarding hundreds of agents who no longer produced useful material or no longer had access to target intelligence. Poor planning, carelessness, lack of training and lack of imagination had taken its toll of once effective networks. Kuznetsov was feared and resented but his backing from Moscow was always unequivocal, and instant.

KGB officers meeting Kuznetsov for the first time were always surprised. The man who had been nicknamed the Moscow Tiger was nothing like they had expected. He spoke very quietly and was a patient listener. He wore rather old-fashioned clothes, was polite and persuasive rather than belligerent, and his questions and responses showed that he was both well trained and very experienced. The senior KGB officers whom he caused to be dismissed or demoted were given state pensions or distant postings and were careful to voice no criticism of Kuznetsov or his decisions.

During his career there were three major checks on his own security. There had been no negative aspects in the reports. No evidence of financial chicanery, not even the slightest indication of nepotism, and no evidence of deviation from the rules governing all senior KGB officers. He took almost no advantage of the quite normal and legitimate privileges accorded his rank, buying little from the privileged shops and warehouses, refusing the services of permanent servants and declining the luxury flat that was his rank's due. He lived alone in a large but one-roomed flat not far from his office in Dzerdzhinski Square.

There was one aspect of his life that had briefly concerned the investigators. Kuznetsov had never married nor had he ever had a long-term girlfriend. The possibility of homosexuality had obviously arisen. But with their usual thoroughness, they discovered that Kuznetsov regularly used the resident girls employed by the KGB. The KGB girls, nicknamed the Swallows, were mainly concerned with the entrapment and blackmail of foreign diplomats and businessmen. The investigators interrogated the girls thoroughly on Kuznetsov's sexual behavior and even tried to find some common factor as to why particular girls were chosen. His sexual behavior appeared to be quite normal but indicated a taste for a few pleasures that were not usual in the Soviet Union. It was assumed that they were evidence of Kuznetsov having used prostitutes in other countries.

He had no hobbies, but he played the piano well and was friendly with a number of professional musicians who played in the prestige Moscow orchestras. He also frequently used his privilege ticket when Moscow Dynamo were playing at home.

Women liked him, not only because he had a quiet charm and none of the usual sexual aggression that important men seemed prone to, but because his lean frame, large brown eyes and hollow cheeks made them eager to mother him.

Kuznetsov saw his parents very infrequently. Once he became a KGB officer the relationship diminished. He no longer lived with them, and although in a way they were proud of his success and independence the pride was tinged with a mixture of awe bordering on fear. He was no longer the boy or young man they once knew. He always showed concern for their welfare and often brought small gifts when he had been to a foreign country.

They were surprised when he once asked them about his mother. He had never seemed interested before. They told him how beautiful she was. A happy young woman with a talent for music that was well above average. There seemed little else to tell him and he asked no direct questions. They didn't mention that she was Jewish because it had never even entered their heads to do so. It was possible that they didn't even remember. But they had given him a postcard-sized photograph of a quintet. They were not actually playing and his mother was talking to the cellist, her violin and bow in one hand. Her face was in profile and barely discernible, but it was obvious that she was smiling. He had kept the photograph though he seldom looked at it. But he sometimes thought about the pretty girl who was really his mother and he wished that he knew more about her.

As Massey walked back to the house he was tempted to phone Chambers. But he couldn't discuss it even on the top-security circuit. It would be too dangerous. And what could Chambers say, except that he should use his own judgment?

When he was alone in his sitting-room next to his office his thoughts went back to that night so many years before when he had first met Kuznetsov. He had been to a concert at the Festival Hall. Rostropovich had played the *Rococo Variations* and at intermission Massey had walked out to the upper foyer and stood looking across the river at the floodlights on the Houses of Parliament. His eye had been taken by a pleasure steamer all lit up, and he wondered if the passengers ever thought about the things that went on in their names. The answer would have been yes if they had been Europeans, but the British weren't really interested in politics, indifferent to what the rest of the world was up to unless it concerned sport or the cost of food. He had been vaguely conscious of the soft mellow warning bells for the second half of the concert but he had gone on standing there, looking across the river.

Suddenly, he heard a woman cry out and turning quickly, he saw one of the attendants helping a man to a chair. The man was gasping for air, his chest heaving and his face almost purple. Massey turned to the nearest window, forced it open and the cold night air came in with a rush. He pulled the man and the chair nearer the window, loosened the man's tie and said, "Don't panic. Relax. You're going to be OK. Relax . . . it'll go." The man's head was thrown back, his chest heaving, and he tried to stand. The rasping hoarse sounds were longer and less frequent, and slowly the spasms subsided. When he opened his eyes there were tears pouring down his cheeks and he was trembling, a ring on one of his fingers knocking against the leg of the chair.

Massey stood there and several people had gathered around. He asked them to move away to give the man air. A man in a dinner jacket said that he was the assistant manager and asked what had happened.

"The man had some kind of bronchial attack. He's recovering OK."

"Should I get a doctor for him?"

"I don't think it will be necessary."

The man in the chair tried to stand but fell back weakly into the chair again, and Massey realized that the man had cursed in Russian, softly but audibly.

Massey said quietly, in Russian, "Are you feeling better?"

The man nodded and asked him to call a taxi. Massey asked the assistant manager to get a taxi and he left hurriedly, only too anxious to be relieved of further responsibility.

As Massey stood alone, looking at the man, he wondered who he was. He could be a diplomat, someone from the Trade Mission, a journalist or even a KGB man. There was a time, when he was first in SIS, when he thought he could tell a KGB man from his face and appearance, but he'd learned how wrong that theory could be.

The man had been ashen-faced but he was able to make his way, with Massey's arm round him, down the stairs, across the foyer and through the doors to the waiting taxi. He stood with one hand against the taxi door, his head bowed. Massey asked him in Russian where he wanted to go. He groaned, and Massey could just hear him say that he wanted to go to the Soviet Trade Mission.

Massey stopped the taxi several hundred yards before the house, paid the driver and stood in the cold night air, lightly supporting the man.

"Walk around for a few minutes. Get some fresh air."

The man took deep lungfuls of air and after a few minutes he seemed almost normal again, apart from the beads of sweat on his forehead.

"It happens sometimes," the Russian said. "Once or twice a year."

"Don't worry. You don't have to explain."

"There's nothing to explain. It just happens."

Massey nodded as he looked at the man's face. "Of course not."

"Why do you look at me like that?"

For a moment Massey didn't reply and then he said quietly, "Because I know what causes it. But just forget it."

"How is it you speak such good Russian?"

"I was at the Embassy in Moscow for some time."

"What's your name?"

"Jan Massey. I was deputy military attaché. Nobody important."

But Massey had seen the recognition of his name on the Russian's face.

The Russian nodded. "And my name's Karelin. I'm at the Trade Mission."

Massey smiled and said quietly, "You're Kuznetsov and you're KGB."

"Were you trailing me tonight?"

"No. I booked a ticket for the concert weeks ago."

"Why did you help me?"

"For the same reasons that I would help anyone. I didn't know then who you were. I didn't even know you were Russian until you spoke."

"How did you recognize me?"

"I've seen photographs of you on the files." He smiled. "And you remembered my name too."

"It's strange. You and I talking together, and yet we are enemies."

"Are we enemies?"

The Russian's brown eyes were intent on Massey's face.

"What do we have in common?"

Massey shrugged. "We're men. We breathe, we eat, we sleep."

"You're a very strange man, Mr. Massey."

"Why?"

"I guess you're SIS. I don't remember what the files said. SIS or MI5, or some such organization. You could have walked away and raised a laugh or two back at Century House or wherever, about the KGB man gasping like a dying fish in public. But you stayed behind and talked. Am I supposed to say thank you by giving you some information?"

Massey laughed softly. "You're being naïve. Or pretending to be. I shall report that we met and the circumstances. But nobody will laugh. We have people with the same problem." He paused. "And for the same reasons."

"What reason?" the Russian said softly.

"They've had the same treatment. The water treatment. They live it over again. Once or twice a year. When they're under pressure."

"I'm not under pressure of any kind."

Massey shrugged. "You'd better get back to the Mission and sleep it off."

"Will this . . . episode . . . be reported in the press?"

"Good God, no. People are frequently taken ill at the Festival Hall and other public places."

"But not KGB officers."

"Nobody knew you were a KGB officer. They didn't even know you were a Russian. The British aren't natural linguists."

"But *you* know now."

"So?"

"So you could inform the news agencies."

"Why the hell should I?"

"To ridicule the Soviet Union."

"How long have you been in London?"

"About five months."

Massey smiled. "If the incident was reported in the British press, readers would wonder why it was even mentioned. And they'd probably start a fund for underfed KGB men. And sweet old ladies would send the Embassy herbal remedies. You've got a lot to learn about the British, my friend."

Kuznetsov shrugged. "Maybe you're right." He paused. "Thanks for your help. It was very kind of you."

"Forget it." Massey smiled. "Take care of yourself and don't get into mischief."

The Russian smiled wanly as he turned and walked slowly away.

It was almost two years later when Chambers got him out of bed at two in the morning. A car was on its way to take Massey to a meeting. No hint of where the meeting was to be or what it was about. As the car went over Putney Bridge, up the hill, to turn right by the common, Massey guessed that it must be the safe-house.

As the car turned into the gardens of the block of flats it swept past the unlit caretaker's kiosk, to the central block of flats. It stopped at the side of the building where the internal road led down to the garage block. Chambers was waiting for him there at the end of the narrow central pathway that ran along the back of the building giving access to the flats through their kitchens. A fir tree and a cypress cast shadows in the moonlight where Chambers was standing.

"Sorry about this, Massey. But it's important. I'd better put you in the picture before we go inside." He paused. "A KGB man has made contact with us. Not a defector exactly, but a potential collaborator." Chambers coughed. "But he'll only cooperate if he can deal with you."

"Why me?"

"He knows you. Says he's willing to trust you."

"Who is he?"

"Goes under the name of Karelin. Used to be attached to the Soviet Trade Mission in Highgate. He's an accredited diplomat at the Soviet Embassy at the moment. Third Secretary."

"You mean Kuznetsov? Is he still here?"

"That's the chap. He is here for another month. Then he's being promoted and sent to Paris."

"Why's he offering to collaborate?"

"I don't know. He refused to give a reason. Said it was a personal decision, not ideological. Maybe he'll tell you more."

"What is he offering us?"

"He offered to act as a contact for what he described as crisis situations."

"What the hell does that mean?"

"I think it's some kind of rationalization. Squaring the old conscience. If he feels that things have reached a crisis point and could boil over, or we do, he'll assist us."

"Sounds a bit naïve, doesn't it? We need the tip-off before it's a crisis." He paused. "What's he expect in return?"

"A safety net. If he ever needs to get out we help him and give him protection. The usual stuff. Pension, new identity and so on."

Massey looked at Chambers's face in the dim light. "Sounds a real dog's breakfast to me."

"You think he could be a plant?"

"No way. Not with a pathetic story like that. It's all vague. No explanation of why he's suddenly decided to help us. No reality to the help he will actually give. He's selling smoke."

"I'd like you to pick up the pieces all the same, Jan. He could be very important, even if he only acts as some sort of reference point for us."

"OK. It's up to you . . . where is he?"

"He's in the bottom flat here. Number thirty-nine. I'll take you in. He's got to be back at his place by eight o'clock and it's nearly three now so there's not much time."

Elaborate arrangements were made for Massey to meet Kuznetsov during the following three months, at first in England and later in a small town on the Seine just outside Paris.

They were difficult meetings because, although he got on well personally with the Russian, he remained unclear about what the Russian was offering. But Kuznetsov made clear that he was prepared to pass on information that would prevent SIS from making substantial errors in combating KGB operations in Britain and the Republic of Ireland. Like most directors he ran the operations in one country while being based in a neighboring country. It was normal KGB practice.

The first sign of Kuznetsov's cooperation came after six months. He advised SIS to remove one of its agents from Warsaw where he worked as a librarian at the British Embassy, but was in fact organizer of sensitive network and about to be arrested by the Poles. And a few days later he gave Massey the name of a KGB man at the Soviet Embassy in London who was successfully manipulating a top MP with the objective of a well-publicized defection to Moscow.

Kuznetsov insisted that his only contact with SIS was through Massey by a complex but efficient system devised for immediate contact at any time. But the system had been almost a one-way system for nearly two years. The information passed by the Russian had become more important as time went by and he was more ready to provide answers or guidance on specific items that were put to him. His good faith had been proved on a number of occasions and at no time had he asked for information in return. But on two occasions Massey had passed on warnings that gave Kuznetsov the chance to avoid danger to his own operations from other countries' intelligence organizations. By then the information the Russian was passing had become important enough to warrant sacrificing minor SIS operations, and even their less important operators.

When both Massey and Kuznetsov ended up on different sides of the Berlin Wall in direct opposition it had been entirely fortuitous, both sides having an urgent need for experienced men in the area at the same time. But from London's point of view it was also extremely convenient.

For Kuznetsov and Massey, however, the locality provided additional hazards in their contacts. It was easy enough for Kuznetsov. A call from any phone box to the tobacconist's shop in West Berlin would indicate a meeting, a seemingly innocuous conversation supplying coded details of time and place. But to protect Kuznetsov, Massey's contacts had to be far more cautious and complex. There was no possibility of using cut-offs or any of the usual procedures. Kuznetsov was on his own, on the other side of the Wall. The Moscow Tiger, who didn't know how to handle his own problem. He'd never said what the problem was and Massey hadn't probed beyond a friendly and genuine interest and a wish to help.

Massey had respected Kuznetsov from the start. Aware of the danger to himself the Russian had guided them away from some irretrievable mistakes. His advice was always negative advice. He had never supplied them with top-security information. Just warned them against following some route that would lead them to disaster. He gave no explanation but the warnings had saved lives and on some occasions had prevented disasters that might have caused a heightening of East–West tensions that could have led to serious consequences. Massey had never got close enough to him to like Kuznetsov but he admired him and was concerned to make sure that he was never endangered through carelessness on his part. He was the only contact with the Russian. Nobody else in Berlin knew of the relationship, and it was accepted that Massey would only contact Kuznetsov at the Russian's request. There would be no contacts initiated by Massey except in a crisis situation.

If Kuznetsov *had* visited Bourget, then something was seriously wrong. His responsibilities no longer covered France but the Russian would know all about Bourget. It seemed strange. But Bourget could have been lying. The unidentified visitor to the SDECE house could be anybody. There was nothing to go on. And nothing concrete to concern him. He and his staff had to evaluate a dozen rumors a week and assess their likely truth. Most of them were gossip, a few were disinformation put out by the Russians or the East Germans, and maybe one a month had some substance. The rules they usually applied were a mixture of the likelihood of the rumor being true and any supporting facts. If there were no actual facts to support the story it was discounted for the time being.

In this instance there was neither likelihood nor a single actual fact confirming the reality. But Massey's success had often come from intuition. A bell ringing in his mind hinting at some long-forgotten incident or fact, a red light flashing that said that something was wrong. And this was one of those occasions. Massey felt deeply uneasy about Kuznetsov. Should he risk endangering the Russian by using their crisis contact arrangements? And on such a slender basis? He knew that such a move was unjustifiable by any normal standards. He decided that he would have to wait and see what happened.

Most intelligence officers—particularly Massey—hated indecision, but it was part of Massey's responsibilities to resist his inbuilt urge for action, or even reaction. It was a burden for which there was no training; expected of him but not openly acknowledged.

Massey found it haunting his mind through the rest of the day's activities. That one doubt. There could be something wrong and he was doing nothing about it.

Fourteen

Massey walked through the series of basement security checks to Cohen's office. Cohen's secretary showed him on the ground plan where he could find him.

Max Cohen was sitting beside an operator in front of a VDU, his eyes intent on the screen. Lines of coded text rolled slowly up the screen, the speed responding to the control button on the computer. The lines were sixty-four characters wide in five-figure groups, alpha-numeric with one digit in each group of lines. A line came up to central screen and the text stopped rolling. One of the groups of figures was flashing slowly and the operator noted the line number. As the text rolled again, Cohen reached over and speeded it up. A few seconds later the scrolling stopped again and another group was flashing. Cohen turned to Massey.

"D'you want me, Jan?"

"I can wait."

"No need." Cohen stood up and turned to the operator. "Warn the cryppies and Evaluation and tell them I want it quickly." He paused. "An hour. Not longer . . . in my office."

"Yes, sir." The operator nodded and turned back to the VDU.

When they got back to Cohen's office he sat down and reached for the phone, pressing two of the buttons as he put it to his ear.

"Is Mr. Mason there . . . Cohen . . . yes." He put his hand over the mouthpiece and looked at Massey. "It's urgent, Jan. I'll only be a moment." His hand uncovered the mouthpiece. "Joe . . . I've just come from thirty-nine . . . there's a whole lot of traffic coming over to you from there . . . it's got both the key-words you were alerting for . . . yeah . . . OK . . . We'll put it on the fast decoder and printer . . . say fifteen minutes . . . OK."

Cohen hung up and looked at Massey. "London's not gonna like this little lot."

"What is it?"

"We had a warning to keep close check on the traffic of three particular Red Army divisions stationed near Magdeburg. They moved overnight to about twenty kilometers from the border at Helmstedt."

"Could be unannounced maneuvers."

"They leave a whole lot of admin staff behind for maneuvers. They've taken everything with them. Those were the orders from Thirty Army and we're just deciphering the orders from Moscow to Thirty Army."

"Won't Cheltenham and Fort Meade have picked it up as well?"

"Probably. I don't know. They always make us work as if we're the only listening-post so far as East Berlin and East Germany are concerned. I suspect that we're just part of a belt-and-braces system but Mason's going to alert Cheltenham right now."

"But they're always shifting units around, Max. Why is this so significant?"

"Who knows? But if it wasn't significant we shouldn't have had prior warning from London and Cheltenham. Anyway . . ." Cohen shrugged. "Thank God I'm only the messenger boy." He paused. "What can I do for you, Jan?"

"How long would it take to bug the SDECE house?"

"Is that the one by the zoo?"

"Yes."

"One room or the lot?"

"The lot."

"Telephone, normal speech and what else?"

"The radio traffic."

"We've got that. It's on the files. There's nothing on it that matters so it probably doesn't get to your summaries. But you should get a routine 'nil report.'"

"I probably do. I haven't checked."

"So speech and telephones." Cohen closed his eyes. "Remind me. Garden front and right-hand side. What about the back?"

"It backs onto a block of flats."

"Back to back? Party wall?"

"Yes."

"I'd guess a week to do a recce and another week before we'd be operational. Could be three weeks. Anything special you're after?"

"Not that you need to know."

Cohen half-smiled and shrugged. "OK. Do you want it?"

"Not yet. But think about it, Max. And just you. It's not for discussion."

"Leave it with me."

The internal phone buzzed and Cohen reached for it. He looked at Massey as he listened. When he had hung up he smiled.

"Evaluation . . . panic over. The buggers were playing radio games—they hadn't moved, just put on a radio exercise."

"For our benefit?"

"Not entirely. They know it causes pandemonium on our side but they do it from time to time to practice deception. Apart from keeping their own radio people up to scratch they get a chance to see if anything appears in the Western press and it gives them a clue to where the leaks might be. We do it to them sometimes. And the Russians do it because they know that it worries our Germans: Makes them realize how close they are across the border."

"Going by the report from my people, they couldn't have shifted artillery and tanks without months of preparation."

"Why not?"

"Lack of spares. Bad servicing. And most units at less than half strength."

"You didn't seem much concerned anyway."

"If it was likely to be for real I'd have had orders from London to go on standby for disrupting their plans."

"I thought the experts at NATO estimated that they'd be at the Channel ports a week after they started."

Massey smiled. "They used to say that when the Pentagon was on the trail of more cash. They've realized that it isn't worth scaring the Europeans for the sake of a few billion dollars."

"You think it wouldn't happen that fast?"

"No way. They wouldn't get far in a week if they tried it. And they know it."

Cohen sighed. "I'm glad to hear it."

"You get asked to the top-secret briefing sessions. You should go sometimes." Massey smiled. "It'd counteract all that Wagner."

Massey had checked every day at the Ku'damm flat. It was three weeks since he had heard from her and he was getting anxious. He had known that it would be difficult but he regretted not having made some simple arrangement that could let her indicate that all was well with her.

He was relieved to find a note from her that morning at the flat. She would be there at three o'clock the next day. That was today. For a moment he was tempted to just stay there and wait for her, but he drove back to the Grunewald house and worked until two, driving back into the city center. It had been difficult in the routine meetings to hide his good mood.

Dead on three the doorbell went and she was standing there, smiling and beautiful.

It must have been just after four as they lay on his bed looking up at the ceiling that she said, "Tell me about your wife."

"I don't have a wife, sweetie."

"Your old wife. How is it said? Your past wife."

"My ex-wife. She was a bitch, that's all there is to say."

"Was she beautiful?"

"Pretty."

"How is the difference between pretty and beautiful?"

"Blondes are pretty, brunettes are beautiful."

He leaned up on one elbow and looked at her. She was naked except for the pearl necklace and when he looked back at her face she was smiling. "I like when you look at me like that."

"Like what?"

She laughed. "Like you're not really looking but you look all the same."

He smiled and kissed her, and said, "How about a coffee?"

She shook her head. "Tell me about your momma. I think she must have been very pretty to give you your nice face."

"I've only seen photographs of her. But she *was* pretty. Very pretty."

"Tell me of her."

"She was Polish, the same as your mother. Born in Warsaw. Came to England from Paris just before the war started. When the war actually started she joined the British Army and was transferred into SOE, Special Operations Executive, because of her languages. She was trained as a radio operator. Dropped in France. Married my father, who was head of her network. Came back six months later. Left the army to have me. In 1944 my father was back in France and seriously ill. She insisted she should be dropped back to care for him. He was badly depressed. She was caught by the Germans before she even saw my father. They sent her to a concentration camp. Mauthausen. With two other captured SOE girls. They burnt them in the ovens."

She lay silent and when he looked at her he saw that her big brown eyes were closed and her cheeks were wet.

He said softly, "Tell me about your mother."

"Give me a paper, a tissue thing."

He wiped her cheeks with a Kleenex and she opened her eyes, still swimming with tears. As she took the tissue she said, "My mother was born in Lwów . . ." she shrugged ". . . in 1939 it became part of the Soviet Union. She hated not to be Polish and she hated all Russians . . ." she smiled ". . . all except one. My father. And she loved him very much. It was like Chekhov. He teaches music and he teaches her piano.

92

She falls in love with him and they marry. You know the rest. She was killed in a car because of the ice."

"Is your father still teaching?"

"Yes. He is professor of composition at the Conservatory."

"Do you see him?"

"Not very often. I told you. He didn't approve of my marriage."

"Tell me again why he didn't like Kholkov."

She shrugged. "Nobody likes KGB men. Especially creative people."

"No more than that?"

She sighed. "He disliked him as a man . . ." she smiled ". . . too much charm, he said, not enough substance."

He was tempted to pursue it but he wasn't sure that he would like the outcome. "When can I see you again?"

"He goes to somewhere . . . I think Dresden . . . on Saturday. So I could see you on Saturday or Sunday. Or both if you want."

He smiled. "I want. You know that."

She looked at his face and said, "Can I ask you something? Something we both may not like."

"Yes."

She said softly, "Where do we end, the two of us?"

"Would you leave him and marry me?"

"For me, yes. For him it would be terrible."

"In what way?"

"He would be disgraced in the KGB. That his wife defects to marry an English KGB man." She paused. "And there is another reason."

"Tell me."

"It would be like a traitor. Someday I tell you. It's not important to you and me."

"Do you love him?"

She shook her head decisively. "I am sorry for him and that is all I feel."

"Does he love you?"

"Not love. Not love. Maybe he likes me. Not more."

"D'you love me?"

"I love you. All my heart. All my body. All my soul. I love you. Always."

"You know I love you?"

She nodded. "Oh yes. I know." And her arms went round his shoulders as she kissed him, moving her mouth slowly on his.

Fifteen

It was ten days since they had had the weekend together and already he had decided that they must plan her final break with Kholkov and then she would come over for good. There should be no problems. He had ready access to everything they would need. Documents, transport and protection until she was safe in England.

It had seemed just one more day. He had slept that night at the house in Grunewald and had just coffee and toast for breakfast before going along to his office.

He buzzed for Howard Fielding, who brought in the previous day's SIS reports. Fielding sat opposite him at his desk, leafing through the typed slips of paper, putting the routine dross into a separate pile before handing Massey the items he thought he should see. He glanced at two sheets stapled together and handed them across.

"You'd better see that, skipper. A new list of staff at the Soviet Embassy in London. The asterisks are suspected KGB."

When Massey had read the sheets and handed them back Fielding was smiling as he read a teleprinter slip.

"Looks like your friend Kholkov's in trouble."

"What kind of trouble?"

"They arrested his missus yesterday. Took her to Karlshorst. Wonder what she's been up to?"

For a moment the room, the building, the whole world seemed to be silent, the air shimmering as if an atomic bomb had exploded on a grainy newsreel film. And then the sweat broke out on his face. He reached out for the slip.

"Let me see that."

Fielding smiled as he handed it over and reached for the next message slip on the pile. Massey was aware that his hand was shaking as he looked at the few lines of type.

SOURCE ZO-17
ITEM 43042

ANNA KATERINA KHOLKOV WIFE OF KHOLKOV A.V.
ARRESTED BY KGB AND TRANSPORTED ZIL NO
809741 TO MAIN ENTRANCE KARLSHORST HQ AT
APPROX 0230 HRS TODAYS DATE. ENDS.

He heard Fielding talking but he didn't hear what he was saying. Then Fielding was reaching across the desk, touching Massey's hand.

"What is it, Jan? Are you OK?"

He shook his head because he couldn't speak, and stood up clumsily, heading for the door. The corridor seemed to be pitching and rolling like a ship at sea as he made for his bedroom.

As he sat on his bed he felt icy cold as the sweat poured down his face. It couldn't be true. But he knew it was. And he couldn't bear to think of what was happening to her in those grim buildings in Karlshorst. He tried desperately to think what he could do, but his mind wouldn't get into gear. It was turning in frantic circles like a rat on a laboratory treadmill. All he wanted at that moment was to be in Karlshorst with a gun, and kill everything that moved before they got him.

Then Andrews came into his room. He didn't hear him knock and he was holding his little black bag. Andrews was the unit's doctor.

"Fielding says you're not feeling too good."

Massey took a deep breath and from somewhere far away he heard his own voice saying, "I'm OK. I'm OK. Just leave me."

The MO put his fingers around Massey's wrist and with his other hand the doctor held a flat metal disc against Massey's forehead to read off the temperature on the digital thermometer. What seemed a long time later he said quietly, "Have you eaten any shellfish in the last forty-eight hours?"

Massey shook his head and the doctor put his hand on Massey's shoulder. "What have you been up to, Jan?"

"I'm OK, doc. Just leave me."

"I'll give you a shot that will calm you down."

"Not a sleep drug."

"No. Something to counteract all that adrenaline rushing round your system. Have you got any cramp in your legs?"

Massey shook his head.

"Stand up, Jan. Let me see you stand."

He tried to stand but his legs seemed like lead. Andrews took off Massey's jacket, rolled up his shirt sleeve and dabbed his upper arm with a cotton-wool swab. Then he stuck in the syringe and pressed the plunger and Massey felt his muscles relaxing so that he could move his legs. Andrews stood looking at him: he was used to dealing with emergencies where he was never told what had happened. Cracked skulls, bullets in stomachs and the ravings of men or women who had been tortured or brutalized. He had grudgingly grown to accept that his questions wouldn't be answered.

"You'll feel OK in about ten minutes. Whatever caused it, don't do it again. And thank the good Lord that you're fit."

Massey wiped his face with the edge of the bedsheet as Andrews packed his bag. The MO glanced back at Massey for a moment as he stood at the door, then, shaking his head slowly, he walked out of the room.

Instinct had driven him to the Ku'damm flat but as he paced around the room he found no peace from the turmoil in his mind. It was crazy. He was the head of British Intelligence in Berlin and he had no idea what he should do. The wife of a senior KGB officer had been arrested and taken to the Soviet military and intelligence HQ in East Berlin. Why? There was an obvious possibility but he couldn't believe that they knew. He hadn't been careless. He had taken all the precautions he would have taken if she had been a highly valued agent. But what other reason could there be for arresting her? If she had offended against some point of KGB protocol she would just have been sent back home to Moscow. A black mark in Kholkov's record, but nothing more. The wives of KGB men and Soviet diplomats did overstep some ideological mark or diplomatic nicety from time to time but he had never heard of a wife being arrested for that. Not even in the Soviet Union, let alone in a Warsaw Pact country.

Massey stared out of the window, unseeing. What would he do if a top agent had been arrested? He knew what the answer was. Clean out their network in twenty-four hours and wait to see what happened. A new file would be opened and a damage control evaluation would be mounted. But nothing more. And this time he had no back-up resources. He was on his own. Even if he could use every resource he had, there was nothing he could do. He didn't know enough. He didn't know anything.

An hour later he drove to the Olympiad offices and sent for several files, including Kholkov's. The others were only so that it wasn't obvious from the records what he was looking at. But there was very little in Kholkov's file that he didn't already know. What a fool he had been not to put a special team on Kholkov right from the start. Like the army always said, "Time spent in reconnaissance is seldom wasted." But it was too late now. Or was it? He felt a sudden relief from the tension as the idea flowered in his mind.

He checked the address in the file and walked over to the map of West and East Berlin that covered one wall. The curtains glided back as he pressed the red button. It was down by the river. One of those pre-war middle-class suburbs that had been left intact by the Red Army, so that it could provide housing for occupation troops. It was still an area where Soviet and East German officials tended to live. And near enough to the Karlshorst HQ to give easy access.

With the Falk street-plan for Berlin he sat at his desk checking and memorizing the area of Kholkov's house. Just doing something had begun to relieve the terrible tension, and his mind pushed away the doubts that crept in as he looked at the map. It was the kind of thinking that he would have dismissed as futile in his official capacity. Dismissed on the grounds that it had no objective. What could he possibly learn from looking at the house when he already knew that she wasn't there? His mind clung desperately to a thin thread of rational thinking. If he could find out why she had been arrested and it was not because they had discovered her relationship with him, then there were things that he could do. Unofficially and, perhaps, even officially.

The need to do something, anything, was overwhelming. He left messages for Cohen and Fielding that he wouldn't be available for a few days. He left no contact number and the messages left it unclear whether he was on duty or taking a few days' leave. He could be in East Berlin by mid-afternoon and back in West Berlin tomorrow morning.

He emptied all his pockets and took the Canadian passport and documents from the small wall safe together with a wad of U.S. and Canadian dollars. He parked his car in the Hilton car park and took a taxi to Kochstrasse and walked to the Friedrichstrasse checkpoint.

He walked twice past the house. It was a pre-war villa still covered with Virginia creeper, its pale blue shutters newly painted, its garden neat and well cared for.

As he approached the house a third time, he opened the wooden gate and walked up the gravel path to the porch. There was a large terracotta pot in the porch, filled with trailing pelargoniums and lobelia, but the bell inside the house rang with that hollowness that bells have in an empty house. He walked onto the small lawn in front of the house and looked through the window.

There was a dining-table with six chairs placed round it, a long walnut sideboard, a food trolley, and in the far corner a glass-fronted cabinet housing china plates, dishes and bowls. On the dining-table was a place-setting for one. Salad still on a side-plate, a dinner-plate with a slice of ham and two boiled potatoes. Several dishes with lids on and a silver coffee-set with a coffee-cup and saucer. It was obvious that somebody had left in a hurry before the meal was even started.

There were only small stained-glass windows along the side of the house, and at the back he looked into a living-room that was elegant and well furnished but with no sign of life. The top segment of one of the kitchen windows was at an angle, held open by a simple window-latch. He could reach down easily and open the main window over the plastic work-surface. For a moment he hesitated, then walked slowly round the house again, back down the front path to the gate and the street.

At the row of small shops he bought a small pocket flashlight and then walked back to the café by the bridge. He had a coffee and slowly ate a ham sandwich, and when he eventually paid his bill it was already dusk, but still too light for what he had in mind. He checked that he was not being followed and then walked slowly toward the river.

The houses along the river had been very little damaged in the war. They looked well cared for and inside there were lights going on in the ground-floor rooms as he strolled past them. He was already aware that he had reacted too hastily. There must be other ways, more subtle ways, that he could have tackled the problem. But subtlety takes time, and his need for action was overwhelming. It left him wandering around in East Berlin with little thought of what he was going to do next. Even at that moment he needed to *do* something rather than think things out, and he turned impatiently to walk back toward the house.

As he strolled past the house there was nobody in sight and no traffic in the street. He turned back quickly and went through the garden gate, down the side passage to the back of the house.

The catch on the main kitchen window was stiff but he levered it up slowly and the window finally came free. There was crockery and cooking utensils on the work-surface and he carefully moved them aside before climbing through into the kitchen. He closed the window carefully behind him.

He walked slowly and cautiously to the front room. There was only one thing he wanted to check in there. The food. For a brief moment he shone the flashlight as he stood by the single place-setting. The smell was almost enough but in the brief light he could see the actual putrefaction of the vegetables.

In the living-room he drew the curtains and switched on the lights. There was a pile of magazines on the settee and a sewing-basket on an embroidered footstool. A bunch of dahlias in a vase was brown and wilting and the telephone receiver was off its hook, lying beside the instrument on a table by the teak desk. The desk was locked. He picked up the phone carefully and put it to his ear. It had the silence of disconnection.

As he left the room he switched off the lights and shone his flashlight in the hallway. The stairs were on his left and he went up them slowly and tried a door at the top of the stairs. The door was locked and he moved along the carpeted landing to the next bedroom. It faced the street and he didn't want to switch on the lights. But if someone saw even the beam from his flashlight they would almost certainly phone the police. He made his way cautiously to the windows and closed the curtains.

As he turned, the beam of a powerful light almost blinded him and as he put up his hand to shield his eyes the room lights came on.

There was a man standing by the light switch at the door. Leaning there, smiling. Another man was sitting on the bed, a Kalashnikov resting across his knees, and a few feet away perched on a dressing-table was a man pointing a Walther.

The man by the door he recognized, and it was he who spoke in excellent English.

"Welcome to the German Democratic Republic, comrade."

Massey said nothing. There was nothing he could say. The Russian was Major Panov, KGB. He was based in Moscow normally and was responsible for some of the operations against the British and Americans in Europe. He had heard about him from Kuznetsov.

He looked at Massey with his eyebrows raised in query. "Shall we go?"

Massey sat in silence as the big black Mercedes drove to the Karlshorst compound. And for the first time he wondered if all this had some connection with Kuznetsov. Had the Russian's contacts been uncovered? Or, even worse, had Kuznetsov found out somehow about him and Anna and decided to expose him because he saw it as a danger to himself? Panov escorted him to a long, low building that was white in the moonlight.

Inside the building was a long corridor with a dozen doors leading off it and Panov led him to a room at the far end that ran the width of the building. It was furnished as living quarters for some senior official and Panov seemed very much at home as he waved Massey to one of the armchairs as he poured two whiskies from a bottle of Glenlivet.

Panov put the drink for Massey on the low table between them before he sat down himself. Smiling, he raised his glass.

"Your good health, Mr. Massey."

Massey ignored both the drink and the salutation, but Panov was very much at ease as he leaned back in his chair.

"And now what am I going to do about you, Mr. Massey? Not the sort of fish I usually catch. What exactly were you after?"

"Just get on with it, Panov. Do whatever you're going to do and cut out the chat."

"Tell me," Panov said, "was it all just a passing fancy or was she more than that?"

"Where is she? Why was she arrested?"

"Oh, come on, Massey. If one of my chaps was having a relationship with one of your officer's wives, wouldn't you take some action? Why be so hypocritical about it? You got her into trouble, my friend, and you must have known that it was possible."

"You haven't answered my question."

Panov pursed his lips. "Where is she? She's in safe custody. Why was she arrested? Because she was having an adulterous relationship with an enemy of the State. To wit, Jan Massey. Officer of SIS."

"What do you intend doing with her?"

"She'll face a court trial. Probably ten years in a Gulag. The wife of a serving KGB officer can hardly pretend she didn't realize the significance of what she was up to."

"Is Kholkov himself in custody then?"

Panov smiled. "Oh, come now, don't let's play games. You've done him enough harm already."

"So get on with whatever you're planning to do."

"What do you think we're going to do with you?"

"The usual press conference to announce the arrest of a British intelligence man. A trial in Moscow for the publicity. A hoped-for confession from me. And then a heavy prison sentence. Twenty years and up."

"And for the girl?"

"Much the same. Enemy of the State. The usual crap."

Panov sat looking at Massey for long moment. "What would you do with me if I'd slept with young Fielding's wife—I know he hasn't got one . . . but if he had, and you'd caught me in one of the flats you people have in West Berlin."

"You've left something out."

"What's that, my friend?"

"We shouldn't have arrested Fielding's mythical wife just because she was fond of you."

Panov raised his eyebrows. "Is Anna Kholkov fond of you?"

"Of course not. We were just friendly." And Massey lied unhappily to help her.

"And were you fond of Anna Kholkov?"

"Forget it, Panov. My feelings are none of your business."

"Why do you think we are talking here together?"

"You've made a good arrest. You're enjoying the feeling, and you're trying me out to see if I'm scared and I'll talk. I'm not scared. And I shall not talk. To you or anybody else."

"Not even for the sake of the girl?"

Massey hesitated and then said softly, "Not even for the girl."

"You wouldn't lift a finger to help her?"

"How could I help her, for God's sake? You'd do whatever you've already planned to both of us. Whether I talk or not. But I repeat . . . I shall not talk."

"D'you think it is at all possible that you and I could speak the truth to one another?"

Massey shrugged. "It's unlikely, but possible."

"Would you answer me just one question truthfully if I offered to release the girl tomorrow?"

Panov saw the immediate response in Massey's eyes and he followed up his question. "A question about your feelings, nothing to do with your work and mine."

"Ask me the question."

"Do you love Anna Kholkov? Genuinely love her?"

"Why do you want to know?"

"If you really do love her I'll set her free."

"Why would you do that?"

"I'd count it as inexperience and foolishness on her part. She's young and she's not in our business. I could see why she falls for you. You're an attractive man." Panov paused. "I can even see how you could love her." He paused again. "If it was not love on your part, then your relationship with a KGB officer's wife had another purpose. A professional purpose."

Massey sat silently trying to sort out the turmoil of his thoughts but Panov leaned forward.

"Do you love her, my friend? If you do, say so now."

Massey took a deep breath and said quietly, "Yes, I love her. It was not a professional relationship in any way. Apart from the fact that we only met because she happens to be Kholkov's wife."

Panov stood up slowly and walked over to the red telephone on the bottom shelf of the bookshelves. He spoke in Russian and Massey listened. Surprised, relieved, but uncomprehending.

"Ployakov? . . . yes . . . Panov. The girl Anna Kholkov . . . yes . . . Release her now if you please . . . yes . . . of course . . . So bring it over and I'll sign the release form. No, no restrictions . . . that's not necessary . . . Leave it to her . . . yes . . . In my room."

Panov hung up and turned, leaning back against the shelves looking at Massey.

"Does that please you, my friend?"

"Why did you do it?"

"I wanted to—" Panov stopped and shouted, "Come in" as someone knocked on the door.

A lieutenant in KGB uniform came in and stood to attention. Panov held out his hand, took the printed form and read it slowly. He took a pen from his jacket pocket and signed the paper. He held it out for Massey to read. It was an official prison release form made out in Anna's name and with Panov's signature authorizing her immediate release.

When the lieutenant had left and they were alone, Panov walked to a small alcove and brought back a tray of sandwiches and a bowl of fruit, placing them on the low table before he sat down.

"I don't have plates. These were intended just for me. Help yourself."

Massey shook his head and Panov smiled. "Don't be so British stiff-upper-lip, comrade. Just eat, for God's sake. We're not children. There's chicken and there's cheese."

Massey made no move but Panov helped himself to a sandwich.

"You don't look like the photographs of you, Massey, that we have on our files. They make you look older." He leaned back in his chair. "And what are we going to do about you, my friend?"

Massey shrugged. "Put me through the mincing machine I expect. Hoping you'll make me talk. And then the Moscow trial and the propaganda rubbish. And then the Lubyanka or the Gulag."

"A bit old-fashioned, Massey. We're not all dinosaurs in the KGB now."

Massey's eyes showed his disbelief and he asked ironically, "When did you all change?"

Panov laughed softly. "We didn't all change. Just some of us. There were cunning minds in Dzerdzhinski Square who thought that we needed a few more . . . what shall I say? . . . sophisticated? . . . sophisticated minds. Subtle rather than crafty." Panov tapped his chest, smiling. "I'm one of the new boys." He spread his arms, shrugging like a Frenchman. "Not an angel maybe, but different."

"Why are you telling me all this? It won't make me go soft under interrogation."

Panov shook his head slowly. "Your file says you're half Polish. Is that why you are so prejudiced?"

Massey smiled. "I've been working against the KGB and the GRU for years, Panov. That's why I'm prejudiced."

"And you don't believe that a KGB officer could be human, too? Just SIS and the CIA are the nice guys, forced to do dirty tricks by the wicked Russians?"

"Tell me why you really let Anna go free."

Panov shrugged. "No point in holding her. She's no risk if she loved you and you loved her."

"You could have used her to bring pressure on me."

"Would it have worked?"

"Who knows?"

"But you don't feel it was . . ." he shrugged ". . . kind, let us say. You don't feel grateful or anything like that?"

"Very cautiously, a little."

"But back to you. What should I do with you? What would you like me to do?"

"You could drive me back to Checkpoint Charlie and see me through the barrier."

"Is that what you would like?"

"Why not?"

"Don't dodge, Massey. Is that what you would like? Yes or no?"

"Yes."

"You would consider it civilized if I did that?"

"Miraculous."

"But not civilized?"

"OK. Civilized too."

Panov leaned forward, his face close to Massey's. "Let me be frank with you, Massey. Moscow doesn't particularly want to raise hell with the British at the moment for various reasons. I'm prepared to do a deal with you. No trouble for the girl. I'll let you go back. But I want a small piece of cooperation from you."

Massey shook his head. "No way, Panov. No way."

"You don't even know what I'm asking."

"I won't talk, Panov. That's final."

"I'm not asking you to talk."

"What is it then?"

Panov stood up and walked over to the bookshelves, took down a large format book and walked back to his chair, putting the book on the table. Massey could see a color picture on the jacket. A close-up shot of a mountainside covered with wild flowers and snow-capped peaks in the distance. The title was *Frühling im Gebirge*—Spring in the Mountains. Panov pointed to the book. "I just ask that you take that back with you and put it somewhere on the shelves in the library at the house in Grunewald when you get back."

"And if I don't?"

"Then you stay here and we have to go through the usual ritual. Just like you described."

"With Anna involved."

Panov shrugged. "Inevitably."

"Can I talk to Anna?"

"No."

"How do I know that she won't be harassed?"

And in that question Panov knew he had won.

"You have my word, Massey. And there's no advantage for me in harassing the wife of a brother officer." He paused. "But you must not contact her again. I'm sure you understand that."

Massey understood all too well. He had no cards in his hand. Nothing to negotiate with. He would have to go along with them for Anna's sake. He wondered what significance the book had, and why they should want it in the library of the house in Grunewald. Maybe some code. But it looked just like a normally printed book. And who at the house would use it? He could check on the register the name of anyone borrowing it. There was no point in bluffing. In fact there was no bluff he could even try.

Panov interrupted his thoughts. "Did any of your people know you had come over today?"

"Why do you want to know?"

"It's not quite midnight. I could have you back on the other side in half an hour. You can't go through Charlie because it's closed but I can see you over through the Brandenburg crossing. You wouldn't need to explain where you have been provided you went back to the house tonight."

Massey stood up slowly and reached for the book. He found it hard to speak at all, but he said quietly, "OK, Panov, let's go."

Sixteen

Massey walked back through the empty streets to the flat on the Ku'damm. He phoned Fielding, who had to be fetched from his bed by the duty officer. He chatted for a few moments, but Fielding had nothing special to report. And he had established that he was around in case it was ever queried.

The book lay on the comforter on his bed and it was almost an hour before he could bring himself to look through it. There was nothing suspicious about the text or the pictures. What he was looking for was taped onto the back cover under the paper jacket. It was just over five inches across. What looked like a thin flexible gramophone record with an extra large hole in its center. In its top left-hand corner was a normal, white label with four lines of typing.

CP/M-861 (tm) VER 1.0 (BRITISH)
SERIAL 3 C86-336-5904
(C) 1982 SIRIUS SYSTEMS TECH.
(C) 1981 DIGITAL RESEARCH.

Although he wasn't in any way a technician he recognized what it was. It was a floppy disk of the kind that Meyer's people used on the Sirius computers. There were a dozen of them always at the side of each computer. Four in use and two sets on standby and they were in use twenty-four hours a day. There were long shelves from floor to ceiling in the computer-room and the disks were filed in slim, gray, plastic cartons of ten. Thousands of them. Maybe tens of thousands. Copies of them were kept at Cheltenham and the NSA's installation at Fort George Meade. Some controlled the functions of the computer and some stored information. Over a million characters on each slim disk. He had no idea what the function of the disk was that he held in his hand. He folded the illustrated cover back over it and put the book on the table beside the bed.

He lay back on the bed and closed his eyes. What a fool he had been. An unprofessional fool. Just like the new boys who charged into some operation like stampeding elephants. Panov sitting there, suave and cool, watching the worm wriggling on the hook. He had taken for granted that neither Kholkov nor the rest of them knew about his relationship with Anna just because Kholkov had never given even the smallest sign of knowing. He had been amiable and normal every time they met, whether it was on business or privately. But once they had known, then he had been a sitting duck.

They had worked out that it wasn't just sex, it was for real, and they had just sat there, waiting for him to come. And breaking into the house would have been enough to bring a holding charge while they sorted out what to do with him. But they had sorted out what they really wanted long before he arrived. Long before they arrested Anna. And whichever option he chose they were winners. A propaganda victory or the five-inch piece of plastic that did something or other that they wanted. And Anna, although they had released her, was their permanent hold on him so that he couldn't just destroy the disk or pass it to Meyer for comment. The bastards had got him, tied and well knotted. Because he had been Polish, impetuous and stupid.

But as Massey lay there he knew that those thoughts were only to block out the other thoughts. The thought that he would never see her again. Ever. Two days ago it had all seemed so decisive and inevitable, and then, in just thirty-six hours, it had ended. Finally and inexorably. Not even loving last words. Just a void. She must have been terribly scared when they picked her up in the dark, early hours of the morning and put her in a prison cell. He wondered if they had told her why she was arrested. She didn't belong in the world of cells and prisons and it was he who had put her there. He had been careless and irresponsible. He had judged it from Western standards. At the worst, they were committing adultery. But to the KGB it would have seemed incredible. As incredible as if he had just walked through Checkpoint Charlie and given himself up. He felt the salt of his tears as they trickled slowly down his cheeks to the corners of his mouth. If only he were a proper Brit so that he could adopt that stiff-upper-lip approach. He remembered seeing the first light of the false dawn before he slept.

"That's about the lot, Jan."

Leeming gathered up his files and shoved back his chair. He sat down again slowly as Massey spoke.

"I want a list of all withdrawals from the library, Peter."

"You mean the technical reference library?"

"No. The general library."

"We don't keep a record, Jan. It's not worth the time and effort. It's cheaper to risk losing a book or two."

"I want it done for the next month at least. Name of book. Name of borrower. Date out and date returned."

"Any particular reason, Jan?"

"Just something I want to check."

"OK. Will do. How often do you want to see the register?"

"Every day. After the shifts have changed."

Still looking vaguely mystified, Leeming nodded and stood up.

When Leeming left, Massey walked down to the library and put the book on the new books shelf. And for the first time he let the thought gel in his mind that there was a traitor in the SIGINT organization despite all the vetting procedures and the constant checks. He had known it when Panov gave him the book but he had closed it all out of his mind. Filed it away for another time. And the other time was now.

There were just over two hundred people who worked at the Signals Intelligence installation. Not more than twenty or so worked on the Sirius computers. But that wouldn't really narrow down the suspects. The disk could be filed by one of the non-technical clerks. What puzzled him was its function. What could it do that wouldn't be noticed and lead to its discovery?

Panov went over the instructions again and again, brushing aside Johnson's questions as to what it was all about. He said that it was too technologically complex for him to understand himself let alone explain it. All Johnson had to do was take the disk from the book, transfer it to the file marked K109-1704, remove the first disk from that file, destroy it and return the book to the library. He would be given two days' notice before the exchange had to be made. They would notify him when to do it. And he would then get further instructions. Johnson complained that it was difficult for him to get access to the room where the Sirius computers were housed but Panov brushed his protests aside. An officer of the KGB, Panov said, as Johnson now was, would be capable of working out some means of doing what was necessary. There would be a substantial financial reward if he carried out this small operation successfully. When Johnson asked how much he would be paid and Panov indicated that it could be between four and five thousand U.S. dollars Johnson was obviously impressed.

Although Heidi Fischer's reasons for wanting to be married to Arthur Johnson had been realistic and practical, she had, nevertheless, vaguely imagined that her married life would bring security and some sort of domesticity. But in fact the relationship had deteriorated. He gave her money spasmodically, barely enough to feed them and pay the rent of their rooms, and most nights he slept at his billet or was on night duty. And his ruttish acts of sex were infrequent. But Heidi Fischer had been a survivor and she was still a survivor. She was young and attractive and there were thousands of British and U.S. servicemen in West Berlin. She was naturally promiscuous and she enjoyed the casual pick-ups and the torrid couplings in cars and deserted alleyways. She kept her earnings in a Sparkasse account in her old name.

It was four o'clock on Wednesday when the doorbell rang and she slipped on the toweling bathrobe to answer it. It was the young man named Klaus. Panov's messenger boy. He was young and good-looking and cheeky. And he was fantastic in bed.

"Is he here, Heidi?"

"No. You know he's not here in the daytime."

Klaus grinned. "I brought you the record you wanted."

"The Viennese songs?"

"Yeah. 'Dr'unt in der Lobau' and 'Kleines Hotel.' All the songs you wanted."

She put her mouth to be kissed and her arms went round him as he slid his hand inside the bathrobe. For long moments his hand fondled her breasts and then he drew back his hand.

"Business first, kid. Important business. Get a pencil and paper."

"Can't it wait, Klaus? I'm all turned on."

"Get the paper and pencil. Get a move on."

She watched as he scrawled on the paper, Friday Sept 12th. Earliest.

He folded the paper, walked over to the fireplace and put the paper under the china dog on the mantelpiece.

"Give it to him the minute he arrives."

"He might not come here tonight."

"So give it to him tomorrow, you silly bitch."

As he walked into the bedroom he was unbuttoning his shirt and minutes later they were both naked on her bed.

He left two hours later and stopped at the door to remind her about the message on the mantelpiece.

Johnson phoned her that evening but she forgot to mention the message. He discovered it himself on Friday evening, asking her what it was. When she told him, he went white with anger, cursing her obscenely as he reached for his jacket. As the outer door slammed to behind him she went to the wardrobe to find the half-empty bottle of whiskey that a sergeant had given her. It was the second bottle she had opened that week. An hour later the bottle was empty, the radio still playing as she staggered to the unmade bed in the alcove. She had had enough of Arthur Johnson. She'd got her passport and could leave whenever she wanted. That dark blue passport with its gold coat of arms that meant that she could be in London in a few hours. All she would need was new clothes, a room where she could take the men and she'd be free of the bastard and independent.

As Johnson reported back at the security checkpoint at the house in Grunewald he looked at his watch. It was ten o'clock already. Two hours instead of two days to carry out his instructions.

He wasn't allowed to go down to the underground section unless he was on duty but he phoned through to Corporal Malins offering to take over his shift. Malins was delighted and ten minutes later Johnson was alone in his office.

The only way he could get through to the maze of inner rooms was with an officer on duty. He checked through the day's duty-roster and the roster for the following day. The fourth shift would come off duty just before midnight and the relief shift would be going through in ones and twos from eleven thirty on. Lieutenant Strauss was duty changeover officer. He was an American on secondment from Fort Meade, the U.S.A.'s own electronic surveillance installation. He was a scientist not a soldier and was easygoing and amiable. He could probably be conned into letting him through. He wasn't security minded and often forgot his own pass and had to go back and search for it in his room.

In the end, it was incredibly easy. Just like Panov had said. Behave like you're entitled to be wherever you are. He asked Strauss if he could suggest the title of a book that would explain simply how microchips work and Strauss put his plastic card into the security lock and walked with him to the library and showed him four or five suitable books. When Strauss left, Johnson took two and the picture book and sat at one of the reading-desks for a few minutes looking through the books. He was alone in the library, and when he had removed the disk he replaced the books on the shelves. He went into the computer-room with three men from the new shift. Nobody stopped him when he walked over to the files and looked for the number he'd been given. He sweated a little as he exchanged the two disks. He put the original disk from the file inside his battledress blouse.

It was Meyer himself who held the security door open for Johnson to go back into his own office as Meyer came through to check the new shift.

He phoned Heidi on Saturday evening but there was no reply. On Sunday he had a twenty-four-hour pass and took the unit bus into Berlin. He walked to her room and let himself in with the key. She was out and the place was a shambles. Two glasses on the table that stank of neat whiskey, a half-burned cigar stub in a saucer, the radio babbling away in German and the sink piled high with dirty crockery.

As he stood there he heard the key in the lock and he watched her come in. Swaying a little as she stood there, looking at him.

"What the hell's going on, you stupid bitch?"

She reached out with her hand behind her and steadied herself against the door.

"They sent a message for you."

"Where is it?"

"It wasn't written down. The chap just told me."

"What did he say?"

"He said . . ." and she closed her eyes ". . . he said to get rid of the disk."

"Nothing else?"

"No." She opened her eyes and saw that he wasn't angry, and leaning back against the door she did the only thing that always worked and pulled up her skirt so that he could see the dark triangle between her legs. He grinned and carried her to the unkempt bed.

Seventeen

For two months Jan Massey had done his best to disguise his deep distress. He had worked long hours trying to concentrate his thoughts on his work but he spent most nights sleeping only fitfully. Hundreds of times he had told himself that there was nothing he could do. And even more times he had recognized that once Anna had been arrested what he had done was the best within his power. But he knew it was a poor best. Somehow he had been careless. He could have sworn that they had not been seen. And if they *had* been seen then the other side must have known from the start that he and both the Kholkovs sometimes met socially from time to time.

There were moments when, on the edge of sleep, he had visions of it all, like brief flashes from some film that he had seen. The uneaten food on the table. The house that she had lived in. Panov's smooth, well worked-out proposition. He would lie there bathed in sweat, angered by his impotence and lost in a sea of misery caused by his thoughts of Anna, trying not to imagine what repercussions it had had for her. And more anger at her misreading of Kholkov's awareness of what was going on.

His senior colleagues had noticed his withdrawal. There were no longer the informal chats after meetings. When a meeting was over he always left immediately. They frequently saw him walking on his own in

111

the gardens. Shoulders hunched and head down, walking but not looking. Oblivious to the rest of the world. Both Max Cohen and Howard Fielding had tried, tactfully, to discover what was wrong but their tentative enquiries had been brushed aside with obvious resentment.

Massey had seen the weekly status report on the KGB units in East Berlin and when he saw that Alexei Kholkov had been promoted to major and transferred back to Moscow it had seemed like the final act that irrevocably closed the drama. A few days later he decided to take a week's leave and spend it with his father.

The main street of Tenterden is one of the most picturesque streets in southern England. Wide and tree-lined with most of its houses and shops genuine Georgian. The others are mainly typical Kentish ship-lapped, timber houses. Even on gloomy days, Tenterden has an air of smiling lightness and summer that lifts the spirits of its visitors from the marshlands and the flat, featureless acres reclaimed from the sea that constitute the Romney Marshes. Dr. Massey's surgery was the front room of one of the Georgian houses.

He could have lived well enough on his pension and savings but so many of his patients were old friends. His list had fewer than two thousand names on it and most evenings he had no more than half a dozen people in the small waiting-room. He had several virtues that were much prized by his patients. He had time to listen and time to talk. He was always there, and anxious mothers knew that he could be called out in the middle of the night. And middle-aged patients knew that he would only smile when the dreaded heart attack turned out to be no more than indigestion. Old people found comfort from him because he had the strange habit of sometimes holding their hands as they unfolded their troubles. It was not a working method that he had deliberately devised. It was instinctive. The need had always been there and slowly over the years he had recognized it and satisfied it.

Jan Massey was sitting in the armchair opposite his father, his arm stretched out in front of him, a slice of bread held on an old-fashioned brass toasting-fork in front of the glowing, coal fire.

The old man watched him and then said softly, "You're burning it, lad."

Jan Massey sighed, turned the bread and held it back in front of the fire.

The older man waited until they were sipping their second cups of coffee before he said, "Tell me about it, Jan."

"Tell you what, Father?"

"Tell me what's troubling you."

"There's nothing troubling me."

"You don't *have* to tell me. You know that. I'm not prying. But you *are* my son and I wouldn't need to be a doctor to know that you're very unhappy. Is it your work?"

"No, Father."

"Is there anything I could do to help you?"

Jan leaned forward and put his hand on his father's knee.

"Don't worry about me, Papa. There's nothing that anyone can do."

"There is always something that can be done. No matter what the problem, there's a solution. Sometimes more than one."

Jan looked at his father's face and said quietly, "I fell in love with someone, Papa. I loved her very much and she loved me. It didn't work out. It did her harm. It was my fault. But now it's over. Gone."

"Have you got a photograph of her?"

"No. An oil-painting. A portrait."

"Where is it?"

"It's on the dressing-table in my bedroom."

"Here or in Berlin?"

"Here."

"Is she in Berlin?"

"I don't know. I don't know where she is."

"Were you happy with her before it ended?"

"Very happy."

"What kind of happiness?"

"Just glad to be alive in the same world with her. Glad of every day."

"Can I recommend a medicine to you?"

"I don't need one of your bottles or a box of pills."

"That wasn't what I had in mind."

"Tell me."

"It's a medicine I've used for many years. It's called love. It can sometimes have a bitter taste but it works. I know it can work because it works for me. When I knew that your mother was dead, and how she died, it was a very dark, cold world for me. I think if I hadn't had you to care for and love I might have decided to die myself. Do you remember when I used to walk up to the parish church here and sit in the churchyard?"

"Yes. I remember."

"There was a book I read. Palgrave. There were some lines of a Shakespeare sonnet that made me realize that my love for your mother had become an inferior love. Maybe you know them:

> Love is not love
> Which alters when it alteration finds,
> Or bends with the remover to remove

113

It goes on in the same vein. It made me realize that my thinking was both selfish and negative. I could love my girl the same way I had always loved her . . . if I chose to. And if it was real love. And if I didn't, then the sick ghouls in Mauthausen had won. Maybe you could find some kind of solace that way?"

Massey half-smiled. "You're a good man, Father. And a good doctor."

"Will you try it? Just look up at the sky sometimes. Day or night. It gives us new dimensions."

"Maybe, Father. Thanks for understanding."

The old man reached for the tuner on the hi-fi and the music was the Barenboim recording of Fauré's *Requiem*.

Massey walked over to the window to draw the curtains. There was a light scatter of snow on the garden and he shivered involuntarily as the bare branches of the apple trees swung and tossed in the first harsh winds of winter. There would be four or five inches of snow in Moscow already.

Eighteen

There was heavy snow as the plane came in to land at Tegel and Howard Fielding had come to the airport with a car to meet him in.

Fielding watched Massey as he passed through Immigration and stood waiting for his bag from the carousel. He didn't look any more amiable than when he had left. It was going to be back to "sir" again, not Jan, and Fielding was disappointed. He was a young man and Massey was his idea of what he'd like to be in a few years' time. It was a mixture of affection, respect and young man's hero-worship. He had seen Massey listening to a report of a failure of some operation. The brown eyes as hard as glass, those muscles tense at the side of his mouth and the deep lines from his nose almost to the stubborn chin. And seconds later calmly telling them all what had to be done next. No apportioning of blame, no apparent anger, just cool, calm professionalism. He had lost none of the respect or affection over the last few months but he was ill at ease in the cold aloof relationship that now existed. He had discussed his feelings unofficially with both Cohen and Harper, who obviously shared his views but were not prepared to comment or criticize. Massey was the boss and his aloofness was his privilege. It was up to them all to get on with their jobs.

* * *

When Bourget phoned, the Frenchman insisted that Massey meet him somewhere where they couldn't be seen in public. Massey suggested Club Chérie and Bourget had agreed.

Despite the great urgency when Bourget had phoned, the Frenchman, as usual, arrived half an hour late at Club Chérie. Massey was playing chess with one of the girls, a pretty young thing who said she was an artist but obviously earned more money obliging the customers at Club Chérie than she did from the sale of her paintings. But she really did paint. She had shown him one of her paintings that Karl, who owned the club, had hung on one of the walls. It was a mixture of Dali and Picasso. The kind of picture that needs a long and explanatory title. She dragged Bourget over to see it and he admired it loudly and fulsomely without taking his eyes from the young blonde's fantastic breasts.

But he came back to the table alone, staring at the pieces on the chessboard as if he were trying to work up some deep and significant comment relating chess to the "game of life" or maybe espionage. Either way he gave up the struggle and came down to earth.

"How much they charge, these little whores?"

"It used to be a hundred and fifty D-marks, Pierre, room extra, but that was a few years ago and inflation may have crept in."

"What's her name, that one?"

"She didn't tell me. Do you want me to ask?"

Bourget shook his head vigorously. A bit too vigorously to be convincing.

"We talk about Kuznetsov, yes?"

Massey hesitated and said quietly, "OK. But I'm not really interested."

"You're not interested, or London is not interested?"

Massey smiled. "Same thing, Pierre."

"How much you know of him in, say, last two years?"

"He's in charge of operations against SIS and CIA in Berlin. Mainly NATO and United States stuff."

"For last two years, maybe a little less, that was only his cover. He specializes in other direction."

Bourget's big brown eyes were full of significance and fatherly concern for a wayward son.

"Tell me more," Massey said.

The Frenchman's big, thick forefinger tapped the table slowly, like the hammer of a piano. "He is concerned now with your people. SIS. He builds a big dossier on all your people in Berlin and the Federal Republic."

"They've always done that, Pierre. They do it automatically."

"He says he knows of top-secret operations. And more."

"What more?"

"He knows of traitor in your organization. Maybe two traitors. They not even know of each other. Not even work to same KGB man."

116

"Do you believe him?"

"Yes."

"Have you really got Kuznetsov, or are you just dreaming dreams?"

"I swear on my mother's grave, Jan."

"Your mother's still alive, you bastard. Lives in Lyon."

"Is just a turn of phrase. I swear I got him."

"You mean that he's physically held at your place right now?"

Bourget shrugged. "He come to me whenever I say the word."

"When did he approach you first?"

"Two months ago. Maybe three."

"He's just visited you and then gone back to the other side?"

"Who knows where he goes?"

"What did he say when he approached you?"

"He identified himself. He says he wants to make a deal."

"What's the deal?"

"He gives us information and in return we talk with CIA for him to go to United States."

"Why doesn't he go direct to the CIA?"

Bourget grinned. "He don't trust them. Wants us to find out which way they jump."

"So why are you talking with me?"

"Two reasons. First is, Paris don't like CIA, and second is, Kuznetsov talks about your people . . . SIS." Bourget grinned. "You not want that he talks to Washington about English traitors, yes?"

"No. We shouldn't like that too much." Massey turned and looked directly at the Frenchman's face. "What was the other reason, Pierre?"

"Which other reason?"

"The one you haven't told me."

"Who say there is another reason?"

"You're wasting my time, Pierre. And yours."

Bourget sighed theatrically. "OK. I tell you. Last time I meet with Kholkov he tell me that if ever we are approached by Soviet intelligence defector he would pay cash to know and more cash if I return him. The cash for me personally. In Swiss bank in code-name. They would pay plenty for Kuznetsov, my friend. He's more important that Kholkov himself."

"They do that sometimes, Pierre, if they've planted some guy on you. They want to make it look like they're desperate to get him back. It's an old trick to divert suspicion and make you feel you've got a really hot guy."

"He talked of a hundred and fifty thousand D-marks."

"Jesus. No. Are you sure you heard him right?"

"I hear him OK." He paused. "I go fifty-fifty with you."

"Was the conversation recorded?"

"No."

"He could be trying to frame you, Pierre. It's been done before. *He* could have recorded it. Have you been doing much against them in the last few months? Anything I might not know about?"

"Maybe. How do I know what you know? You tell *me*."

Massey closed his eyes, trying to remember the French summaries. There never was much worth reporting about the SDECE. They didn't do all that much. West Berlin didn't interest them really except for political things.

"I can't remember much, Pierre. I'd need to check the records. There was that homosexual thing involving one of your Berlin Mission. Then the French girl clerk at NATO Brussels. The cipher clerk at your Embassy in Bonn who was getting drugs paid for by the KGB man through SDECE in Marseilles, or Nice was it? That's all I can remember off-hand."

Bourget nodded. "Is plenty more but nothing special. So what do we do?"

"Have you told Kholkov that you've talked to me?"

"No," he said, and Massey knew that he was lying.

"OK. Tell Kuznetsov that we're interested and that I'm going to London soon and I'll talk about it while I'm there. He'll have to wait until I get back. Maybe another twelve days. I'm not going until Saturday week."

"He will want sooner than that."

"So tell Kuznetsov that we are interested in principle. And tell Kholkov to get stuffed. He's laying a trap for you."

"So I sell Kuznetsov to you people. You pay instead of Kholkov. I need money, my friend. So do you."

"I don't, Pierre. The money's all yours. I don't want to know about it. London might be interested but I doubt if they'd pay forty thousand pounds. For me it's just business. We either want Kuznetsov or we don't. Simple as that. We shall thank SDECE officially for your cooperation whether we take him or pass."

"And if you take him what do I get? Me personally?"

"I'll pay for a night with that pretty blonde."

"Nothing more? No money?"

"Not forty thousand pounds, that's for sure." Massey smiled. "I doubt if we'd pay that for Andropov himself."

"Maybe a retainer. Monthly."

"If Kuznetsov really has what he says he has, then London might authorize me to do something, but I couldn't promise anything."

Bourget sighed. "OK. I leave in your hands."

Without looking at Massey, Bourget said, "One of my guys says he see you twice with a dark-haired girl. Who is she?" And he looked up smiling, but his eyes were intent on Massey's face.

"How should I know? All the girls I know are either dark-haired or blonde. I've never gone for redheads."

118

"They say she not your type."

Massey shrugged. "What's my type?"

"They say you like pretty ones, long legs, big tits, like my Leni. They say this one is beautiful, not pretty. Walks like a dancer and looks at you like she marry you someday."

"I'm not the marrying kind, Pierre. And I must get on my way. Thanks for the drink. I'll be in touch."

As Massey stood up the Frenchman looked at him from under the black bushy eyebrows. But he said nothing. Just nodding as Massey walked away.

He walked back to the flat on the Ku'damm and let himself in. It was nearly midnight and he ran himself a bath. As he lay in the warm soapy water he tried to remember the exact words that Bourget had used. He'd mentioned Kholkov first and then the dark-haired girl, or did he say black-haired girl? Was it a crude attempt at pressuring him about Kuznetsov? It was almost impossible that he should know who she was. Bourget could have put a routine surveillance on him just for the hell of it, but Ridge's people would have spotted them. The SDECE boys in Berlin weren't well trained. But Bourget was obsessed with girls. Maybe he just wanted to know who she was and get an introduction to try his luck. But if it was that, he would have pursued it. He wasn't a romantic, just a lecher.

It looked as if Kuznetsov *had* actually contacted Bourget. He could think of no reason why he should; and a dozen reasons why it was highly dangerous for the Russian to do so. His status in the KGB made any movement by him into West Berlin virtually impossible. Did that mean that Moscow had authorized or even initiated his contact with Bourget? It seemed highly unlikely. But the whole thing was unlikely.

It was a relief to know that the Russian was not with Bourget and Massey decided once more that he could only wait and see what developed.

Nineteen

Massey looked through the pages of the SIGINT summary. A clandestine transmitter was operating out of the French sector, using a code generally used by the PLO, an extract from the transcription of a telephone conversation that indicated that a CDU politician in Bonn was asking for money for supporting the request for a grant to a West Berlin electronics company. A French diplomat in a French Mission car had given a frank view of his opposite number on a Franco-German committee, the Soviet HQ at Karlshorst had circulated the description of a Red Army major who was suspected of having defected to the West through Helmstedt sometime over the weekend. A KGB detachment in Dresden was complaining to Moscow of lack of funds. A West German trade union leader had had three telephone conversations with a number suspected of being a cut-out for a group of low-grade KGB agents fomenting trouble among West Berlin civil servants.

Day after day the pages of two-line summaries came to Massey, Harper and Mason. Mason and his team were responsible for evaluating each item, checking the traffic against previous reports, seeing how they fitted into the general intelligence jigsaw and sometimes warning that the material was deliberate disinformation put out by some section of the Soviet intelligence services.

Harper was responsible for the gathering of intelligence by other means than monitoring and responsible for countering KGB and the Red Army's GRU attempts at penetrating the British and West German intelligence services. All information gathered by technical rather than human means was passed back to GCHQ within hours. For Massey it was a sign of the times that SIGINT, the monitoring service, was more highly valued than HUMINT, the intelligence gathered by Harper's team. It was the official view that HUMINT was subject to all the mental and psychological vagaries of the human source and the human evaluator. SIGINT was fact. It had been transmitted by phone, radio or computer. Sometimes it was false but Mason's evaluation team could spot the phoney material in minutes. Others back at Cheltenham could provide an even finer safety-net. And the NSA at Fort Meade provided one more filter in the assessment of much of the SIGINT information.

Massey turned to the surveillance reports on Bourget's place but there was nothing significant. The mystery visitor had not appeared again. Their telephone and radio traffic gave no mention of Kuznetsov or any other Russian name of significance. Bourget's chatter still disturbed Massey but it looked as if it had been nothing more than a crude attempt to get money. And Bourget had talked as if he were still in touch with Kholkov, who had been posted back to Moscow weeks ago.

He strolled down to Cohen's office and saw him through the glass partitions at one of the Evaluation work stations bending over to look at the screen of a VDU. When Cohen showed no sign of returning to his office Massey threaded his way through the rows of work stations until he was standing behind Cohen. As his shadow fell across the screen Cohen turned irritably, and then relaxed as he saw that it was Massey.

"We're getting an interesting batch from the Soviet Mission HQ. We don't know what it's about but it's showing checkwords we've had on our priority list and have never come up before."

"What does it indicate?"

"Some sort of major event in the Kremlin and with top KGB people involved."

"Who provided the checkwords list in the first place?"

"It's coded as a Foreign Office request. Top priority if more than five of the checkwords come up in the same four-hour shift."

"Any guesses of what it's about?"

Cohen frowned, a meaningful, warning frown. "Not beyond what I've told you." He turned to the operator. "Warn Evaluation that there's top priority material coming their way and get the emergency cryppies on it right away." Cohen turned back to Massey. "Let's go to my office, Jan."

In the security of his office Cohen stood looking at Massey. "It means that either Brezhnev is dying or dead or that they've eased him out. And he's being replaced by Andropov."

"Our Andropov?"

"Yes. One big step for mankind. From head of the KGB to President."

"How can you tell?"

"Sit down and I'll explain."

When they were both seated Cohen said, "We have checkword lists from all sorts of people. SIS, NSA, GCHQ, special units, the Foreign Office and a good number of government departments. We get so much material when we're monitoring, either in code or clear, that if we transcribed it all it would be months out of date by the time anyone saw it. So we have the checkword lists and if those words, in code or clear, come up on the screens, then we transcribe that section of our traffic. Sometimes it has to be a combination of words before we transcribe. One of the words could be somebody's name. The American President for instance. Too common in the traffic if it's standing alone, but if certain other words on the list come up in the same text, then we transcribe.

"The Foreign Office checklist had nineteen words on it. Four were names of Politburo members. Actual names, and the KGB code-names for them. This batch was from the Politburo to the head of the Soviet Mission in East Berlin and the head of the KGB at Karlshorst. The other checkwords had no significance for me but when the list came through I was told—well, it was hinted—that this would cover an upheaval at the top in Moscow, or Brezhnev's death. Andropov's code-name was the only other name in the whole piece." Cohen shrugged. "We shan't be the only station to have picked it up. It'll have gone to all Soviet ambassadors, warning them. But I want to get our stuff back to London inside the hour."

Massey stood up. "I'll let you get on with it, Max."

"Was there something you wanted to talk to me about?"

"Nothing that can't wait."

That night Massey went to the Ku'damm flat. There were days when no matter how hard he tried he couldn't keep her out of his mind. It was the first time he had been there since it happened. He wandered from the sitting-room to the bedroom to the kitchen. There were two coffee cups on the draining board alongside the sink. Unwashed, the dark stains dry and reticulated, a spoon covered with crystals of brown sugar. The air in the rooms was still and dry, and he tried to think of what he had wanted when he had decided to go there again. It had seemed possible that some of the pleasure of his days with her could still linger there and, by some kind of osmosis, make his heart lighter. But it did nothing. He had a small photograph of her portrait that he had brought framed to place on the bedside table. He stared at it, on the edge of tears. Her eyes were still big and beautiful, the neck still slender and graceful. He turned away suddenly. That beautiful face still existed somewhere. In Moscow or Warsaw or maybe Prague. He could find out from Central Archives where Kholkov was. Just a phone call or a single-line routine request. But he was not sure that he could bear knowing. It would be so much better if he could wipe it out as if it had never happened.

He walked to the window and looked across the city. The blue sky was reflected on the snow on the roofs of the buildings. They had never seen snow together. He walked slowly to the bed and lay there, his eyes closed, his cheeks wet.

When he eventually stood up it was dark, and, despite the heating, he shivered as he walked to the door and let himself out.

Signalman Johnson let himself into the flat. It was untidy as always. Clothes on the floor and on the bed, a pile of dirty crockery in the sink and cigarette butts everywhere. He hadn't seen her for a week and he wondered what she'd been up to. The Russkis giving her the fake passport and marriage certificate had calmed her down for six months or so but for the past year she'd grown more and more cantankerous. She shouted back at him now whenever she was displeased and once or twice she'd threatened to leave him. But what was worse was her putting in the dirt about him to the Russians. He wasn't sure what she was telling them but both his usual contact and the major above him had been a bit offhand the last two times that they'd met. Urging him to keep her happy because she was very useful to them.

He'd had a meeting with them that evening and Levchenko had finished up talking about her again. Stressing the importance of keeping her happy.

"For Christ's sake," Johnson shouted. "Whose side are you on? Hers or mine?"

Levchenko touched his shoulder with a friendly gesture. "It's for you as much as for us, comrade. We want to protect you. An angry wife is a danger in this business."

"So what do you suggest I do? I don't start the rows."

Levchenko shrugged and smiled. "A box of chocolates sometimes. Or a bunch of red roses. Women like these little signs of affection."

"You mean when she calls me dirty names I run out and buy her a bunch of flowers? Not bloody likely."

Levchenko sighed and involuntarily glanced at the chandelier where the microphones were hidden. He hoped that the surveillance people were listening to what he had to put up with. "How about you take her on a few days' holiday in London? Show her the sights. She'd like that." He paused. "We could arrange funds for you . . . say, five hundred sterling pounds."

Levchenko was satisfied by the obvious greed on Johnson's face as he said, "If that's what you want, OK then."

"Tell me," Levchenko said, "tell me what you know about Mr. Massey."

Johnson shrugged. "He's the head guy. That's all I know."

"You see him around the place?"

"Not very often. He spends his time with the big white chiefs. The section bosses like Cohen and Harper. Not with the likes of me."

"Is he popular? Does the staff like him?"

"No idea. The people in London must like him or they wouldn't have given him such a top job."

"Who are his friends?"

"I've no idea. How should I know?"

"Has he got a girlfriend?"

"God knows. I don't. He ain't gonna tell me if he has."

"There must be gossip about him. There always is about the top man. What do people say about him?"

"We don't spend our time talking about the nobs. They don't interest us."

"The nobs?" Levchenko looked confused.

"Yeah. The nobs. The bosses."

"What are his interests? His hobbies?"

"I've no idea. I told you. He's way above people like me." With sudden inspiration Johnson said, "Maybe he likes gardening. He spends a lot of time in the grounds of the house. Just walking around, sitting by the pond. Maybe gardening's his hobby."

"I've arranged for you to be given a camera. A little Minox. One of my men is going to show you how to use it. There's some things we want you to photograph."

"I'd never get through the metal detectors."

"You will. It won't register. We've made it so that it won't show up. There's no metal in it."

"What d'you want me to photograph?"

"I'll tell you later." Levchenko paused. "By the way, how did you get the tape out?"

Johnson smiled. "That's a trade secret, comrade."

"Tell me how you did it."

Johnson heard the quiet voice but he saw the hardness in the Russian's eyes.

"Tell me why you want to know."

"I'll tell you when you've told me how you got it out."

"I wrapped the tape round my arm in the toilet and then put a piece of medical plaster round it."

"Why didn't they pick up the metal reel on the detector?"

"The tape wasn't on the reel. I've got empty reels at my place in town. I put it on there."

Levchenko smiled. "Clever thinking, my friend. You're learning the business fast."

"So why did you want to know how I did it? So you can show other guys, yes?"

Levchenko saw the pleasure in Johnson's eyes. He was pathetic, but they needed him. If he wanted a phoney ego trip let him have it.

"Exactly. Now, let's eat before you go over the camera instructions."

As Johnson walked around the living-room at the flat he opened drawers and looked inside. But it was a piece of paper on the bedside table that he looked at longest. He sat on the bed and stared at the figures. They were in pencil and there was the number 31287 followed by a division sign and the figures 3.50. Eventually he screwed up the paper and tossed it toward the wastebasket. It missed and fell to the floor. Three fifty was at that time the current exchange rate for changing D-marks into sterling. But he didn't connect it.

He waited around for twenty minutes, switching on the small color TV they had just bought, but there was only some sort of quiz program in German and a fuzzy picture on the other channel. Finally he yawned, looked at his watch and left. He wondered what she was doing. Not that he cared, but she ought to be there. He wondered if she was screwing for money again on the side.

Mayhew always followed the instructions precisely but he sometimes wondered why they made it all so complicated. He could have put the stuff in a Jiffy bag and posted it and they'd have got it sooner. It was raining as he parked the car and he put up his umbrella before he walked on up the lane. He could hear the water running in the ditch below the hedge. He wasn't a countryman and he found the unlit lane, the darkness and the night rustlings of birds and animals quite frightening. It was almost half a mile to the cottage and they'd told him never to use a flashlight.

He was panting and sweating despite the cold night air when he went through the rickety gate and up the short path to the door. There were no lights on at the front of the stone cottage but he felt for the bell and pressed the button exactly as they had said. He walked back down the path and on up the lane to the telephone kiosk. There was no light inside but he lifted the receiver and dialed the ten digits carefully and accurately. He pushed in the coin and heard the three rings before the phone was picked up at the other end.

"Can I speak to Mr. Jamieson, please?"

"Of course."

Then the phone was hung up at the other end and the dialing tone came back. He hung up his receiver and stood outside the kiosk. Five minutes later the man came, and stood there in silence.

Mayhew felt slightly embarrassed as he said softly, "The red poppies are blooming."

The man said, "All's well that ends well."

They walked back together in silence to the cottage. The door was ajar, the man went inside and Mayhew followed. There was an oil-lamp burning now in the small parlor and Mayhew waited as the man pulled back the worn carpet and lifted the hinged cover that revealed the wooden steps that led down to the brightly lit cellar.

The cement walls were painted white and the plasterboard ceiling supported two strip lights. A strip of chipboard covered with black Formica served as a work-bench. Mayhew recognized the Japanese NRD-515 shortwave receiver but the small transmitter had no name badge and was not a model he had seen before. There was a simple microscope under a plastic cover and a pile of notepads. On the wall above the bench were two digital display clocks. One showed local time and the other, he realized, showed Moscow time.

On a small shelf under the clocks were a few books. Mayhew recognized the faded red-covered copy of *The Town That Was Murdered* by Ellen Wilkinson. It was the old Left Book Club edition. The *World Radio and TV Handbook*, 36th edition, was between the Penguin *Decline and Fall* and a Russian–English dictionary. The Berlitz *Russian for Travellers* was alongside Bertrand Russell's *History of Western Philosophy*.

There were two folding canvas chairs and Rose pointed to one of them and settled in the other himself.

"I hear you've been promoted, comrade." He smiled. "The people at Cheltenham must be pleased with your work."

"How did you hear that? It was only a couple of weeks ago." Mayhew was smiling and relaxed. He liked being called comrade. It was a sign that he belonged.

Rose half-smiled. "I hear. Anyway, how did you get on with the project?"

"The Watch List has been extended very considerably. That's the main thing. The new numbers and frequencies are on my tape."

"Good. Are any of them significant?"

Mayhew shrugged. "How should I know?"

Rose nodded. "Any news on Rhyolite?"

"It's very difficult for me. It's nothing to do with my work but I've heard that there have been two new launchings. One seems to be a back-up on an existing orbit and I've heard gossip that the other is to concentrate on transmissions from the Soviet base at Kabkan."

"Is it now? And what about new helpers?"

126

Mayhew looked surprised. "You told me not to try any contacts."

"Absolutely. But I asked for details of possible targets."

"I see. Well, there's a couple of people you might look at."

"Go on."

"There's a chap named Smallwood. He's due to retire in two years' time. He's a technician but he's not done long enough for a decent pension. He's worried about how he'll manage on what he'll get."

"What does he do?"

"He services the decoding machines."

"Which ones?"

"The American ones—I think they're called Pyramiders."

"They're not decoding machines, they're frequency hoppers for communicating with agents in 'denied areas.' Tell me more about him. Everything you know."

The two had talked until well after midnight and then Rose had walked back down the lane with Mayhew to where he had parked his car. He watched as its red tail-lights faded into the distance and then walked slowly back to the cottage. The quiet, modest little man, Mayhew, was worth an armored division. He seemed to have an instinct for the kind of information that they wanted. He kept him on simple gleanings of information; most of it was no more than double-checking on what they already knew. It was the gossip, those diffident asides, that were so valuable. A man who had serviced Pyramiders was an incredible find. It was almost unbelievable that the British would let a man with that knowledge and experience retire on an inadequate pension and social security handouts. But that was the sort of thing they let happen. Bureaucracy was seldom tempered with imagination.

Jack Rose always said, with a grin, that he was a member of the Bristol Conservative Club only because they had three full-size billiards tables. He was the owner of successful antiques shops in Cheltenham and Bristol. He had never married despite his obvious charm and was much in demand at local dinner parties. He had been a JP for ten years but had declined several invitations to stand for mayor. It was well known that he had no interest in politics. He gave a £50 cheque to both the local Tories and the Labour Party at election times and both felt that he was more on their side than the opposition's.

Twenty

Signalman Johnson had never taken to Fomenko. He'd only been dealt with by him two or three times but he didn't like the Russian's attitude. The other Russians were always ready to put an arm round his shoulder, to crack a joke and show their appreciation of what he was doing for them. But not Fomenko. He was never impolite but he was impassive and only concerned himself with the business at hand.

Johnson had gone through Checkpoint Charlie and walked on as they had instructed to Karl Marx Platz where a black Mercedes had picked him up and taken him to the small office at the back of the hospital where Fomenko was waiting.

The Russian shook hands briefly and motioned Johnson to a chair on the opposite side of the small table.

"Your trip to England, comrade." He handed over an envelope. "Five hundred pounds. Half in sterling, half in dollars." He pushed across a white envelope. "Two British Airways tickets Berlin–Gatwick and return. Seats have been booked on both flights. Return flight eight days later as you asked for. Any questions so far?"

Johnson shook his head. "No."

"Right. Now, a few words of warning. The lady's documentation. Apart from the name the passport is genuine. The marriage certificate is a high-grade forgery . . . not genuine, but it will pass all normal visual scrutiny. It's in your interest, comrade, that it's not genuine. It keeps the lady happy, but as you wished, it does not make her legally your wife. At the same time I want to warn you to be very careful while you are in England. A driving offense, a drinking offense . . . anything of that sort could bring you in contact with the police. If they had reason to examine the marriage certificate carefully you could be in trouble. Serious trouble. Remember that, please."

Johnson bridled. "And you remember, mate, it was your people wanted me to take her to England in the first place . . . not me, comrade." And Johnson jabbed his finger at his chest in emphasis. "I didn't want no holiday in the first place. You people wanted to please *her*, not me. I take the bloody risks but she's the one you always want to please."

Fomenko sat in silence, looking at Johnson's face. He said quietly, "Is that what you really think, Mr. Johnson?"

"For Christ's sake . . . it's not a question of what I think . . . it's facts. Just facts."

Fomenko stood up and held out his hand. As Johnson responded, the Russian held Johnson's hand in both of his as he spoke. "When you come back, comrade Johnson, we will talk about your feelings again. Meantime I must make it clear that you are the one who matters to us—not the girl. Our only reason to please her is to make sure that there is no trouble for you with her. Do I make myself clear? You are the one who matters. That, too, is a question of fact."

Fomenko knew from Johnson's face that he was not merely mollified by what he had said but pleased, and flattered.

He walked with Johnson to the car that was waiting and stood, watching, as he was driven off.

Back in the small office he gathered up his papers, phoned Grushko and arranged to see him at Karlshorst.

Fomenko signed in at the desk, showed his pass and walked down the main corridor to Grushko's office. Grushko was his boss.

Grushko was listening to the radio news from Moscow and he waved Fomenko to a chair and went on listening. He was using headphones, and when he took them off and switched off the set he turned to Fomenko. "His death's official. Andropov will take over in a few days." As he sat down he said, "No comment outside." He paused. "And none inside if you're as sensible as I think you are." He reached for a packet of cigarettes and his lighter. "What's your problem?"

"The man Johnson."

"Johnson . . ." Grushko frowned. "Is he the British SIGINT man or the American sergeant?"

"He's the British SIGINT man."

"And what's the problem?"

Fomenko outlined almost verbatim his conversation with Johnson, and Grushko leaned back in his chair and was silent for several minutes. Then he said, "What do we use the girl for?"

"She does courier work for us. She lets us use their room as an emergency safe-house. And she keeps an eye on Johnson." Fomenko shrugged. "That's about it."

"The rooms, we don't need—we've got plenty of safe-houses that are properly organized. So we can discount that. So far as keeping an eye on Johnson is concerned—I don't like that at all. When I interviewed the girl she struck me as being of low intelligence, cunning but not intelligent. She was—maybe still is—a prostitute, and she had the arrogance that those women have. They are used to being abused by men and that often means they despise not only the men who use them, but all men. Maybe she behaves with Johnson as if she controls his relationship with us. He might have sensed this. The psychiatrist's report said he was of low intelligence but simple in his outlook. Never clever or cunning. Naïve even. So I discount her value in that respect. What courier work has she done?"

"Various officers have used her. Taking written messages and money. Person to person where any other type of communication would be dangerous."

"How often is she used?"

"About once a week. Sometimes more often if it's urgent."

"Who's her contact on this side of the Wall?"

"Usually the KGB girl at Kaufhaus der Osten. Sometimes we have to use the tobacconist shop by the zoo."

"And who is her contact on the other side?"

"The man at *Postamt 301*."

"Any complaints?"

"None."

Grushko leaned forward, his arms on the table. "OK. When they get back from this trip you go on paying her the weekly amount—but you don't use her. Nothing." He looked across at Fomenko. "I don't want anything to disturb our relationship with Johnson. We've got a number of special operations we want to use him for in the future. He may be a sheep but he's a useful sheep so far as we are concerned. Understood?"

"Yes, comrade."

"And in the future you alone will handle him. It's got very untidy over the months. Stick to the rulebook, comrade, and you won't go wrong. Handle him like he is a prize. Maybe he is."

"Yes, comrade General."

* * *

130

Signalman Johnson and Heidi had two days in London. They did all the usual sightseeing from Buckingham Palace to the Tower of London, and then he had taken her to Birmingham and back to his old stamping-ground in Handsworth.

All his old friends had disappeared. Three were in Winson Green prison and one was dead, killed in a knife fight. The only contact with the old days was an ex all-in wrestler named Tony. He hadn't known him well but he'd been a regular at the betting shop and a regular client of one of the girls Johnson had run messages for.

Tony was now running six girls of his own and had offered Johnson and Heidi the use of one of the rooms in the house where he and one of the girls lived.

Johnson and Tony visited the local pubs together, and when she wasn't busy, the girl, who called herself Diana, and Heidi compared notes on their profession. Services, the law, prices and accommodation.

Diana was amazed at what the girl from Berlin told her.

"So how much is thirty D-marks in real money?"

"You divide by three point five."

"I'm no good at that sort of stuff." She laughed. "I can add up and do takeaways but not no more than that. What is it in pounds?"

"Just under nine pounds."

"You mean you do it for nine quid?"

"Yes. But they have to pay for the room."

"And how much is that?"

"Say three pounds for an hour."

"You mean you give them an hour for nine quid?"

Heidi shrugged. "That's how it is for street girls."

"But you've got a place."

"He don't let me take them there. So it's hotels or the backs of cars."

"You could get thirty quid for an hour over here. And they'll have finished in twenty minutes anyway if you help things along. Why don't you move over here? Tony'd take you on if I talk to him."

"He's in the army, we have to stay where he's sent."

"Look, honey. You could be clearing a hundred quid a day here. No trouble at all. *After* Tony's cut. You could rent a room and then buy a house. I've got two houses. All mine. No mortgage on one and only a few thousand on the other. Talk to your fella. He wouldn't need to work. You could both live good on your money alone. He's not daft, surely. Let me talk to him."

Heidi looked toward the window and then back at the girl. "If he said no but I came here on my own, would Tony look after me the same?"

Diana looked at the girl. "Like that is it?"

"Maybe."

"I wondered how you got stuck with him. Looks a right dummy to me. Yeah, Tony'd look after you. How about I tell him in confidence?"

131

"He'll tell Arthur. They're friends and they're men."

"They're not friends. Tony wouldn't have a dimwit like him for a friend. I'll tell him and then you can have a talk with him private, like." She grinned. "You know how to handle him. He's a pushover when he's not drunk."

"I'll phone you from Berlin when I'm ready."

"OK." Diana looked at her watch. "Let's go to town. Buy a dress or something."

They spent two hours in the city and Heidi noticed the bank in the first big street they walked along. She made an excuse in the tearoom to go to the toilets and using her passport as proof of identity she deposited what now amounted to £9,537.64 in her own name.

Twenty-One

Jimbo Vick didn't like New York. He didn't like Chicago or San Francisco either. He was ill at ease in big cities. He maintained that big cities gave out bad vibes. He would have found incredible and laughable the suggestion that his unease was because he was born to be a big fish in only quite small ponds, and that in big cities nobody was impressed by anything he'd got. His money was peanuts compared with the wealth of big cities and his talents were of no interest either to those who were the society trendsetters or the young swingers who were his usual companions.

He spent his free evenings in Baltimore, driving the red Ferrari up Interstate-95, parking it at the Baltimore Hilton on West Fayette. Sometimes he ate at the Hilton but it was generally a few drinks at the bar with that night's lucky girl and then a move to China Doll for a meal, or the Peabody in North Charles Street if she was more that kind of girl. He had a small but luxurious apartment over a delicatessen in a side street off Saratoga, and that's where most evenings became nights.

Everybody in Baltimore knew what went on at Fort Meade. They knew it was the HQ of the National Security Agency. A listening-post that could eavesdrop on Soviet generals issuing orders to tank commanders in Smolensk or Siberia and on Politburo members whispering state secrets to their mistresses as they drove out from Moscow to their *dachas* in the pine forests. And they knew that a lot of the money earned by the thousands who worked at NSA was spent in Baltimore. NSA people were given the respect that would be given by any civilian population to occupying troops who behaved well and spent money locally.

Jimbo had been more successful as the leader of his small group than even those who had recruited him had expected. The notice on the outer office of the suite of rooms in which they worked merely said Math 190. But their work was both exotic and creative in its area of mathematics. Jimbo had never been told what the reports and experiments that they produced were used for or even that they were used at all.

His team were all young and highly committed. They were mathematics glamour boys and they knew it. And although Jimbo Vick could turn nasty if anyone tried to challenge his authority, most of the time he treated them as near equals, relaxed and ready to kid along with them. But they grew to realize that the camaraderie was not between equals but a gesture from the leader to his troops. They respected his skill at their specialty and his tigerlike defense of their status and privileges. He took no nonsense from the bureaucrats, fighting their corner with what was frequently considered as insubordination and impertinence by senior administrators. But Jimbo generally got his way. He worked conscientiously and over long hours and his specialty was of prime importance far beyond the thousand acres of Fort Meade.

When he was told to prepare a paper to read to a seminar in Washington he resented the wasted time, but when he found that the seminar was restricted and that his paper was only one of four to be presented to an audience of only ten top mathematicians who were working on allied areas of mathematical problem-solving, he realized that he was being honored, not relegated.

The seminar was to last for three days and was held in a suite of rooms at the Sheraton Carlton and there were a dozen or more plainclothes security men providing discreet but efficient round-the-clock surveillance.

Jimbo had noticed the blonde the first time the group had assembled. He had assumed that she was somebody's secretary but she had been introduced by the convener as Miss Swenson. She looked more like a Las Vegas showgirl than a mathematician but in the discussion after the first paper had been read, her questions had been searching and she was obviously well informed.

The convener had said that it would be appreciated if the group stayed together during the three days. Eating together in the dining-room provided. He also pointed out that he had not given any details of their jobs and would prefer that such matters were not pursued in private. The seminar was intended to provide the members with a broad picture of how the frontiers of mathematics were being extended by various government agencies. The other members of the group were older than Jimbo and he guessed that at least half of them were academics. At least one he recognized as a professor from MIT who had written a piece for one of the scientific journals on the mathematics of chance as applied to contract bridge.

There were no real contenders for the blonde, and from the familiarity between most of the men he surmised that many of them knew one another and had academic and private reputations to preserve.

Three tables had been set out for meals in the private dining-room, and name-cards had been placed so that the seating could be varied from meal to meal and day to day.

The need to avoid talking about their jobs made conversation difficult, especially for Jimbo. The older men had private lives and interests that could be discussed but Jimbo Vick's private life was limited and, after the necessary expurgation, boring. He was included in the general conversation but was aware that they saw him as young enough, and perhaps naïve enough, to warrant a touch of condescension.

The blonde was at another table and went to her room as soon as the meal was over.

On the second morning Jimbo was reintroduced to the others and presented his paper. During the question period the convener intervened several times to prevent answers on security grounds but Jimbo was aware of the intense interest that his paper had created. He was also aware that the blonde was obviously impressed too. She asked no questions but Jimbo recognized the universal vibes. On that subject he was even more of an expert.

They were at the same table for the evening meal that night, but he had little chance of talking to her because he was constantly answering questions about his paper. There was no longer any condescension. He was the expert and they were the tyros in his area.

He walked over to the table laid out as a bar after the meal was over and the girl walked over a few minutes later.

"Can I get you a drink?"

"Thanks, a tomato juice. No sauce just the juice."

As he handed her the juice he smiled. His little boy smile. "Are you anti-alcohol?"

"No way. I'm not anti-anything. I just don't like the taste of the stuff."

"What about beer or lager?"

"I don't like that either."

"Well, whatever you drink it's obviously good for you."

The girl smiled and shrugged. "Thanks. I was impressed by your paper. Is it going to be published?"

"I shouldn't think so."

"Why not?"

He smiled. "The usual reasons. Security."

"How long have you been working on those theories?"

"Just over a year."

"You've done a hell of a lot of research for just a year."

"I've got a team working with me."

"You're very young to be heading a team on that kind of material."

"How about you? What's your specialty?"

She grinned. "Nobody here admires my work, that's for sure. I specialize on knocking down mathematical theories. Creative negativity my bosses call it." She laughed. "Others are less polite."

"Have you knocked down any theories of any of the people here?"

She laughed again. "At least two of them."

"It must help that you're so pretty. Softens the blow a bit."

"I've always suspected that that's why I was given the job. But I don't think it works."

"It would work with me. Definitely."

The girl laughed. "Let's hope you don't have to test that theory."

"Am I allowed to ask where you are based?"

"Why not? I live in Washington."

"Did you understand my presentation?"

She smiled. "If I say no, then it confirms the dumb blonde theory. If I say yes, then it confirms the theory that all women are liars."

"Typical Women's Lib evasion. There were several men here who obviously had only the vaguest idea of what I was talking about. It's a very narrow area of mathematics."

"I got the general idea. What's your name by the way? Your first name."

"James, but my friends and family call me Jimbo."

She looked at his face, laughing. "They're right. You are a Jimbo."

"Meaning?"

"Bouncy, macho and—shall we say?—young."

"And your name?"

"Kirsten. Kirsten Swenson."

"A nice name. Very Swedish. Very glamorous. Like its owner."

"Thank you, kind sir. Now I'm off to bed."

"How about I take you out to dinner tomorrow night?"

For a moment she hesitated. "OK. But I'm catching a plane at eleven thirty. I need to be at the airport by eleven."

"Which airport—Dulles?"

"Yes."

"No problem. I'll drive you there after dinner."

"OK. It's a deal."

Jimbo was aware that by meeting him at the restaurant she had avoided letting him know where she lived. But she wasn't one of his usual teenyboppers, she was big game and well worth stalking slowly and carefully.

He had booked a table at the Montpelier restaurant at the Madison Hotel and Kirsten Swenson had looked stunning in a pale blue linen suit. Jimbo Vick was aware of the heads that turned to follow them as they made their way to the corner table. She had let him choose the food for both of them. Calf's liver with a good year's Chambertin after a superb soufflé, followed by fresh raspberries and cream. As the meal progressed, he realized more and more that she was definitely very special. Obviously used to Washington society, with friends on Capitol Hill and at several of the embassies, she chatted amusingly of the latest scandals, and seemed well informed on what was going on in the White House.

"Tell me about you, Jimbo. What do you do when you're not beating a path through stochastic math theories?"

Jimbo shrugged. "Nothing much."

"I'd have thought you were a bit of a swinger." She smiled. "And a bit of a ladies' man."

"Why that?"

"You're good-looking, lively, young and active, that's what most guys are who meet that description."

"And you don't like swingers and ladies' men?"

"They're fine in their place."

"And what's their place?"

She smiled and reached forward, putting her hand on his as it lay on the table. "Don't take it so seriously, Jimbo. I'm only teasing." She paused. "How about you meet me from the plane on Sunday night? Arrives at six fifteen."

"And I can take you out for the evening?"

She smiled. "We'll see."

"Say yes."

"Maybe."

Long after she had gone through the checkout and the door to the boarding gate he still stood there. Looking into space and thinking about her. Jimbo Vick was smitten and it was a new and not entirely pleasant experience. Why was she going to Chicago? Who was she seeing there? Where did she work and what did she do?

On Sunday night Jimbo had been at the airport half an hour before the plane was due, feeling faintly embarrassed at the bunch of long-stemmed red roses in the Cellophane wrapping and a small decorated message ticket that said, Welcome back—Jimbo.

She was wearing a black silk dress that clung to her beautiful body like a second skin, and she had obviously been surprised and delighted at the roses.

137

They had had a drink at the airport bar and she had left him for a few minutes to make a telephone call. When she came back she'd invited him back to her apartment with the offer to grill them a steak.

Her apartment was in one of the old brick townhouses in Foggy Bottom. A top-floor attic studio with polished wood floors and chintzy décor and furnishings.

Jimbo was on his best behavior and distinctly ill at ease. For once in his life he was trying to look like an upright citizen. A reliable, intelligent and responsible adult. The role sat on him like a suit two sizes too large and the girl was obviously aware of his efforts—and amused.

He made no pass at her as they sat having a final drink on the divan-settee but she'd let him kiss her good night at the doorway and she had responded, as his tongue explored her mouth, out of habit. When his breathing became heavy she moved out of his arms and said that she had tickets for a jazz concert the following Wednesday if he'd like to take her. He accepted eagerly and she laughed at his boyishness as she kissed his cheek before letting him out.

At the end of two weeks Jimbo Vick was in love. Desperately and painfully in love. Wishing that he had told her about his previous rip-roaring life so that he could lay his reformed character at her feet like a dog bringing a bone.

He seemed to have nothing to tell her about his life since leaving home that wouldn't destroy his new image. He had already told her that he worked for NSA. And she had told him that she worked for a high-technology consultancy in downtown Washington that was part-funded by government departments who required independent assessments of high-technology projects.

He dated her two or three times a week and it would have been every night if she had agreed. It was six weeks before he had sex with her. He was careful not to indulge in any fancy stuff and the missionary position became the norm. Just once in the first three months he had been tempted to phone one of his teenage swingers and make a wild night of it. But after much pacing and indecision he stuck to the strait and narrow. He even phoned his home and made it up with them so that he could go through the ritual of her meeting his parents before he asked her to marry him. They were delighted to hear from him and said that any friend of his was welcome anytime. He suggested the following weekend and they readily agreed.

But Kirsten Swenson didn't agree. Lying there naked and beautiful, she shook her head slowly but emphatically. Long before that night he had told her that he loved her.

"Why do you shake your head so angrily?"

"I'm not angry, Jimbo. I just don't want to be married. Not to anybody. It isn't just you."

"I'll go on asking you until you say yes."

"Don't, Jimbo. Don't spoil it. I like you a lot but I'm not the marrying kind."

"Is there anything I could do to make you change your mind?"

She swung her long legs off the bed and sat looking at his face. There were tears of disappointment in his eyes and she said quickly, "I'll see you whenever you want to see me. You can make love to me. But if you pressure me about marriage I'd want to walk away, Jimbo. Don't ask me. Let's talk about something else."

"Like what?"

She screwed up her eyes, thinking. Then she said, "There's something you could help me with."

"What?" he said eagerly.

"The office wants me to do a consultancy job in San Francisco. I'd have to be away for three months and I don't want to go." She turned her head and the big, heavy-lidded blue eyes were intent on his face. "I thought I could get out of it if I could offer some specialty that I needed to work on." She paused. "Can I heist your subject? Will you tutor me a bit? Just enough to make me look like I know what I'm at?"

"Of course I will."

"Has it got any practical uses or is it just pure mathematics?"

"Of course it has practical uses or I wouldn't be paid for doing it."

"How can I sell the idea to my people? We only deal with practical applications. What kind of client could use your work?"

"How much did you understand of my paper?"

She laughed as she looked at his face. "Not much. It sounded like the mathematics of guessing to me."

"That's not a bad description actually. The word *stochastic* comes from a Greek word, *Stokhastikos*, capable of guessing. Have you ever used decision tables?"

"Yes. We use them a lot for our clients. More or less standard practice."

"Well, the two main definitions of stochastic math theory would be . . ." he hesitated then went on ". . . statistically, a random variable with zero mean and infinite variance. In a process, it could be summarized as involving a random variable whose successive values are not independent. Say of a matrix, that it was square with non-negative elements that add to the unity of each row." He smiled. "Like you said, it's the mathematics of conjecture, of guessing."

She shook her head, smiling. "Now come down to earth. What can I read that will give me enough to sound convincing when I do my pitch for being left in place in Washington?"

"How long have you got?"

"Three weeks, maybe a month."

"There are no books that could help you in that time." He turned to look at her. She was so beautiful. "I'll tutor you. I'll bring you some of our concept work and we'll go over it piece by piece. It'll only be a veneer of knowledge."

"That's all I need, Jimbo. Just enough to impress them."

He laughed softly. "In the country of the blind the one-eyed man is king."

"Who said that?"

"I'm not sure, it sounds like Huxley."

"It was Erasmus. Desiderius Erasmus, 1508."

"My God, what a memory."

She smiled. "Make love to me, Jimbo."

Night after night Jimbo tutored his girl. She was obviously not going to grasp much beyond the application of existing theory but that was all she needed. The consultancy accepted her alternative proposal and that night, for the first time, she let Jimbo stay at her place all night.

Twenty-Two

Chambers's phone call had been brief. He was coming to Berlin the following day with an official of GCHQ. He asked that nobody should be given prior notice of the visit. And that was to include Max Cohen.

Massey met them both at the airport and then drove them to the house in Grunewald. They were intending to fly back to London the same day. Chambers took Massey to one side.

"There's a technical problem come up, Jan. Not on your side but on Cohen's operation. It may be serious, it may not." He paused. "It could even be no problem at all, just a routine cock-up. Listen to what Phillips from GCHQ has to say and listen to Cohen's explanations. I'd like your opinion afterwards. Not in front of Phillips, just for my ears only. OK?"

"Of course."

"What's your present assessment of Cohen?"

"He's enthusiastic, puts in far more hours than he should and he's kept his people happy in substandard conditions. About his technical ability my views would be useless. I'm not qualified to comment."

"What about his loyalty?"

Massey frowned. "A hundred percent. No doubts at all."

"What about his attitude to routine security?"

"As far as I know he sticks to the procedures I originally laid down."

"How do you know he does?"

"There's no way anyone could be a hundred percent certain. If there was a lapse it would almost certainly be picked up at Cheltenham or London. Or by the NSA." Massey shrugged. "There's no such thing as absolute security. You know that better than I do."

"OK. I just wanted to hear your views before we start. Shall we go in?"

Chambers sat with Massey on one side of the mahogany table, Cohen and Phillips on the other.

Chambers leaned forward as he spoke. "A problem, gentlemen. Or to be strictly accurate, maybe a problem. I'll leave it to Mr. Phillips from GCHQ to explain." Chambers turned to Phillips. "It's all yours, Mr. Phillips."

Phillips wasted no time. "The problem concerns traffic on July third of last year. It was the section covering Soviet Army and Air Force traffic from Karlhorst for the period . . ." Phillips looked at a small notebook and then back at Cohen and Massey ". . . thirteen-hundred hours to sixteen-hundred hours." He looked at Max Cohen. "That doesn't have any significance for you, Mr. Cohen?"

"Not until I've checked. Was it garbled transmissions or what?"

"No. Transmission was OK. Reception was OK. The codes used were all routine and standard codes that we broke when they originally started using them."

Cohen shrugged. "If reception was OK what was wrong? Did we misroute it, or what?"

"No. It wasn't misrouted. It went to Evaluation, was extracted for the Ia summary and was passed to Cheltenham about . . ." again Phillips looked at his notes ". . . about sixteen minutes after decoding."

Cohen smiled. "So what's wrong with it?"

Phillips didn't look amused. "We don't know."

Cohen leaned back in his chair. "So why are we here?"

"Because NSA was monitoring that traffic that day and they didn't record the same traffic."

"What did they get?"

"Perfectly routine traffic from Karlshorst. Nothing exceptional. But entirely different from our stuff."

"You mean we both monitored the same wavelengths, at the same time, on the same day and they recorded different transmissions?"

"Yes."

"That's technically impossible. It doesn't make sense."

Phillips's eyes were intent on Cohen's face. "It happened, Mr. Cohen," he said quietly. "It happened."

Massey intervened. "Could it be wrong labeling or incorrect filing? Some office routine cock-up?"

"No, sir. It went straight on disk in both cases and the timing and monitoring details are computer-recorded on the disk. The software does that automatically."

Cohen said, "Have you examined the original disks? Both of them? And have you checked the print-out?"

"I've done all that. The timing and the rest of it is recorded in both cases. Identical. But the traffic is different."

"Substantially different?"

"No part of it is the same. The same codes from the same units but different text."

Massey looked at Chambers. "Maybe we should get Evaluation to look at both texts and see if there is any significance in the two texts."

Phillips interrupted. "Evaluation at GCHQ and Fort Meade have already done that. They've found no significance in either text. It's humdrum routine stuff. Indents for pay, rations and medical supplies. Leave-rosters. Weapon and ammunition returns. Minor movements of troops and armor. The usual sort of stuff. But differing between the two."

"Not one single item the same?"

"On your disk there were details of a promotion that didn't fit. A routine promotion from captain to major of an artillery officer."

"Why didn't it fit?"

"He'd already been promoted. Six months earlier and the words and details were exactly the same as in the original notification."

Massey shrugged. "Could be some admin balls up. Their second echelon is notoriously inefficient."

Phillips didn't respond. He just sat there looking from one to the other. Eventually he said, "We'd be glad of any explanations anybody could offer."

Cohen smiled. "Me too."

The man from Cheltenham was not amused. "We're taking it seriously, Mr. Cohen. It's not a light matter."

Massey moved in. "Tell us exactly what you want us to do, Mr. Phillips."

"We want your people to come up with an explanation, sir."

"And what is Fort Meade doing about it?"

"Checking it out the same as us."

"No suggestions from them?"

"Not so far, sir. But I'm in touch with them daily."

"And GCHQ at Cheltenham? What are they doing about it?"

"They sent me over here, sir."

Massey was mildly irritated at Phillips's manner. "Nothing more than that? What is this—a buck-passing exercise?"

"You'd have to suggest that to the director, sir. He approved my visit."

"Is there anything else you'd like to do while you're here?"

"I'd like to interrogate the operator concerned."

Cohen barely kept the anger from his voice but he said quietly, "I think you mean interview, Mr. Phillips, not interrogate."

"Call it what you like, Mr. Cohen."

"Have you got the operator's name to save checking the records?"

Phillips looked at his notebook. "It was a Sergeant Turnbull. Reginald Turnbull. Royal Corps of Signals."

"You could talk with him in my office. I'll be interested to hear if he's got any suggestions."

"I'd prefer to see him alone."

Cohen smiled frostily. "I'll pretend I didn't hear that, Mr. Phillips." He looked at Massey. "Can I fall out, Mr. Massey, and get on with this."

"Yes. Let me know what happens."

Phillips's meeting with Cohen and his operator had provided nothing apart from irritation to both parties, and Cohen had not done his colleague from Cheltenham the courtesy of driving him back to the airport. He had arranged for a pool car to take him. Chambers had dinner with Massey, after Cohen had reported the essence of the interview to them. Chambers appeared to have lost interest in the problem. He and Massey ate at Kempinski's.

When the coffee had been poured, Chambers said, "How're things in general?"

"We've got seven networks the other side. We seem to be getting what your people want."

"Any problems?"

"No. I thought I had a problem a few months back but it's died down."

"What was that?"

"I had an approach from the top Frenchman. Wanted to sell me a Russian defector."

"Sell?"

"Yes."

"What was the prize?"

"He said he'd got K holed up at his place. Ready to come over to the CIA."

"You mean our K?"

"That's what he said."

"Why didn't you tell me?"

"Because I didn't believe it. I had the French place under intensive surveillance. They hadn't got any Russian there."

"You're sure of that?"

"Quite sure."

"What was the object of the approach?"

"Cash. Personal cash."

"How did you react?"

"Mildly interested. Argued about the amount. Said I'd see what London had to say."

"Has he been back to you again?"

"No."

"And you think it was just a bluff?"

"I'm sure it was."

"Why did he pick on that name, d'you think?"

"K's name sometimes appears in top-secret NATO reports. I didn't want to use the emergency system if I could avoid it. It's not that safe from K's point of view."

"Maybe we should review it. One of the P19 radios might be more efficient."

"They listen just as hard as we do."

"I'll talk to Facilities when I get back."

Heidi had made her plans carefully. She had the money in the bank in Birmingham. She had phoned the girl and spoken to Tony. He would take care of her and get her started. All she had to do was plan her departure. She had no intention of even hinting to Johnson that she was leaving. But she wished she could be there to see his face when he came back to the empty rooms. She would have loved to leave him a note telling him what she thought of him but she knew that it didn't matter. Her new life would make up for all of it. Sometime in the future she'd find out how to divorce him. There were things that she had to leave. The big stuff like the bed, the table and chairs and the old-fashioned wardrobe, but the rest she would take.

There had been no problem getting the plane ticket and booking a seat, but as the day for leaving approached her apprehension grew. He would really beat her up if he found out what she was up to, she had no doubt about that. He could even destroy her passport and the Russians were unlikely to give her another. Especially if Johnson told them what she had been planning to do.

She left the rooms in the early morning and took a taxi to the airport with her three heavy cases. Her passport, plane ticket and her bankbook were in her new Italian handbag.

There was an hour's wait at the airport which she spent in the toilets until the flight was called. She neither ate nor drank anything during the flight. Immobile in her seat, she tried not to think about what she was doing.

There were no problems at Gatwick and she took a taxi to Euston where she phoned Tony, who said he would meet her at New Street station.

The three of them, Tony, Diana and Heidi, went to a local club that night to celebrate her new freedom.

"What would happen if he came over and found me here?"

Tony shrugged. "Nothing. What *could* he do? You can live where the hell you like. He wouldn't do anything anyway."

"He might beat me up."

"Then you go to the cops. That'll stop him. They won't do anything, but it could go on his army record if they called in the military police."

"When can I start earning, Tony?"

Tony grinned. "Tonight if you want. I can make a phone call and the chap'll pay for your taxi."

"How much do I charge him?"

"Make it fifteen. Give him an hour. And ask for the taxi fare. I can lend you a quid or two if you're broke."

She shook her head. "It's OK. I just want to start building up a few clients."

Tony smiled. "You'll be all right, kid. Don't worry."

"Phone the guy now," she said softly.

Twenty-Three

Chambers stood up and walked over to the window, opening it to let out the cigarette smoke. And to collect his thoughts. He looked out of the open window for a few moments, watching one of the pleasure steamers heading up the Thames toward Chelsea Bridge.

Walking back to the table, he took off his jacket and hung it over the back of his chair. Harris from GCHQ sat facing him. Balding and rosy-faced, Harris looked like a cherub from some medieval Italian painting. His pale blue eyes were emphasized by his gold-rimmed glasses. But Harris was the hatchet-man who dealt with GCHQ's major problems.

Casey was NSA. A deputy director of long-standing more used to the buffetings and changes of mind of successive administrations and their committees than his British colleagues. The NSA's secrecy had to be guarded and preserved by top men willing to put their careers at stake to preserve the Agency's privileges and responsibilities. In his opinion the British lived a charmed life with their D-Notices and the Official Secrets Act.

It was Casey whom Chambers turned to. "Tell me what you think, Casey. No tact, no diplomacy, no bullshit."

"Well, sir . . ." he paused " . . . if you put it that way I can only repeat the Agency's attitude. We think that heads should roll."

"Why exactly?"

"Just to show we take a real poor view of what's happened."

"What *has* happened, Joe? Exactly what?" Harris's voice was high-pitched and querulous. "There's something happened that we can't explain. Not yet, anyway. So we chuck out a top man just to show we care?"

"You don't have to lose him, just put him out to grass for a couple of years. Then think again. The same will apply to one of our top guys."

"We virtually accuse a man of treason without any grounds whatsoever? Not a shred of evidence?"

Casey shook his head emphatically. "No way. Treason doesn't even get mentioned. Administrative inefficiency is all. Just like a senior guy in a big public company. He doesn't cut the mustard so he gets the chop or demotion. Nothing against his character."

Chambers leaned forward to look at Casey. "Do *you* think it was administrative inefficiency?"

"No. I'm darn sure it's not. And our internal security people will stay on it until we find out what happened."

Harris said smoothly, "Who's going to get the chop at your end?"

"Do you know Altieri?"

"Yes."

"D'you think he's good?"

"First-rate."

"Well, he's the boy. He's heading for somewhere quiet and unimportant as soon as I get back."

"You've met Max Cohen?"

"Yeah. Several times. Looks a good guy."

Chambers sighed. "What reasons will you give your chap?"

"Somewhere near the truth. Why not? He isn't going to be surprised. He knows his job's on the table."

Harris said, "Cohen will be shocked. Really shocked."

Casey shrugged. "Well, he shouldn't be. He's a top guy. Somebody makes a balls-up in his area . . . so he takes the fall."

Chambers leaned back in his chair. "Your people really think that this is the answer, Casey?"

"It's not the answer, Mr. Chambers. Finding out what happened is the answer. This is just a gesture to show that when such things happen the guy responsible gets the chopper."

"Which version of the traffic do your people find more credible?"

Casey turned to look at Harris. "They're both credible. Both versions are typical. Nothing to choose between them. But they're different. So one of 'em's a phoney. It's as simple as that."

Chambers pushed back his chair. "Let's think about it overnight, yes?"

Casey shook his head. "I've got a plane to catch tonight."

Chambers looked at Harris's grim face. "I think we'd better agree,

148

Harris. Reluctantly." He sighed and looked at Casey. "But our cooperation with NSA is more important than any individual."

"More important than justice, Mr. Chambers?" Chambers tried to
ignore Harris's question.

Casey stood up tucking his shirt back in his trousers. "I'll leave you two
gentlemen to philosophize and get on my way. If we find the answer be
sure we'll contact you right away."

At first Johnson hadn't realized what had happened. He had assumed
that she had gone out for cigarettes or a pack of beer and he had taken
off his jacket and settled down in the wicker chair. It was when he went to
switch on the TV that he realized that something was wrong. There was
no TV. And as he looked around the room he saw that there was no clock
on the mantelpiece and no china vase. The place had been stripped. But
only when he went in the bedroom did he realize that she'd gone. The
wardrobe doors stood open and the rails were bare. There was none of
the usual jumble of cosmetics and trinkets on the rickety dressing-table
and the bedclothes had been thrown in a heap in a corner of the room.
The bed had been stripped down to its mattress.

The bitch had gone. Done a moonlight flit. But where? He wondered if
it was something to do with the Russians. But surely they'd have warned
him.

For two weeks Johnson checked the clubs and massage parlors almost
every night. But there was no sign of her. And nobody had seen her.
They could be covering up for her, but not all of them. Some of the girls
didn't like her but they hadn't seen her either.

It was the first thing he asked Fomenko at the next meeting.

The Russian frowned. "I don't understand, comrade. Why do you ask
me where she is?"

"Because she's gone, mate, disappeared, flown the coop."

"How long has she been gone?"

"Just over two weeks."

"She didn't leave a note?"

"Nothing."

"And you had no idea she was going to leave?"

"If I'd have known I'd have stopped her."

"Had you quarreled at all?"

"No. I hadn't seen her for nearly a week. I was doing extra half-shifts."

Fomenko looked away toward the door and then back at Johnson.

"We've been paying her regularly but after our talk a few months ago
we haven't used her for anything. Did she say anything about that? Did
she complain?"

"No. Never said a word."

"Do you want her back?"

"Not particularly."

"We'd better find her, comrade. She knows too much."

"She's too stupid to talk. Nobody'd believe her anyway."

"They would if they questioned her. We couldn't risk that."

"So what do we do?"

"Leave it with me." He paused. "Did you get the list we wanted?"

Johnson reached inside his jacket and took out a narrow strip of paper that he handed to Fomenko, who looked at it before looking back at Johnson.

"How did you get this stuff?"

"I did the extra half-shifts. I worked in Central Registry. I wrote the frequencies in Biro on my arm. The code programs I memorized over two nights." He reached inside his jacket again and took out what looked like a folded magazine. He handed it to Fomenko, smiling as he said, "A little present from the West, comrade."

As Fomenko opened it he saw that it was a copy of the German edition of *Playboy*. He put it on his desk and turned back to Johnson.

Johnson grinned. "Have a look inside, mate."

"I'll look some other time, comrade."

"Look now. Don't be so bloody obstinate."

Fomenko sighed with exasperation and reached for the magazine. As it fell open he saw the printed cover of the booklet. It was the internal telephone directory of all the SIS set-ups in West Berlin, Cologne and Bonn. When Fomenko looked up Johnson said, "Thought you might find it useful."

"Good initiative, my friend. I'll see that other people are told." He paused for a moment. "Do you know any of the men who service the microcomputers?"

"Are those the ones with the TV screens?"

"Yes. There's an octagonal metal badge on the printers with the letters ACT in the center."

"I don't remember that. I don't go in there except to deliver urgent print-outs."

"What about the service men?"

"I don't know who they are. We aren't allowed to talk about what we do except to chaps in our own sections."

"Maybe you could find out. Just gossip around."

"I'll see what I can do. What if I get information?"

"Just give us the name and anything you get to know about him." Fomenko turned to the papers on the bedside table and picked up an envelope. "There's four hundred D-marks. There'll be more next time."

It was only eleven days before Johnson's next meeting with Fomenko. The Russian had taken a suite at the Berolina and after they had dealt with their routine talk they had eaten together. A meal to meet Johnson's taste. Sausage and chips with baked beans and a fried egg. Fomenko stuck to trout garnished with almonds.

"We've traced the girl, comrade."

"Jesus. That's quick. Where is she?"

"She's left the country."

"Where's she gone—Vienna?"

"She's in England. In Birmingham. A place called Handsworth."

Johnson put down his knife and fork. "The cheeky cow. That's my home place. What made her go there?"

"She's set up as a call girl. She works for a man named Tony. Tony Morello."

"I know him. He's an old mate of mine. The bastard. The two-timing bastard."

"Maybe it's best to just leave her there. What do you think?"

"She could tell Tony and his girl what we've been doing. Everything. Just to make herself more important. Sell her story to one of the newspapers."

"D'you think she would?"

"I don't know."

"Maybe you should go over. Be friendly. Talk to her so that she isn't tempted to be aggressive toward you. She can live her life and you can lead yours and everybody can be happy."

Johnosn didn't reply. He was more in the mood for knocking the hell out of her.

"What do you think, Arthur?"

"I'll have to think about it."

"We'd pay for the trip and some cash for her or a present of some kind."

"I'll let you know."

"See me in a couple of days' time. At the garage office. D'you remember it?"

"Yeah, of course."

He wore his uniform to give him confidence but as he got in the taxi at New Street station his anger came back. She'd got British nationality out of him, and she'd strung him along. She'd been going with men on the quiet. He realized that now.

Probably even used the rooms and done it on their bed. She'd put the poison down with the Russkis and now he was supposed to pretend to be all friendly and nice when he felt more like beating the living daylights out of her. The lying little cow. Calling herself a call girl. A ten-quid whore more like. But the Russkis had been insistent that he should make peace with her as Fomenko put it.

Tony answered his knock on the door. His surprise and embarrassment were obvious.

"Hi, pal. What are you doin' in wonderful downtown Brummagem?"

"Where is she?"

"Where's who?"

"Heidi."

"How should I know?"

"Don't bullshit me, Tony, or I'll go to the police and tell them you're running a knocking-shop here."

"You'd better watch your words, big-mouth."

"So where is she?"

"She ain't here, sunbeam."

"I said where is she?"

"What do you want with her anyway?"

"I just want to talk to her."

"She won't go back if that's what you're after."

"I don't want her to go back. If this is what she wants it's OK by me."

"D'you mean that?"

"Of course I do."

For a moment Tony Morello hesitated, then he opened the door wide and beckoned Johnson inside.

"Are you on the level, mate?"

"Yeah. I just want to talk to her."

"She's at the club."

"Which club?"

"The White Rabbit. It's in the basement of the dry cleaner's by the recreation grounds. D'you remember it?"

"I'll find it. Thanks."

"She may be with a chap, I ain't sure."

Johnson shrugged. "Makes no odds to me."

"Of course it don't. You're dead right. Live and let live, that's what I always say."

The White Rabbit Club was down a flight of cement stairs and an orange light glowed over the door. Johnson pressed the bell and a small hatch opened. A pair of smoky eyes examined him. The door opened slightly, still held by a chain. A tall, thin West Indian looked him over.

"What you wantin', man?"

"I've come to see a girl here."

"What's she calling herself?"

"Heidi. She's tall and blonde. Got an accent."

The man nodded, unlatched the chain and opened the door.

There were four steps down to the club area and he saw her on her own at a table in the far corner. She was lighting a cigarette and she didn't see him until he was standing in front of her.

"Hello, Heidi. How're you doin'?"

She looked up startled and then recognized him.

"Piss off," she said and he saw the anger and defiance in her eyes.

"I'm not here to make trouble, honey. I brought you a present."

"I don't want a present from you, you bastard."

Johnson's anger flared. "You stupid cow, who the hell do you think you're talking to?"

She called out, leaning to one side to look past him, "Tiger. This creep's insulting me."

A big Negro and the tall West Indian walked over and each took one of Johnson's arms. "Come on, lover boy. Let's cool it, eh?"

Johnson turned as they frog-marched him; he saw her contorted face and heard her screaming out, "He's a fucking spy. He's a Russian spy."

As the West Indian closed the door behind him, Johnson stood at the bottom of the steps trembling. Not with fear but with anger and frustration. He slammed the side of his fist against the iron railings that led up to the street. It was their idea not his. He knew her. Knew she'd not cooperate. That bitch who'd pounded the pavements of Vienna screwing for six quid a go. All comers welcome. Sitting there insulting him. Degrading him in front of the niggers. The Russkis may know about spying but they knew fuck-all about hookers. But the bit that mattered was the shout as he left. That was really asking for it. No way was she going to get away with that. Even the bloody Russians would go along with him on that.

Twenty-Four

They were walking back over the bridge from Theodore Roosevelt Island to the parking lot at the Memorial Parkway and she turned quickly to look at Jimbo.

"Say that again."

He smiled. "I asked if you'd like to drive the Ferrari back to your place."

"My God, Jimbo," she said softly, "I never thought I'd live to hear those words."

"So, how about it? Do you want to have a go?"

She shook her head, smiling. "No, *sir*. That would be going too far. It would be like you moving all the furniture around in my place."

"You mean you wouldn't let me do that?"

She pursed her lips, smiling. "If I did, I'd put it right back in its proper place the moment you'd gone."

"But you like the car?"

She shrugged. "Cars I can take or leave. They don't do anything for me. Not even bright red Ferraris. It suits you but it's definitely not me. Not me at all. They're just little boys' toys."

"What turns *you* on?"

She stood still, her eyes closed, thinking. And then she said, "I suppose

154

in a way your darned math turns me on. It's kind of spooky. Mysterious. Forbidden territory."

Almost an hour later they were both naked on her bed. They had made love and she was smoking a cigarette. "What kind of people d'you have in your team? Are they old, young or what?"

"They're all about my age. A couple two years older and three younger."

"Are they all oddballs?"

"No way. They're all perfectly normal. Fanatics, maybe, but not crazy. They're just hooked on being right out there on the frontiers of science."

"Tell me about them. What they're like."

"The youngest is Billy Myers. He's twenty-four. Got a Ph.D. in math at Berkeley. Born in San Francisco. Got a stack of girlfriends. All teenagers. Spends money like a drunken sailor. The oldest is Bert Sayer. He's thirty-eight or -nine. Pillar of the church. Pretty wife. Three kids. Keen photographer. Quiet. Calm. And a brilliant mathematician." He smiled. "Any more?"

She laughed and shook her head. "Do you have to justify what you all do?"

"I don't understand."

"Don't you have to find a use for it? To justify the time and money and talent?"

"The use is in-built in NSA's function."

"I don't see how."

"Well, there are two obvious applications. We can crack complex codes using stochastic theory in hours instead of months and we can use the theory in voice recognition. Even word recognition." He paused. "There are dozens of other uses too."

"Could your work be used in industry?"

"Technically, yes. There's hundreds of applications. Thousands maybe."

"So why aren't you making a fortune with IBM?"

"Because what we do is totally restricted. People outside don't have any access to what we do and few of them realize what stochastic math theory could do for them."

"But you could just leave and you'd be a millionaire inside a year."

He smiled. "Would you marry me if I was a millionaire?"

She laughed and took his hand. "Maybe. Let's make love again."

And as he rolled on top of her Jimbo wondered if that "maybe" was for real.

Howard Fielding had stopped Massey in the corridor.

"Max Cohen's very upset by the news." He paused. "He could do with a kind word."

"What news? What happened?"

"You don't know, sir?" Fielding looked surprised.

"Just tell me what it is," Massey said brusquely.

"He's just heard from GCHQ that he's being moved. Being sent to some outpost on one of the Scottish islands."

"Any reason given?"

"Bad security in his operation here."

"Where is he?"

"In his room."

"I'll be there if anyone wants me."

"Right, sir."

After talking with an indignant and depressed Cohen, Massey had phoned Chambers using the scrambler but had got no joy out of him. He was adamant. Cohen's opposite number at NSA was getting the same treatment. There had been lax security and heads were going to roll.

The following day Chambers phoned and told him in guarded words that he should expect a visitor from Special Branch. It was implied that there was more trouble on the way. Chambers hinted that Max Cohen was probably involved again.

The Special Branch man arrived early that evening and Cohen and Massey took him into Massey's private quarters. He was a sergeant, middle-aged and obviously experienced. Calm, and no sign of panic stations as he accepted a neat whiskey.

"The name's Lowther. Jimmy Lowther. Sergeant . . . Special Branch. Got a small problem. Thought maybe you could help me." He looked amiably at them both, waited for a response, noted the grim faces and pulled out his small white notebook with the royal cipher on the cover. He turned over a few pages and then looked up.

"It's a case of elimination, gentlemen. Not much to go on." He paused. "Have you got any Signals chaps on leave in the U.K. at the moment?"

Cohen shrugged. "Probably got half a dozen. Do you want me to check?"

"I'd be very grateful, sir. Maybe I could have names as well."

Massey and Lowther sat in silence as Max Cohen talked on the phone and wrote out the details he was given. He turned to Lowther. "Do you know what rank? Do you want officers as well as NCOs?"

"The description says no stripes. I've taken it as being a private."

"Signalman," Cohen corrected pedantically, then turned back to the phone. A few moments later he rejoined them.

"Only two. One warrant officer, a sergeant-major, is on a seven-day pass. He left here two days ago. And one signalman. Also on seven days."

"His name, Mr. Cohen?"

"Signalman Johnson."

"When did he leave?"

"On the fourth."

"And it's the thirteenth today." He paused. "Could I have a word with him. Mr. Cohen?"

"I'm afraid not. He's not yet returned. He was posted AWOL this morning."

"I see . . . Has there been any attempt to contact him?"

"Not as yet."

"I read your standing orders and they lay down that you notify local police in their U.K. town in cases of absence without leave. Am I right?"

"That's so."

"So the local police have been notified."

Cohen looked embarrassed. "We generally wait for twenty-four hours before we do that. Sometimes travel to Berlin creates problems."

"I see." Sergeant Lowther looked very much the policeman. Noncommittal but faintly disapproving. "It's Arthur Johnson, isn't it, sir?"

Cohen looked surprised. "How the hell did you know that?"

"Just hearsay, sir. We get a lot of hearsay."

"Has he done something?"

"The local police in Birmingham found a body, sir. A young woman. Was identified as Mrs. Heidi Johnson. The chap who identified her said she was German, married to this Signalman Johnson. Seems she'd left him. Didn't care for his ways. He came over to see her. Seems they had a disagreement and she was found dead in the early hours of the morning. The parties said Johnson was wearing battledress with Royal Corps of Signals insignia. White-on-blue arm flashes and the badge on the hat. The local police in Birmingham got in touch with the Provost Marshal in London and he was traced as being posted to this unit. That's why it was handed over to Special Branch." He nodded. "That's why I'm here."

Massey said quietly, "And now you'll be handing it over to Homicide."

"I'm afraid not. Wish I could do that." He sighed. "Seems like this quarrel was in public. In one of these tatty drinking-clubs. The girl was on the game and when the husband appeared she called the bouncer to put him out. And as he was leaving she shouted out . . ." Lowther looked at his notebook as he read out the words ". . . 'He's a fucking spy. He's a spy for the Russians.'" He looked up impassively. "They don't always get the words exactly right. But that was the gist of it."

Cohen shook his head in disbelief. "If he was a spy, sergeant, then I'm Mata Hari. He was as thick as they come. He could read and write and that was about all."

Sergeant Lowther half-smiled. "Mr. Massey'll tell you that they come in all shapes and sizes. There's no A levels for spies. They're not all Philbys, you know. They also serve who only stamp the pieces of paper."

Cohen looked at Massey. "What do you think, Jan?"

"Sergeant Lowther's quite right, I'm afraid. The KGB wants any information they can get about establishments like this. They can get a lot even from the low-level people like Johnson." Massey turned to Lowther. "What can we do to help you, Sergeant?"

"I'd like to look over his quarters and talk to some of the people who knew him."

Massey turned to Cohen. "Let me hand Sergeant Lowther over to you, Max. Any problems just contact me."

Even in the first few minutes of the meeting with Chambers, Cohen and the man from GCHQ, Massey had realized that the disk in the book was involved. He had checked the library list for two months before he called off the check. Nobody had withdrawn the book. But it was obvious now that the disk had been removed. As they were talking he was trying to work out how he could identify who had taken it, though he was reluctant to pursue anyone who might be able to identify him as the man who had made it possible. Although they probably wouldn't know that. He had had no qualms of conscience about what he had done.

It was something that had had to be done to save Anna. If it had turned out to be more serious than it now appeared, and he had been suspected, he would have lied to cover up. He would do nothing voluntarily that would cause her further harassment. He had done too much damage to her already. He had paid the debt as best he could, and he had no regrets.

The only guilt he ever felt was that Max Cohen was being removed for poor security. But even then some self-justifying mechanism made him rationalize that Cohen's security *had* been inefficient or none of it could have happened. When remorse or guilt seeped into the edges of his thoughts he pictured Anna in the KGB cell at Karlshorst. Terrified, trembling, knowing full well what they could do to her. Sometimes when he was alone with these thoughts he would shake his head angrily to dismiss them, and groan aloud at what he had done to her.

The meeting had reinforced his attitude. Whichever day's traffic was the true version, it made little apparent difference. Both days were routine typical transmissions of no interest to SIGINT in any way.

What didn't fit was the Russians using him as the carrier. That presupposed that whoever they had inside was not sufficiently senior to have taken it unexamined through the usual security checks. But a man without that status would also not have had clearance to visit the disk library unless he was operational and involved in monitoring Red Army signals. And somebody at that level would surely have been able to find some way of smuggling in the substitute disk himself. The metal detectors would not have shown it. The disk was plastic.

Twenty-Five

Sir Peter Tovey had arranged a private room for the meeting at the Reform Club. He had taken over as head of SIS five years before at a difficult time, and times had not changed much. The intelligence services were never praised by the opposition and the media when some Russian mole or active spy was caught, more likely they were blamed for the fact that such traitors existed. But Sir Peter was now reconciled to the vagaries of his career. Balding, with a froth of white hair like a cloud around his head, he had a face like those on Roman coins. An aquiline nose, hooded eyes, furrows on cheeks and brows that had grown deeper from maintaining a passive demeanor, he seldom looked directly at those he was conversing with. He chose his words carefully and listened alertly to what was said to him. Chambers had never decided whether Tovey actually approved of him or not. In fact he wasn't sure that Tovey even approved in general of SIS. It was known that Tovey got on well with the Prime Minister, who made no secret of her dislike of the whole Foreign Office establishment.

When the coffee had been brought Tovey nodded to the waiter. "Tell the club servants I don't want to be disturbed."

"Right, Sir Peter."

When the waiter had gone, closing the door firmly behind him, Sir Peter said, "How long is this going to take, Chambers?"

"Not long, Sir Peter."

"What's the problem?"

"Massey. Jan Massey."

"I thought he was one of your prize specimens. That's what you always said."

"That's true. But time moves on and circumstances change. I'd like to move him."

"You don't need to ask me. He's your chap. Move him where you like." He paused and blinked. "I assume you've got good reasons for doing it."

"There's the problem of our top Russian. He won't work with anyone but Massey."

"Got more faith in Massey than you have, what?" Sir Peter smiled. He knew it annoyed Chambers when he made light of any of his problems.

"We haven't had any contact with the Russian for nearly a year."

"Why do you think that is?"

"He's too important to them not to be carefully monitored. Contact has always been difficult. But the kind of information he has given us in the past has been absolutely invaluable."

"So why the rush to move Massey if he's the only pipeline?"

"I'm a little uneasy about Berlin. Several security breakdowns. Massey seems to be very distant from day-to-day operations these days. I've heard talk that he's become aloof. Remote. Disengaged. Not got the spirit he used to have."

"Happens to all of us, Humphrey, from time to time."

"But you've no views on a move."

Sir Peter blinked the hooded eyes as he always did when he was being less than frank. "I'd go slowly if I were you. Let things ride a bit. Haste was never a virtue in this business. I see examples of it every day. A rush of blood to the head, and then months of shambles."

"I'll remember that, sir."

Sir Peter laughed and coughed. "You mean you'll remember it if I'm proved wrong, eh?"

"I wouldn't dream of it, Sir Peter."

"A cognac or something before you go?"

The hint was broad enough and Chambers left a few minutes later.

It was a phone call from the Berlin city police which had uncovered Johnson's room in the city. The new tenant had cleared out the old furniture and had found an envelope behind the sideboard in the sitting-room. It had obviously fallen down the narrow gap between the wall and the plywood back of the sideboard.

The envelope had faded edges but the contents were well preserved. A list of addresses written in pencil. A plastic card with Cyrillic lettering and a handwritten signature. A menu from the Berolina Hotel and a horoscope for Scorpios torn from an English newspaper.

The plastic card was a Soviet Kommandatura pass valid for any Berlin checkpoint, giving the bearer top priority. And it was that that made the new tenant ring the police. The list of addresses was written in ill-formed capitals and one of them was a known KGB dead-letter drop. Signalman Johnson was only just a Scorpio. One day inside. Twenty-fourth of October.

Sergeant Lowther phoned London and he was instructed to hand over his notes concerning Johnson to Massey to pursue if he thought necessary. His companion on the flight back to Heathrow was an unhappy and silent Max Cohen.

The short inquest on Heidi Johnson found that she had been murdered by a person or persons unknown. The following day she was buried in Witton cemetery and the ceremony was paid for by Tony Morello from the substantial bundle of cash that he had found under the mattress in her room. He was praised as a generous and public-spirited citizen by his friends at the local pub.

The girl and the man stood side by side in Arlington cemetery, looking at the graves of President Kennedy and his brother. It had been raining and they were the only people in that part of the cemetery that afternoon. Already a heat mist was beginning to rise and the man said quietly, "I read your report. It's getting near the time. What do you think?"

"It's up to you, Zak. I don't seem to be making much progress."

"You've done fine, honey. Real fine. It's the relationship that matters right now, not the information. We've got two more names to work on now. Maybe a month from now. What d'you think? Maybe a couple of months?"

The girl sighed. "He's such a pain in the ass. Just a grown-up juvenile delinquent."

The man laughed softly. "Upon such sacrifices, my Cordelia, the gods themselves throw incense." He smiled and said gently, "It's always the end that has to justify the means."

The girl pointed her shoe and jabbed angrily at the gravel on the path. "Shall I leave first or you?"

"Did you bring your car?"

"Of course."

"It's starting to rain again. You go first and take the umbrella."

He passed the umbrella to the girl and watched her as she walked away.

* * *

Bourget had been brusque to the point of rudeness on the telephone. Demanding a meeting with him. Insisting it was held that day. Massey had placated the Frenchman by agreeing to go to the SDECE house, something that he had always avoided.

The house was still and quiet as he walked into the tiled hallway through the open door. Bourget came out of one of the rooms, standing in the doorway, beckoning him inside.

The furniture and décor were surprisingly tasteful. Bergère armchairs and sofas, and modern paintings on the walls. He had little time to look around before Bourget waved him to one of the armchairs and sat down himself in another, facing Massey.

"What was the big idea, my friend? To go behind my back to Paris?"

"I don't know what you're talking about, Pierre. I haven't been to Paris for over a year."

"Don't play the innocent, Massey. You could have cost me my career. As it is, I'm being recalled."

"You'd better tell me what it's all about."

"You told them about the Russian. And the deal. You made me a crook. Why? I ask myself, why?"

"I haven't told Paris anything, Pierre. I haven't been in contact with Paris at all."

"They knew the name—Kuznetsov. They knew the amount of money. How did they know? Only you and I knew about the deal."

"Maybe London discussed it with Paris."

"For God's sake. You told those idiots in London?"

"I told you that I'd have to discuss it with them."

"You told them the whole story?"

"More or less."

"But you didn't come back to me. Why not?"

"For several reasons. Mainly because London wasn't interested."

"What were the other reasons?"

"Only one. I didn't believe you'd been in contact with Kuznetsov."

"Why you not believe?"

"You told me at our first meeting that Kuznetsov was here at your place. That he'd defected and you'd got him." Massey paused, and then said quietly, "You never had him, Pierre. You were bluffing. You were trying to con me."

"Con you? What is that?"

"You were trying to deceive me. I checked up and you hadn't got any Russian here. I wasn't interested anymore. Neither was London."

"So if they were not interested why did they talk to Paris about it?"

"I don't know. I don't know that they did talk to Paris. I'll find out if they did if you want me to."

Bourget drew a deep breath. "You're a fool, Massey. You play the upright Englishman, the man of honor. But you sell your friends down the river."

Massey stood up slowly and Bourget stood up too, his face suffused with anger. He said deliberately, small bubbles of saliva on his lips, "I won't forget this, Massey. I promise you. Don't ever come to me for help. And . . ." he clenched his big fist ". . . you just watch your step. One day I'm going to settle with you. I swear it."

Massey swallowed his anger and said quietly, "Is there anything I can do to help you, Pierre?"

The Frenchman shrugged angrily. "You've done enough damage to me, Massey. Just get out of my sight before I go too far."

As Massey drove back to Grunewald he wondered why Chambers had passed on the information about Bourget to Paris. Chambers would never have let it come out accidentally. And he wouldn't even have talked inside SIS about anything that so much as vaguely touched on Kuznetsov. Kuznetsov was their pipeline, not only to the very top of the KGB but to the Politburo itself. The kind of information that he contributed was far from the normal grist of intelligence. What he gave them was the most valuable intelligence of all—the intelligence of intention. Both he and Chambers had spent hours analyzing the warnings that Kuznetsov gave them, looking for some factor, some rationale in what he chose to pass on. His hints, his warnings had never proved wrong. On two occasions in the early days they had deliberately ignored his advice. On the first occasion it had led to eighteen months when West Germans were not allowed to visit East Berlin or the GDR. The second occasion, concerning the stationing of nuclear-armed warships in the South Pacific, had been "punished" as Kuznetsov had said it would be, by providing the Argentines with satellite intelligence. London had assumed that the Soviets would never assist the fascist Junta in Buenos Aires. They were mortal enemies of the Soviet Union on a dozen major counts, but the aid had been given as Kuznetsov had said it would be.

If there was no movement from Kuznetsov in the next few weeks he would have to take the risk of activating the contact mechanism himself.

He read the investigation reports on Johnson before he went to bed. There had been no trace of him despite extensive enquiries by the Birmingham police and Special Branch at Massey's request. Neither had he been seen in West Berlin. None of his working colleagues knew much about him and none of them even knew that he was married. Superficial examination of Heidi's passport and marriage and birth certificates indicated that they were genuine. Massey passed an instruction for them to be sent to Forensic for a full check.

Twenty-Six

He couldn't understand why she was so aloof and indifferent. She didn't want to go out for a meal, she didn't want to go to the jazz club and she wasn't interested in them driving out of town for the weekend. He'd ended up watching yet another rerun of *Casablanca* on TV while she just sat in the armchair smoking one cigarette after the other, her long legs draped over the arm of the chair, her eyes closed. Finally he got up, switched off the TV and stood looking at her.

"What's wrong, honey?"

"Nothing's wrong, Jimbo."

"It is. I can tell it is. Are you down or something?"

"Why don't you go if you're not satisfied?"

"It's only nine o'clock."

"So what? Have an early night."

She swung her legs down and stood up, frowning. She pushed him away when he reached out toward her.

"Tell me what's wrong, babe."

"For Christ's sake don't call me babe."

"OK. Tell me what's wrong, ma'am."

For a moment she hesitated, then she said quietly, "I'm sorry if I'm being a bitch . . ." she looked at his face ". . . they gave me the sack today. Two months' redundancy pay and out. Some bastard even stood there watching as I cleared out my desk."

"Why did they sack you?"

"They said that I was wasting their time and money and stochastic math theories were mathematicians' pipe dreams."

"They must be out of their minds. In two years' time anybody who's worked on stochastic math will be worth their weight in gold bars."

She sighed. "I'm sure you're right, Jimbo. But meantime I've got to earn a living."

"Let me see what I can do. There's a computer outfit I know who could be interested."

Slowly, he cheered her up and the next day he phoned his contact at the computer company and arranged an interview for her that afternoon.

When they met in the evening she was despondent again.

"What happened at the interview?"

She shrugged. "He talked about a job as a systems analyst and when there was a commerical use for stochastic math I could take over in their software section."

"Maybe that's better than nothing while you look around. Maybe I sent you off in the wrong direction way back and I *was* wasting your time suggesting you move over to experimental math."

She looked at him for long moments and then she said, "Would the Agency take me on?"

He looked surprised and then pleased. "Of course they would. I could hire you myself." He paused. "I always imagined that you thought the Agency was a bit . . . well . . . not your style."

She half-smiled and shrugged. "I did at first . . . the spook stuff . . . but I guess I've got used to it knowing you."

"There'll be some security checking but if you don't mind working for me . . . then that's it. I'll leave it to Personnel to fix your pay and conditions. You'll have to sign a 'Conditions for retention of employment' agreement and you'll be employed in a special section of the NCS. And you may be sent on a course before you work for me."

"What's the NCS?"

"The National Cryptological School." He smiled. "We think it's the jewel in NSA's crown."

"And the course?"

"I'd guess they'd put you on CY-001 which is an indoctrination course and then I guess you'd go on a course titled Intensive Program in General Analysis." He smiled. "That's the equivalent of a Ph.D. in codebreaking."

She looked up at his face. "You're really very good to me, Jimbo. I appreciate it. I really do."

He grinned. "Will you . . ." he shook his head ". . . no, forget it."

"Go on . . . ask me whatever it was."

He sighed and looked very much the small boy as he said, shrugging, "The same old question—will you marry me?"

She looked away for a few moments and then back to his face. "Would it really make all that much difference to you, Jimbo? Is it really what you want?"

"It's what I very definitely want."

"Tell me why."

He sat down on the floor beside the chair and she slid down beside him. "Tell me, Jimbo. Tell me why it matters."

"I don't know. It just does. I was wild when I was a kid. Got into scrapes. And in the end my folks had had enough. I felt they were ready to sell me down the river. I hated them for that. They wanted me to do what they wanted and I left home. More to prove them wrong than anything else, I got myself into a university and without intending to I got myself hooked on this math thing. Till I met you I guess I was a sort of Jekyll and Hyde character. Conforming in the daytime. The wild swinger at night. It pleased me to be defying the Establishment, deceiving them. And in the circles I mixed with at night I was the leader. The guy with money and a special talent . . ." he smiled ". . . and a red Ferrari." He paused. "And then I met you and it all changed."

"Why? Why did it change?"

"I don't know. You just seemed right for me. You were impressed by the Dr. Jekyll bit—the math bit—and you obviously weren't impressed by the swinger stuff or the money. I guess you were the first person I had a real feeling for. The first person I had a real relationship with. I felt at home with you. I always have." He smiled. "And you're beautiful. Really beautiful."

"And me marrying you would make you happy?"

"Nothing could make me happier."

"Would you agree to wait until I've done my courses and then we get married?"

He laughed. "I'd agree to anything, believe me. Do you mean it?"

"Yes." She nodded. "I mean it."

They went out that night for a celebratory meal and he stayed at her apartment for the rest of the night.

He saw little of her during the day but while she was on her courses he went over her work with her night after night. Her security clearance had gone through smoothly and she was on a probationary pay scale that paid her $25,000 a year. It would be almost doubled after she had worked at NSA for a year.

Six months after her start at the Agency they were married. Jimbo's family had come east for the weekend and there were a dozen guests from NSA. Most of those who attended the ceremony were touched by a feeling of sadness for the stunningly pretty girl whose parents had been killed in the car crash so many years ago, and had no family to enjoy the obviously happy occasion.

As a gesture of forgiveness and relief, Josh Vick bought the couple a small townhouse in Georgetown not far from the girl's old apartment. His feelings had always been torn between memories of Jimbo as a small boy and the grim realities of his teenage years. He had heard from third parties of his son's success at UCLA but had only half believed what he was told. But as time passed he gradually accepted the change in Jimbo's behavior and attitudes and when both parents had met Kirsten, they were charmed by her and moved by the obvious sincerity of Jimbo's love for his wife-to-be.

Jimbo was happy at last. And pleased and proud that his wife was as bright and creative as any other member of his team of fanatics.

Chambers wasn't sure why he chose the zoo for the meeting with Redway. It provided good security among the crowds of visitors and nobody could overhear their conversation. And it was a fine day, and he was sick of the sight of Century House and its problems. It was like a marshaling yard for problems, particularly those that had no final answer. And he was tired of problems. They flowed over his desk in a never-ending stream. Was the hint from the Czech minister at the congress in Paris for real or just a veiled threat? Was the monitored telephone conversation between the importer of Russian magazines and the Soviet trade attaché an invitation to launder money for dissidents in the U.K.? And was Kuznetsov's prolonged silence because he distrusted Massey's security in Berlin? He had looked through his checklist that morning. There were thirty-seven specific problems on which somebody expected his views and on fourteen of them it wasn't just his views they wanted, but his final decision.

Massey had certainly changed in the last year or eighteen months. He worked long hours. Chambers had checked on that. But the fire had gone. The inspiration and enthusiasm. For years he had told Massey to be less involved in actual operations. That his talents were best used in directing others. Maybe it was his fault, for that was exactly what Massey had done. But he'd drawn back too far. He might just as well be operating from a desk in London. Was it that? Or could there be something in what that bloody Frenchman had said to his bosses in Paris? Some high-up Russian in the KGB who had hinted to the Frenchman that there was a traitor in the Berlin SIS station. Even two, they'd said. And some gossip about Massey and a girl.

Redway was waiting for him, sitting at one of the outside tables at the cafeteria near the parrot house. He'd waved to Redway, bought two

167

coffees and carried them over to the table. As he sat down it all seemed so normal and ordinary that he was faintly embarrassed at making this rendezvous so artificial. But he'd been brought up on the tradition of open-air meetings when possible. St. James's Park if you were in a hurry. The zoo if it was a fine day and the Festival Hall cafeteria if the weather was bad.

Redway was his opposite number, responsible for operations in the U.S.A. and South America. He had been Chambers's predecessor at the European desk.

"Thanks for coming along, Joe. I need the benefit of a good, experienced mind. Yours."

"What's the problem?"

"D'you remember Massey?"

"You mean Jan Massey—West Berlin?"

"That's the one."

"And now he wants New York or Washington and you're softening me up." He shook his head, smiling. "No way, old friend. I wanna let my sleeping dogs lie."

"I wish it were that, Joe. No, it's more complex than that."

"You look worried. Tell me what's worrying you."

For twenty minutes Chambers detailed his doubts, and even as he was speaking he realized how flimsy it all seemed. Rumor, gossip, hunches, vague doubts. But flimsy or not, they were the only grounds he had for discussing the soundness of a senior man.

Redway pursed his lips. He wasn't surprised by the sparse information that had created the doubts. He had had plenty of such crises to cope with in his time at SIS.

"Nothing more?" he asked, when Chambers had finished.

"No."

"We all come up against these situations but when they land on my desk I've got a rule I always stick to. When in doubt—do something. If you don't and you just leave it and it goes wrong, then it's *your* fault. I don't mind that so much when I haven't seen it coming, but I don't like it at all if I've had fair warning and then done nothing."

"What would you do in this case?"

"I'd move friend Massey. No. Let me go back to square one. I'd have a week off. A break. Just to make sure it's not me that's causing the problem. If it isn't me, on reflection, then I'd move Massey away from Berlin. And I'd *promote* him. Up a grade or two and I'd create some little problem area for him to deal with. No criticism, plenty of pats on the back. His talents being wasted in Berlin and all that crap. And give him a task where he's totally involved. Nothing vital but something needing a lot of ferreting and some opportunity for initiative and creative thinking." He paused. "How's that strike you?"

"It's more or less what I had in mind, Joe."

"Of course," Redway said diplomatically. "Have you got something specific in mind?"

"Vaguely. I'll work on it."

"How about we get out of this damp and you treat me to a wonderful lunch at your club?"

Chambers smiled. "They've got the decorators in. What about the Savoy?"

"That'll do." Redway slapped Chambers's thigh and stood up. "Come on. Cheer up. This place would give anyone the heebie-jeebies. I was in a jail in La Paz once that looked exactly like these bloody birdcages. Brings it all back."

Chambers didn't take a week's holiday but he took a long weekend up at St. Andrews with his wife, who was also an enthusiastic golfer. And when he came back he had spent a week thinking how he could create a place for Massey that fulfilled the conditions that Joe Redway had prescribed.

His solution wasn't ideal but it had the benefits of solving the immediate problem and being actually useful, but a little too obviously contrived. He took another week to embellish a little and devise a suitable scenario to placate Jan Massey. He thanked the Lord that there was still just enough time to work an MBE into the Birthday Honors list. The citation would have to read as "services to industry and commerce," but those who mattered would know what it really meant. An open pat on the back. He had still had enough doubts, though, to leave it for a further month before he put the personal call through to Jan Massey in Berlin.

It was another week before they were due to meet and in that week he swung between determination and indecision. But it was too late now to stop the internal machinery that the change had activated. Fortunately GCHQ had been eager to cooperate with his initiative, suggesting that GCHQ themselves take over the surveillance part of the operation in Berlin. It was a sacrifice that he'd had to make to provide the main reason for the reorganization. It wasn't only Massey he had to convince but others inside SIS. Any hint of his doubts on the grounds of security could lead to another of those ghastly witch-hunts that had haunted the intelligence services from the days of Philby, and more recently, Blunt.

Chambers's office was paneled in bird's-eye maple with ornate brass light fittings and a desk big enough to accommodate six people for a meeting. But there were four leather armchairs arranged round the wide, open fireplace and it was these that Chambers thought more fitting for his meeting with Massey. After a few minutes' social chit-chat Chambers came to the point.

He was smiling as he started his party piece. "I've got a pleasant surprise for you, Jan. Two in fact." He paused and laughed. "I could even claim three." He leaned forward toward Massey. "There's been much talk

169

in the last six months that we were wasting your talents in Berlin. You've got it all bedded down and you've ironed out the initial snags in the system so . . . why shouldn't the organization have the benefit of those talents elsewhere?

"I also wanted to make sure that if we moved you your successor wouldn't be overburdened with the joint responsibilities of Berlin. Then out of the blue—mainly because of the removal of Max Cohen—Cheltenham put up the proposal that GCHQ should take over the SIGINT responsibilities and leave SIS to get on with its normal job. We had a number of meetings about it and it was obviously a little incongruous that an SIS officer should have charge of the Signals section which is not normally an SIS responsibility. They agreed that by good luck you fitted the dual role well but they pointed out that you were an exception." Chambers paused. "So," he went on enthusiastically, "it gave us back our man.

"Almost at the same time we became aware of a lack that we had in Paris. A touchy Embassy staff—particularly His Excellency—a poor liaison with French intelligence, and not much idea of how we could improve things." Chambers smiled broadly. "That's what we want to use you for, Jan."

Massey's face was impassive as he said quickly, "When do you want me to hand over?"

Chambers looked as if he were only just considering when it should be. But he said quite quickly, "How about we make it the end of July and you take up the Paris problem late August—early September?"

"Whenever you want. Was there anything else?"

Chambers beamed. "There's a little something coming your way in the Birthday Honors list. We're all delighted."

Massey frowned for a moment and then said, "My father will be pleased."

As Massey stood up to leave, Chambers stood up too and walked with him to the door. "How is your father?"

"He jogs along."

"Give him my regards, Jan, when you see him. They were a great bunch, SOE. A great bunch."

"I'll be flying back tonight if you don't need me anymore."

"By all means. It's been good to see you again."

Twenty-Seven

They had bought two copper casseroles on the far side of the square and had walked back with the white plastic bag to have a coffee at one of the tables outside the café. It was the first time that Jenny Mayhew had been outside Britain and she loved every moment of it. Albufeira was her idea of heaven. The sunshine, the long golden beach, the awesome rocks and caves, and the people. Men from Manchester wearing Bermuda shorts as if all this were their usual lifestyle. Men who owned garages in Liverpool who smiled as they raked their teeth with gold toothpicks. Men who ordered wine by the bottle, not by the glass. Teenage girls from the Midlands who wore daring swimsuits that had been featured in the *Mirror* or the *Sun*. Blue-rinsed wives of peeling men who sat reading the *News of the World*, their lips moving slowly as the front page kept them in touch with vicars and scoutmasters who had surprised the whole village by running off with bellringers and cub-mistresses. They accepted her, the women nodding and smiling at breakfast, the men having a good look at her sweater.

"We must come here again next year, Eric. If we can afford it."

He was gratified that she was so pleased with their holiday, and she had taken to the foreign ways so easily. Saying *obrigada* and *por favor* like a seasoned traveler.

"I'd thought of giving Rome the once-over next year. But they tell me it's no good in August. Far too hot. I'll think about it." And, leaving Rome to its uncertainty, he said, "Better get back to the condominium."

She frowned and said softly, "What *is* a condominium, Eric? I know they call it that but what is it?"

"They have 'em in the States, love. Apartments grouped together or villas, just a block of flats, really, or a small housing estate."

"You seem to know everything, Eric. It's wonderful being with you."

For a moment he was worried. Why did she say it was wonderful *being* with him? Why not *married* to him? Was she telling people he was just her boyfriend, as if they were just having a dirty weekend at Brighton?

"I love you, Jenny. There's never been anyone but you and there never will be."

She smiled fondly. "Me too neither."

Chambers had been surprised at Massey's apparent indifference to his posting to Paris. If there was any security problem about Massey, his move to Paris would neutralize it. The Russians had almost no interest in the activities of the SDECE and Massey in Paris would be of little use to them. And surely if Massey had been involved with the KGB he would have put up at least some sort of argument for being left *en poste* in Berlin.

He had a twinge of conscience about having given any credence to the gossip of a Frenchman who had been trying to line his own pockets by abusing his official position. But the gossip had had to go down on the confidential file. It had been said, and it had to be recorded. The fact that he had taken swift action would be on the record too. Action that had not prejudiced Massey's career if he were innocent. And action that was not officially recorded as being based on any security doubts could not be used in years to come to earn a fat fee from some newspaper by implying that everybody knew that "X" was a Russian mole but the head of the department had stopped the official enquiry because he was a Russian mole too. Old rivalries and jealousies could be raked up again and again to add a little jam to the meager pension. All in the name of democracy and patriotism, of course.

They were undressing to go to bed and he watched her as she sat naked at the dressing-table wiping off her makeup. She was so young and so pretty it sometimes didn't seem true that she was his wife. But she was.

As he lay in bed with his arm around her, she said, "There was a chap watching us today. I wonder what he was up to."

"What man? Where?"

"He came in the shop when we were buying the cooking pots, and when we were having our coffee he was sitting on a bench by the fountain. He was pretending to read a paper but he was looking at us. And when we were on the beach this afternoon he walked past us twice."

"What's he look like?"

"Fair-haired. A bit like Robert Redford but sort of more podgy."

"How old was he?"

"In his thirties. Thirty-six or -seven."

"Maybe he was looking at you?"

"No. It wasn't that kind of look. It was more like he was keeping an eye on us."

"What was he wearing?"

"Marks and Spencer's plaid shirt, and gray trousers. They looked like Marks and Sparks as well."

"If you see him again point him out to me. I'll soon settle him. Cheeky bugger."

"Maybe I just imagined he was looking at us. It's hard to tell. On holiday people are sitting looking at other people all the time. Just passing the time. Anyway . . ." She turned and smiled at him as his arms went round her, then leaned over and switched off the bedside lamp.

Massey had gone up to London from Tenterden for two meetings with Chambers. At the first he had been briefed on the information currently available on SDECE and its top personnel. And he had been introduced to the London-based SIS officers specializing in French intelligence, and counter-intelligence officers in both Metropolitan France and the French overseas possessions.

At the second meeting Chambers was outlining his briefing for the new posting to Paris.

He stood looking out of the window while Chambers talked on the phone. He had never really understood why he didn't like Chambers. He was urbane and tactful, amiable and efficient, but there was a smoothness about him that Massey had never trusted. Even his calm, pale face was smooth, and his black hair was smoothed back as if Brylcreem was still in fashion. But he knew that if he were honest, what he disliked was that Chambers was such a typical Brit. An Establishment Brit who wore three-piece suits to the office and gear from the via Veneto when he was relaxing at home. He belonged in a Dormeuil advertisement in *Punch* or the *Sunday Times* magazine.

Looking from the window on the fourteenth floor, he could see the gray outlines of the Houses of Parliament and Westminster Bridge in the early morning mist of what looked as if it were going to be another typically English autumn day. It was a relief from the stark modernity of Berlin but it was part of the Establishment that he disliked, despite having served it dutifully for over twelve years. For he was at least half British and he owed them that.

Chambers waved to him to take a chair as he went on talking. A few minutes later he hung up and turned, smiling, to Massey.

"Sorry, Jan. But it's budget time and that always means panic stations all around." He paused. "Are you having a good leave?"

Massey shrugged. "Quiet, anyway."

"You're staying with your father?"

"Yes."

Chambers took a deep breath and leaned forward to indicate that the social chit-chat was over.

"Well now, Paris." He leaned back in his chair until it creaked, fiddling with a gilt letter-opener in the shape of a Spanish sword. "It's more a monitoring job than anything else. And full of pitfalls. Ever since they flounced out of NATO, the French have been very touchy about any kind of cooperation.

"They're barely on speaking terms with the Americans and we've become sort of honest brokers between the two of them. It's a role we don't really want. The CIA trample everywhere in Europe with hob-nailed boots and the SDECE are so corrupt and infiltrated that the CIA treat them as if they were an enemy operation rather than allies. So there's quite a task ahead of you."

"What's our set-up at the moment?"

"Very thin on the ground. Morrow at the Embassy, which loathes having him there. Plumpton at the Consulate, and a string of informers."

"Do they produce anything?"

"Not much more than top-echelon gossip. Most of our information comes from other sources. Mainly NATO itself. It's mainly about SDECE cock-ups. But don't kid yourself about the SDECE and the DST; they treat us like we were enemies too. They'd cut our throats as happily as if we were KGB." He smiled. "Maybe even more so."

"What about offices?"

"No office, Jan. Take a decent apartment. Use the embassy radio set-up. Use Morrow and Plumpton. They are directly under you. When you want to interfere, then interfere. Otherwise just keep us informed. Weekly sit-rep. No copy to the Embassy, no internal copies. We'll give you a P.O. box number. Post it or use the diplomatic bag if it's urgent or necessary."

"Budget?"

"There's an existing budget and we're prepared to increase it by up to fifty percent. If you think that's necessary."

"When do you want me to start?"

"No mad hurry. Next month perhaps. There's no rush." He stood up. "Congratulations on the promotion, by the way. Well deserved." Chambers looked at his watch, then back at Massey's face. "Have lunch with me?" And Chambers smiled at the defensive look on Massey's face. "We needn't go to White's. Why not a sandwich at the Special Forces Club? Say, one o'clock?"

Massey smiled. "OK. I'll meet you there."

As they walked slowly up the High Street in Tenterden and turned into the churchyard he realized that his father had suddenly grown old. No longer standing so upright, he walked with a stoop, and his walking stick was no longer just a decoration or a pointer.

They sat on the bench and russet leaves blew into small heaps at the edges of the larger graves, but there was still a pale blue sky and trailing white mares'-tails that signaled the fact that though autumn might have been late it was here now and making up for lost time.

The old man coughed and put a white handkerchief to his mouth. "I still come here, Jan. After all these years. No justification for it. She'd never heard of Tenterden, I'm sure."

"But it's been a comfort all the same."

"Yes. Stupid, isn't it? Just the habit and the years have made it our place. I used to talk to her when I was alone and there was nobody around. Tell her what I'd been doing." He laughed briefly without humor. "Hernias, hysterectomies, and the gossip. The babies, wanted and unwanted. Nothing more interesting to say, I'm afraid. And now . . ." he waved the stick toward the moss-covered headstones ". . . and now it's just thoughts. Waiting until I see her again." He turned sharply to look at Massey's face. "D'you believe in anything, Jan? God, religion and all that? D'you think I shall see her again?"

"I'm sure you will, Father. You see her every day in your mind."

"What about your girl? Ever see her again?"

"I'm afraid not."

"No chance of putting it right?"

"No."

"I'll be interested to hear what you think of Paris." He smiled. "It will be very different from the old days. The Gestapo and the Sicherheitsdienst. The rumors and the rationing." He sighed. "Your mama loved Paris. We were never there together, but I think we might have lived there, or somewhere in France, if it had turned out differently. She liked the country and she liked the people. They were very brave, the French. Nobody who wasn't there could know what it was like. The humiliation, the fear, the shortages. It seemed as if it would go on forever."

"What about the collaborators?"

"There were very few real collaborators. Despite wars, despite occupation, life goes on for ordinary people. A girl sleeps with a German soldier. But what does it matter? She was probably very young and very lonely. He was probably the same." He shook his head. "I see it in the surgery every day. People can't think about the dangers of nuclear bombs every

175

hour of the day. Nor the class struggle or political parties. A few fanatics have nothing better to do, but people get on with their daily lives. All over the world it's the same. We should be sparing with our criticisms." He turned to look at his son. "Where are you going to stay? Do you have an official place?"

"No. I get an allowance to rent an apartment."

"That's good, my boy. A new life. A new start. Where will you live?"

"I don't know. I'll spend a week or so looking around."

"In my days it had to be Montmartre or Montparnasse. Even in wartime, they were the only places to live."

Jan Massey smiled. "I'll remember that." He gently touched the old man's knee. "We ought to go. It's getting cold."

The old man sighed. "I love talking to you, Jan. It's a great comfort. You were a good boy, really. And you've grown into a fine man. An MBE. Your mother would have been so pleased, despite not liking authority." He sighed. "You lead the way."

Twenty-Eight

Chez Raymond on West 56th Street was never a place to patronize when you were in a hurry, but the onion soup was topped with excellent Swiss cheese and nicely browned. But what he went for was the guinea fowl and the delicious wild mushrooms called *chanterelles*. He finished his meal with an excellent Brie. The coffee was the only drink he ordered. No aperitif and no wine. He checked the bill meticulously, paid on his American Express card and tipped the waiter in cash.

As he walked into the street he looked at his watch. It was later than he thought and he waved down a cab. On West End Avenue he asked the driver to drop him just past 72nd Street and he walked the rest of the way.

It was a tall block, offices and shops in the lower half and residential above. There were five penthouse suites and his was on the corner so that he had the fine view across the Hudson River.

He looked at his watch again as he walked from the elevator along the carpeted corridor. It was nine thirty-five, and he had cut it rather fine. Ten o'clock local time was the scheduled time.

As he slid his key into the security lock and pressed down the two retaining clips he wondered what the response would be to tonight's information. He opened the heavy door, carefully took out the key and slid it back in his coat pocket. It was only when he turned that he saw the two men. One, with an old-fashioned crewcut who was about fifty, was sitting in the armchair which had been turned to face the door. The younger man was standing at the side of the door and he reached out and pushed the door to.

The older man said, "Good evening, Mr. Swartski."

"Who are you? What are you doing here? How did you get in my apartment?"

"The porter let me in."

"That's impossible, the building's regulations say—"

He stopped as the man held up a small, black-leather folder displaying an identity card. There was a photograph and a white diagonal line from corner to corner.

Swartski leaned forward to look more closely and the man said, "My name's Logan, Mr. Swartski. And my colleague is Mr. Curtis. We're both FBI. We want to ask you some questions."

"I want to call my attorney. That's part of my rights."

"You can phone him when we've charged you. Meantime—"

"Charged me with what?"

Logan smiled. "Depends on how cooperative you are. Take your coat off, Mr. Swartski, and sit down."

"Do you have a warrant to enter this apartment?"

"No. We didn't want to attract attention to our visit at this stage. We can get one if you wish."

Swartski hesitated, then took off his coat and sat on an upright chair alongside the small desk.

"Tell what it is you want to know."

"I want you to tell me what you've been doing in the United States with a forged passport, a forged residence permit and using a false name."

Swartski stood up slowly. "In that case, mister, either get your warrant or charge me with whatever you've got in mind."

Logan nodded amiably. "Sit down, Swartski, and we can get down to business. Go on. Sit down." Swartski sat down reluctantly and Logan said, "We've taken your radio and various documents. They're at the DA's office." He paused. "We've also arrested Lipski and Saanen." He looked across at Swartski. "Do you want to cooperate or do you want us to do it the hard way?" Logan reached inside his jacket and pulled out a folded paper. "I have a warrant. It's signed and dated but I haven't filled in the charges yet. It could mean the difference between five years and twenty years."

Swartski was silent for several minutes and then he said quietly, "What do you mean by cooperate?"

"I mean exactly what you think I mean. I want the lot. Names, places, controls, payments. The whole bag of tricks."

"You'd better charge me."

"That's OK by me if that's how you want to play it."

Logan stood up and Curtis took the handcuffs out of his jacket pocket. As Swartski held out his hands he said, "Can I make a phone call to my sister?"

Logan smiled. "Your only sister's in Dublin, my friend. And she doesn't want to know you. The man at the United Nations won't want to know you. You won't get any help from the Embassy either. You're on your own now."

Swartski shrugged. "Just charge me or get the hell out of my apartment."

Logan turned to Curtis. "Take him in and book him."

Curtis had booked Swartski in at one of the downtown precincts and had made sure that Swartski was put in with the drunks and drug addicts. The police captain had been warned earlier of the scenario and didn't like it. He liked it less as the hours passed. He had phoned City headquarters and they'd told him to cooperate but not to get involved. It was 6:00 A.M. when Swartski had had enough and asked for Curtis.

Curtis didn't go in the cage. Swartski was standing there, his clothes covered with vomit and his jacket sleeve torn from the shoulder.

"What is it, Swartski?"

"I want my rights. I want an attorney."

Curtis said, "No way," and turned to walk away.

Swartski shouted to him, his hands on the bars, shaking them. "Let me out of here."

Curtis stopped and turned. "Are you ready to answer our questions?"

"Not here. I'm not a criminal. You know that."

"I'll take you to our offices provided you cooperate."

"Answer questions, yes. Cooperate, I don't have to."

A police car took them both to the underground garage of the block and they went up to the top floor in the service elevator. Logan was waiting for them in the outside office and he took over, leading Swartski into a small room. The room was comfortably furnished and Logan pointed at an armchair. When Swartski was sitting, Logan pulled up a chair facing him.

"Mr. Swartski," he said quietly, "I've been through this situation dozens of times. It's like seeing reruns of old films on TV for me." He paused. "But for you it's different. I'd like you to have the benefit of my experience. There's only two ways these things can end. The first way you get yourself an attorney. Then you go on trial. You get sentenced and you appeal. The appeal is rejected and you do fifteen, twenty years depending on the judge's views as to the extent of your guilt and the consequences to national security of what you've done. Right?" He paused again for several moments. "The second way, you cooperate. And when it comes to the indictment we remember that. You go on trial. You get five to seven and that's the end of it.

"Now, you might wonder why we ask you to cooperate. If we've got enough evidence to indict you—and I assure you we have—why not just go ahead and get the maximum sentence the law provides? Well, let's just say we do that. You'll rot in jail but that won't help or hinder me.

"But if you cooperate I've benefited, the Agency has benefited. We've filled in the little holes in the fabric. We can repair some of the damage. If we can do that with your help, then we bear it in mind. Whatever happens you can do no more harm to this country. Your thing is over— finished. It doesn't help the Agency that you spend fifteen years in jail. Maybe it discourages a few of your friends from trying the same game. But nothing more than that. Do you understand?"

Swartski nodded. "You ask that I implicate other people, is that it?"

"You'll find that most of them are already implicated. We know who they are. What they've been doing. They will be arrested too. Some of them are already in custody as of last night. The ones who matter we know already. There may be minor figures we don't know. They are not all that important. But it helps us complete the picture."

"How long will it take?"

"If you cooperate, Mr. Swartski, we're in a different ballgame. We shall be *talking* to you, very different from interrogating you."

"What kind of things do you want to know?"

Logan knew it was the breakthrough. "Before we talk let me have my people get you a change of clothes. And we can get you a drink and a meal. I'll send in Mr. Curtis. Tell him what clothes you want from your apartment."

The two seven-story blocks were officially known as FANX I and II. Friendship Annex I and II. So called because they were so close to the Washington–Baltimore International Airport. To their disgruntled occupants they were known as the Friendship Leper Colony because of their physical separation from the main NSA complex and their lack of some facilities.

One of the most constant complaints was the state of the parking lot, known as Cardiac Hill. It was frequently ankle deep in water because of an inefficient drainage system.

It was 7:00 P.M. when Jimbo and Kirsten walked gingerly between the night shift's cars to the red Ferrari. Jimbo was just unlocking the car doors when the two men walked over from the gray Mustang. Jimbo nodded to them and flattened himself against the car to let them pass. But they didn't pass, and one of them moved round to the other side of the car, where Kirsten was standing.

The older man on Jimbo's side said, "Are you Mr. Vick? Mr. James Vick?"

"Yeah." Jimbo nodded. "Do I know you?"

"I guess not. I'm FBI. I'd be grateful if you and your wife would come with me and my colleague."

"What is this—a security check?"

"Kind of. We'll go back in the building if you'll both follow me."

Jimbo looked at Kirsten and shrugged. They walked together, the FBI man leading the way, the other FBI man following.

They were shown into an office at the far end of one of the corridors and when they were inside, the older man introduced himself and his colleague. "I'm Rademacher and that's Mr. Pekkanan." Rademacher smiled amiably at Kirsten and said, "He speaks Finnish if that might help you, ma'am."

Jimbo said aggressively, "My wife's family are from Sweden not Finland."

Rademacher nodded and smiled. "You don't say. They all sound the same to me."

Jimbo was surprised at the anger in Kirsten's voice when she said sharply, "I'd like to see your documents. Both of you."

They both held out their identity cards and Kirsten looked at them carefully. Not the quick glance that most people gave them. She looked up at Rademacher. "What's the big idea? This isn't a routine check, is it?"

"What makes you think that, ma'am?"

"Routine checks are done by Agency security men. Not FBI."

"Well, we had a few questions we wanted to put to you both. Is that agreeable to you, ma'am?"

"I want to have my attorney here. I want to phone him. Now. Before I answer any questions."

Rademacher raised his eyebrows. "D'you think that's really necessary, ma'am?" He added slowly, "At this stage?"

"Yes I do. Where is the nearest phone?"

"Well, now," Rademacher said, "how about you take the lady to the phone, Pekkanan, and I'll talk to Mr. Vick while we're waiting. No hurry."

Jimbo said, "My wife stays here. Let's get that clear."

"I'll go with him, Jimbo. You stay here."

"Who're you gonna phone? Do you want my guy's number? He's in Baltimore."

"No. Leave it to me."

She turned, and Jimbo watched her walk back down the corridor with the FBI man. Then he turned to look at Rademacher. "I'm going to lodge a strong complaint with the director himself first thing tomorrow morning. Nobody has to put up with this sort of thing."

"How about we both sit down, Mr. Vick? Let's have a quiet word together."

181

"About what? If it's my work, you should know that it can't be discussed with anyone who hasn't been specially cleared."

"It's not directly your work, Mr. Vick." He paused. "I'm afraid it's going to be something of a shock to you." He looked at Jimbo's face intently as he said quietly, "We're arresting your wife on charges of espionage, Mr. Vick. And I'm holding you on suspicion as an accessory. Does that surprise you?"

"No way. I think you're out of your fucking minds. I'm going to call the director right now."

As Jimbo stood up Rademacher pushed him gently back onto his chair.

"I know how you must feel, young man. I'd better tell you that your wife has been under surveillance for some time. Long before you came in contact with her. She's not Swedish, she's Finnish. And both her parents are still alive. They live in Helsinki. They're both active communists and her name isn't Swenson it's Vaara. Kirsten Vaara. She's been working for the KGB ever since she came to the States."

Jimbo sat stunned. "I don't believe it," he said, shaking his head.

"You had no idea of all this? Not even a faint suspicion?"

"I told you. I don't believe it."

"She never mentioned the name Zak or Zacharia? Or Swartski?"

"No, never. Who are they?"

"He's the next one up the line. He's her controller. Bureau officers arrested him in New York last night." He paused. "He's cooperating." He paused again. "I think you should too, Mr. Vick. It isn't pleasant. But it wasn't very pleasant what they did to you. Stringing you along and all that. We see a lot of it. We get hardened to it. But it's not very nice for the people who've been deceived." He paused. "*If* they've been deceived."

"Can I speak to her, alone?" He shrugged helplessly. "Please."

"I'm afraid not. She'll be already on her way to our place in Washington. She is under arrest. You're only detained for questioning."

"You'll be wasting your time questioning me. I don't know anything, and if I did I wouldn't tell you bastards."

"Let's go, Mr. Vick. We've got some paperwork to do before I've finished with you."

It was the third day of Logan's questioning of Swartski.

"Why did you pick on Vick as the target?"

"We'd only got details of three people working in that area at NSA. He looked the obvious one."

"Why?"

"The life he led. The teenage chicks. The need to impress women. No relatives in the immediate background to get in the way. No close relationships with other people."

"Nothing more than that?"

"No. He just looked a suitable target."

"Where did the girl get her math training?"

"At the university in Helsinki and later at Moscow University."

"And what was the brief? What were they after?"

"Anything on the use of stochastic math theory as applied to cryptology. How NSA was using it. Their attitude to it. Was it important? Did they see it as a real tool? How far had they got? Applications and results." Swartski shrugged. "And after that any information from inside NSA. Names, routines—anything."

"I couldn't understand why you let it get out of hand and you let her marry Jimbo Vick. Why that?"

"Because a husband doesn't have to testify against a wife."

"But she married on false pretenses. The marriage can be annulled. It's void."

Swartski shrugged. "Moscow wanted it that way."

"Who put together her cover story?"

"Moscow."

"And her documentation?"

"Moscow, Ottawa and the Embassy in Washington."

"Who did you pass it on to?"

"Tell me who you think it was and I'll nod if you're right."

Logan shrugged. "Let's come back to you. How long have you been working for them?"

"Since Abel set up in New York. After he was arrested I was on my own for a couple of years."

"And your jewelry business, did they fund that?"

"No way. I built it up myself."

"Where did you get your radio training?"

"In Toronto."

"The place over the newspaper shop on Yonge Street?"

"You know about that?"

"Of course."

Swartski shrugged. "The radio was only for emergencies. I didn't use it much. I never really mastered it."

"What other training did you get?"

"I had a few weeks' general training. Surveillance, codes, inks, photographs and procedures."

"Where was that?"

"In Dresden. I went there to a trade fair. Buying jewelry."

"What made you offer your services way back?"

"The Rosenberg case."

"Why that?"

"I thought they had a raw deal. I thought they were framed."

Logan smiled. "Another sucker for Moscow's propaganda machine."

He sighed. "You weren't the only one, my friend. The bleeding hearts department did a good job."

"You think they were guilty?"

"I know damn well they were."

"When do we talk about me? What's going to happen to me?"

"The way we've been progressing, Mr. Swartski, is going to make a lot of difference to our attitude."

"What's that mean?"

Logan looked at Swartski's pale face for several moments before he spoke.

"I'm considering asking the Justice Department to offer you immunity if you'd become a State witness. How would you feel about that?" He paused. "Not that I'm sure they would agree."

"You mean testify in open court against them?"

"If we needed it—yes. But it wouldn't be just the Vick couple. It would have to cover your whole operation. The people in New Jersey and San Francisco." Logan smiled. "And the girl who works for the AFSAC committee."

Swartski shifted uneasily in his seat. "How long have you people been on to me?"

"Right from when you first contacted the KGB man at the Soviet Mission to the UN."

"So why wait all this time to do something?"

"We wanted to know what they were interested in. If we'd pulled you in before you got going we may not have uncovered your replacement so easily."

"So you know who my controller is?"

Logan smiled. "Was, Mr. Swartski. Yes, we know. He was deported a few days ago." Logan stood up. "Are you comfortable here? Anything you want—magazines, cigarettes or the like?"

Swartski shook his head. "If I testify what happens to me?"

"We'd take care of you and you would be given a short sentence. A couple of years. But you wouldn't serve any of it."

"How long have I got to decide?"

"A couple of weeks."

Twenty-Nine

They had bundled him through the checkpoint in the Wall at Bornholmer Strasse just after three o'clock in the morning. He had staggered as far as the patch of grass about a hundred and fifty yards away. A railwayman coming off the night shift had found him lying with his head hanging over the gutter. When the police came they assumed that he was drunk, but in the van one of them noticed that the man's eyes were wide open but obviously unseeing. They radioed that they were diverting to the emergency service at the hospital.

The young doctor on the emergency detail had checked the man over. He wasn't drunk as they had assumed. The man had been drugged, but some sort of alcohol had been poured over his shirt and jacket; there was no alcohol in the blood sample.

They searched the man's clothing and all the pockets were empty. But when they took off his shoes and socks they found a five-pound note and a British Army identity card taped to the sole of his left foot. They phoned the police liaison squad, and an hour later the one remaining German policeman was joined by a uniformed sergeant from the military police SIB detachment.

It was ten o'clock that morning before the man stirred in the hospital bed and an hour later he tried to sit up.

The sergeant leaned over and looked at the man's pale face. "What's your name, sunbeam?"

The man closed his eyes and shook his head. When he opened his eyes again the sergeant said, "What you been up to, mate?" He paused. "You been and gone AWOL, ain't you? Been naughty, eh?"

"Where am I?"

"You're in jail, mate. You been sniffing coke, ain't you?"

The man sat up, running his hands through his lank greasy hair. He looked at the sergeant's face. "What you done to me?"

"Nothing, mate. I just been playing Florence Nightingale."

"What happened?"

"You tell me."

"I don't know what happened. I can't remember."

A nurse told the sergeant that there was a phone call for him. She plugged in the telephone and he lifted the receiver. "Turnbull . . . yeah . . . yeah . . . OK." He replaced the receiver and turned to the man in the bed.

"I'm taking you to the nick, mate. Seems like you've been a very naughty boy. They wanna talk to you."

"Who?"

"The security boys."

"I'm a civilian. I'm not in the army."

The sergeant grinned. "'Course not. You tell 'em." He paused and looked at the German policeman.

"*Ich* will take him *mit*. To the Britische *polizei*. *Ja*."

The policeman shrugged. "He's one of yours, yes?"

The sergeant laughed. "Yeah. He's one of ours all right."

Lieutenant O'Hara was twenty-six with red hair and freckles that made him look even younger. His pale blue eyes looked at the notes on his pad and then back at the face of the man sitting on the wooden chair.

"How about we cut out the bullshit? What were you doing in the last six months?"

"I told you. I was working on the black market."

"What were you selling?"

"Coffee, cigarettes, blankets. The usual stuff."

"Tell me your name."

"I told you twice already."

"Tell me again."

"Joseph Steel."

"Is that the name they told you to use?"

"Who?"

"The Russians."

"I don't know any Russians."

The lieutenant slid the greasy ID card from under his pad and handed it to the man on the chair.

"What's that?"

The man looked at it for several seconds and his hand trembled as he handed it back.

"What's gonna happen to me?"

"Depends on how you cooperate."

"What's that mean?"

"Your name is Arthur Johnson, yes?"

"Yeah."

"Signalman Johnson?"

"Yes."

"You went on leave to the U.K. and you went AWOL and didn't return to your unit?"

"OK."

"Signalman Johnson. As of now, you are under arrest for the murder of a woman known as Heidi Fischer. Also known as Heidi Johnson. Your common-law wife. You will be taken back to Birmingham and handed over to the civilian police. Do you understand?"

Johnson sighed and nodded. "Can't we do a deal?"

"About what?"

"I been working for the Russkis. The KGB."

"Don't come the old soldier with me, Johnson. You're facing a charge of murder. Telling more lies isn't going to help you."

"I'm an officer of the KGB. Same as you, a lieutenant. Phone 'em up and ask 'em, if you don't believe me."

Lieutenant O'Hara stood up. "You're out of your fucking mind, Johnson. That's what's wrong with you."

The Birmingham City police had questioned Johnson for days and on the fifth day they had called in their Special Branch officer. And Johnson had been transferred from Winson Green prison to Wormwood Scrubs and a top security cell. The interrogations were patient, meticulous and probing. Hipwell, the SB interrogator, was an experienced officer and he slowly drew the threads together.

"When you got back to Berlin after your trip to Birmingham, you went through Charlie and contacted your controller. What was his reaction?"

"He was angry. Said I'd no business to make decisions like that without their approval."

"Then what happened?"

"Two of them interrogated me for weeks. They seemed to think I'd been caught by our lot and sent back in to spy on them."

"Go on."

"When they found out about Heidi they seemed satisfied I was OK. But they said I was no use to them anymore. They found me a job repairing TV sets. I got me a girlfriend and they found out she was on the game. The police took her and after that I got no protection from the Russians. The chap at the repair shop cut my wages and I told him I'd had enough hassle from all of 'em."

"Let's go back over when you were at the house in Grunewald. What kind of things did they want from you?"

"Almost anything. Like I told you, even gossip about people interested them. Names and ranks. Home addresses. Jobs. Equipment and routines."

"Apart from that sort of information, you gave them tapes and other things. What was on the tapes?"

"No idea. I just took anything that was easy to take. They wanted anything."

"Did anybody help you do this? Anyone else at the house?"

"No. I never told a soul."

"The disk you changed. How did it get inside? Did you take the book in?"

"No way. I wouldn't have dared. They just told me it was in the book in the library—and it was there. I changed it over and destroyed the old one."

"How did you destroy it?"

"I burned it in the toilet and flushed it down the bog."

"Have you any idea who put the disk in the book?"

"No."

Johnson shrugged as if he thought it was stupid to think he might know.

But it was one of the many things that Hipwell went back to again and again.

Thirty

Apart from the center of the city, Massey knew little of Paris but his father had often talked about the rue Mouffetard where he had lived for a short time during the war, before the Paris networks had been broken up. His father had made it seem a romantic street and enthused about its raffish inhabitants as being the only real French people in the city.

When he asked at the patisserie, the old lady told him of two apartments that were available in the vicinity, one in rue Mouffetard itself.

He walked from the bottom of the hill by the church, up the steep incline of the narrow bustling street until it became the rue Descartes. The rows of stalls made the street even narrower. He turned back and walked slowly down the hill turning into the passage des Patriarches where the landlord had a workshop near the public baths. The old man had looked him over and only reluctantly agreed to show him the rooms he had to rent.

Massey followed the old man to a doorway between an ironmongery and a dilapidated hotel. The wooden door had to be lifted on its hinges before it would open. The rooms were on the top floor and were better than he had expected. There was one large living-room lit by two mansard windows. The floor was polished wood and the furnishings were sparse but sufficient. A low divan bed, a wardrobe, a variety of mahogany cupboards, wicker chairs and a circular table. The bathroom and kitchen were small but clean. The old man explained that the room had been used as a studio by a painter who had moved to the Midi. The rent was reasonable and when Massey had offered three months' rent in advance the old man had accepted.

For several days he spent his mornings making notes of the things he planned to do and lists of the kind of contacts that he wanted. In the afternoons he explored the area where he lived, and checked the locations of various government offices in the city itself. At night, he ate locally in small restaurants and went early to bed. It was a week before he contacted the Embassy.

For a week he read batches of files from the Embassy on their last twelve months' work. Compared with his operation in Berlin it was a shambles. Not much more than the kind of gossip to be picked up at the usual rounds of Embassy cocktail parties. It was almost all political with very little about the French intelligence services. There were the minutes of monthly liaison meetings with NATO intelligence representatives that all too obviously showed that nobody divulged any information to anyone else. The only original information concerned French military intelligence which was only barely the province of SIS. The military attaché at the Embassy was responsible for armed forces' intelligence.

There was only one really experienced SIS man at the Embassy. An old hand named Morrow, who was obviously trying to ride out his last couple of years before retirement without rocking any boats. And that meant keeping on the right side of His Excellency. Not sending in reports that conflicted with the Embassy's own evaluations. Not offending the French. Not offending anybody. Not doing the job. Maybe it was time to get him transferred back to London.

What surprised Massey most was the lack of information on the French intelligence service, SDECE. Its official title—Service de Documentation Extérieure et de Contre-Espionage—was typical of its obscurity. There seemed little information on its staff and even less on where it was housed and how it operated. He decided that his best source of useful information was the Americans.

The senior CIA man in Paris was Autenowski and the Polish connection had worked its usual magic. They had met the second time in the bar at the Ritz.

"Tell me what you want to know, Jan."

"Anything about SDECE."

"Anything?" The American looked surprised.

"Yes."

The CIA man smiled. "Well, first off it's not called the SDECE anymore. There was a big shake-up when Mitterand became president. They call it the DGSE these days—Direction Générale de la Securité Extérieure."

"How long ago was the change?"

"Six weeks, seven weeks, something like that."

"What else has changed?"

Autenowski grinned. "Nothing. Absolutely nothing. Sometimes they report to the minister of Defense, sometimes the Interior, and in some cases direct to the president."

"Is Bourget still with them?"

"You bet. Bourget's a survivor. He applied for a transfer to internal security—DST—but they wouldn't have him."

"What's he doing?"

"Taking bribes, screwing young girls—same as he always did." The CIA man laughed. "I'm only kidding. He's working in their Soviet section. God knows why. He doesn't speak Russian or have any other qualifications that I know of."

"Where does he work?"

"They've got a floor at one of the buildings belonging to the Ministry of Agriculture. Supposed to be a secret cover but when the buses stop there the ticket guy calls out, 'Spy palace.' Everybody knows so it doesn't matter."

"Can I trade with you for a few months?"

Autenowski shrugged. "Depends what you want and what you've got."

"I want to start building up a detailed picture. Names, ranks, responsibilities. Who matters. What kind of current operations they have. Names of informants."

The American smiled. "Names of informants you won't get. You know that. The rest I can give you." He paused. "What do I get?"

"What do you want?"

"Your assessment of our operation in Berlin. An indication of what your mission is over here and . . . let's call it . . . future cooperation."

"That's OK by me."

"How about we meet in ten days' time? You've got my home address. Let's have lunch together. Say a week from Wednesday. The twelfth. Midday at my place."

Massey had sent a note to Chambers on the change of name of the SDECE and had received a memo back in the bag asking if he was sure of the information. He had ignored it. But it angered him that they hadn't known of the change much earlier.

For a week he had worked on his assessment of the CIA operation in Berlin. He typed it out slowly on a portable borrowed from the Embassy. He had no intention of using Embassy facilities. He was going to build up his own efficient unit as soon as he could justify it. The indifference of London to intelligence out of Paris amazed him. There were Caribbean islands that got more attention.

Rademacher stood to one side as the warder unlocked the cell door. As he went inside he turned and said, "I'll buzz you when I want you. On Channel 16. OK?"

The warder nodded and Rademacher turned to look at Jimbo Vick as the key turned in the lock behind him.

The young man was sitting on the edge of the regulation bed, his arms folded, his elbows on his thighs, his head bowed.

"How are you this morning?"

Jimbo made no reply. Rademacher pulled up the wooden chair and sat down, putting the newspaper he was carrying on the floor beside his feet.

"I phoned your father, Jimbo. Like you asked. He's fixing a lawyer for you. A local guy. He's pretty good."

Jimbo looked up and Rademacher noticed the pale, drawn face and the bloodshot eyes.

"Is the lawyer going to act for Kirsten as well?"

"She's got her own lawyer."

"Who is he?"

"His name's Theodore S. Lewin. You ever heard of him?"

Jimbo shook his head. "No."

"He's from New York."

"Is he any good?"

"Yeah. He's a very tricky operator. Specializes in defending people facing espionage and treason charges."

"Have you seen her recently?"

"I saw her this morning."

"Did she send any message for me?"

"I'm afraid not."

"Did you give her my message?"

"I certainly did."

"What did she say?"

"I'm afraid her mind's pretty occupied at the moment."

"Why are you doing this to us? Just tell me why."

"Have you got any idea why we should be doing anything?"

"None. I swear it. Neither of us has done a goddamn thing."

"You thought she was just a nice Swedish girl?"

"She was." He paused. "She is."

"And like all pretty Swedish girls she just happened to be a very talented mathematician?"

Jimbo shrugged. "Why not, for God's sake? You don't have to be a Plain Jane these days to have a talent."

"Why do you think she told you—and everyone else—that she was Swedish when in fact she's Finnish?"

"It's academic. She's an American citizen. Where she comes from doesn't matter."

"She's not an American citizen, and she never was."

"She is now. She's my wife."

"She's not, Jimbo. She used forged and fraudulent documents. She was never given citizenship and she never applied for it. The papers she used were made in Moscow."

"You can prove that? Because you'll have to. Not just speculate. Not just fish around."

Rademacher sighed. "I'm not fishing around, Jimbo. Forensic has established the forgery. So has an independent expert. The DA's office has accepted it."

"And what does that prove? There's thousands of spics with no documents at all coming over every week. Are *they* all spies?"

"Some of them are." He paused. "What would you have done if you'd found out yourself that she was spying for the Russians?"

"I'd have told her she was crazy."

"Would you have reported it to the FBI or NSA security?"

"No way. She's my wife. I love her."

"Despite how she's used you?"

"How has she used me?"

"Deceived you about her nationality and her background. Persuaded you to employ her on highly secret work. Married you to make sure she'd keep her job at NSA. What more do you want?"

"She married me because I love her and she loves me."

"Are you sure she loves you, Jimbo?"

There were tears on Jimbo's cheeks and his voice faltered as he said, "You're a real bastard, Rademacher. A real bastard."

Rademacher bent down, picked up the newspaper and handed it to Jimbo Vick.

"Read that, Jimbo."

The headline said, "Blonde held as Red spy," and alongside was a picture of Kirsten that he had never seen before. It appeared to have been taken by the Kennedy gravesite in the cemetery at Arlington. Jimbo looked at what was printed beneath it and threw the paper down angrily. "I'll sue those bastards—and you, Rademacher. It's time somebody taught you zombies a lesson."

Rademacher stood up, pressing the alert button on his radio timer.

"Is there anything you want, Jimbo?"

"I want to see Kirsten. Alone."

Rademacher hesitated and then, as the warder unlocked the door, he said quietly, "I'll see what I can do."

* * *

Pekkanan reached over and took the packet of sugar from the saucer of Rademacher's cup, tore it open and emptied the brown crystals into his coffee. As he stirred it slowly he said, "She's a real tough cookie, Pete. Cold as ice. She's a real Soviet. Well trained, well motivated and ready to open those long legs for Moscow."

"What makes you say that?"

Pekkanan shrugged. "She made the offer. That and a life pension and a *dacha* at Peredelkino."

"Was what she said recorded?"

"I assume so. No reason why they should have switched off." He grinned. "I played along with it for a bit. It'll liven up the court when they play the tapes."

"He wants to see her."

"Why, for Christ's sake?"

"He loves her. And he thinks she loves him."

"How can a guy who understands all that way-out math be so stupid? That little gal has never loved anybody in her life."

"He's not the first man to be fooled by a pretty girl."

"Just tell him he's wasting his time. She's never mentioned him. Remember when you gave her that message from him that he loves her? She just rolled her eyes up to heaven and went on talking."

"Maybe he'd cooperate if he knew she didn't love him. That she'd fooled him deliberately."

"I think the poor bastard knows in his heart that she fooled him. If he wasn't party to it, the only help he can give us is on dates and times when she was out of town."

"He's going to take it bad. Real bad."

"So what? Shouldn't have been such a sucker in the first place."

"How could he have known?"

"What made him think a dame like that was interested in him? What the hell's he got that she'd want?" He grinned. "She'd have made Miss Universe if she'd tried. She could have had some millionaire if she'd been straight. Not a little hick like Jimbo Vick."

"What do you think?"

"Let him see her and we can record it. She might give something away. Let me work something out."

They had blindfolded Jimbo for the journey. It took about an hour and he had no idea where they were taking him. But all that mattered was that he was going to see her. He felt loose gravel under his feet as he got out of the car and the two agents took an arm each, warning him of three

194

steps. He thought he heard the click of a magazine being clipped into a gun. They walked him slowly and carefully down a long corridor and he stood, held by Rademacher, as a metal door was unlocked.

He was trembling as the FBI man untied the blindfold and he blinked in the bright lights as Rademacher said, "You've got fifteen minutes, Mr. Vick. If you want to leave before then, just press the bell on the table."

As the door clanged to he looked around the room, and then he saw her. She was sitting in an armchair in the linen suit they had bought in Washington, her long legs crossed, her blonde hair tied in a ponytail with a wide black ribbon. And he felt paralyzed at the look on her face. She pointed to a chair facing her. "Do sit down, Jimbo. You can take it that everything we say is being recorded."

His throat was dry as he swallowed with difficulty. "It isn't, Kirsten, they gave me their word."

The blue eyes looked at him as she said, "Don't be such a fool, man. Why do you think the lights are so bright? There'll be a video camera as well as a recorder."

His eyes were on her face, pleading. "Just tell me you love me, Kirstie. You don't need to say anything else."

"Jimbo. Just listen to what I say." She looked up at the light fitting on the ceiling. "And you bastards listen too." She turned and looked at him again. "You don't know anything, you weren't involved in anything. We are not married. I don't love you." She nodded and said, "Now you can just press that bell."

There were tears streaming down his face. "You did love me, Kirsten, you did, didn't you?"

The blue eyes looked at him coldly, "I don't love you, man. And I never loved you. Now just leave me alone. Just get out of my life."

"Why, Kirstie? Why did you do it to me?"

"Piss off, for Christ's sake. You make me sick. You creep." She leaned forward and pressed the bell on the table.

Rademacher had to virtually carry Jimbo Vick from the room. Behind him, the girl lit a cigarette and threw the match onto the table.

On the journey back Jimbo Vick sat bent forward, his face in his hands, sobbing as if he would never stop.

Jimbo Vick had refused to see his parents and refused to see the lawyer his father had provided to defend him.

Rademacher intended to give him a few days to settle down and then go over the dates and times when Kirsten had been meeting Swartski and the Russian.

Two days after Jimbo's meeting with Kirsten, there was a call for Rademacher at two in the morning. Jimbo Vick had tried to kill himself, slashing both his wrists. But the medics said that he was OK. He'd recover.

* * *

Pekkanan and another Finnish-speaking FBI man interrogated Kirsten Vaara for hours every day for seven weeks, aware that their time was running out. The girl was aware of it too. More acid in her replies, more defiant in her attitude as the days went by.

Rademacher had warned Pekkanan of his suspicions right from the start. What made him suspicious was the fact that the actual arrest of the girl was made by the Immigration and Nationality Service and the indictment made under the IN Act. Why hadn't she been charged with the capital offense of Soviet espionage? Rademacher had his suspicions confirmed when the girl was flown without any publicity to Hanover and taken by car to the border control point at Helmstedt. Only a handful of people would have heard of the man who was exchanged for her but both the Russians and the Americans reckoned that they had the better bargain in the deal.

Thirty-One

They had met at a café near the St.-Michel Metro station and as Autenowski went off to make a telephone call Massey leafed through the file of papers that the CIA man had handed to him.

When Autenowski came back, he gave the American his evaluation of their operation in West Berlin.

"I'll look at it later, Jan. But, briefly, what was your opinion?"

"They do a good job, Bill. No doubt about that."

"No criticisms?"

"Not criticism exactly, but I think they're overexposed so far as the public is concerned."

"In what way?"

Massey smiled. "They're a bit too American. They behave like they're at home in the States, where you have at least a public face."

"What's wrong with that?"

"Well, it's OK in your own country where, on the whole, the public supports you. But it makes for problems in Europe, especially Berlin, where all other intelligence services are very much hidden." Massey paused. "It makes your guys very easy targets. Not just physical targets but too easily identified by people who are up to no good."

Autenowski smiled. "I'll read your papers and maybe we can talk again."

"Thanks for your material. It looks very generous."

"It's not. It's just routine stuff."

"We've got so little it'll help me get a grip on things."

"You asked about informants. Are you interested still?"

"Very interested."

"OK. Let's put the cards on the table face up. I've got a girlfriend. She's a reporter. She's just lost her job. She's been covering the Paris scene—politics, scandals and all that for a couple of years. I'd gladly employ her if she wasn't my girlfriend. She'll keep you far better informed than your Embassy people can do. She knows the inside stuff, not just the gossip." He paused. "If you're interested, I'll set up a meeting."

"How soon?"

"This evening if you want."

"Where? When?"

Autenowski smiled. "Ritz bar at seven, OK?"

"Fine. I'll be there."

If he hadn't already been told that Anne-Marie Loussier was a journalist, Massey would never have guessed. In her late twenties she was both pretty and elegant. As Massey and Autenowski talked, Massey was aware of the girl's gray eyes studying his face, and when she joined in the discussion her voice was as quiet as her views were forthright. Mitterand had come in like a lion but the facts of life and the French were going to turn him into a lamb. She quoted current policies and compared them with the last time they had been attempted by a socialist government. They hadn't worked in the old days, they would be even less effective now.

She knew all the section and department heads of French intelligence personally. Their backgrounds, their responsibilities, and their capabilities. She judged them to be more efficient than they were painted. At least in certain areas.

She met him the next day and he hired her. No contract, no specific duties beyond keeping him informed of the actualities of French policies. He phoned or met her briefly most days and the reports that he was sending back to London were received in silence. But from time to time he was asked for further information on various points and it became obvious that his reports were at least being studied.

She joked with him about his own indifference to Paris outside the fifth *arrondissement* and his lack of knowledge of French people in general. She and Autenowski took him to La Madeleine and the Louvre and were embarrassed and almost amused by his lack of interest. He sat bored for an hour at a nightclub that Autenowski took him to one evening.

It was Anne-Marie who first found something that impressed him—a Polish pâté at Michael Guérard's shop in the place de la Madeleine. In the glamorous shop's cafeteria, Massey came alive as he talked with the Polish waiter.

Morrow from the Embassy brought round the sealed message and handed it to Massey together with the special receipt book. Massey had been about to leave and after he had signed the book he walked back into his rooms.

The message was so cryptic and uninformative that it seemed hardly to warrant the top diplomatic code that had been used. He was to get back to London immediately and contact Chambers. He was not to communicate by any means until he was in London. Just go.

He telephoned Chambers from the immigration office at Gatwick and his call was diverted to the duty officer. He was to go straight to the safe-house in Ebury Street.

An hour later he checked that the small light was on over the bottom bellpush and when he pressed the upper button the door opened immediately. The thin middle-aged woman who everybody knew as Amelia nodded to him without smiling and stood aside to let him into the narrow hallway. Amelia pointed to the stairs and Chambers was waiting for him on the top landing. He looked relieved to see Massey, who followed him into the small sitting-room with its old-fashioned, chintz-covered three-piece suite.

"Have you eaten, Jan?"

"I ate on the plane."

Chambers sighed. "Let's sit down." When they were seated Chambers said, "I apologize for all the mystery but . . ." he waved a hand dismissively ". . . I'd better explain straight away." Chambers looked intently at Massey's face. "Have you got any idea what it's all about?"

"Not the slightest idea. Should I have?"

"No, of course not." He paused before he said quietly, "It's Kuznetsov. He wants to see you. Urgently. I think he's in trouble."

"How did he contact you?"

"A call-box phone call to my home. Late last night."

"How do you know it was K?"

"He used your code-phrase. The emergency one."

"What did he say?"

"As near as I can remember he gave me the code-phrase twice and when I responded he just said, 'Stockholm. Amarantan Hotel. Urgent. Must be my friend.'"

"What makes you think he's in trouble?"

"The crude contact and the fact that he contacted me not you. He probably didn't know where you were and was desperate."

"Is your home traffic still monitored and taped?"

"Yes. I had the voice print cleared. It was K all right."

Massey shrugged. "I'd better get on my way then."

"I've brought you a passport and Swedish kroner and I've had our people book you a room in the passport name at the hotel. We paid a week in advance and they'll hold the room for the week. I had to leave it loose in case you were out of touch in Paris."

"Who's 'we'?"

"I don't understand."

"Who's the 'we' who paid the hotel and booked the room?"

"The travel company."

"Our own?"

"Of course."

"Has there been anything strange out of Berlin in the last few weeks?"

"No. Nothing."

"What about Moscow?"

"The usual stuff about internal tensions in the Politburo but nothing really new."

"And the KGB?"

"No personnel upheavals so far as we know. And nothing at K's level or in his sphere of interest."

"Have you got any anti-KGB operations going on against the KGB that could affect the top boys?"

"Nothing in Europe. Something rather touchy in the Middle East and something in South America—a bit of leftover business from the Falklands' days. But none of them in K's manor."

"How can I contact you from Stockholm?"

"D'you know Marsden?"

"Vaguely."

"You can contact him through the Embassy. Ask for the cultural attaché's office. I'll warn him but I'll use the name on your passport."

"What is it?"

"Mathews. Edward Mathews. Ted Mathews."

"Are there any flights tonight?"

"There's a Scandinavian Air Service flight to Copenhagen and you could go over on the ferry to Malmö and take an internal flight to Stockholm. There's a shuttle that calls at Göteborg and goes on to Stockholm. I can get a car to take you to Gatwick."

"OK. I'll do that. Where's the passport and the cash?"

"It's on the little table. And there's an American Express card in the passport name. Check it all over while I phone Facilities."

* * *

200

Most of the passenger facilities at Kastrup airport were closed, but it was two hours before the first ferry left Copenhagen for Malmö and Massey decided to stay at the airport while he was waiting. He could take an SAS bus into the city and a taxi to the ferry and allow an hour for the journey.

He put a 10 kroner coin into the machine, opened the door, took out the Fanta and the 3 kroner change, and walked over to the almost empty café area. He wondered afterwards if it was the near-medical cleanliness of the airport building that had started his train of thought. Floors, shops, toilets, ticket counters, everything was spotless, and he wondered how Scandinavian governments had managed to instill this orderliness and cleanliness into their people. Or maybe it was the other way around. But whatever its roots the impression it created on foreigners was of orderliness. Not just in outward and physical things, but an orderliness of mind and character. They were sane, stable people, and it showed.

As he sipped the drink and absorbed the atmosphere he started thinking about his own life. There was no orderliness there. For the first time in a long time he looked at his life from the outside and there was nothing about it that he liked. He had no roots. He belonged nowhere. He had no home or relationship to which he could retreat from his work as other men did. His mind went to Chambers and others like him. They kept office hours, they had homes and families. And they used men like him as if they were born to wander rootless from place to place, relying on the initial glamour of the job. The knowing what went on in the world behind the scenes. The follies and greed of well-known people. The machinations of statesmen and governments. The unexpurgated history of the times that would never appear on the record. The feeling of power and superiority. And when all that became no more than routine, there were the incentives of promotion and approval, and the self-assurance that came from experience.

Massey had never been prone to hero-worship but he had respected the experience and knowledge of the top men like Chambers who headed the various sections of SIS. Yet there was something about their meeting at the safe-house that he resented. He had been vaguely conscious of the resentment at the time, but in the brightly lit, clinical atmosphere of Kastrup it seemed suddenly of prime importance. It was, perhaps, the taking for granted that he could be pulled out of Paris at a moment's notice and shuffled off to Stockholm without any thought of whether it was convenient to him. Chambers knew, of course, that he had no wife, no family, so it was rational enough for him to assume that he was mobile and constantly available. But what Massey suddenly resented was that Chambers and the rest of them didn't care that he had no background. Never wondered if he was happy or unhappy with his lot. He was just Massey, a senior man who could be moved around the chessboard to cover any emergency that arose. No problems of wife, children and schools, houses and mortgages. If they thought of him in personal terms it would be as their wild half-Slav, footloose and fancy-free, living the life of Riley and always a blonde in tow. There were some who actually envied him his freedom from emotional ties.

He heard a call on the loudspeaker system asking for an official to go to see the Met officer, and looked at his watch. He gathered up his canvas holdall and walked down to the bus stop. The indicator showed a bus leaving in ten minutes and he bought a ticket and took a seat at the back of the bus. He wondered what Kuznetsov wanted and his mind switched back to his work. He smiled to himself as he thought of what must have been Chambers's embarrassment as he responded to the emergency code-phrase. Using Kuznetsov's nickname, the Moscow Tiger, as a base, Massey had chosen two lines from William Blake's poem as code and response. Kuznetsov's line, "What immortal hand or eye," was mild enough, but the awkward, non-rhyming "Dare frame thy fearful symmetry" would not have come easily to Chambers's lips.

They had booked the room at the Amarantan in Massey's own name but he had not been asked for his passport. At the reception desk he filled in his real name and the cover address that he had been given in London and was given a room in the executive tower. There was a punched-hole coded plastic card instead of a key and he let himself into his room. It was just ten o'clock.

When he had unpacked his holdall he walked down to the hotel foyer and checked the message board. There were no messages for anyone with the initial M. He bought a couple of English paperbacks and went back to his room.

It was almost six o'clock when the telephone rang. No code-word, but he recognized Kuznetsov's voice. He sounded breathless, as if he had been running.

"There's a gas station opposite the Soviet Embassy. Ten o'clock tonight . . . yes?"

"OK. I'll be there."

And Kuznetsov had hung up.

Most of the embassies were clustered together in the same area but the Soviet Embassy was well away from the center of Stockholm. It stood back from the main road, just visible through the big wrought-iron gates, half hidden by tall trees and a grassy mound that had been thrown up on the right-hand side and hid most of the building itself. There were lights on behind the glass façade but none of the social bustle of cars and visitors that usually went on at other embassies.

Massey slowed the rented car, saw the gas station and turned right toward a tall tower block and a block of offices or flats. There were empty parking spaces and he backed the Volvo in carefully and switched off the lights. It was 9:45 P.M.

At 9:55 Massey walked toward the gas station. He didn't know whether Kuznetsov would be arriving by car or on foot but whichever way he came he would be visible from the glass-fronted kiosk at the side of the petrol pumps. The long yellow fascia board above the kiosk carried the Shell logo and the door was half open as he walked inside. He bought a packet of cigarettes and used up time choosing one of the cheap lighters from a display board. As he paid for the goods he saw the gray Mercedes draw up at the pumps. The driver got out. He was alone and it was Kuznetsov. He heard him ask in German for the car to be filled and Massey walked slowly down the side street to stand, lighting a cigarette, beside a large white concrete tub overflowing with geraniums.

A few minutes later the Mercedes drew away from the pumps heading toward him. It stopped in the shadows about twenty yards away. Massey walked slowly toward the car and when the passenger door opened he slid inside.

The Russian spoke very quietly. "I'm in trouble, Massey. I need to talk to you."

"Where can we meet?"

"I'm at a meeting with Swedish officials at the offices of the security services tomorrow. The meeting should finish at lunchtime. I could come to your room at the hotel at about half-past one."

"That's OK. I'll be waiting for you."

Kuznetsov had not looked at Massey while he was speaking, he just stared ahead into the darkness. But Massey could see the tension on the Russian's face.

"It's not that simple, Massey. I may need more than just talking."

"Tell me what you need and you'll get it."

The Russian was silent for several seconds and then he said softly, "I may need to get away. Tomorrow or the next day."

"You mean . . ." Massey hesitated, choosing his words carefully ". . . you mean, leave permanently?"

"Better to say what you were going to say—defect."

"Whatever it is you want, it will be done."

"Is that a promise?"

"Absolutely."

"No matter what my reason is for leaving?"

"No matter what."

"Even murder?"

"No matter what. That's a promise."

"I must go. They'll be timing me."

"I'll be in my room all morning. Waiting for you."

Massey got out of the car and pushed the door to quietly. The Russian backed the car and Massey stood watching as it crossed the main road and waited for the uniformed guard to open the Embassy gates.

It was just after one o'clock when the knock came at his door. Massey jumped up from his chair and opened the door. Kuznetsov's face was pale with the skin drawn tight over his prominent cheekbones, but his eyes looked calmer than they had the previous evening.

There was only one armchair in the room and Massey pointed to it and sat on the edge of the bed.

"How long have you got?"

Kuznetsov shrugged. "Several hours. Whatever it takes."

"What's the problem?"

"There's a lot of problems, Jan."

"Tell me."

"What do you know about Bourget?"

Massey shrugged. "French intelligence. Wild. Not very efficient. He was in Berlin when I was there."

"Do you think he would use blackmail?"

"I'm sure he would."

"He was blackmailing me. Threatening to expose me unless I became a double agent for him."

"He knew nothing about your relationship with us. I swear it. Only Chambers and I know anything."

"I know. He wasn't blackmailing me about that."

"What was he using?"

"D'you remember about a year ago the Moscow Symphony Orchestra visited Paris to give four concerts and one of their players asked the French for asylum?"

"No. I don't remember it."

"The man's name was Abramov. The leader of the orchestra. One of the finest violinists in the Soviet Union."

"Why did he defect?"

"He was a man in his sixties. While they were in Paris he met a very pretty young French girl. He fell in love with her. Wanted to marry her. He spoke to friends. The friends contacted the authorities and eventually he was interviewed by a security officer. The officer happened to be Bourget. The French Foreign Ministry had already decided to give asylum to Abramov and the interview with Bourget was really a formality, for the sake of diplomatic protocol.

"But Bourget isn't a diplomat. He's a lout. And he asked Abramov what he could offer in return for asylum. The Russian protested that he was a musician and knew nothing of politics or state secrets. Bourget told him to go away and think about it overnight and see him again the next day. Abramov was panic-stricken and didn't sleep at all that night.

"When he saw Bourget the next day, he told him that he only knew one KGB officer but he did know something about the man that was compromising. To Abramov's surprise Bourget was delighted with his offering. It seemed that the KGB officer was the son of a couple Abramov had known years ago. They had played music together before Abramov became well known. The compromising information was that the KGB man's mother was a Jewess. This was something that the man had never revealed to the authorities. There were reasons why it was possible for them not to know. Innocent reasons. Stemming from ignorance, not deceit."

"Who was the KGB man?"

Kuznetsov shrugged. "The KGB man was me."

For long moments Massey sat in silence; then he said quietly, "What did Bourget do about it?"

"It took him a long time but eventually he contacted me when I was on a visit to East Berlin. A message hinting that he knew something that could ruin my career, and a place and time to contact him. The message scared me. Not just what was in it but the fact that it was in plain language, no code, in French."

"Was the rendezvous his place in West Berlin?"

Kuznetsov looked surprised. "How did you know?"

"I'll tell you later. What happened when you met him?"

"I met him three times. The first time I told him he was bluffing, that he had no proof of his wild statements. The second time he showed me a notarized statement from Abramov about my parents. The third time was to tell me what he wanted."

"Was it money or information?"

"Money. I think he'd realized that there was not only no chance of me defecting or turning but that I might take steps to have him eliminated. He was happy to settle for money."

"Did you pay him?"

"I told him I'd think about it and pointed out that there were things I knew about him that would interest his superiors in Paris."

"How much did he want?"

"Thirty thousand U.S. dollars." The Russian smiled wryly. "He was kind enough to offer to let me pay it in four equal quarterly payments over a year."

Massey smiled. "Always a gentleman was Bourget." He looked at Kuznetsov. "So what else has happened to worry you?"

The Russian took a deep breath. "Do you remember Kholkov? Alexei Kholkov."

"Yes, I do," Massey said quietly.

"When he was in Berlin he had some kind of deal going with Bourget. They exchanged bits of information. Nothing of any importance. But it was paid for in U.S. dollars both ways. And the payments were far too high for the information supplied. I found out about it a couple of weeks ago and interrogated Kholkov. He didn't admit that he and Bourget were lining one another's pockets but I scared the wits out of him all the same. Bourget's back in Paris now, and the day before I was due to come to this meeting in Stockholm Kholkov phoned me. He didn't say it in so many words but he made clear that Bourget had told him about my Jewish mother." Kuznetsov paused. "I wouldn't trust Kholkov an inch. It's just a question of time before he tries to put the bite on me. He wouldn't be able to resist it. He's greedy, ambitious and ruthless, as you know. To have a top man in his hands would be irresistible. So I want to get out before I'm on the train to some Gulag labor camp."

"Would they really do that, Alexsandr?"

The Russian nodded his head emphatically. "There's never been such anti-Semitic feeling in Moscow for years as there is now. I'd be accused of God knows how many offenses against the State. They would assume that everything was deliberate, right from the start."

"When do you want to come over?"

"Your people will agree?"

"Yes."

"Just like that? No bargaining about what I'll bring with me? Documents? Information and the rest of it?"

"No. No bargaining. So—when do you come over?"

"How long do you need?"

"No time at all. You can leave with me tonight if you want."

"It would be easier tomorrow."

"Why?"

"I've got another meeting with the Swedes in the morning. I can leave there after half an hour and be here by ten thirty."

"Won't the Swedes notify the Embassy that you've disappeared in the middle of a meeting?"

"I'll tell them the truth."

"They might not like that."

Kuznetsov shrugged. "They'll like it better than me asking them for political asylum in Sweden."

"What's the meeting about?"

The Russian smiled. "I've been supplying them with evidence that at least half the suspect submarines bumping along the bottom of the Gulf of Bothnia are NATO not Soviet."

"Did they believe it?"

"Of course. They already suspected it."

"How long can you stay now?"

Kuznetsov looked at his watch. "Another hour."

"Let's have something to eat up here."

"OK."

When Massey had phoned room service, he chatted to the Russian until the food was delivered and served. And then he said quietly, "When you said that Kholkov was ambitious and ruthless you said, 'as you know.' What made you say that?"

For a moment Kuznetsov looked at Massey's face, then he turned to look at the window before slowly turning back to look at Massey again. "I heard about the mistake you made in Berlin."

"What mistake was that?"

"I mean Kholkov's wife. That was an example of his ruthlessness and ambition."

"What did you hear?"

"Very little. It wasn't my area of responsibility. I heard only gossip."

"What was the gossip?"

Kuznetsov shrugged uncomfortably. "I heard that you had been trapped into a liaison with Kholkov's wife and then forced to agree to do something rather than be exposed."

"Nobody suggested that the pressure was applied because I loved his wife and she loved me?"

The Russian shook his head. "No. Nobody could possibly think that."

"Why not? If not that, why the relationship?"

"One assumed it was a matter of sex."

"Why not affection or love?"

"A member of the KGB would not have been allowed such feelings."

"I'm not talking about Kholkov. I'm talking about Anna, his wife."

"What is the difference?"

"Only Kholkov was a member of the KGB."

"That's not what I heard."

"What did you hear?"

"That she too was KGB and a party to the deception."

"I don't believe that."

Kuznetsov sighed. "How could she have gone through the Wall to see you without their agreement? She would be under surveillance just because she was the wife of a middle-seniority KGB man. Wives are not trusted." He smiled. "KGB men themselves are not trusted. It is part of my own responsibilities not to trust even the most senior people." He paused. "I'm sorry to have to tell you this, Jan. But I had to answer your question."

"Would you have told me anyway?"

"No. I assumed that you had already worked it out for yourself."

Kuznetsov looked at his watch. "I must leave, Jan." He stood up. "Will you still help me?"

"Of course. Why shouldn't I?"

"You might have wondered if, when they were sounding me out in London, that I might mention that event."

"Will you?"

"Of course not. It isn't important. And it did no harm to anyone but you." He sighed. "Was it real on your side? Did you love her?"

Massey nodded and said softly, "Yes, I loved her. I still do." He shrugged. "I'll make all the arrangements tonight for tomorrow. I'll wait for you and we'll leave straight away." He smiled. "There'll be no problems."

Thirty-Two

When Massey phoned Chambers, guardedly describing the situation, Chambers sounded incredulous.

"You mean it's all done and decided?"

"Yes."

"For tomorrow?"

"Yes."

"I can hardly believe it."

"It's a fact."

"What's he offering?"

"Nothing."

"You mean he won't cooperate?"

"He didn't say so. We didn't discuss it. I'm sure he'll help where he can."

"And there's no alternative?"

"Sure there is."

"What is it?"

"The CIA would be delighted to have him, I'm sure."

There was a long pause at Chambers's end and then he said, "Anything else?"

"No. I guess we'll be back in a couple of days."

"You'd better take him to the place at Ashford. You know where I mean?"

"Yes. I'll do that and phone you when we get there. Maybe you could warn them."

"Yes. I'll do that."

When Massey hung up he wasn't sure whether he was angry or amused. Angry that the defection of a top man in the KGB's hierarchy should be treated as if it needed justification. And amused at Chambers's obvious pique that the issue had not been left for him to decide.

His mind went over the clothes that Kuznetsov had been wearing. A dark gray two-piece suit, Moscow cut and poor cloth, a white shirt and a black tie. Massey took a taxi to Kungsgatan and bought a cotton, zip-up, showerproof jacket and a pair of jeans. He bought a plastic airline holdall and put in two cotton shirts, a brush and comb, a packet of Bic razors and a tube of shaving cream. Back at the hotel he had asked for a wake-up call at seven o'clock.

He had breakfast in his room and had told the desk that he would be checking out mid-morning and to send up his bill. He checked the items and used his American Express card to pay. After that it was just waiting. The offices of the Swedish security services were at Polhelmsgatan and it wouldn't take Kuznetsov more than a five- or six-minute walk to get to the hotel. He was tempted to take the two bags and wait for him in the foyer but he daren't be away from the phone in case there was some change in Kuznetsov's movements.

And as he sat there waiting, he could feel his heartbeat increasing as the thoughts he had been avoiding seeped back into his mind. He took several deep breaths to calm himself. What Kuznetsov had said about Anna made logical, realistic sense. If she was KGB and part of a set-up with Kholkov, it would explain a lot of things that seemed odd in retrospect. The convenient absences by Kholkov. The coincidence of meeting her in the KO store. And other more intangible things. But he still didn't believe it. A girl can fake sexual pleasure but she can't fake love and loving words.

It reminded him of times when he had had to break the news of an agent's death to his wife. So many of them said the same thing. They accepted that he was dead, but they wished that they could see him just once more. Just two minutes. Just time enough to say how much they loved him. He accepted that he wouldn't ever see Anna again but he would gladly give several years of his life, and everything he possessed, just to be able to ask her if it had been real or only a KGB exercise.

The knock came on his door just before ten o'clock. He made the Russian change into the jacket and jeans as he stuffed his suit into the holdall. Fifteen minutes later they were in a taxi to Arlander. Massey bought two tickets for the domestic SAS flight to Malmö which was already boarding at gate 21. Any Russians looking for Kuznetsov would concentrate on flights from Stockholm to London and the U.S.A. Their resources would be limited and it was highly unlikely that they would check flights from Copenhagen or Helsinki.

At Malmö they had taken a taxi from the airport to the ferry ticket office and an hour and a half later they were in a taxi on their way to Kastrup. Massey booked them on to the Amsterdam plane but they had missed the London connection. After a two-hour wait at Schiphol they landed at Gatwick just before six o'clock local time. There had been no problems at Immigration. Massey had used his own passport, and Kuznetsov the one in the name of Mathews.

As they walked through the green customs section Massey was being paged to go to Airport Information. At the information counter a girl gave him an envelope. His name was typed and it had URGENT in capitals below his name. The note inside told him to go to the Spa Hotel in Tunbridge Wells where a suite for them both had been booked in his own name.

Just over an hour later the taxi dropped them at the hotel entrance. Massey signed in for both of them and they were shown to their suite. He dialed Century House and the duty officer told him that Chambers would be down to see them the next morning at about ten o'clock.

They ate together in the restaurant, took a brief walk in the parklike grounds and then went up to the sitting-room of their suite.

"What was Chambers's reaction?"

"Surprised, of course. I couldn't go into any detail with him on an insecure phone, of course." Massey smiled. "He'll be used to the idea by the time he gets here tomorrow."

"I have to make quite clear to him my position."

"What, in particular?"

"Your people have to understand that I am not a defector. I'm a refugee."

"In terms of your cooperation with them, what is the difference?"

"All the difference in the world. I have no intention of committing treason. No intention of damaging my countrymen."

Massey raised his eyebrows. "Your reason for coming here was that your countrymen might send you to a labor camp because your mother was Jewish."

"The men who would do that are not Russians. They're Bolsheviks. I'm a Russian. I have no wish to die to please such men."

"Was it that certain, do you think?"

"There were four pages in *Krasnaya Zvezda* last month, the official Red Army newspaper. The article was as anti-Semitic as anything the Nazis ever wrote. It suggested that Jews were not only not Russian and non-Soviets but that no Jews should be allowed in any position of authority or decision. It went on to point out how skillful Jews were in hiding their Jewish backgrounds and that it should be the task of a special committee to uncover them, remove them from their posts, and, if necessary, punish them." Kuznetsov sighed deeply. "That piece was a warning. It wouldn't have been printed if it wasn't investigated by the Kremlin."

Massey smiled. "It didn't mention Marx or Trotsky I suppose?"

"It's not a joke, Jan, when you are on the receiving end."

"Do you have any living relatives, Aleksandr?"

"None, thank God. There were times when I wished that I had. But now I am glad."

"It seems a long time ago that we met, that night at the Festival Hall."

"It is a long time." Kuznetsov paused. "I'm sorry I had to tell you about the girl."

"It was just gossip, Aleksandr. Just gossip. One should never believe gossip."

"How could you have imagined that she would not be under surveillance?"

"I'm sure she wasn't. I was very careful."

"When you walk into a trap it makes no difference how careful you are. It's all fixed and arranged before your foot crosses the line."

"You believe Anna was KGB?"

"I do."

"Have you any evidence that she was? Did the people who gossiped say that she was?"

"No. No evidence. Like everybody else I took it for granted that she was KGB."

"Did you hear what they asked me to do?"

"You helped exchange some radio traffic disks."

"Why did they want them changed?"

"We were launching a booster system MHV. It was just possible that your radio surveillance that day could pick it up."

"What's an MHV?"

"A miniature homing vehicle. An anti-satellite missile. It's the main area of space friction between the Americans and the U.S.S.R. One MHV costs about four million U.S. dollars. You have to get your missile up twenty-two thousand miles to hit a satellite parked in its geosynchronous orbit. But if you hit it, then you've wiped out most of your enemy's military control system."

"Was it a successful launch?"

"No. It didn't get beyond one thousand miles."

"So exchanging the disks was of no real value."

"It had some value. It kept the West from knowing that we had not succeeded. Its failure allows the Soviet negotiators to claim that the Americans are the sole aggressors in that particular high-technology area. Andropov had instructed our people to make every effort to get the

Americans to agree to ban the use of anti-satellite weapons." Kuznetsov shrugged. "You carry more weight if you say you come to the negotiating table with clean hands. If you come having failed, and your opponents know that, you might as well have stayed in Moscow."

"I expect the Americans have a good idea of what the Soviets are up to."

Kuznetsov shrugged. "Having a good idea of what they're doing cuts no ice in Geneva or the UN or on the TV screens. Having proof of an attempt that failed is something else." He paused. "The Americans are working on what's called an EMP—an electromagnetic pulse that would destroy all satellites for thousands of miles."

"They're a mad lot—both of them."

"We're part of it, Jan."

"What do you want to do now you're here?"

"Will there be a debriefing?"

"I should imagine so."

"Will it be you?"

"I've no idea. I'm in Paris now."

Kuznetsov looked quickly at Massey's face, frowning as he said, "How long have you been there?"

"A few months."

Kuznetsov went on staring at Massey's face. He opened his mouth to speak, then closed it and stood up, walking toward the window. He stood there, drawing aside the curtains to look outside.

"What time did you say Chambers was coming tomorrow?"

"Ten."

"What sort of man is he?"

"He's very experienced. Well educated. Cool and calm. A desk man. Quiet spoken. Professionally charming and diplomatic. Privately rather withdrawn and reserved. Very Brit. And not given to displays of emotion." He paused. "Probably because there isn't much emotion to display."

"Is he a friend of yours?"

"He's my boss."

"Yes. I know. But does he like you? Is he sympathetic toward you?"

"I've no idea. I think he values my experience and is satisfied with my work. More than that, I don't know." Massey stood up. "He won't be unreasonable with you, Alex, you can be sure of that." He looked at his watch. "I'm going to turn in."

"Does Chambers speak Russian?"

"I'm afraid not. He's not a linguist."

Chambers had talked with Massey alone after having a few polite words with Kuznetsov. Chambers had seemed ill at ease with the Russian. SIS was used to handling the problems of defectors, but the defections were normally expected and arranged, and it seemed as if the sudden appearance of Kuznetsov was an embarrassment. He was undoubtedly the most important defector they had ever had but Chambers's approach was so low-key that Massey wondered what was behind it. Maybe it was just because Chambers spoke no Russian and Kuznetsov's English was very limited.

"Did he give any indication of how he'll cooperate, Jan?"

Massey shrugged. "He made clear that he considered himself a refugee, not a defector."

"That doesn't sound too promising."

"He'll probably prove more amenable when he's settled down."

"When are you planning to get back to Paris?"

"Do you want me for debriefing Kuznetsov?"

Chambers hesitated. "I think not, Jan. I think somebody neutral would be better. Someone who's less involved. D'you agree?"

Massey shrugged. "I don't know. It's up to you. You can always involve me later on if it doesn't work out."

"I hope he's not going to be a problem."

"No reason why he should be. Is there?"

Chambers drew a slow deep breath. "Seems to be taking rather a lot for granted."

"We gave him our word way back. He's just taking for granted that we meant it."

"No sign of gratitude that I've detected so far."

"Why should there be? He's given us far more than we could have hoped for. He's just cashing in on our IOU."

Chambers nodded, but without conviction. "Maybe. We'll see." He stood up. "I'll take him back with me."

Thirty-Three

After months of interrogation it had been decided that Arthur Johnson should be removed from Wormwood Scrubs and taken to a special safe-house in the Midlands. Arthur Johnson had become a problem. He had not been charged with the murder of his common-law wife although he had eventually confessed to killing her. And apart from his own admissions, which were extremely vague, they had no evidence to charge him with offenses against national security that would be acceptable by a court. He himself was not aware of what he had passed to the Russians apart from gossip and a few minor documents. The items that he had photographed and the tapes that he had passed to them were unidentifiable.

What made things more difficult was that if he was charged with the murder of Heidi Fischer his lawyers would inevitably, and justifiably, drag in the security aspects.

Those concerned were thankful that he had no relations or friends who could start quoting habeas corpus and ask by what law he was being detained without being charged with any offense, and without at least being brought in front of a magistrate.

Inspector Hipwell of Special Branch visited him once a week at the special safe-house on Cannock Chase. Like many tenacious interrogators

215

he was loath to give up until he had at least discovered what had been passed to the KGB. Johnson's motives had easily been established but he was puzzled about why they had pushed Johnson back into West Berlin. Their whole relationship with Johnson seemed tatty and disorganized and that wasn't typical of the KGB. It could have been that they were making the best of a bad job, taking what was offered in the hope that it would be useful. And almost anything had some use. But why push him back through the Wall and risk his being picked up?

Hipwell had a sneaking sympathy for Johnson. His upbringing and his lack of education had made him what he was, and his tawdry ambitions and lifestyle were part of the pathetic picture. It was after one of their rather inconclusive chats that Johnson had hinted that he would like a night with a girl. Hipwell had made arrangements with the staff that a girl should be provided. Johnson seemed to be becoming more distant and withdrawn as the weeks went by and Hipwell thought that maybe a session with a girl would help. Johnson seemed not only to be withdrawn but incapable of recalling things that had happened only in the last few months. He was never bright or even alert, but what had been merely a doltish response to questions became an inability even to understand the questions. Johnson and his fate were already a problem and if he became antagonistic it would make things worse. Nobody quite knew what to do with their moronic captive.

The girl who was provided had, oddly enough, been brought from Johnson's old haunts in Handsworth, Birmingham. Nobody had realized the connection with his past and it played no part in the final outcome. The girl's reaction would have been the same no matter where she came from.

The girl was in her mid-twenties and attractive enough for the guard to wonder if she might be willing to engage in a little extra-curricular activity after Johnson was through. But it was not to be. She was only in Johnson's room for five or six minutes before she rushed out angrily.

"You bastards," she shouted. "What do you think I am? Where's the bloody driver? I'm off."

"What's the matter, honey. What is it?"

"Don't you fuckin' honey me, you creep. You know what the matter is."

The guard's surprise was just enough to convince her when he said, "Honest, kid, I don't know what you're on about."

"Have you seen him? Have you seen his crotch?"

"Of course I haven't. Why should I?"

"He's got syph up to his eyeballs. Don't tell me you didn't know."

"Are you sure? Maybe it's a rash or something. Been scratching it."

"For Christ's sake! You must be off your bloody head. Anyway it's your worry, mate. I'm off."

The duty guard phoned Hipwell at his home.

The Special Branch man thought long and hard before he took what he later referred to as appropriate action.

Appropriate action meant accompanying an Army doctor to the safe-house and waiting for his diagnosis in the sitting-room. It was an hour before the doctor came back to him.

"Who is he, Mr. Hipwell?"

"He's . . ." Hipwell shrugged ". . . let's say he's a detainee. Sort of awaiting Her Majesty's pleasure as they call it."

"Well, he's not got long to wait, and Her Majesty's not going to get much pleasure from him. Why didn't anybody notice it before?"

"I don't know. He never complained. It *is* syph, is it?"

"Too bloody true. *Dementia paralytica*. I wouldn't give him more than two months at the outside."

"No cure?"

"No. The tissues are destroyed. I can ease the pain but he isn't complaining of pain. He's past it. He's only half in this world anyway."

"You're sure he's not curable?"

"If I could cure that poor bastard I could be a millionaire by Christmas."

"And he's only got another couple of months left?"

"If he's lucky. Could be less. He's beyond anything that medicine can do. If he was a dog I'd have him put down."

Hipwell had had a long think about the situation. He didn't want to stick his neck out but there was a solution there to all their problems. There was a device in the intelligence services called talking in parables. It consisted of talking about hypothetical situations. What would we do "if"? It was recognized that the situation being described was real rather than imaginary and it allowed questions to be asked and answers given that were official but to all intents and purposes had never been asked or answered.

The inspector talked in parables to Chambers, who suggested that in the circumstances that the Special Branch officer described perhaps no action at all would be best for all concerned. But added a codicil that in those circumstances the doctor who signed the death certificate should be a member of the organization.

Obstinate and anti-Establishment to the last, Arthur Johnson had survived for three months and two days before he finally expired. And Arthur Johnson, neglected child, eager youth, ineffectual protester against fate, mild fornicator, traitor and honorary lieutenant in the KGB, was buried, unmourned by anyone, in Witton cemetery in Birmingham. Not far from where he was born. The only witness to the event was Inspector Hipwell, who rationalized what was really quite a soft heart as merely being the official closing of a file.

* * *

217

Massy settled back into his Paris routine, sending back far more information to London than they had received for years, getting in return unofficial praise and thanks from officers on the French desk, but only silence from Chambers.

He enjoyed his meetings with both Autenowski and Anne-Marie, and after that first visit to Michael Guérard's shop and cafeteria they went two or three times a week. Either the three of them or just him and the French girl.

That day they were lunching alone and discussing a report she had done for him on the DGSE's operations in French territories overseas. He was stirring his coffee when she spoke. She was looking over his shoulder.

She said softly, "I think you've made a hit, Jan. There's a very pretty lady been looking at the back of your head for the last five minutes as if you were Yves Montand or Robert Redford."

Massey smiled. "I'm flattered. If you're not kidding, that is."

"I'm not, my friend. Have a look. She's just got up from her table and she's heading for the door."

Massey turned, reluctantly, to look and for a moment he seemed paralyzed. Then he stood up clumsily, knocking the table so that the crockery rattled.

Anne-Marie saw his face, the perspiration on his forehead, and heard the quick shallow breathing.

"What is it, Jan? What's the matter?"

He looked at her for a moment, unseeing; then he turned and threaded his way through the tables to the door. She saw him looking both ways outside in the street. Hesitating, then breaking into a run as he headed toward the boulevard des Capucines.

He saw her, in the black silk summer coat, walking slowly down the street. Many times he had walked behind girls who looked like her from the back but this time it *was* her. For a moment their eyes had met in the cafeteria as she stood at the door.

She looked over her shoulder and he shouted her name. He saw her looking, then her eyes closed for a moment as she stopped.

Then their arms were round each other, her head on his shoulder, and for long moments neither of them spoke. Then she drew back her head and looked up at his face.

"I used to dream about this, Jan. Night after night. But it wasn't in Paris."

"What are you doing here?"

She shrugged. "He's at a meeting at the Embassy. Tomorrow's my last day."

"Are you being followed?"

"Me? No. They're not interested in small fry like me."

"I've got a room. Can we go there and talk?"

For a moment she hesitated and then said softly, "Of course."

In the taxi they didn't speak but her hand reached out. She was wearing a glove but he could feel the warmth of her hand in his. He told the driver to drop them at the church and he felt his composure returning as he paid the fare and waited for the change. She slid her arm in his and they walked up the hill. A few minutes later as she looked around his room she was immediately aware of its bleakness. It had an air of human despair and loneliness. She had already noticed the tension in his eyes and around his mouth. They stood in the middle of the room looking at each other's faces, each searching for clues or answers to their unspoken questions. Her hands on his shoulders, his arms around her. It was Anna who spoke first.

"I've missed you so much, Jan." Her eyes searched his face. "Tell me what happened."

For a moment or so he was silent, then he said quietly, "Let's sit on the bed."

As he settled down beside her she reached out for his hand. As she laced her fingers through his he said, "Tell me what you think happened."

"Nothing happened. I just never saw you again. I got no answer to my messages." She shrugged. "Just nothing."

"How did you send the messages?"

"Like you said, through the bookshop."

"Where were you living in that time?"

"In the first week I was at the house. I sent one message in that week. Then I had to leave in a hurry to go to Moscow. They said my father was ill."

"Was he ill when you got there?"

"They told me he was in an isolation ward. That he had an infectious fever but he would be OK."

"How long before you saw him?"

"Nearly a month."

"Had he been ill?"

"Yes. He didn't know what it was but he had had a terrible fever."

"Then what?"

"I stayed with him for another ten days or so, then I went back to East Berlin. They had found us a new house because Alexei had been promoted. I sent two more messages to say I was back and giving the new address but there was no reply. About two weeks later Alexei was moved to Moscow and then to Budapest. That's where we are now."

Massey looked at her face. "When you married Kholkov did they make any attempt to recruit you into the KGB?"

"No. Never. I had the usual lecture about supporting my husband but all new wives get that." She paused. "What made you ask that?"

As coherently and carefully as he could, Massy told her what had happened. It was almost dark in the room as he finished, but he could see the pale face and the dark eyes as she looked back at him.

"Did you ever think I was part of it, Jan?"

"No, never."

"I'm glad in a way that I didn't know. It would have driven me mad. It must have been terrible for you."

"What shall we do?"

For a moment she was silent and then she said, "Do you still love me?"

"Of course I do. I've never stopped loving you. What about you?"

She smiled wanly. "You don't need to ask, do you?"

"So what do we do?"

She shrugged and said quietly, "We should do what we ought to have done in Berlin."

"What's that?"

"D'you want me to stay, now, this minute?"

"I didn't dare ask you so soon. The answer is yes. But what about you—your life with Kholkov, Moscow and your father?"

"I always accepted the break with my father. I never owed Kholkov anything. I will sacrifice the pleasure I would have in telling him what I think of what he's done. To me and to you."

"Don't think about him, my love. To him it's just part of his work. They don't have scruples about what they do to people."

"Do you know what I wish this moment?"

"No. Tell me."

"I wish I was twenty years older and we were sitting here remembering the twenty years we had had together. I can't wait to get on with my life with you."

"Have you got your passport with you?"

"Yes, it's in my handbag."

"Let me see it."

Massey looked at it page by page. There was no indication that she was connected with any Soviet organization and there was a year of validity still left.

"Are you hungry?"

"No. I had a snack at the cafeteria."

"I'll pack a bag and we'll go tonight. Where's Kholkov staying?"

"They've got an apartment near the place Vendôme."

"Has it got a telephone number?"

"Yes."

"OK. I'll pack a few things."

"Where are we going?"

"We're going to do the grand tour, honey."

She laughed. "I've been waiting for that."

"For what?"

"For you to call me honey again. I'm so happy, Jan. So happy."

"So am I."

"Where are we going?"

"To Amsterdam, then Copenhagen. And from there to Sweden. When I've found us somewhere in Sweden I'll have to do some work on getting documents for you. Then we'll go to England and get married."

"Will it be legal?"

"Not entirely, but enough for us. Nobody will know anyway. You'll have a different name on the passport and after that it will be my name."

Anna had nothing but the contents of her handbag and the clothes she was wearing. Massey had little more. Only enough to fill his canvas holdall. He left one suit hanging in the wardrobe.

They took a taxi to de Gaulle and there was less than a half-hour wait for the KLM flight to Amsterdam. The plane was half empty and there was no problem about getting seats.

At Amsterdam there was a two-hour wait before a flight to Copenhagen. As they sat in the restaurant Massey asked her to write down Kholkov's Paris number. When she passed him the paper he looked at her face. "You said 'they've' got an apartment near the place Vendôme. Who's 'they'?"

"Another man."

"KGB?"

"No."

"Who is he?"

"His name is Antonov. He's just a young man. About twenty years old."

"What's he doing there?"

For a moment she hesitated, then she said, "He's Alexei's boyfriend. Why do you want the number?"

"I'm going to phone him."

"But why? He could try and have the call traced."

"He might think you're missing for some other reason and notify the police. I want him to know you're with me and if he raises a hue and cry the Soviet Embassy won't like it. He won't be able to trace the call. It wouldn't matter if he did. That's why we're not going a direct route to anywhere." He stood up. "Stay here, order some more coffee and I'll be back in five or ten minutes."

In the kiosk he checked the dialing code for France and put a small pile of guilders on top of the box. Slowly and carefully he dialed the codes and the number. It rang several times before the phone was picked up.

"Who are you calling?"

He recognized Kholkov's voice.

"Is that Alexei Kholkov?"

"Who is that speaking?"

"Massey. Jan Massey."

There were several seconds of silence and then the Russian said, "I wondered if it was you. It's time she was back."

"Have you told the Embassy that she's missing?"

"Missing? What do you mean?"

"She's with me, Kholkov. And she won't be coming back."

"You mean—"

"I mean she's left you for good. If you make a nuisance of yourself there's going to be a lot of scandal for the Embassy. And for Moscow too. Even comrade Antonov won't like it."

There was a long silence and then the phone was hung up at the other end.

It was past midnight when they landed at Kastrup and the tourist desk was closed. The taxi driver had taken them to a small hotel in one of the small streets near the Tivoli. They weren't asked for passports and he signed them in as Mr. and Mrs. Mortimer.

There were no problems in getting seats on the mid-morning ferry from Copenhagen to Malmö and no passport check at either end.

The Royal Hotel in Malmö was in walking distance of the ferry terminal and Massey booked a small suite with a living-room on the fifth floor.

After a bath they took a meal in their suite and as Anna poured out their coffee from a Thermos she said, "What are we going to do, Jan? Have you decided?"

"We'll rent some rooms here in Malmö for a few weeks." He looked at her face. "I'm sorry it's so messy but I've got to cover our tracks as well as finding us a way to live. And I'll have to go to Berlin. It's the only place where I can get you the documents you need."

"What do I need?"

"A passport. A forged passport won't be too difficult but we shall need a birth certificate for the marriage registrar, so the passport has to be in that name." He smiled. "I'll sort it out, don't worry."

"Will you have to explain why you left Paris so suddenly?"

"No. I doubt if London will notice that I'm away."

"Do you think Alexei will do anything?"

"I'm sure he won't. Nothing publicly anyway."

"Will it be illegal for us to marry?"

"Technically, yes. But in normal circumstances you could have divorced him on the grounds that he's a homosexual. Nobody has an interest in exposing us."

"What about your people—the men in London?"

"As far as they are concerned you'll be British and of no interest to them. I shan't notify them anyway."

"But my bad English?"

He smiled. "It's not that bad and people will love the accent." He stood up, reaching out for her hand. "Let's go and look for our rooms."

They moved into the furnished apartment over one of the shops in Södergatan the next day. It was bright and spotlessly clean with well-made wooden furnishings and it was the first bright omen in their disjointed and unplanned flight from Paris.

As they ate their first meal in the apartment that night, Massey suddenly felt relieved. The hurried departure, the disjointed journey had depressed him. He was worried about what they were doing. Not about its rightness, but the way they had moved without a plan, improvising as they went along. His other concern was about the consequences of what they were doing. Despite what he had said to Anna and Kholkov, he knew that he was vulnerable now. He could see nothing rational that could be done against him, but he knew that he had made them both hostages to fate. He wasn't sure what fate he had in mind. It was no more than an all-pervading uneasiness. All his experience told him that such spur of the moment adventures were generally doomed to failure. It was time to do some thinking and planning but somehow his mind was confused. Anna seemed to be taking it all in her stride but he was apprehensive. He'd reacted in exactly the same way as when he'd gone into East Berlin to find out what had happened to her. Not the cool experienced intelligence officer, just the traditional bull in a china shop. All brawn and no brain.

But the neat white rooms lifted his spirits, and he sat down after they had eaten, with a pad and pencil and started listing the things he had to do.

Thirty-Four

Chambers was disturbed enough to fly to Hong Kong himself to interview Max Cohen, who was now second in command of the GCHQ operations in that area. Cohen was resentful of his transfer from Berlin and his attitude to Chambers was guarded to the point of open hostility. He was no longer under any control from SIS and had no intention of becoming involved with them in any way.

As they sat on the verandah of the government guest house that Chambers was using, Cohen closed his eyes as Chambers talked.

"You don't remember Arthur Johnson by any chance? Signalman Johnson?"

"No. I don't. And I don't remember the name of the guy who ran the cafeteria."

"It's a serious matter, Max. He not only murdered his wife but he was working for the Russians for most of the time that you were in charge of the operation."

"At no time was I responsible for any security aspects of the unit. That was your people's responsibility, not mine."

Cohen's voice rose ominously as he spoke and Chambers tried another tack.

"I'm not trying to establish responsibility, Max. I'm just trying to find out what actually happened." He paused. "We need to know if this is one isolated incident or just the tip of the iceberg."

"I'm not stopping you, Chambers. You managed to cast some of the blame onto me in Berlin and you sure ain't going to do that again."

"Johnson said that he got the substitute disk from inside the jacket of a book in the library. Could you suggest how it might have got there?"

"How the hell should I know?" Cohen banged down his glass and swore as the drink spilt over the back of his hand. He looked at Chambers as he dried his hand. "Why don't you ask Jan Massey? He was responsible for security—not me. I ran the electronic surveillance operation. I didn't run agents into East Berlin. I didn't evaluate the signals traffic—and I didn't put the books on the shelves in that fucking library!" Cohen emphasized his words, his finger jabbing in Chambers's direction. "Don't try and get the buck off your desk and stick it on mine. Don't try and involve me or GCHQ. It's your worry, not ours."

Chambers shook his head in mock despair. "Are you telling me, Max Cohen, that the Russians can penetrate a top security installation where you work and you don't give a damn?"

"What you've just said is typical of what's wrong, Chambers. They're just weasel words. Have you stopped beating your wife? If you want to ask me straightforward questions, ask me. But don't, repeat don't, ask me if I know who did it. If I knew, he'd have been in the nick a long time ago."

"OK, Max. Just let me ask for your help. Just your opinion. If the Russians had got into the operation, why all the palaver with putting the disk in the book? Why didn't they just do a straight swap in the disk file?"

"Maybe whoever they used couldn't get into the main operation. Maybe—I don't know—why didn't they get Johnson to do a straight swap at the disk-file shelves? Maybe they didn't trust Johnson. There's a dozen possibilities."

"Who could get into the library and put the disk there, or the book and the disk, but not carry on and do the whole exchange?"

"Anybody who could get as far as the library could go the rest of the way. The real tight security was getting past the inner door."

"Why two people to carry out such a simple operation?"

"There's one explanation. But you won't like it."

"Try me."

"All signals people, every one of them except me, go through the X-ray machine and at random times during the day there's a full strip search. None of that applied to SIS people. Or me."

"What reason would SIS people have for going into the signals installation?"

"None. And they never did go in. They got their paperwork by individual dispatch clerks and the clerks were all my people. Checked in and out every time. I don't think I've ever seen an SIS type in my area, ever. Ask Massey if he agrees."

Chambers looked out toward the bay and then back at Cohen. "Does that mean Massey was in your area sometimes?"

"Yes, of course. We had frequent meetings in my office." Then he looked quickly at Chambers's face and said softly, "Whoever it is, it isn't Jan Massey."

"Why not, Max? Tell me why not."

"For a dozen reasons. First of all, he knows more than anybody about what the Soviets are up to. There's no persuasion and no bribe they could offer Massey that would turn him. He knows the bastards too well."

"You couldn't have a better cover than what you've just described."

Cohen laughed. "For God's sake. OK, let's pursue that scenario. What the hell do they offer him to make him go over? It's going to need to be something fantastic. So let's say they offer him a million dollars in a deposit box in Basel. Yes? And then we come to what they want him to do. Kidnap Sir Peter? Microdots of the most confidential files in Berlin or Century House?" Cohen smiled. "No. They want him to put a floppy disk inside a book in the reading library. A floppy disk that covers all the usual traffic you get on a couple of routine frequencies. So we are brought to our knees by not realizing that the leave schedule for some clapped-out Red Army unit is incorrect. Or that they ain't got any pull-throughs for their Kalashnikovs. No way, Chambers. Whoever it is, it's not our friend. I'd bet my last dollar on that."

Chambers nodded amiably. "Can I take you for a meal, Max?"

"I've got somebody here from Cheltenham. I've got to look after him this evening."

"Top brass?"

"No. A cryppie." Smiling at Chambers's confusion. "A code-breaker."

"What kind of chap goes in for that sort of stuff?"

"Oh, they come in all shapes and sizes. This one's tame enough. He's just comparing notes with his opposite number over here. The routine's the same but pulling in the Chinese dialects isn't as easy as pulling in the Russian stuff. There's God knows how many dialects."

"How wide do you cover?"

"The whole area. We just suck in everything like a giant vacuum cleaner. Private stuff, commercial and official. After that we've got to chew it and spit it out. Phones, radio, telegraphy—the lot."

"How do you get on with the SIS people here?"

"OK. We don't see much of them." He smiled. "What happened to me was a lesson to all of us."

"I'm sorry about that, Max. It was unfair in retrospect."

"It was unfair to Massey too, so I suppose honor was served all round."

"All the same—it was unfortunate."

Max Cohen had not been entirely truthful about his responsibilities for entertaining the man from Cheltenham. The man from GCHQ was neither on Cohen's level nor did he have a personality that would make him good company for an evening out. He looked a bit of a stick-in-the-mud, and Cohen had too many of those in his working life to want them in his free time too.

So Tony Logan, one of Cohen's juniors, prepared himself for a dull evening with his colleague from Cheltenham. As they stood on the hotel steps he said, "What d'you fancy, Eric, beans on toast or the bright lights?"

"What do you prefer yourself?"

Logan laughed. "It's on the old firm tonight. How about a bit of fun?"

"It's your town, Tony. You lead the way."

The garish neon lights of Wanchai winked their various invitations to the strolling tourists but the entrance to the club was discreet, and the sign that said Lola's Club was bathed in a soft pink glow.

The food had been well prepared and Eric Mayhew had gradually got used to having his glass refilled regularly by a topless bar-girl. When they got to the coffee stage Logan leaned forward across the table and said quietly, "You can screw any of the girls, you know."

Mayhew shrugged. "You carry on. I'll wait for you. No problem. I can listen to the music."

"Can't afford it on my money, old chap. Wish I could."

"Are they very expensive?"

"No, about twenty quid. It's the end of the month though—the old till's a bit empty."

Mayhew smiled. "Let me finance you. I've hardly spent any of my overseas allowance. And you've been very helpful the last couple of days."

Logan laughed. "You're a real sport, Eric. How about we take a couple of them upstairs." He winked. "We could swap at half-time."

Mayhew smiled and passed a bundle of HK dollars under the table to Logan, who slid them into his pocket.

"I'll sit this one out, Tony. Maybe I'll join you tomorrow."

"You sure?"

"Of course I am. I'll wait for you. No hurry."

Logan disappeared with one of the girls and he was obviously a regular: a couple of other girls had stood laughing with him trying to persuade him to take them too.

Fifteen minutes later, Mayhew had found the pay phone near the entrance and with his diary open at the page for Christmas week he dialed the number written there, reversing the digits and adding a zero at the end. When the call was answered, he listened carefully and then hung up without speaking.

Half an hour later Tony Logan joined him at the table, smiling as he poured himself a coffee.

Mayhew smiled. "Everything OK, Tony?"

"Fantastic, old boy. She's really something, that kid."

"What's Max Cohen like, Tony?"

"Very efficient. Shit hot."

"I mean, as a man. Is he a family man?"

"No. He's a Jew. All his folk were put in the ovens in one of those Nazi camps. Never married."

"Girlfriends?"

"No steady, but he screws on the side. I know that."

"How do you know?"

"I've screwed his favorite. A Vietnamese girl. A real goer. Uses this place at weekends."

"They're very pretty I understand, the Vietnamese girls?"

"You'd go for May Lai."

"Who's in charge of your maintenance? Is it a chap named Wright?"

"No. I don't know a Wright. Our chap's Helliwell. Came to us from NCR."

"Is he good?"

Logan shrugged. "So-so. Nobody likes him . . ." he smiled ". . . maybe because he leans on us. Who knows."

"A family man?"

"Yes, but the family's in the U.K. Two kids at private schools. Keeps to himself. I'd guess he's stretched pretty tight for cash."

"Must be lonely out here if you're a family man."

"Yeah, I guess so. Most people make the best of it."

"Do you operate the key changes on the coding machines yourself?"

"Yes. Even when I'm on forty-eight-hour leave I come in at seven in the morning and turn the key."

"How long will you be serving here?"

"Another three years, I guess."

"I think I ought to be getting back to the hotel, Tony. I'm a bit tired and we've got a long day tomorrow."

"Fine. Let's get the cloakroom girl to call us a taxi."

Eric Mayhew had absentmindedly slipped the internal telephone directory from Logan's desk into his case along with his own papers when he was clearing up to go back to his hotel after the meeting.

That evening, he walked a hundred yards up the hill to the telephone kiosk. On the wooden frame behind the kiosk he saw the blue chalk mark. Just a short vertical stroke about four inches long. Early the next morning he took the train to Sha Tin and a few yards from the station the man was waiting. He was smoking a pipe like they had said and he took the packet from Mayhew without turning his head and without speaking.

Mayhew caught the next train back to Hong Kong Central and was at the airport two hours later. He phoned Jenny the next morning from Heathrow and was back home late that afternoon. She was delighted with the embroidered silk blouse that he had brought back for her.

Thirty-Five

Before SIS had moved from its old headquarters at Broadway House, the pubs in the vicinity could have provided a useful order of battle for the KGB. Top men were more likely to be seen at some Whitehall club or St. Ermin's Hotel. But lesser lights frequented the local pubs at lunchtimes and, on occasion, in mid-evening when there was a crisis.

One of the most popular was the Ironmonger's Arms where the brewers had shrewdly put in a retired ex-SIS man as its landlord. Jack McAvoy had started his working life as a Shanghai policeman. When he was exposed as the owner of three brothels and their twenty-five inmates he had been discreetly posted back to England where, at one of SIS's stately mansions on the Welsh borders, he taught SIS officers the noble art of self-defense and unarmed combat. Most of them never needed to put any of it into practice but even the academics found him a useful and amiable contact. A blind eye was turned to the obvious fact that Jack McAvoy had connections with the criminal world that from time to time produced items that were otherwise impossible to obtain. Items that ranged from half-price but brand-new washing machines to the as-yet-unmarketed latest version of Ortofon's record-player cartridge and stylus.

Massey had known McAvoy for years and they were mutual admirers despite the fact that Massey never drank in McAvoy's pub. But in the small back parlor in his early days he had sat talking with his informants, patient and persistent as they drank pint after pink or their cocktail equivalents. Bloody Marys had not surfaced in London in those days but there were Pink Ladies and port-and-lemons. Jack McAvoy had admired the tough young man who sat defiantly with a glass of milk.

Massey's one-day trip to Berlin had shown that there was no longer any chance of his getting fake documents from those sources. On the flight back to Copenhagen he had thought of Jack McAvoy and wondered why he hadn't thought of him first.

Massey had done exactly what the KGB were used to doing—checking cemeteries and graveyards for a suitable name and date. He had found two Annas born in the right year and had paid for copy birth certificates in both names. English bureaucracy unwittingly assisted several foreign intelligence services by not linking death certificates with birth certificates.

As he sat in his bedroom at the Park Lane Hotel he realized that he didn't know Anna's unmarried name. He chose the certificate of Anna Lovegrove for no better reason than that he liked the soft name. It was Anna Mary Lovegrove, her father's occupation was registered as Teacher (Grammar School) and the birth had been registered at Keighley in Yorkshire. Anna Mary Lovegrove had died, according to the gravestone in the churchyard in Tooting, when she was two years and seven months old.

Massey had waited until a few minutes before closing time before he went in the Ironmonger's Arms. McAvoy had taken him into his own room behind the bar and had left to lock up. As he sat waiting he looked around the room. Nothing seemed to have changed. The photographs of McAvoy in fake leopard-skin briefs, lifting weights, demonstrating wrestling holds, and the centerpiece over the fireplace that showed a smiling Jack in evening dress with a member of the Royal Family on one side and a well-known criminal on the other. There were a few medals in a glass case hanging on the wall and a framed letter from the royal patron of an orphanage thanking John Kevin McAvoy for the check for £500 sent on behalf of his customers. It was an entirely masculine room and as dreary as the public bar outside. It was ten minutes before McAvoy came back. He sat down smiling in the worn armchair alongside his visitor.

"You on leave, Jan?"

"Kind of."

"Still in Berlin?"

"I was posted to Paris a few months ago."

"You buggers certainly get around." He grinned. "Still plenty of crumpet in the gay city?"

"I imagine so."

"What can I do for you?"

"I want a passport, Jack."

"What country?"

"British."

McAvoy looked surprised. "Why me? Your pals down the road at Petty France can do that easier than me."

"I don't want to use them." Massey paused. "Can you do it?

McAvoy laughed. "I can do anything, mate, you know that. But it'll cost a packet if you want something authentic."

"I want something as near perfect as you can get."

"Visas?"

"No. Just a straight passport."

"Used or new?"

"Brand-new if possible. How long will it take?"

McAvoy shrugged. "A couple of weeks."

"I need it in two days, Jack. But I'll pay whatever it takes."

"For Christ's sake! You must be joking. Let me make a phone call."

"OK."

It was twenty minutes before McAvoy put his head round the door. "Will you go up to a thousand quid?"

Massey nodded. "Yes. But two days."

"They say a week. Can we offer them an incentive?"

"It's up to you. I'll pay whatever it takes."

"Let me talk to them."

When McAvoy came back he nodded. "Twelve fifty but it'll be late on Wednesday night. You can pick it up here. They want the details and the photo tonight."

Massey took out an envelope from his jacket pocket.

"They're all in there, Jack. How are you going to get them to your people?"

"I'll take 'em myself."

"Is it far?"

McAvoy smiled. "Never you mind. Have you got a place to sleep tonight? There's a camp bed here if you want it."

"I'm OK. When do they want the cash?"

"I told 'em cash on delivery."

Massey stood up. "I'll come here at closing time on Wednesday night. I'll phone you tomorrow to check there are no snags."

"There won't be any snags. These guys are the best." He smiled. "It'll be better than out of the basement at Petty France if I know 'em."

* * *

231

Anna had met him at the airport and they took a taxi back into Malmö. Relieved that she now had all the documentation she was likely to need, Massey knew that he would have to go back to Paris alone. Somehow the small Swedish town had begun to feel like their home. They had found real peace there, walking through the Old Town along the canals, exploring the parks and drinking coffee in the square at Stortorget and Gustav Adolf's Torg. Anna spent hours every day in the Lundgren bookshop near their apartment. After two days Massey took a flight back to Paris, and a week later they both flew to Gatwick and drove to Tunbridge Wells.

Dr. Massey sat listening to the cassette on his hi-fi equipment. He was smiling to himself as he listened to Jack Buchanan singing "And her mother comes too." When Jan Massey drew up his chair the old man leaned sideways to switch off the machine.

"Did you find what you wanted in Tunbridge Wells, my boy?"

"I did, Father."

"You look better than the last time I saw you."

"I am, Father. I'm fine." He paused. "Can I talk to you about something?"

"You don't have to ask, boy. You know better than that. What is it?"

"I'm going to get married, Father. A week on Friday. I'd like very much for you to be there."

"And I will be, but that isn't what's making you look so . . . tense. Is it?"

"D'you remember me telling you about a girl I loved and it all fell through?"

"Yes. I remember very well."

"That's the girl I'm marrying. But there are problems. I'd like your comments."

"What are the problems?"

For well over an hour Massey talked to his father and the old man listened without comment or questions. When eventually Massey finished the old man said, "What do you want me to comment on?"

"Am I doing the wrong thing for Anna? She's nobody to turn to for advice except me. I'm not impartial."

"What kind of wrong did you have in mind?"

"Have I rushed her into something she'll regret?"

"It sounds as if you did your rushing a long time ago. When you got yourself arrested in East Berlin. And she seems to be as much inclined to rushing as you are." He sighed. "You seemed to have a very finite amount of calmness and patience all your life, boy. And then you'd be off like a wild thing. It seems a little late in the day to have doubts now. You wonder if she might regret this. Why should she? The worst thing that could happen for her is that you stop loving her. Knowing you, I'd say that's very unlikely. You sacrificed your career when you thought it would get her out of prison."

"And a technically illegal marriage?"

"The marriage isn't a necessity. Just a formality. If that's what you both want, then get on with it."

"Anything else?"

"If they threaten to harm her, those people. What would you do?"

"Protect her."

The old man shook his head. "That's foolish thinking, Jan. You'd better face reality."

"And what's that?"

"You'd have to do whatever they wanted. Just like you did the first time."

"We could move. There are places I know where we could go where they would never find us. Contacts I have."

"Think about it, Jan. Think about it."

"Will you be a witness for us at the registrar's office?"

"Of course I will. Where is she now?"

"We're both staying at a hotel just outside Tunbridge Wells to establish our local address."

The old man smiled. "I'll be there, boy." He paused. "How about you bring her down here for tea tomorrow? Mrs. Hargreaves'll be around."

Dr. Massey had put on his best suit and as he walked her round the small garden he realized what appeal she must have for his son. That calm beautiful face and the lithe young body. Gentle and intelligent, and an obvious strength of character behind the outward diffidence.

He brushed a scatter of leaves from the bench under the apple tree, and as they sat there he said quietly, "Are you happy, Anna?"

"Very happy. The happiest I've even been in my life."

"No regrets? Your father?"

She sighed and shrugged. "I've seen very little of him in the last few years."

"You'll need to be very strong."

She smiled. "Jan is strong enough for both of us. But I will be strong if it's necessary."

"It will be necessary. You can be sure of that."

"Why do you think that?"

"Those people will come back to him. Will want him to commit real treason, not just changing some disk."

"What makes you think that?"

"I can remember him explaining to me—years ago—when he had been on a training course—that when they wanted to use someone they asked

233

for something very minor the first time. Just borrowing a passport maybe. Something illegal but not very important. And once you had done *anything* illegal, you were committed. They had a hold on you. What they asked for next time would be more important."

"You think they will do that with Jan?"

"I'm sure they will."

"But he knows those things better than we do."

"Of course he does. But he's capable of ignoring them if it suits him. Especially where you are involved."

"So what should we do?"

"I don't know, my love. I don't know. Only he can decide when it happens. But it's best you should know that someday it will happen. They are evil people and they already have a hold on him, whatever he thinks."

She walked back to the house with the old man, thoughtful and concerned because she had seen the tears in his eyes.

It had moved her to see where Jan had been a boy. To think of him with his father. Just the two of them. And the influence of those conflicting genes. The reserved, stoical Englishman and the beautiful, impetuous Pole. All influencing the life of the man who looked so controlled and capable but who, she knew, had that gap in his armor. His own people didn't recognize it, but the KGB had seen it and used it. Maybe it took a Slav to recognize that fatal flaw. The impetuous heart that could overrule the head without a moment's hesitation. His father's warning had been perceptive and wise, and she would bear it in mind. When it happened she must be calm, not join him in the turmoil. For both their sakes she must be just a little bit English.

Thirty-Six

Chambers needed time to sort out his thoughts about Massey and he'd booked himself in for a couple of nights at the Compleat Angler in Marlow.

As he sat on the riverbank he watched the tip of the float curve round in the swirl of the tail of the weir. He'd baited the hook with weed from the stone steps and there were roach under the elderberry on the far bank. But the roach, like his thoughts, had been elusive. As he reeled in his line he checked the hook and stuck it into the cork handle, laying the rod alongside him on the grass. It was time to face the thinking.

Why had Kuznetsov been so determined in his refusal to be debriefed by Massey? He'd tried to get some explanation, no matter how vague. But the Russian had just smiled faintly and shaken his head. Then the odd comment from the French way back. A hint about Massey and some girl. When the French gave sly hints about relations with a girl they must really be scraping the bottom of the barrel. And when he'd pressed them for details, the knowing smiles but no more. And then that chat with Max Cohen in Hong Kong. Massey was the only SIS man who had unchecked access into Cohen's operation. And Cohen's vigorous defense of Massey. That was all very well as the attitude of a chap concerned with signals, but in SIS nobody was taken at face value. Burgess, Maclean and Philby had wiped out any lingering temptation to count background, upbringing or outward appearance as proof of loyalty and integrity. Even a man's record of efficiency could be a cover for treason. Loyalty was no longer taken for granted. Civil servants leaked documents to the media and self-publicizing politicians on the grounds that it was in the public interest. People signed their acceptance of the Official Secrets Act and then justified leaking State secrets with no more excuse than that they thought it should be done. Politics, and even government, were now part of an unstable Establishment built on the shifting sands of some clerk's whim of the moment. He had thought that when he used the excuse of GCHQ's deciding to move Cohen and posted Massey to Paris, he would have put him in baulk.

Massey being in baulk meant avoiding another of those dreadful departmental investigations, and the settling of old scores concerning the rivalries of decades long past. The near impossibility of finding positive evidence that would satisfy a High Court judge. And then the traditional media outcry, harking back forty years and more to the shortcomings of people long dead. What possible justification did he have for unleashing such chaos on a hard-working and conscientious group of people? People who knew that there would never be any public kudos for their years of loyalty. And others who continuously risked their lives.

Chambers, after two days' thinking, decided to wait. There was far too little to justify any action against Jan Massey. Instinct, or maybe wishful thinking, told him that something would happen that would resolve the problem. He was sufficiently on edge to wonder if it was significant that in two days he had spent fishing, he had not taken a single roach. He needed a sign. From God, or somewhere.

In Paris Massey, too, was looking for a sign. For two months he had spent five days a week in Paris on his own, flying back to Malmö on Fridays.

He never went straight to their apartment from the airport and he never allowed Anna to meet him when he flew in. The airport buildings were quite sparse and open and gave him plenty of opportunity to check if he was being followed. He waited for the other passengers on the flight to take the airport bus or drive off in waiting cars and there was never a sign of anyone watching him.

He had apologized to Anne-Marie for his sudden disappearance from the cafeteria and although she had smiled she had made no comment nor asked any questions.

The material that he was sending back to London came partly from Autenowski but mainly from Anne-Marie. He had repeatedly asked the French-desk officer for some indication of what areas particularly interested them, but there was very little response.

Massey was aware that his role had changed substantially. What was expected of him was no more than top-grade hack work. The kind of work that old faithfuls of SIS were given when they were working out their last couple of years before retirement. But he was too much the professional to just coast along, and through Anne-Marie he had built up a small network of useful informers who provided a wide spectrum of information that could be expanded easily into a well-based intelligence network. He had sent a memo and report to Chambers showing what could be done if the budget was quite modestly increased. There had been no reply beyond an acknowledgment that his report had been received.

Autenowski had obviously sensed that he was frustrated and had made a discreet and tentative suggestion that he might like to join the CIA. There were top jobs that he could be offered and it was clear that Autenowski had discussed the possibility with CIA headquarters at Langley before sounding him out. But the complications of Anna virtually ruled it out, and Massey settled down to accepting that he was being made to work his passage back into SIS's favor. He wasn't sure why he had to do it but was well aware that such things were not uncommon.

He also had Anna for consolation. He telephoned her daily and their weekends together made up for his arid existence in Paris. She was well aware of his desperate need for the calm, peaceful routine of their weekends. She asked no questions about his work but knew instinctively that he was in a state of uncertainty and turmoil. Although it was in her life that the greater upheaval had taken place, she had coped with it more easily. Even before she met Jan Massey she had considered leaving Kholkov. She wondered sometimes why she had married him. He had not been KGB when she first knew him: he had been a not-very-successful actor with the Bolshoi reserve group. She wondered later if perhaps he had been KGB even then. Maybe just an informer on his colleagues. He had been charming and diffident and undemanding. They had been married for three months before she discovered that he was homosexual. She had been resigned to her situation and her acceptance had, in fact, made their relationship more relaxed. She no longer saw him as a husband but merely a man whose career would be jeopardized if she broke off their relationship. She neither sought nor expected to find another man to share her life. When she first met Jan Massey it was like being a teenager again. He was handsome and intelligent, and she was conscious of his being an exceptional man. A big, calm, quiet man, who was too sure of himself to need the macho devices that most men adopted. And right from the first words they exchanged she had sensed the great depths of his emotion. Bottled up, as hers were.

When she lost touch with him after her visit to Moscow she had been hurt at first and confused. But gradually she had grown to accept that because of his work something serious could have happened to cause him to cut off the contact with her. She was quite sure that it was not a question of his ceasing to love her. But as the months went by she found herself more often daydreaming about him, wondering if perhaps she had done something or said something that had caused him to have doubts. But the daydreams just as often involved imaginary scenarios of their meeting. The meeting was always in a wood, sunshine slanting through the trees. Jan walking toward her down a narrow track in the slender birch trees, unaware that she was waiting for him at the end of the path. The daydreams always ended at the moment when their eyes first met. She never knew what happened after that.

The actual meeting with him in Paris was nothing like her daydreams. Nothing like anything she had imagined. It was so ordinary that it seemed as if they had arranged it beforehand. She had needed no time to think about staying with him. It was no more than putting the clock back to the time in Berlin when they were so near to grasping the nettle but had waited for a sign. For her the lesson had been painfully learned and she didn't hesitate. She knew instinctively that he loved her and she believed implicitly what he had told her of what had happened. Apart from believing him, it all fitted in with what had happened to her. Despite her knowledge of the KGB, she was shocked at what they had done and angry with Kholkov's duplicity. But it didn't matter anymore to her. She was with Jan and that was enough.

She had known that it would create problems for him but she knew that he would be able to cope with them. But as the weeks went by, she realized that despite his obvious pleasure in their being together he was tense and uncertain about what they should do. She made no suggestions, just following his lead without question, and as the weeks went by he seemed to regain his old confidence. On the telephone during the week his voice was always tense despite his reassuring words but on the weekends he relaxed as soon as he was with her. They were both used to a rootless existence and they found the small Swedish city friendly and civilized.

Their weekends together were no more than most couples could take for granted, but for both of them their pleasure in the ordinariness and routine of their weekend lives was almost the first real pleasure that they had ever experienced. It was as if they had both come in from the cold.

Thirty-Seven

Massey had given up his room in the rue Mouffetard and had taken two rooms at a small hotel near the place Vendôme. He was putting on his bathrobe when he heard the knock on the door and he walked across the room slowly as he tied the belt. When he opened the door he saw a man in a well-cut dark blue suit. Tall and slim with a tanned, smiling face that for a moment Massey couldn't place. As the man smiled at Massey he said softly, in Russian, "Fomenko, comrade . . . may I come in?"

For a moment Massey hesitated, and then he stood aside to let the Russian into the room.

Fomenko stood in the center of the room. "I apologize for coming unannounced . . . but I thought it might be more tactful this way . . ." He shrugged. "And easier, of course."

"What do you want, Fomenko?" Massey said quietly.

Fomenko smiled, his eyes amused, his head slightly tilted as if he were interviewing Massey for a job. "Could we sit and talk for a few moments, do you think?"

Massey nodded and pointed to an armchair, seating himself on the arm of a chair facing the Russian. Fomenko made himself comfortable before looking up at Massey.

"It seems a long time since we last met. I was looking forward to seeing you again as soon as I got the news."

"What news?"

Fomenko smiled broadly. "Kholkov's news . . . you really do provoke our little friend." He smiled. "A touch of Oscar Wilde—losing your wife once is unfortunate, but losing her twice is just careless." He paused. "Anyway—I thought we should talk."

"What about? Get on with it."

Fomenko waved toward the other armchair. "Do make yourself comfortable, my friend. You look so tense perched up there."

"Just say what you've got to say, Fomenko."

"Well, I'm really more concerned to hear what you've got to say to me."

"About what?"

"Oh, Massey, be a good chap. You ride off into the sunset like young Lochinvar with a senior KGB man's wife and you wonder what there is to talk about." He leaned forward. "You don't imagine that we shall just let you walk away with it, do you?"

"Do what you like, Fomenko. Moscow would be the laughing-stock of the world if you publicize that the wife of a KGB officer prefers an SIS officer instead."

"Of course. I can visualize the cartoons right now. Even our Warsaw Pact colleagues might manage a smile at our expense. But I wasn't thinking along those lines." Fomenko flicked a nonexistent speck from his immaculate lapel. "I was thinking more about the very, very senior SIS man in Berlin who cooperated with the KGB." Fomenko paused. "Some misguided people might see it as treason, might wonder what kind of men they were who chose, as head of a vital intelligence operation, a man who is prepared to commit treason for the sake of a pretty girl." Fomenko sighed, taking a deep breath. "So what do we do about it, my friend? Do we lash out at one another in public, or do we find some way to avoid this? Compromise?"

"Go on."

"You told me . . . that night in Berlin . . . that you loved Anna Kholkov . . . Do you still love her? . . . Or are you just paying off an old debt . . . a debt of honor, let us say? What is it?"

"Forget the questions, just say what you want."

"Do I detect a hint of willingness to cooperate, my friend?"

"If you do you'd be wrong, Fomenko. You've got no hostage now. No phoney scenario of a young girl held in prison on fake charges as a trade for what you want."

Fomenko said softly, "We've got two hostages this time, Massey. The two of you." His face was grim as he looked back at Massey. "I give you fair warning, my friend. No matter how long it takes, we'd find her. And when we find her we'll settle the score. I'm not bluffing, Massey, I mean it. I want you to believe me. We'll get her wherever she is. We've got all the time in the world. And every time you kiss her goodbye you'll wonder if that's the last time you'll see her alive." He shrugged. "If that's what you prefer to cooperation just say so and I'll walk away right now."

"What is it you want?"

"Right now, nothing. I just want to establish that when we call for your cooperation again we shall get it."

"What kind of cooperation?"

Fomenko shrugged. "Who knows? It's not been thought about. Maybe we never ask you for anything."

"You just wanted to make the threat."

"Put it like that if you wish. Let us say that I'm pointing out that you can't play games with us without paying the entrance fee. If you put your hand in our mincing machine don't complain when we turn the handle."

"So. You've made your point. You'd better go."

"You sure you've got the message, my friend? If you want her to stay alive. If you want to live undisturbed, you toe the line. It's a kind of insurance policy, Massey. And it doesn't cost you a cent. *You* cooperate with us if we ask you to and . . ." he shrugged ". . . you both live happy ever after."

Fomenko stood up, walking slowly to the door. As he put his hand on the lock to open it he turned and said, "If you wonder if we could find her, just work out how I traced you here. Think about it."

The Russian nodded and then let himself out, closing the heavy door quietly. Massey walked to the door and pushed down the catch on the lock, and then, realizing how pointless it was, pushed it back up again.

In a strange way Fomenko's visit had cleared his mind. He was a professional, back in the world he understood. It was part of the card game that he had been playing for years. Not the classic bridge game that top desk men played, but poker, where temperament was almost as important as the cards you held. Up to now there had been an unacknowledged deadlock. They had taken the kitty in Berlin and now, with Anna, he'd just got his money back. So they were dealing the cards again. He had little doubt that they would be prepared to wait for years if necessary to carry out their threats, either against Anna or by exposing him. But they were aware that if he chose he could retaliate by embarrassing them—by exposing the pressures they had brought to bear on him with all the charade they had gone through in Berlin.

Fomenko and others would have worked out the play quite carefully. Branding him as a traitor would mean being exposed themselves. His downfall wasn't worth that to them. So they had raised the stakes. Not exposure but a death threat. So it must matter to them not to be exposed. The move to involve him further was probably no more than a pre-emptive upping of the stakes just to see how he responded. A fishing expedition, to which he had no need to respond. There was a vague feeling at the back of his mind that there was another card in his hand to play, but he couldn't, at that moment, recognize what it was. In a way Fomenko's visit had cleared the air. He hadn't been sure what their reactions would be to Anna's departure, but now he knew. She was back in her original role as a useful pressure point. But it had been threats, not action.

There had been no signs of his being followed in Paris or on his weekend journeys. He recognized that this pattern of life could only be temporary but he had doubts about how to solve the problem.

He had his sign when he walked through Customs and Immigration at de Gaulle on a Monday morning a few weeks later. Two men had closed in on him as he walked through to the taxi rank, one on each side. The jab in his back unmistakably from a silencer. When he stopped, the man on his right said, "There's a white Citroën just ahead. Comrade Fomenko just wants to talk to you. If you make trouble I'll shoot. Those are my orders."

For a moment Massey was tempted to lash out but he took a deep breath and walked to the car. The rear door opened as he got there and Fomenko beckoned him inside. When the other two were in the car and the doors closed, Fomenko nodded to the driver.

He turned to Massey. "I must apologize for the crudity but it seemed the only way."

Massey said nothing as the car was driven toward the city. When they turned right at place de Colombie into boulevard Lannes he guessed where they were going and was amazed at their arrogance.

The gates of the Soviet Embassy stood open and the car swept inside and down to the far end of the building.

Fomenko led the way through a small door in a stone wall, along a short corridor to a room that was furnished as a living-room. He held the door open for Massey and pointed to one of the leather armchairs.

"Do sit down, my friend."

Fomenko nodded to the two other men to leave and as they closed the door behind them he turned to Massey.

"Please believe me when I say I don't wish to harm you or disturb you in any way. But we need your help." As Massey opened his mouth to speak the Russian held up his hand. "Let me finish, comrade." He paused. "If you would assist us on this occasion I have been authorized to tell you that we give a solemn undertaking that we shall never ask for any assistance from you again. We should leave you and Anna in peace. You may not like us but you know enough to know that when we make a bargain we keep our word. Always." He paused again. "As an indication of our attitude, let me say that we learned only by accident of your flight back this morning from Sweden. You have not been under any surveillance by us and . . ." he smiled ". . . perhaps more important to

242

you . . . let me say we have no idea where Anna is. We have not tried to trace her."

"So why today's little show?"

Fomenko smiled and shrugged. "Forgive me. It was the only way I could be sure of being able to talk to you."

"I'm not going to help you, Fomenko. You're wasting your time."

The Russian's brown eyes looked at Massey's face as he said quietly, "Would you really like her to be killed? I can't believe that."

He saw the anger on Massey's face, the white knuckles and the deep breath to control himself. Fomenko went on.

"We've been putting together one of our jigsaw puzzles. It's taken us quite a time and a lot of work. We've only just begun to see the picture. And the picture's very disturbing. A very senior KGB officer disappeared while he was at meetings in Stockholm. You may have heard of him. Aleksandr Dmitrevich Kuznetsov. There seemed to be no reason why he defected. He was not under suspicion. In fact he was due for yet another promotion. Now, in our investigations there are two threads. Threads that lead to two different men. One is a Frenchman—Bourget. A man who you knew in Berlin. The other is you." Fomenko waited for a moment and then went on. "All I want to know is which one of you it was. We've traced contacts by Kuznetsov with both of you. You and the Frenchman." Fomenko spoke very quietly. "Which one of you made him defect? And how did you do it?"

"Have you asked Bourget?"

"No. We don't trust Bourget. Maybe we shall talk to him but either way he would say it was you." He paused. "This is a serious matter for us and for you too. We are prepared to give you time to think it over."

"I'm not going to answer your question, Fomenko. You're wasting your time."

"You will, Massey. Because if you don't, the girl will die. Wherever she is we will find her. It would be just a question of time. It didn't take us long to trace you to the hotel or to check that you would be landing at de Gaulle this morning."

"You're not on your home ground this time, Fomenko. We're not in East Berlin now."

"Oh, come, Massey. You know us better than that." He looked at Massey's face. "Let's leave it for a week, yes? You think it over and we meet again." Fomenko smiled. "I'll contact you."

"If I told you it was Bourget what would you do?"

"I'd believe you," the Russian said softly.

"Why?"

"Because you might as well kill the girl yourself if you told me a lie." Fomenko stood up. "You have nothing to lose provided you tell the truth. If it was Bourget, then that is the end of the matter for you. If it was you it is still the end of the matter for you. Either answer and our account is squared. All we want is the answer." He paused. "You're free to leave—there are no guards on the door."

Massey bent to pick up his bag and was tempted to wreak his anger on the Russian, but there was no point and he straightened up and walked to the door.

Outside he let the first empty taxi pass and hailed the second. He had no doubt what he must do. He must warn Kuznetsov.

Massey phoned Chambers as soon as he got back to the hotel and was taken aback by Chambers's reaction when he said that he wanted to talk to Kuznetsov. He thought at first that Chambers didn't understand who he meant because when referring to the Russian he used just the initial letter, but it became clear that Chambers knew exactly who he meant but was reluctant to agree to a meeting. When he asked why he shouldn't talk with the Russian, Chambers asked him what he wanted to talk about. Massey said that he had heard several pieces of gossip concerning the KGB that he would like to discuss with Kuznetsov, and Chambers grudgingly agreed. He would like a meeting himself with Massey before Massey saw the Russian. Massey suggested that he would fly over straight away and they could meet that evening, but Chambers said it was not convenient, suggesting the afternoon flight the next day and adding that he would meet Massey at Gatwick.

As the plane started its descent to Gatwick Massey went over in his mind again how he would pass the warning to Kuznetsov. He took it for granted that there was a strong possibility that wherever they met would be bugged. Chambers's reluctance to agree to the meeting could only mean that they were still debriefing Kuznetsov. The Russian was an experienced professional who would need the truth of what had happened to convince him. It would be up to Kuznetsov to demand even higher security protection without revealing why. It had to be between Kuznetsov and himself. There mustn't be the vaguest hint that the request for higher security came from anything that he had said.

Thirty-Eight

Chambers, looking tired and pale faced, was waiting on the tarmac and had walked him through Immigration and Customs with a familiar nod to the officials. As they were going toward the exit they passed a small crowd of people waiting for passengers. A young woman with a scarf round her head stared at them, checked something in her handbag and walked toward the public telephones.

As they got in the car Chambers said, "I've arranged for us to go to one of the safe-houses. It's not far."

"Which one is it?"

"I don't think you know it. It's just outside East Grinstead. It's a pleasant little place and we should be comfortable there."

"Is K there?"

"We're bringing him down from St. Albans. Tomorrow."

Chambers didn't respond to his attempts at conversation but was friendly enough once they were at the house. He showed Massey to a pleasant room and left him to settle in while he went to check if there were any messages for him.

There were only two messages for Chambers. One from his wife and one to phone the duty officer at Century House immediately after he arrived.

He dialed the CH number.

"Duty officer."

"Chambers. I got a message to phone you."

"Ah, yes, sir. I took a phone call about fifteen minutes ago. The caller asked for you and I said you were not available. They asked for a message to be passed to you urgently. Do you want to go over to a scrambler?"

"Is it necessary?"

"I don't think so."

"Go on then."

"The message was quote tell Mr. Chambers to ask Massey about Anna Kholkov unquote. End of message."

"Is that all?"

"Yes, sir."

"Any name given?"

"No. None, sir. It was a foreign accent."

"A recognizable accent?"

"I'd say it was Russian, sir."

"Do you speak Russian?"

"Yes, sir. I was at St. Anthony's."

"OK. Thank you."

Chambers hung up and stood in the paneled hall. He'd been waiting for a sign. This looked like the sign. He sighed and picked up the phone again. Radford would be down in about an hour.

They had dinner together in the annex and Chambers talked about his recent visit to Buenos Aires. As they got up from the table Chambers said, "Let's go up to my room and talk about things."

As Chambers opened the door of his suite Massey saw a man sitting there. He recognized the face but couldn't remember who he was.

Chambers said, "Let me introduce you. Jimmy Radford, Jan Massey."

Radford didn't get up but he smiled as he put out his hand. "You won't remember me but I took over a defector named Kinsky from you about six or seven years ago."

Massey nodded as he shook Radford's hand and sat down as Chambers pointed to one of the chairs. It was Chambers who started them off.

"I've been worried about several things recently, Jan. All of them concerning you. I thought it was time to get them off my chest." He waved toward Radford. "I thought it might be sensible for Jimmy Radford to be here too. Any objections?"

Massey shook his head. "No. None at all. Is this an official enquiry?"

Chambers shrugged. "Not quite, but it could turn into that."

Massey nodded and said quietly, "Please go ahead."

"I'd like to go back to when Kuznetsov came over." Chambers paused and looked at Massey's face. "I suggested to him that as he knew you for so long that you should debrief him. He was adamant that he wouldn't be debriefed by you. I asked him why not you, and he wouldn't answer. Just shook his head and smiled. Why do you think he didn't want you to debrief him, Jan?"

"I've no idea. I'm surprised to hear it."

"Any suggestions why he took that attitude?"

"Could be several reasons. Maybe he preferred to start fresh with somebody different."

"Go on."

"How should I know why? Maybe he doesn't like me, or remembers how we first met. He was embarrassed about that at the time. Thought he'd lost face."

"Could it be that he doesn't trust you?" Radford said quietly.

"If he didn't trust me why did he want me to help him defect?"

"You and I were his only contacts, Jan," Chambers said. "And I don't speak Russian."

"He speaks good enough English to make contact with you."

Radford said, "Is there any possible reason why he shouldn't trust you? Maybe a misunderstanding?"

"Not that I know of."

Chambers said, "Let's go back to when you were in Berlin and we had that trouble about the disks . . ."

They questioned him for three hours. Politely, persistently, going back over his answers again and again, but they got nowhere. Jan Massey was a professional and he knew more about interrogation than the two of them would ever know. He guessed right from the start that they were fishing. They had nothing to go on and they got nothing from him. It was one in the morning when the confrontation broke up. The atmosphere was strained but no direct accusation had been made. They agreed to talk again the following morning at eleven.

Neither Chambers nor Radford slept that night. They had a lot to do.

Massey sat in his room going over what had obviously become an interrogation. He had no intention of giving them an inch. He was aware that he was now under pressure from both sides. From the KGB and SIS.

In Paris, Fomenko had fumed when he got the message that Massey had flown to London and that the man who had met him at Gatwick was Chambers. He assumed that Massey had gone to report the Russian offer in the hope that it would give him SIS protection. He also assumed that Massey would not divulge past events or his relationship with the girl. But there was no hope now, Fomenko assumed, of getting what they wanted from Massey. His sudden flight to London was answer enough. And now all he could do was finish Massey off as an SIS officer.

Chambers had driven back to London and the name Kholkov had been run through Central Archives's computer. It had thrown up two Kholkovs. One at the Soviet Embassy in Cairo and the other a KGB officer who had been in Berlin and was now in Budapest. It had not taken long for Berlin to confirm that an Anna Kholkov was the KGB man's wife. There was no photograph on file but there was a detailed description.

Kuznetsov was roused from his sleep at the safe-house in Kensington and led to believe that Massey had told SIS of his relationship with Anna Kholkov, and asked what he knew. Kuznetsov was suspicious and refused to go beyond the fact that he knew that the girl and Massey had had an *affaire*.

Massey walked round the garden of the safe-house that had once been a vicarage and saw Chambers drive his car through the guarded gates and park it at the front of the house.

At a few minutes before eleven he knocked on Chambers's door and walked in. Chambers was alone and on the telephone, nodding as he listened to what was being said at the other end. Finally he said he had a meeting and hung up. He turned to look at Massey and Massey took some comfort from the troubled look in Chambers's eyes.

Chambers pointed to the chair and sat opposite, his hand reaching up to loosen the knot of his tie.

"How did you sleep, Jan?"

Massey shrugged. "Not too well."

Chambers sighed. "I thought it would be better . . . more constructive . . . if we talked alone."

Massey nodded but said nothing, his face impassive.

Then Chambers said quietly, "Tell me about Anna Kholkov."

There was a long silence. Two or three minutes. And then Massey said quietly, "I want to resign from SIS. As of today. And I refuse to answer any more questions."

Chambers shook his head slowly and emphatically. "Jan, Jan. It's gone too far to be that simple. You know that. Please talk with me. I'll do all I can to help."

"And if I don't?"

"I'll have to charge you and take you to a magistrates' court. You know the drill. You've done it enough times yourself. But, I beg of you, don't . . . just once in your life . . . think before you jump. There are compromises that can be arranged. You know that too."

"You mean you want me to do a Blunt?"

"Yes. If that's how you want to describe it."

"It's a game I've not played. Tell me the rules." Massey saw the relief on Chambers's face.

"Let me tell you the reasons so that you'll understand that it's not some device to incriminate you. We strongly suspect that you have worked with or for the Russians. With the KGB. There is a lot of circumstantial evidence pointing that way. Given time we could almost certainly come up with enough evidence to convince a court.

"It is more use to us to know exactly what has been going on than to have you sitting in a cell for the rest of your life in Wormwood Scrubs. And you don't need me to tell you that the media and the politicians would have a field day at SIS's expense if you went on trial. We've had a bellyful of them the last few years. We've been whipping-boys for so-called investigative journalists and the militant left doing Moscow's bidding." He paused. "What do you say, Jan?"

"Just let's assume that I cooperate. *If* I do—how do I come out of it?"

"Early retirement on health grounds. Full pension but no gratuity. And we'll leave you in peace. No messing about."

"What protection would I get?"

Chambers looked surprised. "Is it that bad, Jan?"

"It could be. I don't know."

"Let's say that if you cooperate and it looks like we need to warn off Moscow, we'll do it."

Massey knew already that he had no choice. His career would limp on if he didn't cooperate, but Anna and he would live like nomads, constantly under tension as they waited for the blow to fall.

"OK, Chambers. I'll tell you what's happened. It started in Berlin . . ."

They had hired a car and driven out to Skanör and then walked down to the shore. The beach was almost completely deserted, just two anglers casting for bass.

They found a sheltered inlet in the bank and opened the haversack with their Thermos and sandwiches. There were small flocks of sand-pipers at the edge of the sea and snipe on the bank behind them. Great clusters of willow-herb covered the sheltered side of the bank, its fluffy seeds already visible where the long thin seedpods had begun to split. It reminded Massey of his walks on Romney Marshes with his father. Almost as if she had read his thoughts she handed him a sandwich and said, "Have you told your father?"

"I told him about you and me and what had happened but I haven't told him about the present situation."

"Why not?"

"It would depress him and he's too old to face this kind of thing. He was always afraid that I would do something hotheaded and land myself in trouble. He'd start thinking that he is in some way responsible for letting what he calls the Polish influence affect me.

"He never knew what I was actually doing and as far as he's concerned he'll assume that I'm still doing the same job but somewhere else."

"And what about you?"

Massey turned to look at her face. "All I want is to buy us some peace."

"What do you have to pay for peace?"

"I've told them what they wanted to know. They've given me most of what I asked for."

"What did you ask for?"

"Guaranteed permanent immunity to prosecution. Full pension. No disclosure internally or externally. No harassment of any kind."

"Why should they do a deal, Jan?"

Massey shrugged. "A lot of reasons. First of all, despite what they said, they couldn't have provided anywhere near enough evidence against me to satisfy a court. In fact they didn't have a shred of evidence. Just a few shrewd guesses. Nothing a court would accept for a moment. And exposing me would have been an embarrassment. For the department and for the government.

"And it means they can do what they call a 'damage limitation' exercise. They can go back to the moment when the disk was changed and look at all the decisions that were made subsequently and check whether they were influenced by the changeover." Massey shrugged impatiently. "It hasn't affected anything really. It was out of the mainstream of intelligence."

"Why did the KGB go to such elaborate lengths to trap you if it wasn't important?"

Massey shrugged. "That was only the beginning. Once you've committed an illegal act on behalf of the KGB they've got a hold on you. The first time can be some very small offense. But once you've committed *any* offense, that gives them an extra hold on you. Next time it's something more important."

"And Fomenko and the KGB?"

"Well, they refused to give any guarantee when Chambers first contacted them but he had obviously made his point. They came back a week later and said they'd reconsidered and they would agree to leave us alone provided I was no longer active in SIS." He smiled. "They really wouldn't have liked their part of the game to be published in the press. It was in the KGB's interest to call it a day. And in Moscow's interest too."

"What *didn't* you get that you asked for?"

"I asked for genuine British citizenship for you. They agreed to that, and I asked that our marriage was made legal. They wouldn't agree unless Moscow agreed to allow you a legal Soviet divorce. Moscow would never agree to that because it would provide documentary evidence of what had happened if it was ever investigated. That's the only thing I couldn't get."

Anna looked at his face and said softly, "Do you ever wish you'd never met me?"

"Of course I don't. The unpleasant things that happened were nothing to do with us. I behaved very stupidly and they cashed in on it."

"Where shall we live when it's over?"

"I'd got in mind New Zealand or Spain."

"Why New Zealand?"

"It's a long way from Europe. They're nice people and it's a lovely country. The only snag is that they speak English and still have some ties with London. People over there could look into my background and start putting two and two together. In Spain we would lose ourselves. They wouldn't care enough to check on me. Why should they? Even if they found out that I was once SIS I doubt if they'd care. There are scores of British criminals there. One British traitor wouldn't matter."

"You're not a traitor, Jan. Nobody could say that."

"I am, my love. I'm afraid I am."

"And all those years of service in SIS count for nothing?"

"I'm afraid not. To everybody except us, I'm a traitor. That's how they would see me. The government, politicians, the media have a vested interest in ignoring any human factor. Loving you would be no excuse. It would be misrepresented. Deliberately. It would be in their interest to make it a question of sex not love."

"But why? Why couldn't it be for love?"

Massey smiled. "Because some people, some of the public, would feel sympathy for you and me if it was a question of love. When a man is exposed as a traitor he must be shown to be *all* bad. Not just a traitor but a pervert, a bad father and husband. A man whose friends always found him strange and aloof. A man who cheated at school. If possible a homosexual or a child molester. And a man who was motivated by hatred for his country and his countrymen. Whatever you do, you mustn't let a traitor look human. If he is intelligent you must make his intelligence mere cunning, any qualities or virtues he has as a human being must be made to seem malevolent. Otherwise some people might sympathize with him, even identify with him. He must be a monster not a man.

"And this is not just the attitude of the Soviet Union or Britain, but every country in the world. Even a spy can be allowed admirers. Provided that he's working for his own country. The KGB's Abel in the United States, Sorge in the Far East—they have their admirers. But not Philby or Alger Hiss, or Gouzenko."

"And you think that nobody would say good things about you? Not even Chambers and the others who know you well?"

Massey laughed, shaking his head. "They would say that they hardly knew me. If they wanted to be kind. If not, they would recall some incident that showed them I was always ruthless or maybe mentally sick."

She shivered despite the sunshine. "When can we go to Spain?"

"I think it will be all over in about ten days. You could go ahead if you like and start looking for a house."

She shook her head. "I'm not going anywhere without you."

Thirty-Nine

The court case against Jimbo Vick had dragged on for several months. He refused to go into the witness box himself. His attorney argued that he was not avoiding cross-examination but was not prepared to give evidence that could affect his wife's reputation. The prosecution claimed that there was no valid marriage and that Jimbo Vick had no wife and was unmarried. They produced all the necessary documentation to substantiate their claim. And day after day Jimbo Vick sat at the table, his wrists still strapped, staring into space as if he was oblivious to everything that was going on around him.

When eventually he was sentenced to ten years he showed no emotion as he was led away, and refused to let his counsel mount an appeal. There were the usual background reports on his life in the media, with emphasis on the wilder episodes. A few newspapers suggested that it was an injustice that allowed a proven spy, a foreigner, to be deported while an American citizen got a long prison sentence as a mere accessory.

Jimbo refused to see his parents both during the trial and after sentencing. He was given a cell on his own and was under more or less constant supervision.

It was over six months after he had started his sentence before Mary

Holland and her editor were able to get permission for Mary to interview Jimbo Vick, and over a dozen letters to him before he agreed to see her.

As he sat opposite Mary Holland in the interview cell that was provided for lawyers to meet their clients, she knew that she would have to tread very carefully with her questions. Jimbo Vick's mind was a long way away. But he made no move to stop her as she pressed the record button on the small Sony tape recorder.

"Do you mind if I call you Jimbo, Mr. Vick?"

He didn't reply, just a shrug of his shoulders that she treated as an assent. She glanced at her shorthand notes and then back at his face.

"Did you feel your sentence was rather harsh, Jimbo? A bit unfair in the circumstances?"

"No."

"Why not?"

"It was the price that had to be paid."

He spoke slowly and quietly.

"For what?"

"If I'd defended myself it could only be at the expense of Kirstie. That's what the bastards wanted me to do."

"Did you never have even the slightest suspicion of what she was doing?"

"No. Never. You don't have suspicions about somebody you love."

"You must have loved her a lot."

"I did. I still do."

"Despite what she did and despite her attitude to you?"

"If an American had done what she did about some Soviet secrets, she'd have been praised as a heroine."

"And her attitude to you after you were both arrested?"

"If you love somebody, they don't necessarily have to love you in return."

"What was it about her that made you love her so much?"

"That's a very perceptive question, you know."

"So tell me."

He took a deep breath and then sighed. "I've no idea. No idea at all. I just loved her."

"Do you ever wish you hadn't met her?"

"No. Never. She was my fate. Nothing else could explain it." He sighed. "Despite what happened, we were a pair. A rather odd pair—but a pair all the same."

"Your answers are unusually honest and frank. Why?"

"You think you're using me, don't you? But you're not. I'm using you."

"How come?"

"When your paper, magazine, whatever, prints this interview she'll see it eventually. This is my way of telling her that I really did love her."

"Let's go back to the beginning. How did you first meet her?"

He smiled very faintly. "It was at a seminar in Washington, she was there too and . . ."

Forty

It was only twenty-four hours after Tom Bartram arrived that the first piece appeared. Just a few lines in the *Standard*'s gossip column.

Yet another mystery in the ongoing troubles of BBC TV's Current Affairs department. It seems that a project being worked on by top interviewer Tom Bartram has been stopped in its tracks by the new Head of Current Affairs Stanley "The Knife" Dillon. It seems that several thousand pounds have already been spent on planning an investigation into the perennial problems of the security services. We understand that an Opposition MP is to raise the matter with the Home Secretary next week. Supporters of veteran Tom Bartram at the BBC TV Center hint that this is, in fact, just one more shot from Dillon at his old rival Bartram, and that the program was, in fact, a light-hearted look at how some of the alleged British criminals are now living it up on the Costa del Sol.

The *Daily Express* carried the follow-up the next day:

Members of the opposition are suggesting that a new *Belgrano*-type campaign is to be expected soon, raising doubts about some of the activities of MI6, the Secret Intelligence Service. Since the Blunt affair the Foreign Office has constantly denied that any similar deals have been done with Moscow's moles and sleepers. But at least one Opposition MP is convinced that both MI5 and MI6 are riddled with what he calls the "Cambridge closet communists."

The next day's *Times* parliamentary report recorded an exchange at Prime Minister's Question Time.

Mr. Paul Schubert (Lab. Otterly West) asked the Prime Minister if it was true that an immunity-from-prosecution deal had recently been offered to an officer of MI5 or MI6 suspected of passing top-secret information to the Soviet Union or one of the Warsaw Pact countries.

The Prime Minister said that no such deal had been done or contemplated.

Several Opposition MPs indicated dissatisfaction with the Prime Minister's reply and said that the matter would be pursued through other channels.

It was a typed slip pushed in front of the late-night ITN newsreader that started the next phase.

Tomorrow's *Sunday Express* carries a report on an investigation that a team of reporters has compiled on a man who is alleged to have been a senior officer of MI6 who was working at the same time for the Russian intelligence service, the KGB.

The report in the *Sunday Express* covered two pages except for a few advertisements. There was a large photograph of the Foreign Office and a large and grainy photograph of a man who had once been head of MI6. He had been dead for almost ten years. He stood awkwardly in the bright summer sunlight, facing the camera, a tennis racket in his hand, a cocker spaniel at his feet and a mass of hydrangeas just visible in the background.

The piece was by-lined to Jason Armitage and Ruby Edwards, and a few short sentences claimed a long history of investigative successes to the pair.

The headline was heavy and across the two pages. "Is the Fifth Man still doing Moscow's work?" A boxed paragraph explained in bold type:

Due to the protection given by our ridiculous libel laws we have been advised not to publish the name of the MI6 suspect. Neither are we allowed to give a description that would lead to his being identified. We ask—why not? Moscow knows who he is. The Cabinet knows who he is. MI6 knows who he is. We know who he is. But under our archaic libel laws, you—the public—are not allowed to know.

The first two columns of the report were in heavy type.

We have talked with ex-officers of the security services and the Secret Intelligence Services and there is no doubt in their minds that Burgess, Maclean, Philby and Blunt were only the tip of the iceberg of the Soviet penetration of these two services on which our national security depends.

The more we talked to these experienced officers, now in honorable retirement, the more disturbing was the picture that emerged. To prevent accusations of bias or misunderstanding we asked for the name of one such suspect who we could investigate ourselves. The man whose name was given to us was given the code-name Lucifer for our investigation.

We have visited several European countries during our investigation of Lucifer and interviewed literally scores of people who knew the man concerned. At no time did we divulge why we were making our enquiries. What we have discovered makes a horrifying story of incompetence and falsification. We asked for interviews with the present bosses of both services. And were refused. We asked for various pieces of information to be confirmed or denied. All our requests were refused. It seems that the intelligence services are better at keeping their own guilty secrets than defending our national interests. Ex-members of SIS refer to the department as the Firm. We would call it, more appropriately, the Club.

Let us look at this one single case. The man concerned was a senior officer in SIS. His mother was born a national of a Warsaw Pact country and was at one time an intelligence agent for one of the British wartime espionage and sabotage departments. We were not able to trace her present whereabouts. The man concerned had frequent meetings with KGB officers using his official position as a cover. He speaks fluent Russian.

In an interview with his ex-wife she told us something of his character. She described him as ruthless and aggressive. In several interviews with a psychiatrist, when we described details of some of the incidents in his married life, the psychiatrist, who has appeared as an expert witness in several court cases, confirmed that the behavior described was typical of some kinds of psychopath. In the divorce proceedings it was admitted by "Lucifer's" counsel that he had, on three separate occasions, brutally attacked his wife's friends. It was suggested in court that this was due to his "Slav temperament."

As head of station for SIS in a key European city he was in a position to pass to the Russians every detail of the massive radio surveillance organization under his control. There was recently a token clean-up of our intelligence operations in this important city and the man concerned was removed virtually overnight and posted elsewhere to a different country where there was no possibility of his gaining top-secret information of interest to his paymasters in the KGB. Why, if this man was not suspect, was this hurried move necessary?

One of the men previously under his command was later found to be a double agent for the KGB with the rank of lieutenant in that élite Soviet organization. There is little doubt that the protection provided by his commander gave the best possible cover that a double agent could wish for.

There were unconfirmed suggestions through the intelligence organization of another country operating in the same city at the same time, that our suspect was involved in offers of money bribes for the release of KGB agents under arrest.

Any one of these revelations should have been enough to alert our security forces. And even now they should be investigating this man and the others like him. "No comment" is not good enough.

The stone-walling by the Establishment is not confined to us. Members of Parliament, alarmed by the state of affairs, have raised questions in Parliament about this specific case. The government's replies have been devious to the extent of denying all knowledge of the circumstances.

Few people realize the powers and responsibilities of the two organizations still known as MI5 and MI6 and the following section of our report gives a complete summary of both intelligence departments.

The rest of the article consisted of charts showing the chain of command from the Home Secretary to MI5 and the Foreign Secretary to MI6. And then the internal chain of command of both organizations. There was nothing that had not appeared in a dozen or more books over the years. The exploration of the two organizations' responsibilities and history repeated what was already on the public record, including the usual errors.

The subheadings on the rest of the article promised more than the text delivered. Facts went unsubstantiated and where the omissions were too obvious it was implied that proof would be given later in the piece. The proof never quite caught up with the allegations.

People long dead, unable to defend themselves, were accused of treason and conspiracy on no more grounds than having been at a school or university which some renegade had attended years before or after them. Their motives were impugned without a shred of evidence, their characters assassinated because they had once lived in the same city as some communist suspect. They might never have met but the implication was that they could have.

Nowhere in the article was there a word of praise for men who risked their lives, saw little of their families and who knew enough to expose a score of public figures as hypocrites or worse, yet kept silent.

Jan Massey, despite his long experience, found the media hunt and its distortions only confirmed his dislike of the British Establishment. But Tom Bartram knew that Massey's defiant attitude hid real wounds.

G

Forty-One

A report on the mounting media coverage had been phoned through to Tom Bartram twice a day. His instructions fluctuated, from advice to be very cautious to insistence that he should get as much material as possible and try and ensure that it was all exclusive.

His talks with Massey had been extended over ten days and his outside broadcast team had been sent to fill in their time getting stock film of the Costa del Sol from the gates of Gibraltar to Malaga and on up the coast to Nerja.

On the tenth day Tom Bartram had been told by BBC TV Features that he had only three days left in which to film or call it a day.

He stood with Massey at the side of the house as Massey turned on the pump to fill the water tanks from the well, and Bartram turned to look again across the bay. It was a view he had seen so many times now but the lushness of the flowers, red, purple, bright orange and white margue-rites, still held his eye. And the blue of the Mediterranean was a perfect background for an opening shot. You could pull back from the long-shot and fill the lens with a single bloom. A marigold, the ornate head of a geranium or the purple bracts of bougainvillea.

He turned slowly to look at Massey's face. For long moments his eyes traveled over it. The strong bones, the brown eyes, the full sensual mouth would look marvelous in close-up. And he knew in that moment that he wouldn't do it.

"When can I fetch the team up, Jan?"

Massey shrugged. "It's up to you." He turned off the pump switch. "Let's go back on the patio."

When they were sitting, drinks in hand, in the wicker chairs, Bartram turned to Massey and held up his glass. "What is it you and Anna say?"

Massey smiled. *"Na zdrowie."*

"Na zdrowie." He paused. "I'm going to leave you two in peace, Jan."

"What's that mean?"

"I'm going to pass. I'm not going to finish the assignment. No filming."

"Why not?"

"I just don't want to."

"Tell me why."

"I'm not sure it would end up as good material."

"I don't believe that. You asked me a few minutes ago if you could bring your chaps up to start filming."

"I wanted to see if you'd refuse."

"Why?"

"Then I could have justified myself in persuading you to let me do it."

"And?"

"And I would have done it."

"So why *didn't* you do it?"

"Because you so obviously trust me."

"Is that a bad thing?"

"It is for me. I don't want to be trusted." Bartram looked at Massey. "You're going to get a rough ride, Jan. I think you know that already. You're a professional, and you know how these things go." He paused. "I don't want to be the guy who puts the first boot in. I made a tactical mistake when I started chatting with you. I ought to have stayed at arm's length. I've got involved with you both."

"Or do you mean your bosses wouldn't give your stuff screen time if it didn't point an accusing finger at me?"

"No. It's more than that. They'd probably accept whatever I did. But I *would* have to point an accusing finger at you. You did what you did. There's no use pretending you didn't. The reasons why you did it won't be acceptable to the Establishment. They'll make them seem tawdry if they let them get mentioned at all. If I hadn't got to know you so well they wouldn't be acceptable to me either." He sighed. "But I *have* got to know you and that rules me out." He shrugged. *"Tout comprendre c'est tout pardonner.* I'd either end up as a bad reporter or a bad friend." He paused. "And I don't want to be either."

Massey smiled. "I understand. I'm sorry for your sake."

"Can I give you some advice, Jan? Professional advice."

"By all means."

"Nobody else seems to have tracked you down yet. But they will. Don't talk to them as you have talked with me. Refuse to be interviewed. Refuse to answer any questions. Just give them the old 'no comment' routine. And stick to it."

"Why do you say that?"

Bartram turned to look over the bay before he turned back to look at Massey. "You know why, Jan, as well as I do. They'll all have a vested interest in destroying you. No editor will give them orders to do it and no cabinet minister will threaten to reduce the BBC's license fee. But the media will know by a kind of osmosis what's expected of them."

"A hatchet job?"

"No . . . well, I can think of a couple who might do a hatchet job, but the majority will just make you look like a first-class bastard."

"Won't it be even worse if I refuse to talk at all?"

"It'll be speculation then, Jan. That's different. It's mere gossip-column stuff. A few paras here and there. They'll have difficulty getting their libel lawyers to let them mention your name if there's no official statement implicating you." He smiled. "It'll be a thing that so-called investigative journalists ferret away at for years. Long double-page spreads in the heavies—all hints but no facts—no facts that prove anything, anyway. You'll just have to sit tight, both of you, and let it wash over you. Get yourself a good lawyer right away." Bartram grinned. "You might even end up with a nice libel settlement out of court."

Bartram stood up and held out his hand. As Massey took it he said, "Did *you* understand, Tom?"

Bartram nodded. "Yes, I understood, Jan. But don't be tempted. Stay silent. Give my love to Anna when she gets back from the market."

"She'll be disappointed."

"She won't. Your Anna may be a romantic but she's also a realist."

Bartram waved from the wrought-iron gates, closing them carefully and snapping the padlock closed on the links of the chain. He waved again as he got into his car but Massey was looking out across the bay. He turned slowly and walked back into the house. Almost without thinking he switched on the radio. They were playing the "In Paradisum" from Fauré's *Requiem*.